M.C. H

THEY'RE DESTINED TO FALL IN LOVE...
IF THEY DON'T KILL EACH OTHER FIRST.

BORN OF BLOOD AND MAGIC

BOOK ONE OF THE LIGHTLESS SERIES

ISBN: 978-1-7382538-0-7

Born of Blood and Magic - Book One of the Lightless Series

Copyright© 2024 M.C. Hutson

All rights reserved. No part of this book may be used or reproduced in any manner whatsoever without written permission except in the case of brief quotations embodied in critical articles and reviews.

This is a work of fiction. Names, characters, places and incidents are either the product of the author's imagination or are used fictitiously. Any resemblances to actual persons, living or dead, businesses, companies, events of locales is entirely coincidental.

Cover design: MiblArt

For questions and inquiries, please contact: mc@mchutson.com

*I couldn't do it with without you:
Michelle, Rachel, Wendy, Jenna and Arqam*

Note for Readers

- This book contains profanity, violence, gore, mentions of drug use, sexual assault and explicit sex scenes.

- This book is written in Canadian English.

- If you would like to receive free bonus content and updates on future works, sign up for M.C. Hutson's mailing list here: mchutson.com

M.C. HUTSON

They're destined to fall in love...
if they don't kill each other first.

BORN OF BLOOD AND MAGIC

BOOK ONE OF THE LIGHTLESS SERIES

MC Press

Prologue

December 2009

Petra sat on the ledge of a large bay window in Kate's bedroom, and the more she stewed, the more she thought about leaving.

Staring beyond the frosted glass, she tried to distract herself by watching the flurry of snow drifting down from a black backdrop of sky. She was fighting the impulse to look over at her best friend, because the last thing Petra wanted to see was Kate smiling stupidly at her BlackBerry while she exchanged BBMs with her latest boyfriend, Clyde.

Petra's jaw clenched. *If she was just going to ignore me, why'd she invite me over?*

Kate disregarding her was nothing new, and for the last year, her friend's shoulder had turned ridiculously cold. Petra feared that it'd never thaw, but maybe that was for the best. After what had happened, maybe it was impossible to go back to how things were.

They used to be inseparable, and they got on so well that they could finish each other's sentences. Back then, no one could make Kate laugh the way Petra could and no one understood Petra the way Kate did.

It's crazy how one night can ruin everything. Petra sighed. Suddenly, she was more sad than angry, and her heart ached like a pin had pricked it.

Everything had gone to shit on New Year's Eve. Instead of a hopeful beginning, it had marked the start of their end.

Sure, Petra and Kate still hung out all the time—they did share the same friend group. However, ever since that night, Kate avoided meeting Petra's eyes. And to Petra, it seemed that invisible sludge had gummed the cogs of their ability to communicate with one another. Words came out awkwardly. Jokes didn't land. The distance between them expanded like the universe.

Their friends were all very much cognizant of the shift in Petra and Kate's dynamic. Yet, both Petra and Kate insisted nothing was wrong, and over time, their group came to accept the disfunction as the new normal—all accept Georgia.

Georgia didn't know how to leave things alone, and she kept digging for the seed of their discord. But Petra wasn't going to tell Georgia anything, and Kate's lips seemed tighter than hers.

When considering everything, Petra had been more than surprised when Kate had approached her with an invitation to sleep over and catch up on a few episodes of their favourite anime series. "It'll be like old times," Kate had promised.

Old times my ass. Petra snorted and crossed her arms. Her irritation mounted again as her thoughts turned back to Kate's relationship with Clyde.

The only solace Petra had was that Kate grew bored easily and was quick to cut ties with love interests. Clyde likely wouldn't last a month. Still, his very existence grated on Petra's nerves.

If only Petra could hit rewind. Then she could change the past. Then Petra could have her best friend back. Then Petra wouldn't be in love with Kate.

Unfortunately, there was no such thing as time travel.

Petra bit her lip as she recalled the events of that fateful night—how she had confessed to Kate that she was gay and how Kate had arched an inquisitive dark brow before telling Petra to prove it. "Kiss me," she had dared.

Before that moment—before their lips had touched, leading them down a thrilling yet awkward exploration of each other—Petra had only thought of Kate as her childhood friend. Ever since, however, Petra's thoughts about Kate were anything but friendly.

Petra didn't like that her mind was consumed with thoughts of Kate. More than anything, she wished she could block them, as she was discovering that unrequited love was possibly the most helpless state to be left stranded in.

While Petra kept telling herself that one day the feelings would pass, she also feared that she'd go on forever examining past interactions with Kate, searching for any signs of reciprocated affection. But, so far, there was nothing to find. If anything, Kate had only shown Petra how much she was trying to forget.

Unable to resist the pull any longer, Petra looked away from the window to peer at Kate. Instant regret punched her in the stomach.

Sure enough, Kate had that dumb lovestruck look on her face. Her bright brown eyes were glued to the phone as her thumbs deftly typed on the miniature keyboard.

Clyde's a tool. What does she even see in him?

Rolling her eyes, Petra hopped off of the window ledge and shoved her hands in the front pockets of her jeans. "I think I'm gonna call my mom to pick me up," she said.

Kate lifted her face from the glowing screen, and she let the device slip from her slender fingers onto the mattress on which she sat with her legs crossed. She frowned. "I thought you were sleeping over."

And I thought we'd be watching Bleach. Petra shrugged. "Just remembered, I have some stuff that I need to do." Petra was proud that her tone came out even and calm—like she didn't give a fuck. She'd gotten quite good at feigning indifference. But the act was tiresome to keep up.

Kate pouted in the cute way she did when she didn't like an answer. "Like, I don't see what could be so important that you'd wanna jet in this weather?"

"It's not snowing that much."

"Ugh, you're so annoying," Kate whined, dropping onto her back on the bed.

"Don't sit there and pretend you care if I leave." Irritation crept into Petra's voice.

From where she lay, Kate's brown eyes narrowed on Petra.

"What's that supposed to mean?"

"I got here like an hour ago, and you didn't even say hi."

"I totally said hi."

Petra shook her head. "No, you didn't. You've been on your fucking phone—chatting with Clyde this whole time!"

"First, there's no need to yell. Second, I'm not chatting with Clyde—I'm talking to Georgia," Kate said, rolling off her bed. She moved towards Petra until they stood toe-to-toe. "And it isn't like you tried talking to me. You've been sulking since you arrived."

"I don't sulk."

"You totally sulk—like all the time. You've got the worst temper ever. It's a wonder I put up with you," she said, chuckling softly.

At the sound of Kate's laughter, Petra felt a rush of warmth blossom across her chest. She looked into Kate's eyes, framed by perfectly curled lashes, and her heart raced while her fingers itched to cup Kate's face. Every fibre of Petra's being sought to lean forward and capture Kate's mouth with her own, but she didn't have it in her to act on her desires. It was too much of a risk. She feared rejection too much.

Petra's shoulders slumped.

"Petra …"

"What?"

Kate tucked a lock of her black hair behind an ear and bit on her lip. "Do you ever think about New Year's Eve?"

Petra's pulse quickened. *All the time.*

"Look, I know we laughed it off, and …" Kate's gaze dropped, and she wrung her hands. "I know we blamed it on the vodka we pinched from your mom's liquor cabinet, but …"

"But … what?" Petra asked. Her heart hammered.

"Sometimes I think about it—actually, I think about it a lot," Kate admitted. She blew out an exaggerated breath of air, and continued, saying, "Anyways, Georgia told me that if I didn't tell you, she'd rat me out, so here's me being honest for once. Okay, I'm just going to say it. Petra, I think I might be in love with—"

Petra didn't wait for Kate to finish—she kissed her.

When Kate melted against her and kissed her back, Petra swore she finally found heaven after traversing hell for nearly a year.

Petra groaned, wrapping her arms around Kate's waist to pull her in closer.

The two teenagers soon found themselves topless and intertwined on the bed—and that's how Kate's mother found them.

Shrieking, the pious Ms. Chen stormed into the room with a red face. "By Christ, get off my daughter!" she shouted, fanning her flushed face with both hands. "No-no-no, this is not happening."

Embarrassed and freaking out, Petra quickly found her shirt and pulled it over her head.

Meanwhile, Kate pulled the bedsheet up to cover her bare chest. Tears brimmed in Kate's brown eyes as her mother continued to shout and make a scene.

More than anything, Petra wanted to console her friend, but Ms. Chen was not having any of that. Ms. Chen wanted Petra to leave—immediately.

Petra was banished to the foyer to await pickup from her own mother while Ms. Chen continued to scold her daughter upstairs.

Petra sat on the narrow bench near the front doors while she waited.

The argument upstairs continued and was mostly audible. Petra wished she couldn't hear it. She didn't like the vehemence in Ms. Chen's tone that was normally warm and inviting. The evident pain in Kate's voice made Petra's heart sink.

"How did you turn out like this? I raised you to be proper. I raised you to be good," Ms. Chen cried. "I don't even recognize you."

Kate must have mumbled something her mother didn't like, for Ms. Chen's next words were, "I forbid it—I forbid you to see her. Give me your phone—now. You are grounded."

"I hate you," Kate wailed. A door slammed, and then Dumpling—the family toy poodle—began to bark and howl.

Petra's gut wrenched as the dread built up in her system—her own mother was a devoted Catholic and shared similar views to Ms. Chen.

As the minutes ticked by, her leg bounced, and the feeling of unease in her stomach intensified to the point where she felt sick. This was not how she planned on coming out to her mother—in fact, it had never really been her intention to come out to her.

When Helda Malkovitch finally arrived, Ms. Chen launched into a rant. Her usually kind face fumed with anger and spittle flew from her mouth as she went on and on about how Petra had defiled her sweet and innocent Kate.

All the while, Petra's mother stood erect and unmoving like a mountain—almost appearing calm. But Petra knew better than to mistake her silence for anything other than fury. Helda always got really quiet before losing her shit—she was like a bubbling volcano just waiting to blow.

It was not until they stepped out into the cold and the front door slammed behind them that Helda erupted. "I did not raise a sodomite," she spat, stomping through the snow that had built up on the walkway. "You will repent for your sins, and this cannot happen again. Do you understand?"

Petra stopped walking. She felt her eyes prickling with tears. "That's not how it works, Mom."

Helda turned and cast her daughter a disdainful look. "God did not create a woman to lie with another woman."

"Good thing I don't believe in God," Petra said, tears running down her face, dripping from her chin.

"Who are you ... you cannot be my daughter." The look her mother gave her then was steely and sharp as a blade—it cut Petra deep.

Turning away, her mother continued to sputter insults while trekking through the snow.

Petra noted that Helda's silver BMW was nowhere in sight, and the narrow residential streets were crowded with parked cars that were quickly disappearing under growing mountains of snow.

Petra stood, arrested by her feelings, and watched as her mother stormed around a corner and disappeared beyond a tall wooden fence.

Even as the snow continued to pelt against her face, burning the tips of her exposed ears, and the cold soaked through the thin canvas of her Converse sneakers—annoyingly wetting her socks—Petra felt that there would be nothing worse than climbing into the warm cabin of her mother's sedan. The car was too small for the two of them, and the ten-minute drive back home was sure to be an eternity filled with Helda citing bible verses and uttering phrases meant to shame Petra out of who she was.

For a second, Petra wondered about Kate—whose mother was almost as bad as Helda. She doubted that the night's debacle would change a thing between them. If anything, Petra felt that the conflict would only strengthen their feelings for each other. After all, Petra and Kate had initially bonded over the dysfunction of their families.

According to Kate, Ms. Chen had always been a zealous evangelical. Helda, on the other hand, only began to frequent mass after the death of Petra's father. He'd died in a car accident when she'd been eight—a drunk driver had run a red light, T-boning her father's vehicle. Petra had taken his passing hard, but Helda had taken it worse.

A newly minted widow, Helda had latched onto the church for stability. Fellowship became the pill to ease her grief, and just like a drug religion consumed her.

Even so, Petra was sure Helda's love for her trumped any devotion to the church. She'd not be forsaken for being gay. Her mother would come around—someday—hopefully.

Just then, her mother's cry rang out into the night, breaking Petra's train of thoughts. She broke into a sprint, fearing her mother might have fallen on ice.

Sprinting past the fence, Petra rounded the corner. She spotted the silver sedan and then she froze—but not from the cold.

The creature straddled her mother's torso; its face buried in her neck. In the dead of night, the smacking of lips sucking on flesh was a terrifying soundtrack that was louder than the howl of the wind.

Petra's mind screamed at her—telling her to flee—telling her that she'd be next. But trembling was the only movement her body remembered. Even her breath caught in her throat.

The monster tore away from its prey with a hiss. Blood dripped from its mouth in globs, staining the greyish slush on the road. Sharp fangs glinted like razors in the dim streetlights. No white could be found in its obsidian eyes. The frightful sight imprinted on Petra's psyche and would haunt her for years to come.

When it fixed its black stare on her, Petra had been sure that it would launch itself at her.

But it didn't.

Instead, it blinked a few times, almost as if confused. Then, its eyes changed—the deep black receding. As its fangs retracted, its crazed expression dissolved. And when it stood, wiping the blood away from its mouth, Petra saw it was a pretty Black girl—about her age—looking back at her.

The monster-girl dropped her gaze to the unmoving body at her feet and made a face that was indiscernible to Petra. "I'm so sorry," the creature whispered so softly that Petra decided she must've misheard. And her eyes had to be tricking her too. Vampires didn't exist, and her mother couldn't be dead, not when she'd already lost her father. Fate would never be so cruel.

But when the creature fled with unnatural speed, Petra was left alone on the empty street, and the truth began sinking into her bones like the cold of that night. Everything suddenly seemed so quiet, the blanket of snow muffling the world.

Relearning how to move, Petra's legs were stiff as she crossed the street. Tears welled in her eyes when she took in the blood pooling around her mother's head, mixing with the slush. Helda's face was so pale, and her lips were blue.

A cry tore from Petra's throat, and the weight of her sorrow drove her to her knees.

Chapter One

Spring 2019

It was dinnertime at the Finch residence, but Vy had no place at the table.

For the last ten years or so—since the age of fifteen—she'd been presumed dead, and while Vy found the duplicitous act painful and onerous to keep up, it was better for everyone if she stayed missing.

From her usual perch—in a large linden tree, whose hefty branches and foliage offered seating and coverage—Vy looked on as her half-sister, Ginger, set a steaming platter of pot roast in the middle of the dining table before taking a seat beside her beau. Scalloped potatoes, green beans and breadsticks were being served as accompaniments.

Despite human food not being to her taste, Vy licked her lips. It was a visceral reaction, a remnant behaviour from the days before her change.

On nights when Vy was feeling particularly lonely, she would often make the journey back home.

Sometimes being near her family had a replenishing effect, but if Vy was ever truly honest with herself, she'd realize that seeing their faces usually did nothing but add to her pervasive sense of isolation.

Through the brightly lit window, Vy watched as her father piled his plate high with meat, potatoes, and breadsticks. Unsurprisingly, he avoided the veggies. Vy worried about him; over the last few months, he had grown quite thick around the midsection, but at least, he had cut the booze.

The more Vy thought about it, a little weight never hurt anyone. What really mattered was that his colour was back, and he seemed to laugh a lot more lately. Indeed, it had taken a very long time, but it seemed to her that Malcom Finch was putting the past behind him. Which was a good thing. Though, Vy selfishly hoped he wouldn't forget her.

Tess was a big reason for Malcolm's turnaround and recovery. Vy couldn't say that she was Tess's biggest fan. Her father's fiancée was a little too young, too happy, and too good. And there was something off about Tess that Vy couldn't quite discern. Yet, if Vy really wanted to know what *it* was, she could. If she was up to it, and had a little spare energy, Vy could pretty much find out everything there was to know about anyone.

But for now, she was not going to rock the boat. Everyone appeared content, and Vy wanted things to stay that way.

As the household began eating, Vy's teeth began to ache dully.

Usually, the thirst came on slowly, as it did at that moment. First, there would be a faint throbbing of her teeth. Then, Vy's throat would constrict and go dry. Then, Vy would incrementally lose control; fangs would protrude, and common sense would blur until all that mattered was relief.

For years, Vy had worked hard to tame her cravings, and for a short stint, she had even felt triumphant. However, more recently, the thirst was raging its ugly head more frequently and with more intensity. It was a cause of great concern—the first and only time that the thirst had sat in the driver's seat, it drove Vy to kill someone. She did not want to see what else might happen if she gave up the wheel again.

Sometimes, Vy felt like a bomb ticked inside her, threatening to blow at any moment, uncaring of the casualties. For that reason, Vy tried to limit her contact and attachment with humans. It was why she couldn't be with her family.

A sad sigh escaped Vy's lips as she withdrew a tiny resealable plastic baggie from her pocket. The small package held a powdery neon-blue substance that had many names, but was most often referred to as chem.

The more prim and proper unhuman factions turned their noses up at and forbade the use of dusts and potions. And about a century ago, the beasts—specifically snobbish werewolves—began decommissioning any low-to mid-grade level spellcaster found to be producing the stuff.

Generally, fangs had no use for anything spellcasters cooked up—blood was the only rush they needed. But Vy was not your average leech. Dubbed by the unhuman community as an illblood—a being of two factions—she was essentially an abomination and was therefore shunned.

While the many factions were divisive in their tolerance for the use of dusts and potions, they were all in agreement about intermixing bloodlines—it should never happen.

About ten years back, when Vy had traded up her sham of a human life, she quickly discovered that to be an illblood meant you were pretty much on your own. Members of her mother's faction fell into two groups: there were those who were wary of Vy and therefore ignored her, and there were those who were just hostile towards her.

On the flip side, Vy wanted nothing to do with the vampire coven—not that fangs would welcome her with open arms any time soon. In fact, fangs were almost as fucking elitist as the wolves.

Looking towards the house, Vy saw her father lean over in his chair to kiss Tess on the cheek while her sister gleamed at her boyfriend as he helped himself to more food. More than anything, Vy wanted things to go back to how they were before her transition.

In the past, that dream had seemed impossible, but Vy had recently come to believe that there might be a way to rid herself of her vampirism. All she needed was something of value that she could gift Mistress May with in exchange for a foretelling.

Opening the tiny plastic baggie, Vy shook a bit of chem on the back of her hand and lapped up the fluorescent powder with her tongue. The effects of the dust hit her almost immediately. A numbness fell over her body like a weighted blanket and away went the aching of her teeth. The feeling was comforting.

Vy's ears pricked at the sound of rustling leaves. Her eyes darted to a branch below her and to the right. A shadow sat in silence on the limb.

"Alice," Vy said with surprise. Though her friend had a bad habit of showing up randomly, Vy was always taken aback when she unexpectedly appeared. It was uncanny that Alice always seemed to know where she was. "How long have you been sitting there?"

The shadow popped up to its feet, and with the grace of a cat, Alice easily manoeuvred to take a seat beside Vy. "Not so long. Although, if your faculties were not impaired, you would have perceived me far earlier," she said in a cold, flat tone.

Rolling her eyes, Vy shifted on the branch to face her friend.

Alice was not the oldest fang in the city, but she was old enough to be terrifying. If anyone questioned Alice's kinship with Vy, they knew better than to openly express their disgust.

In considering her misfortunes, Vy would never count herself as lucky. However, she could not deny that Alice's presence in her life was a blessing. When the world had seemed so dark and Vy had been on the brink of ending it all, Alice had shown up, not only offering shelter and guidance, but also kindness—something Vy had needed more than anything else.

As of late though, Alice and Vy disagreed on just about everything.

"Why were you looking for me?" Vy asked, meeting Alice's piercing blue eyes. While she was over her infatuation, she still felt the tug of lust as her gaze took in the beauty of her friend's face.

Vy often mused that Alice had the look of a vampire love interest in a Hollywood flick. With her porcelain complexion, full lips, and killer cheekbones, Alice was devastating. She was smaller than Vy and had a thin frame. Her short blond hair was always styled the same—slicked back.

Like most fangs, Alice's fashion sense could be boiled down to two words: black and leather. On that cool spring night, Alice sported her usual leather jacket, halter, and leather pants get-up. But even decked in leather, her presence was regal and superior.

"Belisarius received word that the wolves have come to possess a talisman," Alice answered.

Vy raised an eyebrow. "What kind of talisman?"

"I am uncertain of its nature, but does it even matter?"

It probably didn't. A talisman was a talisman—a rare magical item that bestowed unique power and ability upon its possessor. One of Vy's earliest lessons from her mother had been that power was everything and that securing more was the true mission of each faction.

"So, the wolves have a new talisman—whoop-di-do. And I care why?"

"It crossed my mind that if you obtained this talisman and gifted it to Belisarius, he might grant you a place within the coven," Alice responded.

Vy snorted. "You know I want nothing to do with the coven."

"Yes, but it is unwise to remain unaffiliated. There is safety within a collective," Alice said. "Are you aware of what is transpiring in New York?"

Vy nodded. She had heard rumours about a planned coup, but she'd never thought they carried any weight to them. After all, Silas, the coven leader in NYC, was very, very old, and thus freakishly strong. And apparently, it was a renegade of younger fangs—with ambitions of outing their existence to the human world—who were leading the movement. "Why does it matter what is going on over there?" Vy asked.

"I am being sent to New York, and I do not know when I will be back," she replied. "I will not be here to watch over you."

Vy shook her head in disbelief. She couldn't believe that things were that bad. "Is Belisarius shipping you there to back the resistance or support Silas?"

Alice ignored the question and returned to their previous topic, saying, "It is dangerous to remain unaffiliated."

"You worry too much," Vy said with a shrug. "Besides, it's been over nine years since anyone's made a try at me."

Pale-blue eyes narrowed on her. Alice's mouth was set in a tight line. "You worry too little."

"How many times do I have to say it until you get it? I don't want to join the coven. I don't want to be another henchman for Belisarius. I won't be forced to do things." *Like drink human blood.* Vy crossed her arms.

"Foolish girl." Alice's eye flashed with annoyance. "Like it or not, Violet, you are a vampire. With every year, your power grows and your hunger grows with it. Before long, your diet of squirrels, hamsters, and rats will not suffice. Your sickness and aversion is all in your head. Make peace with what you are. Your denial is not serving you."

Vy's fists clenched. "I am not in denial. I have a pla—"

"I will not listen to you prattle about time travel again," Alice said, holding up a hand. Her blue gaze fell to the home with its brightly lit windows and its inhabitants. "It is as if you are addicted more to your own misery than to chem."

"You're such a killjoy."

"No, I am pragmatic," the vampire corrected. "There is no cure for vampirism, and the hourglass likely does not exist. Surely, it would have been found already if it did."

"May knows something," Vy said.

"It perplexes me, the lengths at which you trust that sorceress."

"Trust is not what I'd call it," Vy mumbled. In fact, she didn't trust May at all. But what she knew was that the sorceress had the sight and divulged information for the right price.

"If May knew where the hourglass was—it would be hers," Alice stated. She shook her head. "Why are we discussing this?"

"We don't have to," Vy said.

Standing up on the branch, Alice cast Vy a somber look. "Quit being thick-headed. Acquire the talisman for Belisarius." With those words, she leaped away, disappearing into the darkness of the night.

Feeling slightly annoyed, Vy glanced back at the window. It saddened her to see that the table was empty, the dishes cleared away. Her gaze shifted and fell upon the decorative grandfather clock, which sat in the middle of the Finch dining room, just behind the recently vacated table. It always surprised Vy to see it. Not only because it was broken, but mostly because it belonged to her mother. It was the only relic that belonged to Camellia that hadn't been banished to the basement.

Vy shook herself; she didn't want to think about her mother. She'd rather contemplate an alternate reality for herself. One where she could keep her family. One where she wasn't constantly battling thirst.

Suddenly, a thought popped into her mind that made her smile. Vy decided that she would indeed steal the talisman, but she would not be stealing it for Belisarius.

Chapter Two

Kayla Clay awoke to shooting pain. She clenched her teeth and sat up in her bed. The incessant ringing in her left ear made her feel nauseated and slightly off balance. She momentarily closed her eyes to fight off the wave of sickness that came with every morning.

Over twenty years of service with the Order of Light had been unkind to her body. Fighting the good fight came at cost. She'd broken more bones than she could count, and it was in moments of stasis that her body liked to remind her of that fact.

Reaching over, Kayla switched on the light and opened the drawer of her bedside table.

She removed her pain medication, shook out a few pills onto her palm and swallowed them easily, without water. It would take roughly thirty minutes before she felt some form of relief.

Kayla flinched as she rolled out of bed and flexed her stiff fingers before massaging the tight muscles of her neck and shoulders.

Physical agony encumbered her as she got ready for the day. Alone, within the confines of her chambers, she allowed herself to groan and complain, but once she left her room, she always made sure to mask her discomfort.

As the first female commander in the Order's history, she was already scrutinized to a higher degree. It wouldn't do to show any sign of weakness, especially not now when she was so close to achieving what her predecessors had not—what her father had not.

It was minutes to 0600hrs when Kayla stepped into the harshly lit corridor and winced. The ceiling mounted LED lights were much too bright and made for an almost blinding experience when coupled with the shiny white floors and the matte white walls that were standard across the entire base.

Locking her door, Kayla started towards her office.

Crisp, cool air greeted her when she exited the barracks building. On that early spring morning, it would be another hour before the sun rose, and so the lampposts were still on, illuminating the gravel road that looped the vicinity.

Kayla's tactical boots crunched on the path as she walked, and her blue eyes swept over the quiet landscape that slowly crept to life. Usually, at such a time, there would be swarms of trainees out and about, but exams were in progress. With no classes to attend, trainees tended to sleep in.

Nearing the chapel, Kayla eyed the domed and columned edifice with contempt.

The chapel was the oldest of seven structures that made up the Order's Canadian base, and being that it was the symbol of the

Order's faith, it was justly positioned at the centre of everything. Just north of the church was the main building. The main building contained the admin offices, training facilities, health ward, and dining hall. The motor pool and airfield were to the west. The barracks were to the east. And to the south were the cellblocks, where the lab was located. The cellblocks also housed the base's most valuable assets—magical relics and unhuman captives whom the Order dubbed the lightless.

From an aerial view, Kayla knew the base looked much like a Celtic cross because of the layout of its roads. A deep forest encircled the grounds that boasted perfectly manicured lawns, a variety of trees, and well-pruned bushes. Given that every building was made up of white sandstone and fashioned in the neoclassical style, it would be easy to mistake the site for a university campus.

When Kayla reached the main building, as usual she opted to climb the four flights of stairs instead of riding the elevator to get to her office. Years ago, Kayla had determined that activity lessened her pain while stillness made it flare. For that reason, she avoided sitting and she was prone to pacing.

Moments after walking into the spacious and sparsely furnished room that was the commander's office, Peggy Richardson entered, holding a steaming cup of black coffee and an almond-flavoured protein bar.

Richardson was a pleasant faced middle-aged woman who had occupied the role of executive assistant for the last two decades.

"Morning, Commander." Richardson's warm brown eyes sparkled as she handed Kayla the java and the protein bar.

Kayla acknowledged her assistant with a nod and took a sip of the bitter drink. She then went right to business. "Any new contract requests or leads?"

"Unfortunately not, but I am sure something will come in the inbox soon."

Kayla made sure not to show her dismay. Over the last few months, things had been remarkably calm—the lightless seemed to be on their best behaviour, which wasn't good for her numbers. They'd gotten few requests recently; the majority she'd had to turn down given their ludicrous and dangerous nature. Kayla wasn't in the business of selling livestock. Lightless were meant to be killed, not kept as pets made to perform.

The Canadian base had been in a ruinous state when Kayla had taken the helm a little over a year ago. Under her guidance, costs were cut and profits were up for the first time in years. Not only that, her region was finally closing the gap in recruitment.

But her efforts and milestones meant nothing to those she reported to—the board of directors and the chief commander held her to a much different standard than her male counterparts.

Kayla knew that there were several commanders who failed to meet quota month after month. She knew that Commander Smith, who oversaw the base in Australia, had not met his targets once in his entire twelve-year tenure. Not to forget that her predecessor, Commander Folkes, had held on to his position for half a decade despite being an idiot who revelled in pissing off brokers, who were possibly the Order's most important stakeholders. And recently, from a source, she found out that Commander Rothschild, who ran the US operation, only consistently surpassed his numbers because he worked *with* lightless filth.

Even so, it was only her figures that were constantly picked and probed at.

Were Kayla a weaker person, she'd have cracked under the burden of all the bullshit. But she'd be damned before she let a feeble cohort of old impotent men impede her plans. She lived to see the day of their reckoning—the day she disrupted everything.

Of course, there were some hurdles she'd have to jump in the interim. She was well aware that her head was on the chopping block at the end of the fiscal year, when the board met to review the books and appointments. Ultimately, she only had nine more months to get all her pieces into place.

Kayla took another sip of her coffee and eyed Richardson over the rim of the cup. "Any word from the scouts?"

At that, her assistant perked up. "Yes," she replied with a smile. "There are six likely candidates that have been identified. I will bring their profiles over for your review."

"Good. I will look them over as soon as I get them," Kayla said. Given that soldiers of light (SOLs) retired early—in their mid-forties—the demand for new recruits never waned. There was always a deficit, and it didn't help that workforce planning was nigh impossible when management could not predict how many trainees would make it to the end of the ten-year training program. "Ideally, I'd like to send our recruiters out today or tomorrow to contact those I deem a good fit," she continued.

Richardson nodded and left the commander's office shortly

after.

Kayla dimmed the overhead lighting to its lowest setting and walked over to the nearest of the many large windows. She unwrapped the protein bar from its blue foil and ate it relatively quickly. By the time she had finished her coffee, the medication had begun to work—dulling but not eliminating her pain.

The sun rose, and Kayla welcomed the natural light as she reviewed the printed profiles Richardson had brought her. After careful review, Kayla decided that only four of the six would be contacted, and she advised Richardson to notify the recruiters.

At 0945hrs, Kayla left her office to make her daily visit to the lab. While she disliked any interaction with Dr. Raz, checking in on the progress of his research was always the highlight of her day.

Heading south down the ringed road, sergeants, SOLs, trainees, and general staff saluted Kayla as she passed them. Each she acknowledged with a courteous nod. Such rituals were second nature to her, and she found value in rank that was earned.

Kayla knew she had earned her station and the respect that came with her new title, yet sometimes a tiny voice in her head deceived her into questioning whether she was good enough. The voice always got louder in the weekly conference calls, led by the chief commander, where everyone spoke over her and gave no thought to her suggestions.

At 1000hrs, Kayla walked through a sallyport and entered the lab. The mechanized door clanged shut behind her.

Raz sat on a stool staring at a large computer screen that displayed a multitude of graphs. He didn't look away from the monitor to greet her—not even when Kayla cleared her throat.

Annoyed, Kayla moved in his direction and booted the leg of the table upon which the computer rested. It wobbled slightly, and Raz turned from observing the charts to glare at her.

Surprisingly, he did not open his mouth to mutter one of his tagline insults. Instead, his eyes softened, and he smiled at her, flashing straight white teeth.

He wants something. Kayla's blue eyes narrowed on the doctor's handsome face. She was not the slightest bit interested in hearing his latest request—his last one had been nearly impossible to fulfill.

Frankly, Kayla was still unsure how Olivia had managed to tag and bag a hopper—a lightless with the ability to teleport to any point on the planet in a blink. Hoppers were master evaders. In all of the Order's history, Kayla had only heard of one other being caught.

The brat is resourceful. I'll give her that. Kayla mused as she folded her arms over her chest.

As if summoned by Kayla's thought, Dr. Raz's office door swung open and Olivia stepped into the lab, looking dishevelled as ever.

Kayla fought the urge to grimace. The young SOL irritated her to the point of near insanity, and it had nothing to do with *what* the girl was. Sometimes merely being in Olivia's presence made Kayla want in fall back on old habits.

In her heyday, Kayla had not been known to be so cool headed—far from it, in fact. But a hard lesson had been jammed down her throat a few years back, and she now let reason drive her actions. Emotions were better left out of any decision-making. They were far too messy, and sometimes the consequences could be lethal.

Kayla's mouth became a thin line of dissatisfaction as she eyed the young woman. Olivia's person was never in order: hair long and unbound, shirt untucked with sleeves rolled up past elbows, pants baggy, and boots loose and untied. The woman always looked like she needed rest. Dark circles were a permanent fixture under her mischievous hazel eyes. Olivia's skin was too pale, and her frame was thin like a child's. Nonetheless, she was far prettier than most, and despite her small stature, she was one of the fiercest soldiers on the base.

"S'up Clay," Olivia said with a mere cock of her blond head.

"Put your uniform in order," Kayla directed, her tone sharp.

Olivia blew out an exaggerated breath of air and made a show of rolling down her sleeves and tucking in her shirt. "Happy now?" she asked, gesturing at her uniform with a flourish.

Kayla eyed the woman disapprovingly. "Where's your belt?"

"Don't have one—I am allergic to anything I find constricting."

Before Kayla could respond, Dr. Raz spoke up. "Let's drop the topic of Olivia's state of dress—there is something of import we need to discuss," he said, pushing his glasses up the bridge of his nose with an index finger.

Kayla wanted to ignore Raz and tear into the kid. However, she knew she walked a fine line when it came to addressing Olivia's behaviour.

For whatever reason, Raz was fond of the girl. Kayla didn't understand their relationship, nor did anyone else on the base. The rumours about them were rampant.

Dr. Raz was in his mid-forties. Olivia was twenty-four. The doctor was a good-looking man with his salt and pepper hair, neatly trimmed goatee, and grey eyes partially obscured behind thick black frames. He was the type who kept himself and kept his space tidy. More often than not, he spoke in a soft tone that could coax a nun into sinning. Though, when speaking to Kayla, his voice always held notable tartness.

When considering that Olivia was his exact opposite—sloppy, obnoxious, and wild—they made an odd pairing. While many speculated that the two were sleeping together, Kayla would wager that whatever was going on between them was purely platonic. Her running theory was that Olivia liked the special treatment she received from being Raz's favourite, and Raz kept Olivia close because—unlike the other members of the Special Operations Tactical Unit (SOTU)—the young woman was a willing guinea pig.

Whatever the case was, Kayla knew from experience that any firm disciplinary action taken against Olivia could result in Raz choosing to delay his work. And, given that Kayla needed the serum completed within nine months, she couldn't risk any procrastination on his part.

Gritting her teeth, Kayla looked at Raz. "What do you want this time?"

"I learned many things from the hopper, and I have made significant progress," Raz replied, swivelling on the stool to face her.

"But …"

"But the serum is still … unstable," he said.

"What are the side effects?" Kayla asked.

Raz shot a quick look at Olivia. For a moment, sadness tinged his eyes. "Cardiac arrest."

Kayla's gaze drifted towards Olivia. The young woman had taken a seat atop a desk. Her booted feet dangled above the ground as she leaned back on her hands. Kayla's heart had stopped once before—she recalled how unpleasant it had been. She met Olivia's eyes. "How are you feeling?"

"Peachy," Olivia said with a blank expression.

"I'll put you on light duties for the next little while," Kayla said.

At that, Olivia hopped off the desk. "I'm fine. I don't need to be babied."

"Clay is right," Raz said, nodding. "It will be good for you to rest."

Olivia's hands clenched into fists, and her face flushed. "Fuck that!"

"Language!" Kayla warned.

Olivia angled her chin defiantly. "I am not some fucking child who needs to be coddled after scraping their knee. I know my limits, and I'm fine."

It didn't seem that long ago that Kayla had once thought the same. In her mid-twenties and throughout her thirties, she had constantly pushed herself past what her body could handle. Back then, if anyone questioned her or told her to slow down, she shut them up. Now, at forty-six, her body rebelled against her as if to punish her for all the years of mistreatment.

Kayla did not bother to enlighten the young woman—she knew her words would not sink in. Olivia was brash and thought she knew better. Only time, experience, or death would humble her.

"Nobody is calling you a child," Raz said. Rising from the stool, he moved towards Olivia and placed a reassuring hand on her shoulder.

Olivia looked up at him, and the anger melted from her face. "I know how important this is to you," she mumbled. "I feel like I can bag the illblood faster than anyone—I should be the one who bags her."

Kayla arched a brow. "Illblood?"

At that, Raz walked briskly to a desk and picked up a manila folder. He brought it to Kayla and held it out for her to take. "I think this lightless is the key to stabilizing the serum—and she is finally unguarded and ripe for the picking."

Kayla flipped open the file, her blue eyes scanning the profile. She knew the name well. More than that, she had plans for that lightless in particular, but it was far too early to execute them. "No," Kayla said. "If you need an illblood, I can find you another." Illbloods—lightless of mixed blood, possessing abilities of two unhuman factions—were quite rare, but Kayla was certain they'd be able to find another one for Raz to experiment on.

Raz shook his head. "Another will not do—I need *her*."

Kayla frowned. "Why?"

"I believe this illblood may have been born a vampire," he responded.

"Impossible." Kayla snorted. "Vampires can't be born—they are the reanimated dead."

"Yes, but if you flip through Violet's profile, you'll note that she has aged over the years. She has some other interesting attributes as well. For example, the illblood has an aversion to sunlight but can go about in the day."

Re-opening the folder and turning the pages, Kayla wondered how she hadn't noticed before—the illblood had indeed aged over the years.

"So as you can see, I need Violet—another won't do," Raz stated.

Kayla nodded. "Do you need the illblood alive?"

Raz seemed to think about it. Then, he said, "No, but I need her body as intact as possible."

I can work with that. Kayla didn't like that she'd have to bump up her timelines, but in her line of work flexibility was a must. Plans often needed to be revised at the last moment. Failure to do so could be detrimental.

"I will send Malkovitch and Clay Junior to retrieve the illblood as part of their final," Kayla stated. "As you are likely aware, Malkovitch is the highest ranking trainee—I expect that she shouldn't have much trouble with this task."

The doctor seemed pleased enough with Kayla's words. Olivia was not.

Livid, the brat kicked a stool across the lab, and it collided with a cabinet. A beaker rocked to its side and rolled onto the floor with a smash.

Kayla moved towards the SOL to address the behaviour, but Raz held up a hand in a placating gesture. "Olivia is very passionate about our mission—you must understand she has been through a lot recently," he said.

While the doctor spoke softly, Kayla heard the hidden warning of his words. His expectation was that Kayla would overlook Olivia's outburst. The lab fell silent as Kayla weighed her options. Then, she said, "I agree with you, Raz, she has been through a lot. I will see to it that she is only assigned light duties for the next two weeks."

"That might be for the best," he replied.

Standing behind him, Olivia's eyes flared. Her face was very red with anger, and her breath came in heaves.

Kayla's phone buzzed. She removed it from her pocket. When she saw the message pop up, she resisted the urge to roll her eyes.

Tim Just now

Holding an auction tomorrow. Got some news and a contract I need filling :) Hope to see you XOXO.

Kayla slid her phone back into her pocket and turned to leave the lab. She clutched the manila file under her arm. It was only 1024hrs and already she could tell that it was going to be a long day.

Chapter Three

Petra Malkovitch sidestepped, dodging the open palm strike that was aimed at her head. In a quick movement, she grabbed her attacker's extended arm and twisted it—hard. Wrinkles of pain etched her opponent's face, and the lines deepened when she exerted more pressure on the limb.

From the corner of her eye, Petra caught movement. Her body on autopilot, she released her hold and rolled away in time to evade a second assailant's advance.

With a cocky smirk, Petra dropped to the floor, shooting her leg out. She swept the feet from under both, dropping her two contenders with a resounding thud.

Popping up to her feet, she elbowed a third challenger in the face, which made them stagger and drop to a knee.

In that moment, Petra's smug expression bloomed into a toothy grin. She was pleased with herself—pleased with the progress she'd made. She was strong now, equipped with the skills needed to take on and eliminate the world of its evil. And once she passed her final test and was sworn in as an SOL, she knew exactly which lightless she'd target first.

Petra's expression darkened when the image of obsidian eyes and razor sharp fangs flashed in her mind. In the past, the recollection of her mother's murderer had stirred a crippling panic within her. But now, when Petra remembered, all she felt was blinding rage and a deep desire for vengeance.

Groaning on the floor—a mere foot away from the polished toe of her tactical boot—Petra's two fallen foes, Hardy and Miller, scrambled to their feet while Khan continued to kneel and squint from the hit she took to the face.

"Fuck, Malkovitch's got that look in her eyes again," Hardy said, wiping the sweat from his forehead. "I'm out."

Miller's eyes narrowed on him. "You can't be serious."

"Exams are starting," Hardy said with a shrug. "I don't care how bad the food has gotten. I've waited ten fucking years—ten! I'm not risking getting injured. Nope, not today."

"Hardy's right," Khan said. Lowering herself down on the sparring mat, she stared up at the gymnasium ceiling and rubbed her temples. The area around her right eye had begun to darken and swell. "I don't even want to think about repeating the last year or getting assigned to the cellblocks. I need to pass my final."

"Exactly," Hardy agreed. "Petra, you can take your vouchers and shove them up your ass."

"You sure?" Petra arched a brow. "I hear tiramisu is coming up on the menu this Friday."

Miller groaned and licked her lips. "Seriously, Malkovitch, you have like a million of them, and we've been at this all week. Can't you just give us our cut already?"

While a million was definitely a stretch, Petra had amassed quite the stockpile.

The Order was big on rewarding performance. Every week, the highest performing trainee from each class was awarded with a voucher, which could either be traded in on Fridays, when the kitchen prepared dessert, or at the end of the month, when two could be swapped for a meal from the outside—like pizza or McDonald's.

For the last six years or so, Petra had consistently outperformed her classmates week after week, and they were all bitter about it— especially since Petra rarely used her vouchers.

Since the murder of her mother, Petra had come to perceive the world through the lens of a bleak filter. For the most part, she felt numb, but also colours didn't seem so vibrant, and food had lost much of its taste.

Petra didn't crave sugary treats or fast food; she yearned for her mother's cabbage rolls and borscht. She believed that she'd never find joy in food again and came to view it as mere sustenance—only eating as needed to maintain her muscle mass.

So the food did not bother Petra. Though, to call the Order's cafeteria meals bland would be to compliment them. Frankly, the food was gross, and it had only gotten worse in the last year when Commander Clay, for some unknown reason, changed suppliers. Before, there had been variety and the apples hadn't been mealy.

At present, it was the same lukewarm chunky slop being served day after day. It was no wonder vouchers were so valuable to trainees. Even SOLs were pissed at the commander for the cuts, and they were constantly bad-mouthing Clay for halving the stipends they received to feed themselves when executing missions off base.

The way Petra saw it, the commander probably had a good reason for her decisions. Either way, she didn't care.

"Your cut? That implies I owe you something," Petra said, addressing Miller's question. "The deal was that you would get ten each if you bested me."

"Well, that's not going to happen," Hardy said, rolling his eyes. "How about you give us five each instead? Be fair."

Petra's green eyes darkened. "Life's not fair."

"Whatever, I'm out." Hardy threw Petra a middle finger. "Go fuck yourself, Malkovitch," he swore, storming out of the gym.

"Ugh," Miller exclaimed. She looked as if she were ready to pull out her hair.

If Khan was upset, Petra couldn't tell, which wasn't surprising. Khan wasn't the type to complain. At a little over five feet in height and weighing a hundred and twenty pounds soaking wet, she also wasn't the best combatant.

But what Khan lacked in brawn, she made up for in smarts. She was also pretty in a way that wasn't immediately evident at first. Khan had the kind of face that was a little too distinct—the kind of face that grew on a person overtime. Over the years, Petra had discovered beauty in Khan's strongly peaked brows that were very thick and dark against her olive-toned skin. And occasionally, Petra had even found herself wondering what it might feel like to kiss her classmate's pouty lips. Whenever such a thought occurred, however, Petra quickly scolded herself before feeling guilt's embrace.

While Petra knew she wasn't to blame for her mother's death, she couldn't help but feel slightly responsible. It was hard to look back on that cold winter night and not play out a different scenario—one where Petra hadn't kissed Kate and where her mother stayed home instead of driving over to the Chen household to pick her up.

In the year following Helda's death, Petra often found herself tumbling down the mental rabbit hole that followed whenever she asked herself, "What if?"

Back then, it had always been a laborious effort to shrug off the state of ennui that emanated from such a question. But over time, Petra had learned that nothing good came from examining and re-examining her past decisions. She also determined that it was best to never think of Kate and what could have been. It was too painful and much too distracting.

There was no way to change the past, and so it was best to try to forget. It was best to put all her energy into becoming the best soldier she could be.

Petra knew that she would only be able to avenge her mother if she could outmatch her foe, and to do that she needed to be strong and shrewd.

Relationships—like the act of reflection—were a hindrance to progress. For that reason, Petra had long ago erected a wall between herself and her classmates.

On the few occasions where she felt herself being pulled closer to Khan, Petra had made sure to stack her bricks higher. In another life, Petra saw herself and Khan getting along quite well. But for now, Petra didn't have the luxury of navigating the complexities that came with friendships or lovers. All her waking hours were devoted to training—nothing else mattered.

A sudden hush fell over the gym. Conversations ebbed. The clinking of weight machines ceased. Runners slowed to a walk on their treadmills—some abruptly stopped.

Petra noted dozens of eyes staring at her. Most, however, focused in the direction of the double-doored entrance. Looking over her shoulder, it became apparent why.

Petra crossed her arms and turned to face the woman who stalked towards her.

Isolated and starved for entertainment, most of the base's inhabitants clung to rumour and any form of personal drama with fervour.

Petra and Olivia's rivalry wasn't the juiciest headline. However, it was going on five years since the two women exchanged blows, and many eagerly awaited the day when they would fight again. Petra knew that there was a lot of money and vouchers on the table. From what she'd heard, the majority picked her as likely to win in a second bout.

It pleased Petra to know that most thought she would redeem herself in a future head-to-head against Olivia. Though, she secretly questioned whether she could.

Not only did Olivia have the advantage of having served on SOTU for the last four years, but it was going around that Olivia had single-handedly tagged and bagged a hopper.

Meanwhile, I am still a fucking trainee. Petra clenched her jaw, and her eyes narrowed menacingly on the woman who advanced like a predator towards her. The closer Olivia got, the hotter Petra's blood boiled.

Some would say she was a sore loser. But she knew most agreed that Olivia had cheated in that first match by bringing a knife to a fistfight. Then again, Olivia's behaviour was to be expected. The tiny woman was ruthless, and Petra should have accounted for that.

What Petra found unforgivable was the reaction from base management.

Shortly after Olivia had cut Petra up within an inch of her life, Commander Folkes had made the decision to fast-track Olivia through the SOL training program—essentially rewarding her misconduct. And then, a year later, Olivia was again promoted to work on the special ops team.

Smirking, Olivia halted about five feet away. She mirrored Petra's stance, folding her arms over her chest and standing with her feet wide.

To be expected, Olivia looked like hot mess. Her white shirt was only half tucked in, and the arms of her sleeves were rolled past her elbows, partially displaying the finely detailed tattoos that consumed both her arms. Every member of SOTU boasted the same tattoos. Ambitious as she was, Petra hoped to one day also bare the markings.

"Ran into Hardy in the hallway. He's on a rant, calling you a voucher-hoarding bitch," Olivia stated.

"That's because she is," Miller muttered. Petra shot a glare at her, and Miller's face reddened.

Petra turned her attention back to Olivia. "It's been a while since I've seen you on the base," she said. "Did you finally push Commander Clay's buttons a little too hard? You finally get the boot from SOTU?"

Olivia snorted. "I don't think Clay has ever had her buttons pushed. My theory is that Junior is adopted."

A few snickers came from the crowd that had gathered around the sparring mats.

Petra snapped. "Have some respect. You shouldn't talk about the commander that way." Petra regarded Commander Clay very highly. The grizzly woman was a fucking legend and had one of the greatest track records within the history of the Order.

"I forgot about your hard-on for Clay." Olivia grunted.

Petra gritted her teeth. "I don't have a hard-on for her."

Olivia shook her blond head, her hazel eyes glinting with amusement. "Tell that to your reflection," she said, gesturing with a hand at Petra's muscular form. "You used to be so pretty. Now you look just like Clay—like a man."

The snickers got louder, and Petra's face burned. More than anything, she wanted to knock the laughter from Olivia's face. Frankly, Petra liked the way she looked. She didn't care to be insulted, especially not in front of her peers.

"That's low Liv—even for you," Khan said softly. She had risen some time ago and stood to Petra's left. Khan's peaked eyebrows drew together in a frown. Her right eye was very swollen, and Petra felt slightly bad about it. "You're stirring more shit than usual. Is something eating at you? We can talk about it."

"Nothing's eating at me. I'm just peachy," Olivia barked. "I'm here to give the people a show."

Khan blinked her surprise. "Liv?"

Olivia ignored Khan and stared straight at Petra. "How about it, Malkovitch?"

Petra was also curious to know what had gotten into Olivia, but she didn't care that much. She wanted to fight Olivia. She wanted a real challenge for once. She wanted to test how far she'd come.

Cracking her neck and rolling her shoulders back, Petra smirked. "We can finally put all those bets to bed."

"My thoughts exactly," Olivia said with a chuckle.

Petra dropped into a fighting stance. Her green eyes sparked with excitement. Not bothering to wait for Olivia to get into position, she struck out fast and hard with her fists.

Olivia easily evaded Petra's attack by dodge rolling. Smiling, she sprang to her feet and brushed her loose blond hair out of her face.

The crowd in the gym had grown, and it erupted into cheers as the two women circled each other like sharks on the sparring mats.

Petra went on the attack again, throwing a flurry of punches and kicks at Olivia. None landed. Olivia was quick—she bobbed and weaved, effortlessly avoiding being hit. However, she did seem to lag. She wasn't moving as fast as usual. *Is she injured?*

As if deciding that she was sick of playing defence, Olivia bolted over to the weight-training section and ripped a ten-pound barbell from its stand. Swinging the weight like a warhammer, Olivia went on offence, slashing and hacking at Petra.

With the weight in hand, Olivia was significantly slower, and Petra had no trouble dancing around her opponent's assault. Petra was banking that Olivia would tire herself with the weight soon. *I'll go back on the attack when she looks out of breath.*

An odd thing happened.

On a swing, Olivia flinched and dropped the weight. She staggered back as if in pain. Her left hand grasped at her chest.

Petra didn't know what to make of Olivia's faltering, but she used the opportunity to go back on the attack. Throwing a punch, her fist satisfyingly connected with Olivia's face.

Petra motioned to throw another punch. But she caught a flash of metal from the corner of her eye. Side stepping, Petra just barely missed the dagger aimed at her midsection.

The blade cut through Petra's shirt and grazed the skin of her stomach. A thin stain of blood marred the white fabric.

Petra shuffled back, putting some distance between herself and the blade, which Olivia clutch firmly in her right hand.

"You and your fucking knives," Petra sneered.

Olivia spat a glob of blood onto the floor and wiped her mouth. She looked like she was about to say something, but then the gym doors burst open.

Sergeant Dukes—who managed trainees in their tenth and final year—stepped into the area with a look of displeasure on his face.

The mass of rowdy spectators quieted instantly.

Dukes's steely grey eyes swept over the space, and Petra could tell that he quickly discerned what the whole commotion was about. The sergeant looked at Olivia sternly. "You should not be sparring—I've been advised you are on light duties," he stated.

Olivia glowered but said nothing. She sheathed her blade.

The sergeant's hawkish stare settled on Petra next. "Malkovitch, your presence is needed in the commander's office. Come with me."

Dukes turned and left the gym. Petra had no choice but to follow after him.

Before she walked through the double doors, Petra snuck a peek back at Olivia. *Next time, I will wipe the floor with your face.*

Dukes insisted they stop by the medical ward to get Petra's cut treated before they headed to the commander's office.

Petra sat on the examination table as she waited for the nurse to return with materials to bandage her up.

Dukes stood with his arms crossed by the door of the examination room. "I don't know what you were thinking," he said suddenly.

"What?"

"Sparring with Olivia when finals are beginning," he replied. "Don't you remember what happened to you the last time you faced off against her?"

Petra's body went very stiff. "I wouldn't have lost this time."

"I think you underestimate her. The girl might be half your size, but she never goes into a fight without a trick up her sleeve," Dukes said. "My advice—stay clear of her."

"I have tricks too," Petra retorted.

Dukes snorted.

The nurse returned with antiseptic and a large bandage.

Petra lifted her shirt, and the nurse got to work cleaning the small cut and applying the dressing. When the nurse finished, Petra thanked her and hopped down from the examination table.

Dukes led the way out of the medical ward. Together, they walked down the brightly lit white halls.

Passing groups of trainees and SOLs, Petra noted the way her colleagues looked at her before diving back into their conversations. *Seems everyone knows about the fight already.*

Petra and Dukes climbed four flights of stairs and then walked down another long hall until they arrived at the large set of doors that led to the commander's office.

Richardson, the commander's assistant, frowned at them from behind her desk that was positioned just outside the office. "What took you so long? Never mind—just go inside. The commander has been waiting for you."

Dukes opened one of the two doors and stepped into the dimly lit office. Petra followed him, and he closed the door behind them.

Commander Clay paced by the large windows on the other side of the room. She stopped, and her blue gaze swept over Dukes and then Petra. The intensity of Clay's eyes used to make Petra squirm, but she was no longer intimidated by the woman. Instead, Petra revered the commander. She sought for Clay to see her as competent and strong.

Ten years ago, after being primed by her caseworker—who she'd later learned to be a scout for the Order—Kayla Clay had recruited Petra.

Back then, Petra had shrunk back when the beast of a woman

had joined her on a park bench. Despite wearing a cast on her right arm, Kayla came off as threatening to a younger Petra, who had escaped to the park to be alone with her thoughts and to get high to numb her pain.

When Kayla had taken a seat beside her, Petra had quickly outed her joint.

Before her mother's murder, Petra hadn't dabbled much with weed. But she'd picked up the habit as a way to cope with the shattering of her life. It hadn't help much though. It hadn't fogged her brain enough to forget. It hadn't quelled the flood of tears that came with every night.

Nights had always been the worst. A deep despair had always taken hold of her when the lights in the group home went out in her shared room. And even in the day, it had followed her around, making it impossible for her to speak to anyone—even to Kate.

Before long, Petra had started skipping school. Her hopelessness had felt like a collar, tightening around her neck a little more each day.

But then, her caseworker had said the most unexpected thing. "I believe you," she had said. "I know nobody else does, but I do—and there are others just like you and me who have seen the darkness that hides in this world. There are even those who fight against it."

Petra had blinked up at the woman. And for first time in weeks, she was able to breathe a little easier. "What if I wanted to fight too?" she had asked.

In response, her caseworker had smiled at her and said, "I would say that is a very noble thing to want to do."

Not long after that conversation with her caseworker, Clay had found Petra in the park and sat down beside her.

For many moments, Clay hadn't said anything, but Petra would forever remember her first words, "It is unfortunate what happened. I can empathize. I have lost somebody too."

Petra had looked up at the woman, tears brimming in her green eyes. "Does the pain ever go away?"

Clay had shaken her head. "No, not fully. But I have found that there is no better medicine than revenge."

"Revenge," Petra had repeated.

All in all, it hadn't taken much convincing on Clay's part. Petra had agreed to join the Order minutes into their discussion.

Now, meeting the commander's icy blue eyes, Petra hoped that Clay would forget the anxious and weak girl Petra had once been.

Petra raised her hand and saluted the commander.

"Have a seat Malkovitch." Clay nodded and gestured towards the seats that were opposite the great desk. Petra saw that one of the two armchairs was occupied by Dustin Clay, the commander's son.

Petra followed directions and sat down. Nearby, Dustin turned in his seat and leaned towards her on the armrest. "Hi Malkovitch," he said with a bright dimpled smile.

Dustin was possibly the prettiest boy Petra had ever seen outside of television—he looked nothing like his mother. Where Dustin possessed a boyish appearance and soft blue eyes, his mother's face was all deep wrinkles, faint scars, and hard angles. Where Dustin was lean, his mother was built like a Viking. Where Dustin's blond hair was full and wavy, his mother's was thin and straight.

Petra didn't return the smile. Instead, she glared at him. She figured that if she scowled at him enough, he'd get it into his head that he would never have a chance with her.

His continued crush on her was baffling. Years ago, maybe it had made sense. She'd once been quite pretty with her long red hair and her blossoming feminine physique.

When she'd been a new recruit most of the boys in her class had taken a liking to her. But Petra had chopped her hair off a long time ago, and she now packed more muscle than what most would think appropriate for a woman.

All but Dustin had lost interest in her. His continued infatuation was ridiculous and made no sense.

Commander Clay walked behind the massive desk but did not take a seat. She gripped the back of her chair with her hands and looked over at Dukes. "Thank you, Sergeant, you may leave."

Dukes nodded and left.

"What happened to your shirt?" the commander asked.

Petra looked down at the bloodstain. "I was sparring."

"And who is it that got that close to you?" Clay raised a brow.

"Olivia."

"I see." The commander fell into thought. Her brows furrowed. Seconds ticked by where the only sound was humming from the vents. Then, Clay cleared her throat and said, "I have invited you two here because you are to work together to complete your final exam."

Dustin's a fanatic and a fucking idiot. He'll only get in my way. Petra shot Dustin a dark look. He beamed at her.

"This is your mission," the commander said, sliding a manila folder across the desk towards Petra.

Annoyed, Petra reached over and grabbed the folder. She flipped it open without a thought. When she looked down at the profile, her heart stopped.

Instantly, Petra was taken back to her lived nightmare. She saw blood mixing with slush. A pair of soulless eyes mocked her. Fangs glinted like sharp steel. And she recalled her terror—the way her entire body froze.

Petra's pulse began jackhammering in her ears. Her fingers crumpled the pages in the folder.

The woman in the profile picture did not look like a monster. No, she was stylishly dressed and had a radiant complexion the colour of black coffee with a splash of milk. Her hair was long and black and curling. Her dark and sultry eyes did not hint at the vile creature within.

"You are to bring the target back—alive," the commander stated. "I hope you are up to the task, Malkovitch."

"I've never been more ready," Petra said through clenched teeth.

"And you understand that no harm should come to her?"

Petra blinked her confusion—it dawned on her that she hadn't initially heard what the commander had asked. *Clay expects me to bring the fang back alive?* Petra fought against the cruel laugh that bubbled in her chest. *There is no fucking way.*

Contrary to her thoughts, she responded, "Yes, I understand."

"I do not find your response convincing, Malkovitch."

You once told me that there is no better medicine than revenge.

Petra cocked her chin forward and stared intently at the commander.

And you expect me to let the fang live?

Petra willed her tone to sound indifferent when she finally said, "I will bring the target back alive."

The commander didn't appear to look convinced, but said, "Good."

Chapter Four

Magic Ink was May's front business. Toronto's most revered sorceress owned the tattoo shop that catered to both humans and unhumans.

Vy was curious to know why May provided services to humans at all—inking them was not that lucrative, and it posed the risk of exposure. Sure, there were some unhumans who took no real steps to hide what they were from the world, but May was not one of them. From what Vy knew, the sorceress was a huge advocate of the status quo and had a hard stance against the enlightenment movement that was gaining momentum within some factions.

For a moment, Vy's thoughts turned to Alice, who had been sent to New York, where the movement was really picking up steam amongst the youngest of fangs within Silas's coven. Vy wondered what motive Belisarius had for sending Alice away—the Toronto coven leader was known to thrill in stirring pots. She hoped that whatever he was cooking up didn't get Alice burnt.

If it weren't for Vy's chem habit, she would have actively avoided going anywhere near May's tattoo parlour. The place was riddled with unwanted memories. But, since May didn't allow for bulk purchases, Vy had to drop by weekly for her fix.

Approaching the entrance, Vy looked inside the shop and groaned when she saw Poppy's unpleasant face. Her hand hesitated to reach for the door handle. *Maybe I should come back later when the spellcaster isn't working.*

Vy liked to think that her skin had thickened over the years; after all, she'd endured so much—the mysterious departure of her mother, the monstrous change that came with puberty and the horrific realization that she was a slave to the thirst, which she could not fully sate without falling ill.

Deep down, however, she knew that she walked a tightrope when it came to her emotions. So, as best as she could, she tried to avoid situations that had the potential to throw her off.

Vy felt that she could handle Poppy's hostility, but the aggression coupled with being in the establishment was awfully unbalancing for her. It was hard to be in the shop and not think of Nick.

Sure, a couple months had passed, but Vy was still struggling to come to terms with the fact that he was no longer part of her life.

Exhaling a deep breath, Vy pulled on the door and entered.

As she walked towards what used to be Nick's workstation, she bit her lip. A new artist—a spellcaster with a neon-green mohawk and too many piercings to count—now occupied the space next to the bubble-gum pink graffiti wall.

The green-haired unhuman was quick to look away when their eyes met, and Vy told herself that she didn't care if the spellcaster ignored her.

Upon reaching the checkout counter, Vy cleared her throat to get Poppy's attention. When the ill-tempered spellcaster looked up from her phone, Vy asked, "Is May in?"

Poppy set her phone aside and leaned against the counter. The look she shot Vy could have frozen the Great Lakes. "We're out. Come back tomorrow."

Vy gritted her teeth. "I'm not here for that."

The spellcaster snorted her disbelief. "My mistress has no other business with the likes of you. Scram—there'll be a fresh batch tomorrow."

Vy dropped her voice so that the nearby patrons would not hear when she said, "I'm not looking to purchase chem. I need to speak with May."

Poppy pushed off the counter and stepped towards Vy. "My mistress is busy." The spellcaster stood almost a full head taller and loomed over her.

Vy craned her head back and locked eyes with the witch. "Just tell her I'm here. What's the big deal?"

"Get the fuck out of here, fang!"

A few human patrons turned their heads towards the counter with a questioning look, and Vy commented softly, "Wanna say that louder? I don't think everyone heard."

Poppy folded her arms and grunted. "I don't know what Nick ever saw in you."

Vy's body flushed with heat. Her teeth tingled, itching to extend and tear through Poppy's flesh. In her mind, she even saw herself doing it, pouncing on the spellcaster and sinking fangs into the thin skin of her neck. The thought alone was enough to send a wave of nausea through Vy's body.

As the feeling of sickness washed over her, Vy reached for the counter's edge to steady herself. Holding on to it, she closed her eyes and waited for the image to clear from her head.

"What the fuck is wrong with you?" Poppy said, the disgust in her voice evident.

Releasing a deep breath, Vy opened her eyes when the sickness passed.

Vy opened her mouth to answer, but before she could utter a word, the door behind the counter opened. The great sorceress stepped out into the parlour.

May's dark-brown eyes said everything there was to say and nothing at all as they swept over the bickering pair.

While age was not a true indicator of a spellcaster's strength, it was usually a decent guide. By appearance alone, Mistress May looked to be in her mid-to-late twenties, but Vy knew she had to have at least a couple of centuries under her belt. There was something about the sorceress's presence—the way she took up all the air in the room, the way she captivated the eye, the way she assertively moved—that hinted at her years and prowess.

Vy only knew of one other who possessed such an aura—her mother. But the similarities ended there.

Mistress May was not one to conceal her natural bronze

complexion—a feature of all spellcasters. The flowing magenta dress she wore left nothing to the imagination with its plunging neckline and contoured fit. As usual, the sorceress's long dreadlocks were tied back neatly with a golden scarf. Large gold hoops hung from her ears, and gilded bangles jiggled on each wrist as she shifted. But the amulet she wore about her neck was said to be her most cherished possession. The long chain with its hefty red stone was thought to be the source of May's soothsaying abilities. Some even thought that it was a talisman fashioned by the Great Architect, creator of all.

Having only interacted with May on a couple of occasions, Vy wasn't sure what to think. All she knew was that May was her best bet for getting her hands on the hourglass, and she hoped that the bauble she had snagged was of enough value to entice the sorceress to grant her a foretelling.

May flashed a smile that didn't match the predatory glint in her eyes. "In my office, the two of you—now!"

To Vy, Poppy looked a hundred times smaller as she scurried through the open door.

When all three of them were in May's office, the sorceress shut the door, dampening the sound of chatter and the buzzing of tattoo machines.

Before Vy could register what was happening, May lashed out, smacking the lesser spellcaster with a force that drove her to the floor. "What do you have to say for yourself?"

Struggling to her feet, Poppy wiped her mouth with the back of her hand—it came away red with blood. A metallic tang scented the air.

Vy licked her lips while simultaneously feeling the nausea return.

It was such an odd thing—Vy could rip into a squirrel or rat with ease. But spotting or smelling human or unhuman blood made her stomach turn. Every time she had tried to go hunting with Alice, the outing always resulted in Vy puking her brains out.

Vy was convinced she was allergic to human and unhuman blood, but Alice believed it was all in Vy's head. Whatever the case was, Vy swore off drinking blood from anything that was bigger than a raccoon years ago. And the thirst raged at her for doing so—but the way she saw it, she didn't have a choice in the matter.

"My apologies. I never meant too—"

"You don't even know what you did," May sneered.

Poppy's glittering eyes couldn't quite meet her mistress's steely gaze.

"What, by the Architect, did I do to deserve to be surrounded by imbeciles?" Sighing, the sorceress rubbed at her temples and then motioned with a jiggling hand for Poppy to depart. "Remove yourself from my sight. I will deal with you later."

Nodding frantically, Poppy rushed out of the room but made sure to gently close the door behind her. Suddenly, Vy was alone with May in the tiny office.

With its white walls and standard dropped ceiling, the room was a stark contrast to the loud pink-and-black scheme of the Magic Ink's main area.

Looking around, Vy doubted that May spent any time in the drab space, and she stifled a laugh that arose from picturing the daunting sorceress seated behind what had to be a desk from IKEA.

Vy's theory was confirmed when May proceeded towards the only item in the room that warranted any attention—a gilded full-length mirror whose surface shimmered in a peculiar way that spoke to its true purpose.

"Come now, illblood. I am eager to see what you have brought for me." With those words said, the sorceress stepped into the mirror and disappeared.

While Vy hated portals, she heeded May's directions and followed her through the mirror. Reaching the other side, Vy stumbled but quickly righted herself. Despite having travelled thousands of times via portal, she'd never gotten used to the feeling of being swallowed and spat out. To her, portals were more disorienting than teleportation. But they also reminded Vy of a time she'd rather forget.

Taking in her surroundings, Vy determined that the grand drawing room, where she presently stood, was much more to May's taste.

The floors were polished natural stone. Cream-coloured walls were ornately panelled and inlaid with gold. High arching windows looked over a giant terrace and a beautifully landscaped garden with a grand sputtering fountain. The vaulted ceiling was decorated with a gaudy fresco that depicted the Great Architect creating the universe and the worlds in-between.

Vy could see how some—maybe most—would look upon such a room and marvel. In her opinion, however, the style was much too extravagant and dated. It gave seventeenth-century French château vibes. For a moment, Vy wondered if the portal had transported her to France.

Deciding that it didn't matter where she was, Vy turned her attention to May.

The sorceress sauntered over to a Victorian mahogany chaise with buttercream upholstery and sat down, beckoning with a rattling hand for Vy to do the same.

Vy crossed the room and sat in an adjacent armchair.

"Now, you must forgive Poppy—the girl is not right. All the same, she will be punished accordingly," May said, leaning back comfortably in her seat.

Vy couldn't help but grin slightly. It tickled her to know that Poppy would be getting a taste of her own medicine. May was rumoured to be cruel—though less cruel than most sorceresses who headed a ménage of spellcasters.

Having eavesdropped on countless conversations, Vy came to understand that May ruled by withholding wisdom. She manipulated those who served her with frivolous promises of sharing insights on how to execute complex magic. And when a spellcaster within her ménage pissed her off, May was known to take a skill away from them.

Vy was not sure how this was possible, but she'd overheard enough spellcasters complain about May erasing an ability to believe it to be true.

A sigh escaped the sorceress's lips. "It is as if history has taught you nothing," she said. "You younger unhumans grow too bold, saying whatever is on your mind without a care. You never think about who might be listening—who might be watching."

Vy didn't know how to respond, so she kept quiet and clasped her hands together in her lap.

"So, tell me, what are your thoughts about these whisperings?" May asked.

Vy blinked her confusion. "Whisperings?"

"Do you think that humanity should be enlightened to the existence of unhumans? It would seem that is all that is ever talked about these days."

Oh, those whisperings. Vy met May's brown eyes. "There is a reason we stay hidden. While we may be stronger, their numbers are greater." The words were not her own—they were her mother's.

"Wise words. I wonder where I've heard them before?" May cracked a smile, and to Vy, it seemed genuine. It disappeared when she added, "Not to forget that the few mortals who are enlightened want to kill us all."

Vy knew that the sorceress was referring to the Order of Light—a fanatic organization that hunted unhumans for profit and sport. In the past, Vy had had a few run-ins with the Order. Each time, Alice had quickly made mincemeat of their soldiers.

Vy's last encounter with the Order had been about nine years ago. She was pretty sure Alice had scared them off her for good.

Shifting in her seat, the sorceress leaned over to grab a dainty golden bell that rested on an ornate end table. She rang it twice.

The chime summoned a beautiful spellcaster dressed in a stylish white dress with puffy sleeves. Vy bit her lip as she eyed the figure.

"She is pretty, isn't she?" May said.

"Yes," Vy replied with annoyance. It irritated her that the sorceress could read her desires so easily.

"Casey, bring myself and the illblood something to take the edge off," May directed.

The spellcaster left momentarily and returned with a gilded platter that held a decorative box and a miniature spoon. Vy's eyes followed the woman closely as she approached and presented her mistress with the tray.

Opening the lid, the sorceress removed a spoonful of neon-blue dust and snorted it.

Soon, the box and its contents were before Vy, and she had to work to pull her gaze from the spellcaster's bosom long enough to focus on spooning a dose of chem upon the back of her hand. But Vy didn't dare snort the powder. While the sorceress seemed quite unaffected, Vy knew from experience that chem packed a greater punch when inhaled, and she much preferred the weighted feeling of calm that came from a simple taste.

With the flick of her tongue, Vy lapped up the powder. Quickly, the tension in her body melted away, and the rumbling of her thirst ebbed with it.

"You may take your leave now," the sorceress said, dismissing the younger witch with the wave of a jingling hand.

With heavy-lidded eyes, Vy watched the pretty spellcaster leave the drawing room. She wondered if Casey ever frequented the Sappho Lounge. Likely not—Vy went often, and she hadn't seen her once.

Of course, even if she did see her, it wouldn't matter. Vy was an illblood. Casey was sure to ignore her, as most spellcasters did.

"You are lucky I am in a good mood today," May said. "I should take offence at the sultry looks you cast my paramour—yet not a single glance sent my way."

When pointed out, it was weird that Vy was not attracted to the sorceress.

May appeared as a goddess in the flesh, and the reek of glamour was nowhere to be found on her. At least, Vy could not perceive that May was shrouding any flaws behind a magical veneer.

"I am sorry," Vy said.

"Save your apologies for someone who wants to hear them." The sorceress cackled. "Now, I know you have something for me, but I could not *see* what it was. Show me what you have brought."

Nodding, Vy reached into the inner pocket of her jacket and withdrew the iridescent black bead—the talisman she had stolen from the high and mighty werewolves. She held it out in her palm for May to see.

The sorceress's eyes widened. "Where did you get that?"

"Thought you knew everything." Vy shrugged. "I found it on the sidewalk."

Another cackle escaped May's lips. "You should know the sight has its limits. Even so, I do recall Mackenzie was bragging to anyone who would listen that he came into possession of such an item. So, the real question is: how did you manage to pilfer it from the beast?"

It was a question Vy couldn't answer. She was sworn to secrecy.

"So, it's a pretty big deal? What does it do?" Vy asked, deflecting the question.

"It does nothing, and the wolves are as dimwitted as they are arrogant."

Vy felt her heart crash to the floor. "It's worthless?"

"Not entirely," May responded. "It does have some magical properties and can be ground and mixed into pigments for rune tattooing." It was common knowledge—even to the wolves—that May supplied dusts and potions, but her main source of wealth came from charging exorbitant fees to ink enchanted marks onto unhuman flesh.

The tattoos were a form of glamour and frequently served the purpose of augmenting an unhuman's physical appearance. But Vy knew the capabilities of rune tattooing to be endless. What truly mattered were the magical elements of the ink and the intricacies of the spell behind the design.

Vy eyed the glittering object she held and felt at a loss. She had been banking on it being of value.

"Let me see it," May said, holding out a perfectly manicured hand.

Vy leaned over in her seat and dropped the insignificant pearl onto the sorceress's outstretched palm.

Gripping the tiny orb between her index finger and thumb, May observed it closely. "Tell me how you managed to come into its possession?" she asked again.

"I don't see how that matters."

The sorceress did not seem pleased with Vy's answer, but moved on to a new question. "What is it that you want in return for this?"

Vy arched a brow. "So, you do want it?"

"I am always sourcing petty magical items that can be broken down for ink," May answered in a clipped tone. "Out with it now—I don't have all day. What is it that you want?"

"About a month ago, I was in your shop. I guess I looked sad because you commented that the past is not completely set, and I should not fixate on what can be changed."

"Did I now?" May's eyes sparkled with bemusement.

"Yes, you did," Vy replied. She frowned. "I think you were hinting to me that there is an alternate future for me."

"Was I now?"

"Were you?"

"Maybe. It depends."

"Depends on what?"

"Depends on what you say next," May said.

"Tell me where I can find the Architect's hourglass."

The sorceress exploded with laughter. When she sobered, she said, "your naïveté is refreshing. If I knew where a talisman of such power was, why would I ever tell you?"

May's words left Vy's spirit feeling extinguished. "What did you mean, then, when you told me not to fixate on what can be changed?"

"So many questions, but how do I benefit from answering?"

"A trade. I will give you the item."

"This pitiful thing? Illbood, you will have to do better."

"What is it that you want?"

"I want what everyone wants—power," May said. "Tell me how

you stole the stone from the beasts."

Vy gritted her teeth. "I can't."

"Why?"

My mother swore me to secrecy. "I just can't."

"You know you owe her nothing—she left you."

Vy's eyes narrowed on May. "How did you—"

"I have the sight, remember? Is that not why you are here?" the sorceress asked. "It is a fair trade. Tell me how you pulled a fast one on the wolves, and I will tell you how to get the hourglass."

"How do I know I can trust you?"

"You can't."

Vy bit her lip, and a thick silence fell over the room as she thought about and weighed her options. Was it really a fair trade? Vy wasn't sure.

May broke the quiet. "My patience is wearing thin. I need an answer."

Vy's brows furrowed, and she met the sorceress's eyes. Then her gaze dropped to the polished stone floor. "I can't. Sorry I wasted your time," she said with a shake of her head.

"The only time you waste is your own. It'll take you an eternity to find what you think you want," May said, leaning back in her seat and steepling her hands. "But by then it'll be too late."

Vy's brows drew closer together. "What do you mean?"

"You will never see your mother again."

The drawing room's walls felt like they were closing in on Vy. Her breath caught in her chest. She looked up at May—the sorceress seemed quite indifferent, like she couldn't care either way.

Meanwhile, Vy was in turmoil. How could she divulge the knowledge she had vowed never to share? Then again, perhaps May was right. Did Vy really owe her mother anything after she'd left years ago and without a word?

A sigh escaped Vy's lips. What did she have to lose? She had already lost everything, and the thirst was getting worse with every passing day. It was only a matter of time before she lost her grip on the wheel again, and she did not want that day to come. She needed to rid herself of her vampiric affliction, and the hourglass was the key to finding out how to do that.

"Okay, I will tell you," Vy whispered in defeat. Her gaze dropping to her lap, she began divulging her secret. When Vy said all there was to say, she stared up at May and asked, "So, how do I find it?"

The sorceress smirked. "I have foreseen a path where you will enter Present's Gate, but you will not do so without Petra Malkovitch willingly at your side."

"And?"

The sorceress raised a brow.

"That's all you are going to tell me?" Vy felt heat rushing through her body.

"That's all you need to know."

Vy bolted to her feet with clenched fists. "Who the fuck is Petra? Where do I find her?"

"You don't have to worry about that—she will find you." With those words, the sorceress erupted into another fit of laughter.

Livid, Vy wanted to jump on the sorceress and scratch her eyes out. But she knew that wouldn't end well for her.

Of course, she'd been duped. Alice had warned her about May. Why did Vy always have to learn the hard way?

Chapter Five

Kayla stepped down from the helicopter into the cool night air. Over the course of the hour-long ride, her muscles had grown stiff and achy.

Two of Tim's men greeted her with thin smiles. Both bald brutes were suited in black and were armed with pistols at their waists. They escorted her off the rooftop without a word. Kayla passed through a heavy weighted door and descended a few flights of stairs. She was met by the melodic notes of smooth jazz.

Kayla gritted her teeth. She hated jazz. Actually, she'd come to hate music in all of its forms. It exasperated the constant ringing in her left ear.

Five years ago, she'd been diagnosed with tinnitus. The condition was a parting gift from a beast—specifically a werehyena—who'd smacked her around a few times before Kayla had managed to lodge a silver bullet between its feral yellow eyes.

One of the guards held open a door for her. Kayla didn't bother thanking him as she stepped into the dimly lit room.

The opulence of the club was revolting. Persian rugs lined marble floors. Coveted art pieces hung upon intricately panelled mahogany walls. Guests dressed in the world's finest sat comfortably in plush velvet armchairs, sipping from crystal glass that brimmed with dark-red liquid.

Disgusted, Kayla looked away from them. Seeing humans consuming vampire blood always turned her stomach.

While 99.9 percent of the world was unaware of the nightmarish fiends who stalked in the dark, the few who were enlightened tended to be obsessed with the supernatural and sought to find a way to taste immortality by any means possible. More often than not, the 0.1 percent were the obscenely rich, and brokers like Tim liked to spin tales to them that grating bits of a fang's tooth in their morning coffee would keep them forever young and vibrant.

Having been brought up in the Order, Kayla learned early on that when a person had everything money could buy, it was only natural for them to reach for the unattainable. It was only natural to want immortality.

Kayla found their sort deplorable, and she hated doing business with them. Unfortunately, were it not for their money, the Order would have dissolved long ago.

The Order had been formed in sixteenth-century England by a group of witch-hunters who tore away from Christianity to embrace a new faith devoted to serving a new God—the Light Almighty.

The origin of the Order's doctrine was unclear, and Kayla had always wondered about it. Though not one to care too much for theology, she never went looking for the answer.

She was, however, well versed on how the Order pivoted from a mission devoted to eviscerating darkness from the world, in the name of the Light, to a framework more focused on raking in cash.

After experiencing years of expanding membership throughout the centuries, the Order's influence suffered a steep decline during the First World War. Too many of its followers were conscripted, and too many died. Those who were lucky enough to have escaped the trenches with their lives seemingly washed their hands of the Light.

Suddenly floundering, in the 1920s, the Order's leaders determined that the survival of their belief depended on becoming financially independent instead of relying on tithes.

And so, a model was developed where the organization began to monetize its services, taking on contracts to kill or capture lightless. And, of course, now and then, a client would make an odd request for the retrieval of a supernatural tome or relic.

It hadn't taken long for the new model to pay off, but in changing everything, the Order had created a rift within itself. There was still a great majority amongst its constituents who balked at the shift away from core principles. Then there were those like Kayla, who found the church to be an archaic hindrance.

All in all, if it were not for the filthy rich and their fascination with the paranormal, the Order's house of cards would have toppled decades ago.

But even if Kayla owed all she had to her clients, she couldn't help but despise them. A taste of immortality should not be reserved only for the rich. In Kayla's perfect world, everyone who wanted immortality could possess it. In her perfect world, magic would be a tool for all of humanity to use to finally eradicate lightless filth from the planet.

"Oh, you made it."

Kayla's thoughts were interrupted by a shrill of a voice that was all too familiar to her.

Swallowing a groan, Kayla turned to see Tim Harding approaching her with his thin arms held out wide, as if to embrace her. She held up a hand—a warning to let him know that he touched her at his own risk.

Her gesture made him smile, and for the slight moment where laugh lines crinkled his beady brown eyes, he almost appeared handsome.

Tim was a slimy man, and there was something oddly reptilian about him. He was very pale with slicked back black hair. While Tim was shorter than Kayla, his crocodile leather shoes had a heel that gave him a slight edge on her. That night, he wore a perfectly tailored cream pinstriped suit with a white turtleneck beneath.

Tim always wore turtlenecks. Kayla was one of the few who knew why—unfortunately.

Tim stopped walking when he stood a handshake distance away. He had an entourage of three guards behind him.

Kayla cocked her head towards the squad at his rear. "You've beefed up your security?"

Tim didn't acknowledge her statement. Instead, he said with a smirk, "I would like to speak to you—privately."

Of course he does. Somehow, Kayla prevented her disdain from showing on her face.

Tim turned and beckoned for Kayla to follow him. She did so—not willingly, but out of necessity. It was important for Kayla to know what was going on around her, and Tim had eyes and ears all over the place. For now, she had to play nice where he was concerned.

Once they were alone in his lavishly decorated office with the door shut and locked, Tim wasted no time.

He shrugged out of his cream jacket and tugged his turtleneck over his head. Beneath the expensive clothes was a hairless and bony man who had patches of scaly, dried skin around his elbows. Dressed down to his sleeveless undershirt, Tim came off as docile as an alligator with broken legs and a loose jaw.

Excitement sparkled in his brown eyes. His breaths came quicker with each passing second.

Kayla's eyes drifted to the band of dark bruises about his thick neck—Tim had a thing for being choked. He liked to be strangled to the point of almost suffocating. But he only got a hard-on if a woman did it.

Most women, naturally, didn't have the strength to take down a man like him. And so, Tim had set his sights on Kayla from the moment they'd first met. When he hadn't been able to woo her with gifts and kind words, he had propositioned her. Knowing that it would be helpful to have a man like Tim in her corner, Kayla had accepted.

"I am ready," Tim said, licking his lips.

Without hesitation, Kayla approached him from behind and wrapped her arms around his neck like a vise.

It wasn't long before Tim began to squirm. But even as he started to thrash, attempting to pry her forearms away, Kayla could tell that he enjoyed every moment. The closer Tim got to the black precipice of no return, the more he revelled.

How easy it would be to snap his neck? Kayla often found herself resisting the temptation to maintain her grip a second too long. If she were put in this same position a few years back, she likely would have given in. But reason outweighed her desire to see Tim dead, and so she released him moments after the fight leaked out of him—when his body started to go limp while the bulge in his pants was evident.

Coughing and gasping for air, Tim's knees hit the floor. His face and the whites of his eyes were very red.

Despite the symphony of throaty coughs, he wasted no time and unzipped his fly.

Kayla turned her back on him. "Seriously? There is a washroom right over there. It'd be nice if you'd do that in there for once," she grumbled, walking over to his desk.

Tim didn't reply—he was far too engrossed with jerking off. It wasn't long before his coughs mixed with moans to create the most disgusting soundtrack Kayla's ears ever perceived. The ringing in her ear intensified, making her feel slightly off balance.

Turning her attention elsewhere, Kayla picked up a catalogue for the auction from off of Tim's desk.

The auction was slotted to start at 2200hrs—in roughly thirty minutes.

Kayla began to thumb through its glossy pages. At first, she was not at all impressed with the offerings—vintage bottles of fang blood, an assortment of fang teeth, a pelt sheared from a werebear, a fire demon horn. Then she came to the last item and frowned.

Kayla heard Tim let out a groan, and soon after he was zipping up his pants.

Setting the catalogue back down, she turned to face him and propped herself against the side of the desk. "A spellcaster?" she said, her tone cold and penetrating.

Tim rose to his feet and reached for his discarded turtleneck that was strewn across a coffee table. "Impressed?"

"No," Kayla lied.

Truth be told, nabbing a witch was quite the feat. In all her years, she'd not once been able to track one down, despite there being countless leads. Spellcasters were a cautious and secretive bunch, and they integrated with humanity, which only added to the difficulty of identifying them. Moreover, they casted glamour about themselves, shielding their appearance.

Often labelled as the black sheep within the unhuman community, spellcasters were hated by most of the lightless factions.

Beasts—werewolves primarily—despised them for their ancient practice of culling any male infants they birthed. Fangs were wary of them for it was said that there once existed sorceresses who could control the dead and living dead. And many of the other groups resented that some spellcasters could nullify their abilities with the utterance of a few words.

"They are dangerous," Kayla said. "I think you should reconsider auctioning a live one."

"The spellcaster is a class D mute. Her tongue has been torn out. I doubt she will be sputtering spells anytime soon," Tim replied. Turtleneck back on, he began slithering his arms into the sleeves of his cream jacket. He continued, saying, "Not to mention that she is heavily sedated. I don't anticipate that she'll be capable of much trouble. Of course, were she to ever get out of hand, I'm sure the buyer would enlist the Order's services."

Kayla shook her head. "You shouldn't be selling livestock." The practice was relatively recent. When Kayla first learned of it, she'd voiced her opinions to the chief commander. When he hadn't cared, she'd gone to the board with her concerns, and the old men seemed to care even less. All that mattered was profit.

A few contract requests had come to the inbox asking for the capture and delivery of a live beast or demon. Kayla had turned them all down. The only good lightless was a dead one. They were too dangerous to be kept alive.

But all the rage amongst their clientele was purchasing lightless to show off and bet on in ostentatious unhuman cockfights.

"Fortunately, what you think doesn't matter," Tim said, straightening the collar of his jacket.

Snorting, Kayla decided to change the direction of the conversation. "You said you had something for me?"

Tim nodded, and then coughed. "Yes—and it is a doozy."

Kayla arched a brow.

Tim smirked. "Apparently Commander Rothschild has struck a

deal with Silas."

"What kind of deal?" Though Kayla asked, she felt she knew the answer. Word on the street was that a slew of juvenile fangs—tired of living in obscurity—wanted to break free from the NYC coven and out their existence to the world. It was kind of a big deal.

For far too long, Silas had allowed his children to create new vampires unchecked, and now he had a problem on his hands. The new generation of bloodsuckers were entitled and not keen on taking orders.

"Would you believe me if I told you that it is a hundred-million-dollar contract?"

Yes, she would. The infestation of newly blooded fangs in NYC was bad, and at a million dollars a hit, it was very likely that Silas had a hundred fangs that needed exterminating.

Even so, a hundred million was only the amount Rothschild would be taking in for the contract. There was a lot more profit to be made from harvesting the blood, organs, and teeth from the corpses.

Kayla couldn't stop the frown from forming on her face. While she struggled to meet her quota of twenty-five million a month, Rothschild was unjustly making four times that amount with a single contract.

Fuck him and fuck the board. There's no way those geezers don't know what Rothschild's doing.

But what could Kayla do about it? Nothing—at least not now.

"Anything else I should know?"

"About Rothschild? No." Tim replied. "But I know you recently came into possession of a hopper."

Kayla stilled. *How the fuck did he find out already?* "Who told you?"

"Don't mind that," he said. "What's important is that I am willing to pay you a hundred and fifty million to take it off your hands."

Kayla snorted. "Don't insult me with such a lowball offer. Hoppers are rarer than even your mute spellcaster," Kayla said, "and they are far more useful."

"You forget that I run a business. I need to make a cut too."

"Sounds like a pretty hefty cut."

"I love a woman who bargains." Tim chuckled. "I can give you two hundred million for it."

The offer was better. If she took it, the board would have to get off of her back. But Dr. Raz needed the hopper for his research, so Kayla was not in the position to sell. But even if she was, she would not sell him the live hopper.

"No."

"No," Tim repeated, blinking his shock. "It is a very good offer."

"I don't sell livestock."

Tim's jaw clenched, and his beady eyes narrowed. "Two hundred and ten million—it's my final offer."

"You can shove that offer up your ass," Kayla said.

"I wonder what your board of directors would say if they ever found out that you turned down such a lucrative offer?"

Kayla pushed herself off of the desk and stepped menacingly towards Tim. "Is that a threat?" *He is definitely threatening me.*

"No, it was just a thought I had," he said with a demure smile.

"I was also thinking about what I heard the other day. A little birdy told me that morale at your base is low. Your men are pissed about the cuts you've made."

Kayla's eyes narrowed on him. She wanted so badly to smack the smug expression from his face. More than that, she wanted to know who his informant was.

"I imagine that an influx of cash is just what you need to keep your men well fed and happy," Tim went on to say before looking down at the Patek Philippe on his wrist. "It is almost ten—I have business to attend to. We can discuss this transaction further when I see you next."

Kayla hated the sureness in his tone—he was so confident she'd be back. He was so sure she'd sell the hopper.

Kayla couldn't wait for the day to come where his services were no longer needed. When it did, she'd snap his neck.

The day would come once Dr. Raz stabilized the serum. Kayla just hoped she hadn't massively screwed everything up by sending Malkovitch to secure the illblood.

As she exited Tim's office and headed back for the door that led to the roof, she tried to shake off her unease. Malkovitch would bring the illblood back to the base, she told herself. There was just a high chance that it'd be brought back dead instead of alive. Which was okay so long as its body remained intact.

But Kayla sought to be wrong for once. It'd be a miracle, but she wanted Malkovitch to surprise her.

Chapter Six

Trailing their target, Petra's grip on the steering wheel was tight.

Up ahead, a red Ducati peeled in between two cars parked on the curb. The rider cut the ignition and slid off the bike with an effortlessness that marked them as a lightless to a trained eye.

Petra's breath caught in her chest as she watched the rider's helmet come off, revealing a face imprinted on her memory.

Hot anger burned through Petra's blood. Her entire body throbbed from the heat of her rage and blurred her ability to think straight. She had the insane compulsion to jump out of the SUV and shoot the fang dead between its eyes, but she fought against the urge. It wouldn't do to strike without certainty that her attack would land lethally.

Vampires were known for their strength and speed. To bring one down—even a young one like the target—Petra would need to strategize. She couldn't afford to let her emotions drive her to sloppiness. Also, there was the issue of witnesses—there were way too many people about tonight.

Slowing the SUV to a crawl, Petra looked on with hawkish eyes as the fang tousled curly black hair and strutted away from the motorcycle like a fashionista. The fang had on a sheer black button-down with a black crop-top beneath. She wore tight-fitting jeans and black leather boots with a thick high heel. Bits of gold jewellery accented the outfit.

The fang headed towards a block of bars and clubs, blending in with the herd of partygoers and bar-hoppers smattered across the pavement.

To Petra's luck, a car drove out of a nearby spot. With expertise, she easily manoeuvred the white SUV into the tight space and parked.

Peering out the window, Petra saw the fang cut to the front of a queue leading to a venue that was the consolidation of two Victorian row houses. The exterior of the club was like nothing Petra had ever seen. The entire structure—even the windows—had been assaulted by graffiti.

A sign that read "Sappho" in hot-pink neon letters was mounted above the entrance. Even from within the confines of the SUV, Petra's ears could perceive the loud bass booming from within the establishment.

Petra looked on as the fang exchanged a few words with a large female bouncer who stood at the entry. While she could not hear what was being said, the two women greeted each other with casual familiarity, which led her to believe that they knew each other well.

The waiting patrons, standing idly behind the fang, appeared disgruntled—it did not go beyond Petra's notice that women made up the entire line. Most sported undercuts, beanies, and flannel shirts, but some didn't. Some women wore beautiful dresses beneath their coats. Some had long hair and didn't appear to have tattoos or piercings.

When the fang finally disappeared into the venue, Petra turned to look at Dustin, who sat in the passenger seat. His eyes were fixed on a tablet, and there was a blush of pinkness on his clean-shaven cheeks. She assumed he was trying to be helpful and was scrolling through their target's portfolio.

Petra had gone through the paper file that had been in the manila folder, but it had only been a summary. There was a lot more information on their target to be found on the Order's database, which Petra and Dustin had only been granted access to about an hour before departing the base. Over the years, Petra had sought to look up information on the fang who had upended her life, but she'd never found an SOL willing to sign her into the database.

Petra wasn't sure why the Order restricted trainees from accessing the intranet and database. She'd deduced that there likely was no reason other than to keep trainees in the dark. The organization liked to keep its members ignorant. The lower one was on the hierarchy, the more was kept from them.

Petra aspired to be more than an SOL. She sought to join SOTU, and maybe one day become a sergeant. If she ever hit that rank, she'd finally be privy to the inner workings of the organization.

But if Petra went ahead with her plans—and didn't follow

orders—perhaps becoming a sergeant would never be in the cards for her. Insubordination was a serious misconduct and would result in disciplinary action, but Petra wasn't sure to what degree.

Sighing, Petra rotated in her seat and faced Dustin.

During the long drive, she'd had time to reflect upon the predicament Commander Clay had so purposely put her in.

It pissed Petra off that Clay was putting her in the position where she had to choose between avenging her mother and her loyalty to the Order. Ultimately, she felt that there was no real choice in the matter—she couldn't let the fang live.

But, at the same time, she dreaded what would come when she returned to the base with the fang dead instead of alive.

Clay was a discerning woman, and she would likely not buy the story Petra fabricated—no matter how logical.

Failing the mission likely meant that she'd flunk her final year, which would suck. There was also the possibility that Petra would face discipline if Commander Clay determined that she had purposefully killed the target. There was also the fact that Petra did not want to lie to Clay, a woman she so admired.

However, Petra knew that she could never live with herself if she gave up the opportunity to exact revenge on the creature who had taken everything from her.

Yes, there really wasn't a choice. That being said, Petra was considerably less aggrieved by the fact that Dustin was assigned to attend to the matter with her. Given his unexplainable crush, she felt that he would go along with whatever cover story she came up with. Also, everyone knew that Dustin didn't want to be an SOL—

he sought to join the Church of the Light instead.

Frankly, Dustin should have flunked several years of the SOL training program, but his mother had always pulled some strings to get him through to the next year.

The apple had fallen very, very far from the tree where Dustin was concerned. Having been raised by the late Chief Minister Wu, the pretty boy was much too virtuous to be an SOL. He was spineless and got sick at the sight of blood. Hell, even Khan could outmatch him in a fight.

In a way, by going against orders, Petra would be helping him out too. There was no way he'd get in her way.

"Anything worth sharing in the database?" she asked.

Dustin looked up from the tablet and met her eyes. "No … not really," he stammered.

Arching an eyebrow, Petra reached over and snatched the device from his fingers. On the screen, Petra saw a long list of women's names and corresponding photographs. Many were quite attractive. "What the fuck is this, Junior?"

"A list of the target's … um, conquests." His face turned a shade redder. "The fang fucks women—lots and lots of women."

Petra didn't bat an eye. The information was unsurprising. Younger lightless were known to have ridiculous libidos—it was a weakness that could be exploited. And when it came to sexuality, most lightless factions were fluid. Though, the beasts tended to lean on being strictly heterosexual, while spellcasters—a faction made up entirely of women—only bedded the opposite sex when they wanted to breed.

Angling the tablet, Petra clicked on the first tab and scanned the profile on the screen. Much of the cover information was the same as what had been in the manila folder.

```
Name: Violet "Vy" Finch
Location: Toronto, ON, Canada
Address: 2201-88 Dorrisville Avenue, North York
Sex: Female
Date of Birth: September 29, 1994
Age: 25
Faction: Illblood (Vampire/Unknown)
Affiliations: Alice Hébert
Rank: Unassigned
Notes: Chem user; Observed not to feed on humans
```

Petra gritted her teeth upon reading the last entry on the cover profile. *Doesn't feed on humans—what bullshit!*

When Petra had read that line in the commander's office, she'd wanted to hurl the file. Sitting in the SUV, she wanted to toss the tablet.

She didn't, though. Instead, Petra stabbed her finger on the record log button, which brought her to a new page that outlined the Order's observances of the target over the years.

Reading the log, it became apparent to Petra that the Order had been keeping tabs on Violet since winter 2009—since the incident with Petra's mother.

There had been three attempts to tag and bag the fang, but all had been unsuccessful. The first effort had been around the holiday season of 2009—two SOLs lost their lives during the mission.

Then, the Order tried again in the spring of 2010. Four SOLs had been sent, and all four were lost. The final operation had been back in the fall of 2010. Six SOTU agents were sent to capture the target, and all six had died.

Ever since that last mission, the Order backed off, settling for regular surveillance.

In all previous attempts, it hadn't been Violet who had thwarted the Order. It had been a class A fang, Alice Hébert, who had done the butchering.

Petra tapped on Alice's name and scanned her profile when it popped up.

Noting that Alice was the right hand of Belisarius—the head of Toronto's coven—Petra's brows drew together. Petra wondered why a powerful fang like Alice would ever align herself with an illblood. It was common knowledge that all lightless factions abhorred illbloods.

Petra checked the record log on Alice's profile. It turned out that the Order also spied on the class A vampire. The most recent record log was from two days ago, and it reported that Alice was out of the country and in New York.

Leaving Violet unguarded. Petra smirked and shimmied out of her jacket to remove her double holster, which housed two guns. One was a 9mm handgun holding silver rounds that could take down most lightless with a well-aimed shot to the head or heart. The second gun was a tranquilizer gun developed by Dr. Raz. A single round could knock out a weak-ranking lightless. At the other end, an entire clip could be emptied into a high-ranking lightless and it'd only have the effect of slowing it down.

Holster removed, Petra shrugged back into her light jacket, untucked her shirt from her waistband and roughed up her short red hair. While she was dressed in civilian clothes—sporting a black windbreaker, a white T-shirt and grey cargo pants—she figured that if she looked a little dishevelled it would help her fit in.

"Why are you removing your holster?" Dustin asked. "Going somewhere?"

Petra cocked her head in the direction of the lounge. "I doubt the bouncer will let me in with a handgun." When Clay smiled and clicked out of his seat belt, Petra held up a hand. "Where the fuck do you think you are going?"

His expression was one of confusion. "Inside—with you."

"No, you'll stay here," Petra said curtly. "You'll likely blow our cover if you come in with me."

"I don't see—"

"You have a dick," Petra interjected. "It's a girl bar."

"Oh." Dustin went still. "I don't like the idea of you being in there alone, without back-up."

Petra snorted. "I don't see how you would count as back-up."

"I don't like the idea of you going in there alone," he repeated, his jaw clenched with determination.

For a moment, Petra wondered if she'd been wrong. Was it possible that Dustin might try to get in her way?

Petra exhaled a breath. "Look, I won't be long. I'm just running inside to grab some intel. But you need to stay here," Petra stated. "I want to have the fang tagged and bagged by tomorrow, so we can't waste time twiddling our thumbs."

"Tomorrow?" Dustin seemed surprised. "You think we will have enough intel that soon to conduct a safe capture? What I mean is … our target is an illblood, and we only know what one part of her is. She doesn't even have a rank assigned. She could be quite dangerous."

Petra shrugged. "The fang is in her midtwenties. How strong could she really be?"

"Well, if she is half-beast … that would be pretty strong—and fast," Dustin argued.

He did raise a good point, but Petra was confident that their target didn't rank high.

The various lightless factions all had their strengths and weaknesses, and all experienced and gained power differently. Ages ago, the Order developed a ranking system to make classification and threat level easier to ascertain.

The weakest of the bunch were class D. These tended to be your newly blooded fangs, dim spellcasters who could only mumble the simplest of incantations, and ghouls.

Class C lightless were not seen as much of a threat either, but they could be considerably more dangerous—many demon factions made up this rank.

Class B lightless were quite dangerous to engage with. A wide range of beings fell in this category, such as hoppers, fangs with over a century under their belt, beasts of common blood, and most novice spellcasters. Usually, it was SOTU that handled missions involving any lightless ranked B or higher.

Class A lightless were few and far between. Usually beasts of noble lineage, fangs of significant age, and sorceresses made up this group.

Class S was the highest tier, and the Order was only aware of a dozen or so beings who might rank at such a level—all were sorceresses.

What quickly became evident to Petra—through her studies—was that age was the most relevant factor when it came to strength for fangs. Bloodlines were what mattered for beasts. Knowledge was what differentiated a pitiful spellcaster from a sorceress. And for some lightless, they just fell in the middle, no matter their age or ancestry.

"If the illblood were part beast, I am sure that is something the Order would know—beasts are so easily identifiable," Petra said, debating Dustin's concern. "If I had to guess, our target is probably part demon, and she likely ranks just above class D. I doubt the Order would have us tagging and bagging anything higher than a D for our final."

"You're probably right," Dustin mumbled with a nod.

Of course, I'm right, Petra thought as she rolled her eyes.

She opened the door, and the night air breezed into the stuffy SUV cabin. "I'll be back soon. You stay here," Petra directed.

Dustin didn't seem pleased. He looked as if he wanted to argue some more, but he kept his mouth shut.

Exiting the vehicle, Petra jogged across the street and approached the club with the glowing neon sign. The queue had died, so she was able to walk right up to the entrance.

More than a handful of women stood just outside the club on the sidewalk. Most smoked as they chatted. Upon spotting Petra, they quieted. She felt their eyes on her, but she didn't spare them another glance.

As Petra stepped towards the bouncer, a thrill of excitement—perhaps anticipation—gripped her, melding oddly with her ever persistent rage. Her heart pounded in her head, and her stomach flipped in her chest. Her entire body tingled.

The world around her seemed more vivid and bright. Going on the hunt and being that much closer to achieving her goal was exhilarating. For the first time in years, Petra felt alive.

The large female bouncer held out her hand toward Petra. "ID?"

Petra handed over her licence. After looking at the card, the bouncer proceeded to frisk Petra, briskly patting down her arms, back, and legs.

"I ain't seen you here before," the bouncer said, stepping aside and holding open the front door.

Petra did not respond. Instead, she brushed past the woman and walked into the lounge. Behind her, she heard the bouncer mutter, "Rude."

Making nice with people was not something Petra cared about anymore. It was too much of a chore to put up a polite front.

Petra surveyed the area. Inside, the bass was intense, and she could feel it reverberating through her body. The room was dark apart from strobing lights that beamed and flashed intermittently.

Petra searched for the fang, but had no luck. She began wading through the tight mob of partygoers who thrashed their bodies to the pulse of the music. Given there was no designated dance floor, the entire room was packed and difficult to navigate through.

The room was stifling from the heat radiating off the crowd, and beads of sweat began trickling down Petra's back. At one point, Petra opted to remove her jacket and tie it around her waist.

As she continued to push her way through the mass of bodies, Petra couldn't help but notice the intertwined couples exchanging sensual touches and kisses. A few times, Petra caught herself staring.

On the base, it had been easy to discard her wants and desires. But there, surrounded by women who loved women, Petra was finding it hard to ignore the tug of longing.

Get a fucking grip—you are here for one thing and one thing only, she told herself.

Releasing a deep breath, Petra refocused her mind and worked to block out what was going on around her.

Despite standing taller than pretty much everyone, between the overcrowding and non-existent lighting, it took Petra longer than she would have liked to locate the target.

She found the fang on the second floor of the club. The upper floor was much less packed, and the music wasn't as loud. Comfy lounge chairs edged the walls, and Violet sat in one of them with a beautiful woman curled up in her lap.

With the fang in sight, Petra felt the world grow still around her. Seconds seemed to slow to a stop.

Images flashed before her. Petra saw sharp, glinting fangs and crazed obsidian eyes. She saw greyish slush stained with blood. She saw her mother's lifeless body and recalled her pain and shock and fear.

I'm not that scared girl anymore. Petra shook off the memories and clenched her jaw.

Every bone in her body ached for revenge. She felt compelled to do something irrational, but besides the silver-plated dagger concealed in her boot, she was unarmed. There was no way she'd be able to out-power a fang with a dainty blade.

Petra stared up at the creature with hate in her eyes. Almost as if sensing Petra's gaze, the fang stopped making out with the beautiful brunette sitting in her lap and looked up from her black lounge chair, locking eyes with Petra.

Chapter Seven

Vy looked into the most unsettling set of green eyes she'd ever seen. Their possessor was tall, with broad shoulders that stretched a white T-shirt tight across her chest. The woman's posture was strict, her expression severe. Her hair was very red against her pale skin. Something about her face seemed familiar, but Vy couldn't place it.

Years ago, Vy had determined that she much preferred to bed soft, feminine women, with ample breasts and curvy hips, like Isabella—who had a bodacious physique, a flow of long dark-brown hair and a sultry gaze enhanced by perfectly applied makeup.

Isabella wriggled in Vy's lap and bent her head to lay a trail of soft kisses up Vy's collarbone and neck. Usually, such an act would drive her crazy with desire. But Vy was distracted—she was too preoccupied to revel in the feeling of her date's soft lips on her skin.

The woman with the menacing stare was intriguing. *I wonder if she fucks as hard as she looks at me.*

Vy noted that quite a few women in the bar were ogling the tall woman—likely, none would have the guts to make an advance. She didn't seem approachable. If Vy had to guess, she was probably military or some branch of law enforcement.

Vy licked her lips as her eyes continued to drink in the sight before her. The woman was a dichotomy of beauty and strength. A short and rugged hairstyle framed a classically attractive face. She was all hard muscle, but there was a lingering femininity to her figure that Vy found appealing.

The more Vy's eyes consumed, the more she liked what she saw.

It didn't take long for her intrigue to flip into rampant lust. Vy wanted to feel the woman's strong fingers dig into her waist. Vy wanted to feel the press of the woman's powerful body against her own. Vy wanted to climax, looking into those intense green eyes. And, after the day she'd had, Vy felt she more than deserved a good fucking.

May had screwed her over—and not in a good way. Vy didn't see how a single name—Petra Malkovitch—would bring her any closer to finding the talisman. She also didn't find May's assurance that Petra would find her helpful.

Even so, Vy was determined to remain hopeful—she had to be. If she succumbed to thinking negatively, thinking that she'd never find the hourglass, then she knew what the outcome for her would be. Vy could not go on as things were—period. She needed to rid herself of her vampirism. She was so over feeling sick and tired and starving.

Sighing, Vy pulled herself away from her date.

Isabella pouted and tried to wrangle her back. Vy shrugged away from Isabella's grasp and stood.

"Where are you going?" Isabella whined.

Vy's gaze drifted momentarily to the tall stranger. "I don't want to be with you tonight," she admitted, immediately regretting her choice of words.

Isabella's head knocked back as if Vy had hit her, and she rose from her seat in a huff. Grabbing her beer from off the floor, she took a deep swig from the bottle. "And I don't want to see you again. Don't text me," Isabella spat, purposefully bumping Vy's shoulder as she pushed past her.

Vy almost grabbed for her, but she decided to let Isabella go, watching her leave down the stairs.

It was probably for the best. Vy should have ended her stint with Isabella weeks ago. They'd been hooking up regularly for over a month, and Vy knew that nothing good could come from getting attached. Vy needed to keep her contact with humans at a minimum. If she lost her control and harmed Isabella ... Well, Vy knew she wouldn't be able to forgive herself.

For a moment, Vy deflated and wished she hadn't bothered going out that night. Then, she caught sight of the stranger in her peripheral, and her lust fired again.

The woman leaned against a wall with her arms crossed over her chest. She exuded an air of confidence and danger that lured Vy towards her.

Before Vy knew it, she stood toe-to-toe with the imposing woman.

Beneath the thumping of music, Vy heard the woman's heart rate accelerate. Unwelcome, the thirst reared its ugly head. Vy's teeth began to ache, snapping her from her desire-driven trance.

Reflexively, she clenched her jaw. Nothing annoyed Vy more than having to fuck on chem as it dampened the experience. But she'd have to take some if her hunger continued to escalate.

Ignoring the irritating pulsating of her teeth, Vy lifted her chin to look into the stranger's eyes. Even in the darkness of the club, they were so green.

Vy swayed sensually to the music and held out a hand. "Dance with me?"

To Vy's confusion, the woman recoiled from her and frowned. "I don't dance," she barked.

Vy almost shrank from the harshness of the woman's tone. *Is it possible she's not attracted to me?*

Vy understood she had many faults, but one of the few things she had going for her was her looks. She knew she was hot. Yet, she was also aware that, even in this modern day and age, there were some humans who would think less of her because of their perception of her race.

A hard lesson Vy had learned early on was that some human ethnicities were just not down for women with darker skin. While the fact sucked, Vy didn't think she could really judge—everyone was entitled to their preferences, just as she had her own.

Because of her bronze complexion, Vy had been subjected to a multitude of insults throughout her life. Over the years, she had lost count of the number of times she'd been asked if her hair was real.

Or been told that she was pretty for a Black girl.

In some ways, Vy was thankful she was not subject to humanity in its entirety. She couldn't fathom working a nine-to-five job and putting up with micro-aggressive bullshit all day.

Then again, she'd take being a Black woman in a human world over being an illblood any day. At least, in that scenario, she'd fit in somewhere.

It almost pained Vy to think that she might not be the woman's type. And she decided that she needed to come to a conclusion about this woman immediately. So, she opted to be bold—rising on her toes, she spoke into her ear, "I want to take you home with me—I want to know if you fuck as hard as you've been staring at me."

This time, the woman did not recoil. Even so, Vy was having a hard time reading her.

Naturally, if Vy wanted, she could find out what the stranger was about—Vy had the means to find out everything there was to know about anyone.

However, exercising that ability was quite the power drain. Not to mention her mother's warning that overuse could result in a fracturing of self. "We are only meant to live one life," her mother had often said. "You will lose yourself if you live too many."

The stranger seemed to be struggling to find words. Her eyes glinted with a flurry of emotions, and Vy was not sure passion was one of them.

Annoyed and feeling the hot sting of rejection, Vy decided to cut her losses and gave the woman her back. She motioned to step away, but then felt a strong hand take her wrist.

Vy looked down at the woman's grip and released a breath she hadn't known she'd been holding.

"Take me home with you," the woman said in a tone that was soft but raised the hairs on the back of Vy's neck. She wondered what it was about this woman that elicited such an effect.

Biting her lip, Vy nodded and slid her fingers between the woman's. Without another word, she guided them downstairs. As they shoved through the crowd towards the entrance, Vy spotted Isabella making out with a cute blond who wore a Blue Jays snapback.

Vy knew she had no right to be jealous, but she felt a twinge of it. She always felt a little pained when she broke things off with someone and later saw them with someone else. Letting go was not something she was good at.

Vy exited the club still holding the woman's hand.

The chilly night air felt good against her skin, but it was apparently too cold for the human, who pulled away to untie the thin jacket about her waist and put it on.

"Caught a new one, eh?" Vy heard Yvonne ask.

Vy turned towards the bouncer. "I don't know why you sound surprised," she replied with a faint smile.

"I thought you were getting on well with Isabella," Yvonne said, throwing a stern look towards Vy's latest catch.

Vy gritted her teeth. She didn't want to get into it with Yvonne again. She wasn't in the mood to bicker about why she couldn't settle down. It was the kind of conversation that tired her beyond means, and she always left the discussion feeling shittier than usual.

Vy wanted to be honest with Yvonne, whom she considered a sort-of friend. But she couldn't tell Yvonne the truth. She couldn't admit to wanting to have a relationship. She couldn't admit that she yearned to fall in love. She couldn't admit that, above all else, she craved the connection. Because there was no way to say these things without explaining why it was not an option.

"I will see you tomorrow night," Vy said suddenly, turning away from Yvonne and reaching to take back the stranger's hand.

"Night," her friend muttered.

Vy led the woman over to her motorcycle—parked across the street on the curb. When they reached the candy-red Ducati, Vy dropped her hand. "Did you drive here?"

The woman shook her head. "No."

"You okay with motorcycles?" It had been Vy's experience that some women weren't comfortable getting on the back of her sports bike, so she always made sure to ask.

"Yah."

Vy smiled. She tossed the woman a spare helmet. "Need help putting it on?"

Instead of answering, the woman slid the helmet over her head and fastened it without any trouble.

While Vy didn't like being ignored, she decided to let the rude behaviour slide. A one-night stand was not marriage—she didn't have to like the woman.

Vy put on her helmet and raised the face shield. "I'm Vy—by the way."

"Jane," the woman said after a moment's silence, her face

hidden behind the tinted shield.

Nodding in acknowledgement, Vy mounted and straddled the bike. She knocked back the kickstand, revved the machine to life, and beckoned for Jane to join her.

The motorcycle sank under the bulk of the added weight when Jane climbed up behind her. A shrill of excitement jolted through Vy's body when she felt Jane's strong hands about her waist.

Vy twisted the throttle. She took off with smooth expertise, shifting from gear-to-gear.

Bobbing in and out of traffic and managing to avoid most red lights, Vy made it to her condo building in under ten minutes. She zipped into the underground, where she parked in her assigned spot and cut the engine.

Jane hopped off the bike. Removing the helmet, she ran a hand through her short red hair. In the harsh overhead lighting of the garage, Vy made note of the light dusting of freckles across the bridge of her nose and cheeks. There was something inexplicably sexy about a woman who could pull off looking that good without a hint of makeup.

Vy got off the bike and took off her helmet, combing her curly black hair with a free hand. "Was the ride okay?" she asked.

The woman fixed her with a strange look and then shrugged.

Vy didn't know what to do with that response. Jane's lack of fruitful communication was starting to grate on her nerves.

Sighing her annoyance, Vy started walking towards the elevator lobby.

The ride up to her floor was awkwardly silent, and Jane fell into step behind Vy as she led the way to her unit down the carpeted hallway.

As she slid her key into its lock, Vy couldn't put a finger on the unease she began to feel in the pit of her stomach. She wanted to blame the feeling on her creeping thirst, but she didn't think it was the culprit for her nervousness.

Opening the door, Vy stepped inside and zipped down her high-heeled boots. She pulled them off and stepped to the side to make space for her guest to enter.

Jane moved inside and shut the door behind her. Vy didn't like the way the woman's eyes scanned her home. The foreboding feeling in her gut worsened.

Maybe I should tell Jane that I've changed my mind. Vy bit down on her lip as she debated the situation. A part of her thought she was being silly. After all, Jane was human. Vy was the actual threat. In a flash, and with little effort, Vy could snap every bone in Jane's beautiful body.

Vy decided that she was being paranoid for no reason. "Do you want a drink?" she asked, walking towards the kitchen. "I have beer and some seltzer."

Jane shook her head.

"Water?"

The human shook her head again.

Folding her arms, Vy leaned against the kitchen island and fixed the woman with a cold look.

A thick quiet filled the room. The only sounds were the soft whirr from the fridge and the faint hum of city life leaking in from the outside.

"I keep getting the feeling that you are not DTF," Vy said finally, breaking the silence.

Just then, there was a buzzing—it was Jane's phone.

When the buzzing didn't stop, Vy arched a brow. "You gonna get that?"

"No."

A few seconds later, Jane's phone quieted, and the space once again fell into a hush.

The human appeared to be thinking of words to say. Vy could hear the beat of the woman's heart speeding up.

The sound was hypnotizing, and Vy's eyes drifted to the pulse ticking at the woman's neck. She envisioned herself piercing the thin flesh beneath Jane's ear.

A flash of sickness followed the thought. She winced.

The nausea subsided as fast as it came, but her thirst was more pronounced, scratching her throat and making her teeth ache. *I need a hit of chem.*

When her own phone vibrated, Vy looked away from Jane. Happy for the distraction, she removed the device from her pocket and stared down at the message.

Isabella Just now

Fuck you

Swallowing a groan, Vy set her phone down on the counter.

"I need to use the washroom," Jane said.

Vy cocked her head towards a door near the bedroom. When Jane moved towards the washroom, she asked, "Mind taking off your shoes?" Vy hated dirt or mess of any kind. She affiliated dirt with bugs and insects, which she feared. Vy's aversion was so bad that she usually donned a magical repellent when she ventured anywhere outdoorsy or when she sat on her favourite branch to observe her family.

Jane went very still, but then crouched down and removed her boots rather slow—almost methodically. Once she'd taken them off, she went to the bathroom.

Upon hearing the click of the door shutting, Vy fished out a tiny sachet of chem from her pocket. Shaking some of the vibrant blue dust on the back of her hand, she quickly lapped it up with her tongue.

The effects of the powder hit her instantaneously. A heavy calm fell over her as the thirst faded, the knots in her stomach untying.

Yes, Vy despised fucking on chem, but something told her that without it, she'd have a hard time relaxing around Jane. The woman was too intense.

Chapter Eight

What am I going to do? Hands set on either side of the sink, Petra leaned forward on the bathroom vanity and looked at herself in the mirror. Her face was flushed, her expression dark.

It had been unwise of her to come home with the fang, especially with her only weapon being the dagger. Fuck. She'd give anything to have her gun.

After running a shaking hand through her hair, Petra slid the hidden blade out from the sleeve of her jacket. Earlier, she'd taken a huge risk, pulling it from her boot when the fang had asked her to remove her shoes.

Careful to keep any noise at a minimum, Petra opened one of the large pockets located on the side of her cargo pants and dropped the blade into it.

Her phone buzzed—she knew it was Dustin calling her again. She grabbed the device and shut it off.

Petra stared at her reflection once more and told herself to get a handle on her emotions.

She couldn't go back out there with her hate etched so clearly on her face. The fang already sensed something was up. If Petra wanted to kill it and survive the night, she'd need to get her act in order.

Counting backwards from ten, Petra exhaled a deep breath. *You can do this. If you can set aside your feelings for a while, it'll all be over soon.*

Petra took another deep breath and continued her internal pep talk until she felt a calm come over her. Yes, she could do it. She would play the part of a lover, and when the opportunity presented itself, she would strike.

Petra flushed the toilet and then flipped on the faucet for effect. All she could hope was that the fang hadn't been listening too keenly to take notice that Petra hadn't used the toilet.

Shutting off the water, Petra threw open the bathroom door and stepped back into the main area. The fang sat on the couch and slowly rose to her feet when Petra emerged.

It became apparent that something was off about the fang. Her pupils were dilated and her movements lagged. Petra recalled the fang's profile—it had listed that she was a chem user.

She's high. A smile crept across Petra's lips. *That should make this easier.*

The fang hesitantly approached until they were within inches of each other. She placed her hands about Petra's hips, tugging her forward.

Every fiber of Petra's being wanted to recoil from the touch.

But she couldn't do that. She couldn't give herself away. And so, she stood very still and looked down at her adversary, meeting large brown eyes that seemed almost imploring.

Biting down on her lip, the fang stilled. "I'm really confused," she admitted. "I'm feeling these mixed signals, and I—"

"I have never done anything like this before," Petra blurted. It was the truth. She had never kissed a lightless before. She had never killed before.

"Oh," the fang said, blinking. A look of maybe disappointment crossed her features as her dark brows drew together. "You know we don't have to do anything? If you want to go, I can give you a ride home."

It's now or never. Petra's heart pounded in her ears. Her hands were clammy. *I can do this.* She blew out a deep breath before saying, "I want to do this—with you." Petra forced her hand to cup the fang's face. The skin of her cheek was smooth and astonishingly warm. It irritated Petra how beautiful the creature was. The fang looked so human. Nothing about her screamed lightless. Nothing hinted that she was a monster.

Petra wanted so much to drop her hold to the fang's neck and squeeze until it snapped, but she knew that wouldn't bode well for her. Vampires were incredibly fast and strong. Petra could be dead in a blink if she gave away her intentions too quickly. She needed to distract the fang and only strike at the opportune time.

Petra strained to run her thumb gently over the definition of the creature's jawline. The fang leaned into her touch, and Petra knew that was her cue to do the same. Her stomach knotted tightly, making her feel somewhat nauseated. *You can do this.*

Closing her eyes, she bent her head. To dull her repulsion, she tried to envision that it was Khan that she'd be kissing.

When their lips touched, the fang melted against Petra, and a low moan escaped the creature's throat. The press of a soft body against her was not at all unpleasant, and the sickness she'd felt dissipated.

Petra's mind began to drift as the kiss sparked memories she'd actively tried to forget. Thoughts of Khan faded and were replaced by thoughts of Kate. It had been so long since she'd allowed herself to think about her first love. But in that moment the recollections consumed her, making it almost effortless to play her part.

A switch had been flipped inside Petra. Whatever hesitations and reservations she'd had converted, becoming raw desperate hunger.

And it wasn't at all one sided. The fang seemed just as frenzied as their lips mashed together and fingers bit into skin to pull their bodies closer together. Breathing became a struggle.

Petra knew it should have felt wrong. It should have been harder to feel such desire in the embrace of her greatest enemy. But it felt right. It felt good. Too good. And Petra was losing herself in it all.

The fang's skin and hair were like silk to touch. Her scent was intoxicating. Inhaling deeply, Petra basked in the subtle floral fragrance.

Overtaken by feeling more than reason, Petra lifted her quarry into her arms and navigated them over to the couch.

Setting the fang down onto the seat, Petra positioned herself on top of her, breaking their kiss to place her lips against the fang's neck.

"Fuck," the fang groaned as Petra continued to graze the area with her teeth. The fang's gasps and sighs were an enticing soundtrack to Petra's ears, though it was somewhat drowned out by the voice in her head. It screamed at her. It told her that she was enjoying this far too much, that she should act now, while her enemy was distracted. But Petra's will was surprisingly weak—she didn't want to stop.

The voice instructed her to reach for her blade. But she instead undid the buttons of the sheer black top and ran her hands over the smooth expanse of the fang's abdomen. It wasn't enough to just touch, Petra needed to taste every part of her.

What the fuck is wrong with me? Petra recaptured the fang's lips and snuck a hand under the black crop-top to touch the breasts beneath.

The fang sucked in a breath and pulled back. She smirked and then rasped, "You sure you haven't done this before?" The fang trailed a finger down Petra's cheek. "It crossed my mind that I should take it slow with you, but I'm too impatient."

Before Petra could think to respond or react, they were kissing again, and she felt the fang undo the button of her cargo pants. A hand slipped into the waistband of her underwear and rubbed against her in a way that sent a shockwave of pleasure through her entire body. Petra was so wet, and the fang's expert touch awoke a sensation so intense that Petra couldn't help but writhe from it. "Fuck," Petra said, wincing.

"You like that."

Nodding, Petra was barely able to mutter yes. Her eyes squeezed shut as the pleasure inside her continued to build.

"I'm going to make you come so hard," the fang whispered in Petra's ear before amping the stroke of her fingers.

The mounting pressure became too much. Petra exploded.

Crashing down from her climax, Petra's head spun. Her hearing felt impaired for several moments. The only audible sound was her thundering heart.

When Petra opened her eyes, it was to see the fang smiling with satisfaction.

What have I done? A chill ran down Petra's spine. She couldn't believe that she allowed herself to be touched in such a way by a lightless—and not just any lightless. The worst one possible.

Guilt wrenched Petra's gut. She wanted to puke.

Seemingly noticing the change in Petra's mood, the fang frowned and brushed Petra's face gently with her hand. "Is everything okay?" she asked, concern evident in her tone.

Panicking, Petra scrambled for her dagger. In a quick and messy movement, she stabbed the fang in the chest.

When Petra realized she missed the fang's heart, she grabbed the hilt of her blade, wrenching it free from the creature's chest. Blood gushed and sprayed.

Petra motioned to strike down again, but the fang was faster and shoved her. The force of the push sent Petra flying.

Smacking against a wall, Petra grunted in pain. She recovered quickly though and dropped into a fighting stance, holding up her knife.

Appearing pained and confused, the fang touched the fresh wound. The creature looked down in puzzlement at the blood coating her fingers. She blinked. "Why?"

Petra opened her mouth to say something. The words died on her tongue when the door to the unit burst open.

"Malkovitch—what the fuck?" Dustin shuffled inside with his gun drawn.

When the fang turned to look at the intruder, Petra saw another opening. She launched herself at her foe. Petra saw her target clearly. She knew with certainty that her blade would hit its lethal mark. But then, something hit her in the arm.

An instant dizziness fell over her. The world went dark as she collapsed.

Petra felt like she was buried in sand. An uncomfortable heaviness weighed down her body. It took great effort to crack her eyes open slightly. The challenge to lift her head was even greater.

"You awake?" someone asked.

Blinking, she turned her head and saw Dustin. He sat behind the wheel of the SUV. Dustin glimpsed at her briefly and shot her a boyish smile before turning his attention back to the road.

Petra glanced out the windshield. It was still night, and even with high beams on the country roads were pitch black. The SUV cabin was dimly illuminated by the glow of the dash.

Head lolling back down, Petra noted the cuffs on her wrists and ankles. A wash of fiery anger flooded Petra's body, pushing aside the fog in her mind. She remembered now what had happened. She'd been about to kill the fang and then ... Dustin had shot her.

"What the fuck is this, Junior?" Petra snapped, shoving her restrained hands in his direction.

Dustin's grip tightened on the wheel. "Insurance."

"You fucking tranqued me!"

"You gave me no choice," he said. "We were told to bring the target back alive. I couldn't let you kill her."

"You don't even want to be an SOL! What the fuck do you care if we fail our exam?"

Petra noticed the firm clench of his jaw. "I don't care about the exam—I care about you," he said, sparing her a soulful look.

"The fuck you do." Petra snorted.

"I know what the illblood took from you. I know how much you want to avenge your mother, but we can't go against our directive." Dustin sighed, and his expression became somber. When he spoke again, his tone was very soft. "The Order doesn't take insubordination lightly. And, if you couldn't tell already, my mother is an exceptionally sadistic bitch. I don't know why she is setting you up like this, but it seems to me that she is banking on you disobeying her."

Petra had never heard Dustin speak so bluntly before. Part of her wondered if she'd misjudged him all these years. Perhaps he wasn't the complete doormat she'd marked him to be.

"I don't care if Clay is setting me up. I don't care if I'm punished."

"Figured as much," Dustin said with a nod. "That's why you're cuffed."

Petra snorted. "You're fucking ridiculous. You shouldn't have gotten in my way. I couldn't give a shit if Clay wants to condemn me to work in the cellblocks for the rest of my career—it's not like she'd kill me."

"If you believe that, you are fooling yourself," Dustin mumbled.

Petra stilled. "What do you mean? What are you trying to say?"

"You're smart—I don't think I need to explain," Dustin said. "You might be right, but it's a risk I'm not willing to take."

Petra stared at Dustin intently and wondered why his views about his mother were so negative. Sure, Clay was a grumpy old woman, but Petra had never gotten the sense that the commander was cruel. Clay always seemed rather cool headed, and she gave the impression of having absolute control. Petra couldn't see the commander doing anything rash or doing anything without a reason.

Which begged the question: why had Clay sent Petra to tag and bag Violet Finch—the fang who had destroyed her life?

Had Petra been wrong to admire the commander as much as she did? Was Junior right? Was Clay setting her up? Petra didn't want to think that was the case.

The cab fell silent. Petra's gaze drifted to the rear-view mirror. She grimaced when she spotted the fang's limp form crumpled on the backseat. Unconscious, the creature appeared harmless and very small.

Dustin's had fastened one of Dr. Raz's motion activated shock collars about her neck. He'd been wise enough to also shackle her hands and legs, but Petra noted that he had forgotten to gag her, which was best practice.

Petra hoped the fang didn't wake and begin to prattle about what happened between them back at the condo.

Not that it would really matter—Petra could easily downplay the event, and she knew that her version would ring truer to Dustin or anyone the fang blabbed to.

Looking away from the mirror, Petra clenched her jaw and tried to push the recollection from her mind. She didn't want to think or reflect. It was embarrassing how she'd reacted.

She was utterly disgusted with herself for allowing her ploy to go on much longer than it should have. And She also couldn't ignore the possibility that she might have been successful in her attempt to kill the fang had she struck sooner.

Petra looked out the passenger window at the vast plain of darkness. The thoughts in her head refused to recede and kept playing over and over. She remembered the fang's hands on her body and the soft press of her lips.

Nauseated, Petra opened the window slightly to bring fresh air into the cabin. She was suddenly looking forward to getting back to the base as soon as possible. She needed to shower and scrub away the memory of the fang's touch from her skin.

Chapter Nine

Vy's mother was the kind of woman who didn't need to lift a finger to command the world.

Unequal in beauty, grace, and power, when she arrived, every head turned in her direction as if manipulated by a puppeteer's strings. Be it human or unhuman, man or woman, adult or child—all were drawn to her. When in the great sorceress's palpable presence, all one could do was hold their breath and hope that the enchanting Camellia might spare a fleeting look their way and notice them.

An anxious and nervous child, Vy's days had been spent pining for attention or praise that never came. Camellia was far too concerned with uncovering hidden knowledge. With so much out there to be found, there was barely any time left to devote to her daughter.

Camellia never had anything good to say to Vy, especially when it came to magic. Whenever Vy conquered a particularly difficult incantation, her mother always found fault with something.

"The words are right, but I can sense a wavering in how you are channeling the flow of magic," she'd say.

"Finally, you did it—now do it faster," she'd say.

Camellia had never been satisfied with Vy's progress. It seemed to Vy that Camellia expected to have birthed a prodigy, but Vy was not that. Maybe that was why her mother had abandoned her.

Slowly, Vy's eyes blinked open, and thoughts of her mother dissipated. Her chest pulsed agonizingly, and her head felt like it was stuffed with cotton. A part of her wanted to drift back off to sleep, but even in her state of drowsiness she subtly understood that she was in danger.

Vy laid uncomfortably in the back of a moving vehicle. The seat, where her head rested, had a strong odour of feet. Outside, the sky was pitch black. Cool metal encircled her neck. Her hands were shackled behind her back, and her legs were bound as well.

Rewinding the night's events, it didn't take long for Vy to remember how she got to where she was. Frankly, she was surprised to be alive.

She recalled Jane stabbing her, and then a man bursting into her home and felling Jane with a shot from his gun before turning the weapon on her.

Vy's teeth throbbed as painfully as the wound in her chest. She didn't have to look down at it to know that it hadn't fully healed—it wouldn't heal until she fed.

Her energy was depleted, and she was ravenous. Protracted fangs and a burning throat were evidence of her severe thirst. It had been a long time since she'd suffered such hunger. She was on the brink of losing control.

Vy touched a sharp tooth with the tip of her tongue. Repulsed, she clenched her fists and motioned to sit up. A big mistake. With the movement, a scalding electric current bolted through her body, making her cry out.

"Fang's up, Malkovitch," the driver said, turning his head to look at Vy briefly before focusing back on the road.

Did he say Malkovitch? Ignoring the pain, Vy frowned and recalled that he had called Jane earlier by that name—Malkovitch. Could it be that Jane was related to Petra Malkovitch, whom May had predicted would assist Vy with tracking down the talisman?

"Where are you taking me?" Vy rasped, her voice cracked. It hurt to speak.

When she didn't receive a response, Vy tried to think of who might want to hurt or kill her. As an illblood, she wasn't on the radar for any of the factions—her existence was of little importance in the unhuman community.

She quickly deduced who it might be. And the mere probability made Vy's blood run cold.

"I can't watch over you like I once did," Alice had told her in their last conversation.

Fuck—Fuck—Fuck! Over nine years had passed since the Order had last attempted to capture her. Vy had determined that Alice had scared them off for good—apparently not, if her hunch was right.

Had they been waiting this whole time for an opportunity to try again? Did they know Alice was away in New York? The timing was really too perfect—obviously, they knew.

Vy's mind flew back to the recent arguments she'd had with Alice.

Almost as if knowing danger loomed in the background, Alice had begun to preach to her more and more, telling Vy over and over that she needed to find an in with Belisarius. Each time, Vy's answer had been a firm, resounding no.

There was nothing positive that could come out of taking a blood oath and swearing fealty to Belisarius. Given her illblood status, joining the coven would not grant her the sense of community she craved. After all, Alice was the only vampire who didn't look upon Vy with hate and disgust.

Being part of Belisarius's coven meant that when he called, you answered. If the coven leader ordered you to do something, there was no choice—you did it.

Vy did not have much going for her, but she valued her agency above all. She did not want anyone controlling her life, dictating what she could or couldn't do.

But being captured by the Order—the unhuman boogeyman—was definitely a worse outcome for her.

Exhaling a deep breath, Vy's mind turned to how she could get herself out of the mess she was in.

While she had quite a few tricks up her sleeve, there was one obvious choice, but Vy was not in the best state to execute it. The spell required a lot of energy, and Vy was weakened from her injury.

Magic was simple at its root and was found in all things. It was a nebulous element that could be manipulated like water, fire, earth, and air. However, only those born with the ability to channel its flow could sense and apply it—though, they all did so in different ways.

Hoppers possessed the innate capability to harness magic to carry them to any point on the planet with a single thought. Demons of the varying castes used magic to change into their altered states. Because of magic, the elusive fae were able to move about the world unseen.

But spellcasters, above all other factions, possessed the greatest influence over magic. Their abilities were seemingly endless—that is, if they had the instructions and could follow them with exact precision.

In a lot of ways, a spell was akin to a recipe, and the spellcaster was a mere chef. Though, within the art of sorcery, there was always a trade-off. Sometimes the demands of magic were small—a minuscule pilfering of energy. But for the more complex incantations, the cost could sometimes be greater than the payoff.

The spell Vy was considering fell into the latter category.

It was old magic—dark magic. The kind that the Ancient Ones decreed forbidden out of fear that it might be used against them.

Whenever Camellia had spoken about the wisdom lost due to the actions of the Ancients Ones, she always did so vehemently. The unhuman rulers had systematically eliminated nearly all sorceresses versed in the art of dark magic, and they'd set fire to any texts referencing it.

With the mass annihilation and destruction, and with the rise and fall of civilizations, the feats of dark magic fell into obscurity—only living on in the form of myths passed down over generations.

Vy's mother had made it her mission to find all there was left to find. She'd often stated that there was always truth that could be found in folklore—no matter how outlandish.

From an early age, it became obvious to Vy that her mother took great pride in deciphering fact from fiction. Camellia had thrilled in proving that any means could be accomplished via magic. "Nothing is impossible. You are only ever limited by what you know," her mother had often stated.

Vy believed her mother's words, and it was why she needed to find her. Camellia would know how to rid her of the parasitic affliction. Camellia knew everything there was to know.

But I'll never find her if I don't escape this situation.

Vy directed her attention to the driver. Her body went very still as she gathered the magic around her and moulded it with her mind, shaping it into the form it needed to be in to execute the spell.

She had never attempted such sorcery while her tank was so low—or while on the cusp of being overtaken by her thirst.

However, she didn't have a choice—it was her best option. She had to take the risk and suffer through any possible ramifications later.

Her decision made, Vy spoke the words to initiate the spell.

When the last word left her lips, her consciousness was catapulted into the driver's mind—his very soul.

Merged that way, she became Dustin Clay.

A bombardment of his memories, thoughts, and feelings came at her like a swarm of angry hornets. Every time before, when Vy had used the spell, she'd avoided being stung. But in that moment, she was weak and didn't have the strength to brush off the onslaught.

And so, she felt the prick of Dustin's spirit puncturing her all over—devouring her.

Camellia had always warned her of the double-edged nature of this particular sorcery, stating that overuse could result in a fracturing of self, but Vy had never really seen the verity of that warning. In past use, Vy had always been able to jump in and out of a person pretty much unscathed.

This was the first time that Vy grasped the graveness behind her mother's caution.

Vy finally managed to stop the assault and commanded Dustin to sleep. When his consciousness receded, she was in control.

Suddenly, she saw what he saw—the dark stretch of country road, the clock on the dash reading 4:16 a.m.

Petra, the love of her life, sat cuffed in the passenger seat, staring bleakly out the window.

Vy shook herself. *Those aren't my feelings ... Wait, Petra? Fuck!*

Turning Dustin's head, Vy looked at the brooding figure. From his memories, Vy knew why Petra had attacked her. It all made sense now.

Back at Sappho, Vy had thought Petra looked familiar. But, overtaken by lust, Vy had failed to make the connection. Then again, Vy wasn't sure that she would have recognized Petra in another scenario. The menacing woman looked nothing like the pretty girl who stood stunned and terrified on that cold winter night.

Vy hated to think of that night—the night she'd lost control and killed a woman by accident. For a decade she'd pushed the memory to the back of her mind. But now she was being forced to remove it from its corner.

Dustin's fingers tightened on the steering wheel as Vy teased out the dilemma she was in.

She should be happy to know that May's assurance that Petra would find her was true, but the reality of the situation was ludicrous. It was no wonder May had erupted into a fit of laughter.

Vy did not see Petra *willingly* working with her. Why would she? Vy had killed her mother. It was an impossible circumstance. But Vy had no choice in the matter. She would have to try to persuade her.

Vy brought Dustin's foot down hard on the brake. The vehicle skidded and lurched forward.

Beside her, Petra whipped angrily towards him. "What the fuck, Junior?"

Vy made Dustin draw the tranquilizer gun from its holster.

Petra's green eyes widened when the barrel was pointed at her. "What the actual f—"

Vy got Dustin to pull the trigger. Almost immediately, Petra slumped unconscious in her seat.

Next, Vy had Dustin exit the vehicle and open the back door.

From his eyes, Vy saw her limp body and shrank back from the sight. Her hair was a tangled mess. Dried blood crusted her skin and clothes. Her face was pale like a corpse.

Vy set Dustin's fingers to the task of deactivating the shock collar and freeing her limbs from their restraints. Then, she directed him to point the tranquilizer gun at his neck and fired.

Vy retreated from his mind before his body hit the pavement with a thud.

Breathing heavily, Vy wiggled her fingers and gave her body a shake. Her muscles felt stiff and heavy from the energy spent to use the spell.

Scooting out of the back seat, she tried to rid herself of traces of Dustin. Unfortunately, his essence clung to her like a bad smell. She hoped his influence on her wouldn't be a permanent fixture, but she got the sense it might.

Vy had no time to dwell on her predicament. She would sort out everything later.

There was a much more pressing matter to deal with—the thirst banged against her skull and clawed at her throat.

Dustin's exposed neck called to her. She saw herself biting him, drinking in her fill. Her usual sickness followed the thought. The world tilted.

Vy fell against the SUV, her entire body trembling. She shut her eyes and willed the nausea to subside.

When it finally did, she spared a look at the young man lying unconscious on the pavement. She decided that she couldn't leave him as he was and dragged his body off the road and into the safety of a grassy ditch.

Then, she got into the driver's seat and took off.

Chapter Ten

Wind brushed against Petra's cheek, making her stir. Her eyes slowly opened to the musical notes of birds chirping and the flow of nearby water. Weak threads of light peaked through the trees of a thick forest.

Why the fuck am I in the woods? Petra turned her head. Looking around, she tried to order her memories. She recalled Dustin slamming on the brakes. He had aimed his tranquilizer gun on her. He had shot her—again.

Why? Petra frowned. It made no sense.

She noticed that her hands and ankles were still bound. Someone had positioned her on the ground, propping her back against the rotting stump of a cut down tree.

"Finally, you're up."

Petra's head darted in the direction of the voice.

Anger burned up her neck, turning her face red, when she

spotted the fang. Petra's nostrils flared.

The vampire was seated high up on a hefty tree branch with her bare feet dangling. She looked wild with her curly black hair fluttering in the breeze and her clothes tattered and soiled with blood. In her right hand, the fang gripped a lifeless brown squirrel about its neck.

With supernatural athleticism, the fang launched herself off the branch and gracefully landed in front of Petra without a sound.

A large beetle scuttled up a root that was about a metre away from the fang's right foot. The fang made a face that looked a lot like disgust.

Pulse pounding, Petra used the stump to support her as she rose to her feet.

Staring down the enemy, Petra revisited her darkest memory—the fang's mouth buried in Helda's neck, globs of blood staining the snow, a pair of obsidian eyes.

Bellowing, Petra charged.

Effortlessly, the fang dodged the attack with a side-step.

Pivoting quickly, Petra tried again to tackle her foe, but her legs got tangled in the shackles. She fell and recovered quickly, rebounding to her feet.

"You're definitely not going to make this easy for me, eh?" The fang tossed her kill to the side.

"What did you do to my partner, fang?" Petra snapped.

"Nothing. I'm sure he's fine," she said with a shrug. "Like you, he is probably just waking."

"Where is he?"

"I really wouldn't know," she replied. "To be honest, I'm not sure where we are now."

Petra eyed the fang with suspicion, and a thick silence fell between them.

Her mind toiled as she tried to think of a way to best the fang, but chained and without a weapon, her odds weren't good.

Not knowing what else to do, Petra hollered and propelled herself towards the fang again, attempting to hook the handcuff chain about the fang's throat.

Naturally, the leech was too fast and jumped out of range. "I know why you want me dead Petra," she said.

Those words made Petra freeze. How had the fang uncovered her identity? "Fuck you!"

The fang fixed her with a somber look. "It was an accident."

"The fuck it was!"

"It was. It was a horrible accident. And I am so sorry for what—"

"Your kind does not feel regret," Petra spat, feeling the sting of tears in her eyes. "I don't want to hear your bullshit apology. Your words mean nothing. You are less than nothing—fucking lightless."

Flinching, the fang nibbled on her lower lip. "I don't expect you to forgive me. And if I was in your place, I wouldn't forgive me either," she said softly.

The two women's eyes met. A gust of wind rustled the branches overhead and sent forest debris scattering. The drumming of a woodpecker cut through the quiet.

Petra gritted her teeth. She had so many questions. How had the fang managed to escape Dr. Raz's shock collar? Why had Dustin shot her? Why the fuck had the fang carried her off to the fucking woods?

Petra's hands squeezed into fists. "If you are going to kill me, just fucking do it."

The fang blinked. "I'm not going to kill you."

Petra snorted.

"Really, I have no intention of hurting you," she said. "I want to make things right."

"Make things right," Petra repeated, chuckling bitterly. "The fuck you do. And even if you did, there's nothing you could do." There was nothing that could be done. Petra's mother was dead— the fang had killed her.

Petra felt a ball forming in her throat as the pain from ten years ago resurfaced. She remembered the feeling of her mother's cold body and the serene expression on her lifeless face. The memory tore at her heart, and her eyes pricked. She could feel herself shattering, but she'd be damned before she did that in front of the fang.

Petra wiped her eyes and clenched her fists. Her mind turned to what she could do in the moment to get an edge over her enemy, but then the fang said, "I can bring her back—your mother," and all her internal deliberations stopped.

Back? Petra closed her eyes and shook her head. She couldn't have heard the fang right. There was no way to bring her mother back—Helda was gone. Despite her efforts to hold them back, tears began to stream from her eyes. Petra quickly wiped them away with the back of her hand. She hated that she'd let her adversary see her cry.

"There's a way to bring her back," the fang said. She fiddled with her hands as if nervous.

"Impossible," Petra said bitterly. But even as she said the word, she wished the fang's statement could be true.

"Nothing is impossible," the fang said. "We are only ever limited by what we know, and I know a way to change everything for you—and for me."

"I see what you are doing fang—you wanna get back at me for stabbing you," Petra said. "I won't fall for your games."

"I'm not playing games."

"The fuck you aren't! Kill me—get it over with!"

"I told you already, I'm not going to hurt you," she retorted. "I need your help."

"You need my help?" Petra arched a brow and then laughed harshly.

"I'm serious." The fang bit her lip. "I need to find a talisman, and I need you to help me find it."

Petra stared down the fang. There was an air of earnestness to the creature's expression, but she wasn't buying it. "Why the fuck would I ever help you?"

"It is a time-travelling talisman," she answered. "With it, I could go back. I could change what happened. Your mother doesn't have to die."

Impossible. Petra frowned and shook her head. The fang was definitely playing a sick game, but Petra was not a fool. "I don't see how you need my help."

"A powerful sorceress divined that I would find it—but not

without Petra Malkovitch willingly at my side."

Petra grunted her disbelief. She knew about talismans from training. Sure, they existed, but that didn't mean what the fang was saying held any substance. *But what if she is telling the truth?*

How many nights had Petra dreamed of changing the past? How many nights had she lain awake crying and wishing for a chance to go back? How many nights had she envisioned a scenario where her mother stayed home instead of driving to the Chen household to pick her up? There were too many to count.

Petra's features softened. *Is there really a way to go back?* She met the fang's eyes. "I don't believe you," she said. "I would never work with you."

"Even if it meant you could have your mother back?" The fang crossed her arms over her chest. "I can tell you are miserable. Things don't have to be this way. Your whole life could be rewritten."

"You're a fucking liar," Petra sneered.

The fang sighed and removed a firearm from the back of the waistband of her jeans. She lobbed it over to Petra, who caught it effortlessly despite her bound hands. Petra noted that it was her gun.

What is the fang playing at? Blinking her confusion, she checked the magazine. It was loaded with its silver bullets. One well-aimed shot to the head or heart was all that was needed to take the fang down for good.

Flipping off the safety, Petra pointed the weapon at the fang's chest. *One shot. One shot and she's dead.*

"You want to kill me, here's your chance," the fang said, her voice shaky. "But killing me won't bring your mother back—it won't make you feel better."

"You're wrong, there's no better medicine than revenge." Her finger brushed the trigger.

"We can change everything, if we work together," the fang pleaded.

Petra itched to pull the trigger—why didn't she pull it?

"You could be happy."

Closing her eyes briefly, Petra thought again about all the nights she'd dreamt of such a possibility—her mother back, a different life.

A loud crack filled the air as the gun went off.

The silver bullet merely grazed the fang's arm, and a thin line of blood dripped from the gash. At the last moment, Petra had shifted her aim.

They stared at each other with intensity. Petra's green eyes glimmered with a mix of raw emotion, while the fang's brown eyes overflowed with what could only be described as relief.

She didn't move out of the way. Petra stood, perplexed. It shocked her that the fang hadn't attempted to dodge the bullet. If she hadn't misdirected her shot, the fang would be dead. *Maybe she isn't lying ...*

Petra cocked her head at the cuffs about her wrists and legs. "Get these off of me," she barked.

Hesitant, the fang closed the distance between them slowly. She then broke off the shackles easily with her hands. When Petra was freed, the fang backed away with caution.

Petra focused the barrel of the gun on her. "On the ground," she directed, wanting the fang in a position of disadvantage. "Tell me more about this talisman."

The fang stared at the forest floor, but she made no move to sit. "I told you what you need to know," she said.

"I will be the judge of that." Petra cocked her gun. "On the ground—now."

For a second, the fang looked like she was about to argue, but then she knelt with a defeated sigh. "How long do you have?" she asked. "I can drone on about the Great Architect's lore. Or do you want the watered-down kid version?"

"Don't get smart with me, fang."

"Okay, watered-down version it is," she said, rolling her eyes. "Wanna make yourself cozy on the ground with me, SOL?"

Petra gritted her teeth. She didn't bother correcting the fang. The creature didn't need to know that she wasn't officially an SOL yet. "No."

The fang shrugged. Clearing her throat, she began her tale, "When the Great Architect laboured to form our universe, her brother, Change, looked on with envy, for he could not create from nothing."

Petra raised a questioning brow. "Don't tell me you believe in this myth."

"There is some truth to be found in all stories," the fang replied. "You were the one who said you wanted to know more about the talisman. I can stop if you want."

"Whatever." Petra snorted. "Get on with it."

The fang released a breath and then continued, "Once the Architect finished her work, she looked down upon her design, with its laws and intricacies, and was satisfied. Everything was perfect—just how it was.

But, while she slept, her brother touched the universe and set off a domino effect until Change was everywhere. Then, when the Architect awoke and looked down upon her creation, she recognized nothing and flew into a rage.

The Architect conceived of the stewards and tasked them with going about the universe and setting all things back to their original state.

For longer than can be imagined, the stewards worked endlessly to reset the universe. Yet, no matter how fast they laboured, Change was always three steps ahead of them—touching everything.

Despising that her brother's corruption was observed in all things, the Architect retreated to another void to conceive of a new cosmos.

A few stewards did not take her abandonment well, and they defected over to the side of Change.

Time was one of the many stewards to reject the Great Architect, joining the side of Change.

And, when Change touched Time, they birthed three children—Past, Present, and Future.

Caring more for Past and Future, Change granted these two children the ability to influence Present.

Angered by the inequity, Present went against his father, reaching out to the Architect for her assistance.

Surprisingly, the Great Architect answered Present's call, gifting him with a vessel—an hourglass—that possessed the power to entrap and hold Past and Future in perpetuity. The hourglass also granted Present the ability to manipulate his siblings. However, the Architect made Present vow that the hourglass would never be used to steer the Past or Future. Present agreed and quickly locked his siblings away.

To ensure that he kept his word, Present enlisted the help of stewards—still loyal to the Architect—to watch over and protect the hourglass.

According to legend, were one to wield the power of the hourglass, they would be hunted and killed by the stewards charged with watching over it. The end. Happy now?" Vy asked.

"Very," Petra replied stiffly. "The tale of Past, Present, and Future was never my favourite—Death and Life are Change's more interesting children."

The fang frowned. "If you knew the story already, why'd you make me go over it?"

Petra shrugged, dismissing the fang's question. Frankly, she had forgotten about the tale. But it was somewhat assuring to know that the fang had recounted the myth accurately.

"So you want to get your hands on the hourglass?" Petra said. "And you want my help?"

"I don't want your help. I *need* your help," she corrected.

"Why do you want the hourglass?"

"To go back in time."

"Why do you want to go back in time?"

"It's the only way for me to find someone—someone who can help me change my situation."

"What situation?"

"I'm not answering that."

"If you want me to work with you, you'll answer the question, fang."

"I don't want to be a vampire—an illblood." The fang's jaw set tightly. Her dark eyes sparkled. "I want a cure."

"There's no such thing."

"You know nothing," she snapped. She quickly softened her tone. "Sorry, I didn't mean to get cross."

"I stabbed you. Aren't you pissed?"

"You had your reasons, and I understand them. I'm sweeping it under the rug," she said. "The real question is: can you?"

"No." Petra's brows drew together, and though she considered her options, there was only one that called to her heart. If there was a chance that her mother's life could be spared, she had to explore it. "I can never forget what you did, fang, but I want to see where this goes."

Petra lowered her weapon, and she wondered if she wasn't the biggest fool in the world.

Chapter Eleven

When the SOL lowered her weapon, relief flooded Vy's system.

While she knew Petra wasn't technically an SOL—that the woman was still in training—the title fit. Besides, if Petra hadn't had a vendetta against Vy, she would have likely been sworn in that day.

"Can I stand now?" Vy asked. She wanted off the ground. Not even two feet away from her, there was an army of ants picking apart a dead worm. The insects being so close made Vy terribly uneasy. She'd barely been able to keep herself together as she had recounted the lore of the hourglass.

Vy didn't wait for a response, she bolted to her feet, brushing debris from her legs. More than anything, she wanted a shower. Vy hated bugs. She hated dirt. She didn't like feeling so unclean.

The human's green eyes canvassed the area. "Where the fuck are we?"

"I don't know. I told you this already. I don't have my phone."

Vy rubbed her eyes with her palms. "Without Google, I am lost."

"How'd you manage to escape the shock collar?" The question was direct and sharp.

Vy wasn't inclined to answer and quipped, "My, aren't we talkative all of a sudden?"

Petra threw her a dark look. "Answer the question, illblood."

Vy flinched at the word—illblood. She hated being called that. She knew what she was, and she didn't need verbal reminders. "I have a name. It's Vy."

"I don't care what your name is—what the fuck are you, anyways?" Petra asked, redirecting her questioning.

A smug smirk formed on Vy's lips. From Dustin, she knew that the Order hadn't figured her out entirely. "It takes a special kind of incompetence to be spying on me for so long and not figure it out. Wouldn't you say?"

"My patience is thin. Keep dancing around my questions, and I will change my mind about working with you. What's your other faction?"

Vy met Petra's intense stare. There really was no reason to withhold that information. If they were going to work together, Petra would find out what she was soon enough. "My mother is a spellcaster," Vy answered.

If the SOL was surprised by the revelation, she couldn't tell by her expression.

The forest got much brighter suddenly, the sun's rays filtering through the trees in an almost thematic way.

There was a calmness to the woods that Vy might have enjoyed under different circumstances. Then again, maybe not. Vy had never cared much for the outdoors.

In the not-so-far distance, the lake swashed and babbled. Around them, birds chirped, flitting from branch to branch.

Vy's eyes narrowed on a squirrel about twenty metres away. It carried a large acorn in its wee hands, which it crunched on voraciously. Vy licked her lips—her thirst was not quite sated. Then again, when was it ever?

When Vy had been younger, a single nibble had been enough to hush her cravings. But things had changed. Now she had to feed constantly, and she depended on chem to help tame her hunger. Alice liked to drone on and say that things would only get worse with time—a fang need to feed more with every passing year. This reality was greatly unsettling—Vy was barely managing as things were.

"So what now—where do we go from here?" Petra asked.

Vy blinked and turned her attention away from the rodent. "Not sure."

"You're telling me you don't have any leads?"

"The lead I got was you—maybe you know something?"

"I don't know shit," Petra said coldly, her hand tightening around the grip of the gun that she held at her side. "I should just shoot you and be done with this."

Vy stilled. Maybe she wasn't in the clear just yet. Biting her lip, she tried to think up a way to further sway the irritable woman to her side. She'd already utilized her best ploy, tricking Petra into thinking she'd sacrifice her own life to prove her earnestness. In actuality, Vy's life hadn't been at risk when she had tossed Petra the firearm.

Planning ahead, she had cast invisible magical armour about her heart and head to protect her vital organs. In her weakened state, she hadn't had enough juice to protect her entire body, which was probably for the best. Being grazed by the bullet gave an air of authenticity to the act.

Even so, Vy could tell that Petra was teetering, but she wasn't sure what else she could do to win the human over.

Willingly—that word made everything more difficult than it needed to be. If it weren't for it, Vy could enchant Petra, forcing her assistance.

Vy sighed sadly. She needed that hourglass. Living in a state of perpetual malnourishment was not sustainable. And she was dying to find acceptance amongst her mother's faction. She dreamed of having the type of connection that only came with belonging.

To Vy, loneliness was the worst presence. Though invisible, it was palpable and pervasive. There was a heaviness to its company that sometimes felt suffocating. And maybe it was asphyxiating—a slow death wrought from a million hostile glares and even more cold shoulders.

If Vy ridded herself of her affliction, she'd no longer be despised and ignored. She'd no longer have to fear getting too close to humanity. She could have her family back. She could even find love.

It didn't sit well with Vy that all her hopes hung on Petra's choice. Of all the people in the world, it just had to be her.

Through Dustin, Vy understood how deep Petra's hate for her

ran. The woman saw Vy as her greatest enemy and less than nothing. She'd called Vy a lightless—a being without a soul.

Where Petra was concerned, Vy needed to tread carefully. She couldn't give Petra a reason to flip. Vy needed a lead—and soon.

Her dark brows creasing, Vy tried to think of something. An idea came to her. "You think the Order's database might have information that can help us?"

"How do you know about the database?" Petra asked.

Dustin was the answer, but Vy was not going to tell Petra that. Shrugging, she replied, "I was guessing. I figured your organization would have a repository for its data."

Petra apparently bought her answer for she said, "There might be information about the hourglass—I would have to check. What did you do with the SUV?"

Vy cocked her head to the side. "It is near the road—about a ten-minute walk."

Without a word, Petra began walking in the direction Vy had pointed to, her tactical boots crunching on the twigs and organic waste that made up the forest floor.

Vy followed her.

When they reached the SUV, Petra flung open the door to the driver's seat and climbed inside. She slammed the door behind her.

Vy's hand hesitated on the passenger-door handle. Releasing a deep breath, she opened the door and hopped into the cabin of the vehicle, gently shutting the door so as not to rile the woman further.

Petra didn't spare her a look as she grabbed a tablet that was wedged between the driver's seat and the centre console bin. She proceeded to stab at the touchscreen with her index finger.

Minutes ticked by, and Vy spent the time picking at the grime under her nails. She hated how dirty she was and craved a shower.

When there was no more dirt and blood to pick at, she turned in her seat and asked, "You find anything yet?"

"No."

A few more minutes passed. Vy craned her neck to look at the screen, but the glare was preventing her from getting a good look. "Still nothing?"

Petra's jaw clenched, and she fixed her with a dirty look.

Vy bit her lip and then held out a hand. "Mind if I try?"

Petra snorted, but tossed the device in Vy's lap before folding her arms over her wide chest. She turned and glowered out the window.

Picking up the tablet, Vy looked down at the screen. The Order's database was on the display.

Because of Dustin, Vy recognized the interface and was easily able to navigate it. Also, because of him, she was able to log out of Petra's account, and log back in under a different user—his mother's.

Years ago, Dustin had worked tirelessly to discover his mother's password. He had wanted to know what had happened to the man who had raised him, Chief Minister Wu. After numerous failed attempts, Dustin had found success and was able to uncover the dark truth.

Wu had been accused of being insubordinate, and his mother had killed him as a result. Specifics about the incident had been disconcertingly sparce. A good man's death had been limited to a single sentence written in an occurrence report submitted by his mother. It had read: *on Saturday, April 6, 2008, about 0905hrs, I attended the Church where Chief Minister Wu failed to follow directions, and I was required to use lethal force.*

There was no scenario that Dustin could envision that would warrant lethal force being used on Wu. Dustin hated his mother for what she had done. Even so, he made a point to keep his contempt hidden. There was a lot more to Dustin than he let on. He had ambitions to rise in the ranks of the Church, and he was wise enough to understand that he'd never achieve his goals if he made an enemy out of his mother.

Using the commander's credentials, Vy essentially had unrestricted access to everything.

Vy tapped on the cellblocks tab—one of many labelled as classified.

In the search bar, she typed *talisman*. A few hits popped up, but after scrolling through them, she determined that they were not relevant.

From the corner of her eye, Vy observed Petra. The woman's face seemed to be getting redder by the second.

What if I can't find a lead? Vy shook her head and focused her attention back on the screen.

In the search bar, she typed *Present's Gate*.

A single result came up. Vy tapped on the link and was taken to an occurrence report dating back to the year 1997. It was written in what looked to be Japanese.

Vy muttered a few words of magic. The spell was one of the first Camellia had ever taught her, and it granted Vy the ability to read, write and converse in any language known to man. Soon, the symbols on the screen were not foreign, and Vy could read report.

```
Sir,

On Sunday, March 2, 1997, about 2300hrs,
I was tasked with overseeing the capture
of Itachi Yamamoto, a class C earth demon,
in a covert mission in Machida, Tokyo.
From previous intel, it was believed that
Itachi knew the identity and whereabouts of
a class S sorceress, and so we recognized
the importance of executing the operation
successfully.

Before we closed in on the target, it was
noted that the demon seemed erratic. It
was exhibiting displays of self-harm, and
muttering over and over, "Without honour—
helped you find Present's Gate."
When we closed in on the demon, it did not
heed our orders to remain still. Instead,
it attacked SOL Tanaka.

My platoon and I had no choice but to
shoot it dead.

                    Respectfully submitted,
                    Sergeant Yoshida
```

"You found something?"

When Vy nodded, Petra leaned over to pluck the tablet from her fingers. Looking down at the screen, the human scowled. "This looks like Japanese—I can't read this."

"It's an occurrence report from Tokyo base," Vy said. "It dates back to 1997, but it references Present's Gate."

"Present's Gate?" Petra repeated.

"The threshold that traps the past and future," Vy explained.

"Whatever." Petra snorted. "What else does the report say?"

Vy relayed the information, and the woman was clearly not impressed with her finding, for she gritted teeth and said, "That lead died with Itachi—dead and gone."

"Dead doesn't mean gone. We need to go to Tokyo. If we can find Itachi's resting place ... there might be something I can do." She noted a distinct change in Petra's expression—the woman's features grew less hard and her lips parted slightly. In that moment, she looked very beautiful, and Vy found herself wishing that she could kiss her.

What was even more disconcerting was the blossoming of warmth that spread across her chest. It wasn't the familiar feeling of lust, but an odd sense of longing—Dustin's love for Petra, which had latched itself to Vy like an unwanted parasite.

She stabbed you. Think of the pain that caused you. She wants to kill you, Vy told herself, hoping she'd be able to talk the invasive emotion away. It didn't work, and looking at Petra was not helping. Not helping at all.

Vy felt her body flush with heat, and her face burned hottest. Annoyed, she turned her focus out the car window.

"Tokyo," Petra said, her voice sounding soft and distant. "I don't see how you can do anything if Itachi is dead."

When Vy was certain her words wouldn't come out jumbled, she said, "Don't worry, I have a plan."

"And what's that?"

Deciding a little honesty might go a long way in bridging the gap between them, Vy went over her plan and did her best to not stare or stammer.

"That's not possible—you can't do that," Petra said.

"I can. You'll see."

Chapter Twelve

Repositioning, Olivia cranked the office chair's recline all the way back and propped her booted feet on the desk. She chuckled at the sitcom playing on the computer screen. Blanche Devereaux always cracked her up.

She was rewatching one of her favourite episodes of the *Golden Girls*—the one where Sophia's brother Angelo, a priest, visits and Blanche pretends to be a nun collecting undergarments for needy, sexy people. It was a classic.

Olivia was a sucker for sitcoms. Particularly *Golden Girls*, *Seinfeld*, and *Frasier*, as they had been her mother's favourites. Consuming the familiar content was always bittersweet.

In one way, the nostalgia was cozy, like a blanket. But at the same time, Olivia was reminded that she would never again snuggle beside her mother on the couch with a bowl of buttered popcorn to share between them.

Olivia tore open a pack of Skittles and poured a third of the coloured candy into her mouth. She chewed quickly, swallowed, and gorged on more.

She was just about to tip the last of the fruit-flavoured candies into her mouth when her ears pricked at the sound of the lab's sallyport door clanking open.

Olivia looked up at the wall mounted clock. It was 0955hrs. The commander was early.

Odd. She frowned.

Spinning the chair around, Olivia stood up and tossed the unfinished red package on the desk. She stretched her arms over her head and rubbed her fatigued hazel eyes.

Sleep didn't come easily for Olivia. She was lucky if she got four hours rest in a night. Her constant state of exhaustion made her irritable and slightly delirious at times.

Olivia grabbed her opened energy drink and downed the rest of the over-caffeinated beverage. Wiping her lips with the back of her hand, she tossed the empty blue and silver can into the recycling bin. She didn't bother fixing her uniform before urging her sore legs to move.

Every step hurt as she shuffled out of Raz's dark office and into the fully lit lab.

Olivia squinted against the brightness of the room. She looked at the commander and smirked. "S'up Clay."

The burly woman grimaced at her, and Olivia's lips quirked into a wide smile. Nothing pleased her more than getting under Clay's skin. The commander was so uptight and easy to rile.

"How many times do I have to tell you to put your uniform in order?" Clay spat before looking around the room. She frowned. "Where is Raz?"

Olivia didn't motion to tuck her shirt in or unroll her sleeves. Instead, she shrugged and replied, "It wasn't my turn to watch him."

The commander's expression darkened, and she folded her large arms over her chest.

Olivia strode over to a worktable and hopped up to sit on it. Leaning back on her hands, she noticed the way Clay's blue eyes watched her closely—too closely. Olivia doubted that the commander realized how intently she stared and what undertones her deep gaze carried.

Olivia was a people watcher. Over the years, she'd devoted a good chunk of time to observing Kayla Clay. For the most part, the commander was better than most at presenting an outward image that she wanted to show. But Olivia saw what no one else seemed to see. Under the armour of cold bravado was a woman in pain, a woman who sought acknowledgement over everything, and a woman who was warm at her core. Clay was especially soft when it came to her son.

Dustin should not be on the cusp of graduating from the SOL training program. There were more than a couple years he ought to have failed, but Kayla had pulled strings to push him through. Like most mothers, Clay wanted her son to succeed. Olivia assumed that the commander only saw success in the form of advancing through the Order's ranks.

"Do you have any idea when he will be back?" Clay asked, her annoyance evident.

Olivia shook her head. "Nope."

The commander frowned, and then said, "I know about the stunt you pulled yesterday."

"What stunt?"

"Sparring with Malkovitch."

Olivia threw up her hands and gave the commander an innocent expression. "Malkovitch started it."

"I don't believe you—not for a second."

Olivia pouted. "You wound me."

Clay moved towards her and leaned on an opposing table. She crossed her arms. "Can you level with me?"

"About what?"

"Your behaviour," Clay said. "Why do you insist on going against the herd? Unlike Commander Folkes, I run a tight ship, and there is only so much I will put up with."

"Thought you knew I'm an outcast," Olivia said, before adding, "It's my nature to not fit in."

"I want to understand. What do you want? What would it take to get you to behave?"

Olivia blinked her surprise. The questions seemed out of character for the commander.

Regarding her wants, more than anything, Olivia sought to slaughter her father—along with anyone else complicit in her mother's decision to die by suicide.

But there was no way the commander would assist with that—it was too dangerous. Not to mention that Olivia had long ago accepted that her father might never pay for what he had done.

Aside from that, Olivia desired nothing. Actually, that was wrong—there was something else. Olivia wanted to see that Dr. Raz's dreams came to fruition. And already, the commander was going above and beyond to aid his research and developments.

Frankly, there was nothing of substance Clay could offer her. Even so, Olivia feigned mulling over a response before saying, "Guess it'd be nice to be promoted to Sergeant of SOTU."

Clay looked to be considering her answer seriously. "That could be a possibility, but I'd need to see a dramatic change. For a start, you can dress appropriately."

"Big ask. I will have to think about it." Olivia yawned. Their conversation was starting to bore her.

Clay was back to glaring at her. "It's not wise to make an enemy of me."

"Ditto."

The commander gritted her teeth. A few moments of silence passed between them, and then Clay said, "I need you to go out today."

Olivia arched a quizzical brow. "Thought I was on light duties."

"You are. One of our recruiters has come down with a stomach bug. I need you to make contact with the candidate as soon as possible."

"I don't do recruitment," Olivia said cooly.

"That was a direct order—I wasn't asking."

Olivia clenched her jaw. She considered saying that she refused to go, but thought better of it. She was sick of being on base. The outing would be good for her.

"Fine, I'll go," she said exasperatingly.

"Good," Clay replied curtly. "Richardson has the information you'll need."

"I hate that woman." Olivia snorted and slid off the table. She winced when her feet touched the floor. Every time she'd used Dr. Raz's serum, her legs became ridiculously sore. The pain and bruising sometimes lasted for over two weeks. But a little discomfort was worth it if it meant that Raz got closer to his aims.

"Are you okay?" the commander asked.

With a roll of her eyes, she replied, "I'm just peachy." Olivia smiled tightly and walked past Clay towards the sallyport. She pressed the button near the door to alert control that she wanted to exit the lab. A few seconds ticked by and then the mechanized door glided open with a loud thunk.

Olivia stepped into the sallyport. The door entering into the lab slammed closed, and then the door leading to the hallway began to open. When the gap was wide enough, Olivia slid through it and proceeded down the blinding-white corridor.

She exited the cellblocks building, and it took her longer than she would have liked to get to the main building. But the walk had been good for her stiff joints, and her legs didn't hurt as much.

Oliva rode the elevator up to the fourth floor and swaggered towards the desk positioned just outside the commander's office.

A plump Richardson gave her a dirty look. In Olivia's opinion, the woman had the look of a strict supply teacher.

"S'up Rich," Olivia said.

The much older woman did not return the greeting and held out a manila folder for her to take.

Amused, Olivia grabbed it. Sliding the file under her arm, she turned to walk back towards the elevator and began to whistle a chipper tune. Once, she'd overheard that Richardson despised whistling because it reminded her of her late husband, who had had a habit of cheating.

Olivia rode the lift down to the first floor and exited the main building.

Walking southwest, her boots crunched on the gravel as she headed towards the motor pool. When she reached her destination, she signed out her favourite vehicle—a black Hummer H1. It was large, impractical, and drew too much attention, but Olivia loved driving it. Behind its wheel, she felt like an action movie badass. She also quite liked that no one else signed it out—probably for the reasons listed.

Before climbing into the front seat, Olivia threw open a back door and grabbed an energy drink from the pack she had hidden under the passenger seat. Olivia closed the door and cracked the can open. Taking a long swig, she threw open the driver's door and hopped inside.

With a few quick gulps, she finished the rest of the caffeinated beverage and burped. Crushing the aluminum can, she tossed it on the floor on the passenger's side, where a mountain of trash was slowly growing.

Olivia took a quick look at the file Richardson had given her and entered the location on the GPS. Starting up the Hummer, she rolled out of the car lot and took off from the base.

About forty-five minutes into the drive, Olivia noticed a figure walking towards her on the opposite side of the country road. As she got closer, she realized that she recognized the face.

Well, if it isn't Dustin. Olivia slowed the Hummer, pulling over to the side of the road and stopping. She put down her window and called out, "Rough night?"

Clay Junior looked up at her. From his dark expression, she could tell that he was not glad to see her. But he crossed the street and approached her window.

He peered inside the vehicle before meeting her eyes. "Alone—not on a SOTU mission?" His brows creased.

"I'm on light duties." Olivia snorted. "Doing a bit of recruiting."

"Recruiting," Dustin repeated with a nod. "Where are you headed?"

"Windsor." She cocked her head to the passenger side and then grinned mischievously. "I'll let you tag along—for a fee."

Understanding her proposition, Dustin frowned. "You can't mean now?" He gestured to the road. "Here?"

"Shy all of a sudden?" she quipped, raising a brow. "I reckon there's more privacy here than behind the main building."

Dustin's face blushed with embarrassment. Then he exhaled a deep breath. "I'm not in the mood."

"Seems like you're never in the mood," Olivia said flatly. Though, for once, she actually believed him.

Olivia sensed that his current state of gloom had everything to do with why he was walking back to the base. She knew he was supposed to be out on assignment with Malkovitch to capture the illblood—the assignment that should have been hers.

She didn't have to be a rocket scientist to guess what had happened—Dustin was a hindrance, and Malkovitch likely unloaded herself of his dead weight.

Everyone on the base knew that Dustin was head over heels in love with Malkovitch. If Malkovitch ditched him, he was probably reeling from heartbreak.

"I can take a rain check," Olivia said. "Hop in."

Dustin hesitated for a moment and then walked around the front of the vehicle. He opened the passenger door and scowled. "There's a heap of cans and candy wrappers on the floor."

Olivia rolled her eyes at him. "It won't hurt you. Push it to the side."

Muttering a curse, Dustin climbed into the passenger seat and slammed the door.

Olivia swivelled in her seat and looked at him. "Anyone tell you that you're adorable when you're angry?"

He clenched his jaw and stared straight out the window. "Can you just drive?"

Chuckling, Olivia shifted the vehicle into drive and started back onto the road. "Want to tell me what happened?"

"No."

"Well, I'm dying to know, so spill it," she said. "I promise not to tell anyone." Olivia made a motion of sealing her lips.

Dustin snorted. "I don't even know where to start…" From her peripheral, she saw him run a frustrated hand through his blond hair.

Olivia drummed her fingers on the steering wheel. "How about you start with how you wound up heading back to the base on foot?"

"I'm not sure ... I think Malkovitch tranqued me. I woke up in a ditch."

Cold move—even for Malkovitch. "Why would Malkovitch tranque you?" Olivia asked. Sure, she had a theory, but she wanted Dustin to confirm it.

Dustin released a loud sigh. "I'm worried Malkovitch will do, or has done, something very stupid."

Olivia couldn't help but smirk. The thought of Malkovitch fucking up tickled her. She wasn't Malkovitch's biggest fan. The woman was so smug and full of herself. Malkovitch strutted around the base acting like she was the only person to have ever experienced loss. But anyone who joined the Order carried painful baggage.

It also didn't help that Malkovitch's first name reminded Olivia of her father's name—Peter. And, if Olivia was honest, Dustin's infatuation with her bugged her a bit too. Though she'd never admit to being jealous.

"And what's that?"

Dustin stayed quiet for a while before answering. "We were given directions to bring an illblood back to the base alive and unharmed."

Alive and unharmed. The words repeated in Olivia's mind. She recalled the commander asking Raz if he needed the illblood alive, and Raz had indicated that all he needed was an intact body.

"Okay, so you guys were given a directive, and ..."

"And turns out the illblood is the lightless who killed Petra's mother," Dustin said.

Olivia's mouth gaped. She hadn't been expecting that. *What is the commander up to? What was her intention behind sending Petra?* Her hands tightened on the steering wheel as she pondered.

Everyone knew how committed Malkovitch was to getting her revenge. All Olivia could hope was that Malkovitch brought the illblood's dead body back to the base. If Malkovitch didn't, Raz's research would be put on hold.

"Fucking Malkovitch!" Olivia snapped. She took her frustration out on the steering wheel, hitting it repeatedly until the wick of her anger burned out.

When she was back to feeling calm, she could feel Dustin's eyes on her. "What was that about?"

Olivia didn't answer.

Chapter Thirteen

Autumn 2004

A ten-year-old Vy stood by her bedroom window and watched as her father and half-sister hopped into the navy-blue sedan. Malcolm was off to work, but on the way, he'd be dropping Ginger off at school.

Vy wished she could go to school. She thought it'd be nice to have friends and play tag on the jungle gym. She wanted to be a kid.

Being cooped up all day, with only her thoughts and daydreams to keep her company, was no fun at all.

It had been her mother's idea to homeschool her. Vy knew her father disagreed with the decision but he hadn't had the nerve to voice his opinion. Where Camellia was concerned, her father was mindless putty.

That was how it was with Camellia, though—whatever she wanted, she got. Nothing was too much or too out of the question.

The world was Camellia's candy jar, brimming with sweet possibilities, and the lid only closed when she chose to twist it tight. That being said, as ambitious as Camellia was, Vy had often wondered why it was that her mother restricted herself, choosing to play at human. Her father was a good man, but he wasn't worthy of the sorceress's affections. And Camellia didn't pretend to love him. So why did she stay with him?

On one occasion, Vy had been bold enough to ask, but Camellia had ignored the question, like she avoided most. Much about Camellia was shrouded in mystery, and even though Vy spent day after day with her mother, in some ways, the woman was a stranger.

As the blue sedan backed out of the driveway, taking off down the street, Vy's shoulders slumped. She was not looking forward to the continuation of the torture she'd endured for the past couple of months.

While her mother's lessons were never a walk in the park, blood magic—necromancy in particular—was, without a doubt, the most difficult so far.

Vy feared she'd never be able to grasp it. There were too many instructions, too many elements that had to be executed with perfect precision.

For example, when uttering the incantation, not only did one's cadence need to be just right for the complicated outpouring of words, but one's heartbeat and breathing needed to mirror the rhythm as well. Then—not a moment too soon or a moment too late—one needed to slice through the heel of their palm at a specific depth and angle so that the blood dripped in the most particular of ways.

Vy had failed at this—over and over and over. All the while, her mother sat like a stiff gothic portrait with legs crossed and eyes fixed on a giant tome.

If ever Vy erred and dared to vocalize her frustrations, Camellia's cutting tongue would be quick to lash out like a whip, cracking through the air and re-opening mental wounds that were still healing from the previous day. "How can you expect to channel magic if you cannot control yourself and your emotions?" she'd snapped. "It really is not so hard." After issuing her chastisement, Camellia always returned to her reading, and Vy was left trying to sew herself back up.

Exhaling a deep breath, Vy shuffled her feet out of her bedroom and towards the descending staircase. At a timid pace, she made her journey to the main floor and then down another flight of steps that led into the basement.

Leaning against an unfinished wall, towards the back of the open space, was a large mirror with an ornately jewelled frame. To the human eye, it would appear normal, but the keen unhuman eye would note the way its reflective surface shimmered oddly, revealing it to be a portal.

Vy stepped through the mirror and gritted her teeth. She hated the way it felt to be sucked into the portal, only to be shot out a mere second later.

Camellia's study was on the other side of the gateway.

Vy's gaze swept over the room. It was a large and richly decorated space. Paintings and tapestries hung on the floral-patterned wall. Dark wooden floors were covered with rich rugs with elaborate designs. The furnishings looked as if they had been pulled from a Georgian ancestral home.

The office was a chaos of books. Two entire walls were devoted to hulking built-in bookshelves that were over packed. Tiny mountains of books littered the large oak desk. Some more stacks were strewn upon a chaise and piled in a corner opposite her mother's favourite chair.

As usual, Camellia sat near the heat of a burning fireplace—a large crumbling volume lay open on her lap. She did not look up from the pages or acknowledge her daughter's presence. The expectation was that Vy would continue her training—unheard and unseen.

Vy walked towards her designated area by the large drafty window and took a seat on the floor. About a foot away was a gilded platter upon which lay a crow whose iridescent dark wings hadn't flapped in over two months.

Camellia had enchanted the dead bird, preventing it from decaying. It was Vy's task to bring it back to life.

Beside the crow was a delicate knife with a decorated porcelain handle and a thin razor-sharp blade. Vy's hand shook as she reached for it, her small fingers wrapping around the handle. She had probably cut herself over a thousand times in the last two months—it never got easier, and the first slash of the day somehow always felt the worse.

Releasing a soft quivering breath, Vy began to recite the words locked into her memory, awaking the magic around and within her. She could perceive it flowing in her veins and weighing down her breaths.

Given that it was old magic—dark magic—it was the kind that bared down on her like a plate of iron. The burden of her load intensified with each word that spilled from her lips.

When Vy had first attempted the spell, she'd only been able to say a single verse. Her mind had been too weak then, and it had screamed at her to release the building power. Over the weeks, she'd built up quite the endurance, and she could finally manage the load without flinching.

Her troubles now came towards the end. She faltered at the point where she cut herself. Always, she found herself distracted by the blood welling to the surface of her skin. At the sight of it, she'd lose her rhythm, her heartbeat increasing and her breaths coming quick. Sometimes, she even felt sick.

It happened every single time. Vy didn't know why. There was something about the sight of blood that bothered her—distracted her.

As she neared that point of the spell, she felt dread rising within her. *If only I didn't have to see it,* she thought.

Vy reached the end of the incantation and cut herself. As usual, she slipped up when she sighted the bubble of blood. The moment she stumbled, the rising tide of magic washed over her like a wave, making her gasp in pain.

Curling herself into a ball on the floor, Vy tried to calm her quick breaths. For many moments, she focused on recovering. When she felt well enough, she muttered a few words to heal her bleeding hand.

Vy had a revelation as she sat up. *Maybe ... maybe I don't have to look.*

She exhaled a deep breath and reached again for the porcelain handle. She wiped the blade off with a cloth and then tried again. This time, however, right before she slashed into her flesh, Vy closed her eyes. She felt the pain, but didn't see the blood—she did not falter.

When the final word left her lips, she opened her eyes and hoped for a miracle. *Did I do it?*

She looked at her palm. The trickle looked right—the way her mother had shown her. But more than looking right, it felt right. She could feel the power she'd built up seeping out of her with each red drop.

Without further hesitation, Vy dipped a finger into the magic-infused ink and painted a marking on the crow.

Having failed too many times to count, Vy did not expect it to work. And so, when the crow blinked and moved its head, she gasped her shock and delight.

With soiled hands, Vy gently picked up the bird.

It stood up in the cup of her bloodstained palms, and its head darted around the room. When it cawed, Vy smiled in amazement. *I can't believe I did it!*

The bird stretched out its beautiful dark wings. They appeared colourful in the gleam of the sunlight streaming in from the window. Vy marvelled at the creature, and her sense of awe intensified when it took off and flew about the office.

Vy's smiled widened as she watched it flap about. She giggled and sought to call it back to her.

A loud snap of fingers cut the strings of Vy's spell. The crow froze mid-flight. It dropped to the floor with a soft thud.

Vy gazed up at her mother with sad eyes, but looked away quickly, staring at the fold of her legs. Tears burned in her eyes, and she knew better than to let one fall.

"I did it," Vy muttered when she knew her pain wouldn't be evident in her voice.

"Took you long enough," her mother said flatly. "Now your real training in the art of blood magic can begin."

Chapter Fourteen

Spring 2019

Petra followed the fang out of the elevator and into the dimly lit hallway, keeping a measured distance.

"Fuck." Vy swore. Bending, she inspected her front door. The hinge was broken, and the door opened with a gentle push of her hand.

Petra crossed the threshold, entering the fang's home. Her eyes swept over the space. Evidence of their early skirmish was written in the chaos. There was an indentation in the wall Petra had been forcefully shoved into. There were spatters and streaks of blood. Couch cushions were strewn about the floor.

Making a point about not removing her shoes, Petra moved into the kitchen area and leaned against a counter. She folded her arms and tried to ignore her discomfort. Her body was still feeling the effects of the two tranquilizer darts. She felt weighed down, and her eyes burned with fatigue. And fuck she was hungry.

Petra made sure to keep her discomfort to herself. She didn't trust her new partner. It wouldn't be wise to show any signs of weakness.

From her spot, Petra saw Vy mutter a few indiscernible words—a spell that fixed the door in a blink. In witnessing magic for the first time, Petra couldn't help but stare in wonderment and fascination. Though it didn't pass her notice that the use of magic seemed to take a physical toll on the fang, who stood to her feet with a huff of exhaustion, looking paler.

Once the door was fixed and shut, Vy headed to the small living area where she spoke more foreign words that resulted in righting the space. In a matter of seconds, the quaint living room was back in order—nice and tidy.

As with the first spell, Petra could see the cost that came with casting, what she presumed to be, a simple spell. The fang's cheeks lost some of its fullness, and the rings beneath her eyes were suddenly more pronounced.

Given that Vy looked like she wanted to pass out after muttering two spells, Petra again found herself doubting the possibility that the fang could pull off any form of sorcery—especially not necromancy, the kind supposed to exist only in myth.

During the entire drive back to Toronto, Petra's mind had wrestled with uncertainty and hope. For the most part, she was skeptical. It made the most sense that the fang was trying to dupe her.

So why not end it here? Petra's fingers brushed against the cool metal of her gun. It sat comfortably in her holster underneath her jacket. She shook her head and sighed.

Yes, the desire to kill the fang was fierce, but Petra longed for a different life to a greater degree. And she owed it to her mother to see where this path took her—even if it meant collaborating with the very creature who had killed her.

"Are you hungry?" Vy asked. She stood at the opposite end of the kitchen. Her slender fingers reached for her phone that rested on the counter.

"No," Petra said, keenly observing the fang type in a code to access the device.

The fang's face dropped to the screen, and she bit her lip. Her thumbs worked quickly to type out a message on the keyboard.

Frowning with a sigh, she set her phone back down and looked up at Petra. Her eyes were a very dark brown, almost black, but they were nowhere near the crazed obsidian that had haunted Petra for years. It irked Petra that Vy didn't have the face of a monster—even disheveled and fatigued, the fang was magazine-cover beautiful.

Looks can be so deceiving. Petra dropped her gaze.

"Besides beer and seltzer, I don't have anything in my fridge," Vy said. "Are you sure you aren't hungry? I can order you whatever you feel like."

Petra shot her a dirty look. "I don't need anything."

"Fine, whatever. I'm going to take a shower," the fang said. Her eyes slid over Petra's body, almost lingering. "You might want to take one too, or at least change your stained clothes."

Vy crossed her arms, waiting for a response. Petra didn't say anything and turned her attention to picking at her cuticles.

The fang made a noise of annoyance and moved out of the kitchen. Moments later, the door to the bathroom clicked shut. Soon, the spray of the shower was heard.

On the counter, Vy's phone buzzed.

Without hesitation, Petra walked over and picked it up. She entered the code she'd spied the fang using, and the device opened to the chat application.

Petra scrolled up and read the recent thread of messages.

Isabella 1:32am

Fuck you

Isabella 2:28am

sry, what did I do?????

Isabella 4:16am

Heyyyy, u up?????

Call me ... pls. Why u being like this??? :(

I want to b wit u ...

Isabella 9:05am

Sorry for all the messages. Disregard, I was drunk. But I think we should talk. Call me.

Ivy Just now

It's better if I don't. Sorry.

Petra closed the chat application feeling almost sorry for the girl who was obviously smitten with the fang, but mostly she felt irritated by Vy's cold text. Why it irritated her, she wasn't sure.

Looking down at the phone's home screen, a logo caught Petra's eye. She remembered it. In high school, everyone had been addicted to the social media platform. Though, back then, she'd accessed it on the computer.

It had been years since Petra had had unrestricted access to the internet. Against her better judgement, Petra tapped on the application, and she scanned the fang's profile.

Vy used an alias on the app and only followed two people—her father and half-sister, who Petra knew to both be human. The fang had zero posts and zero friends. Her profile picture was a stock photo.

Petra stared at the search bar. The tiny magnifying glass called to her.

Heart hammering in her ears, she typed Kate's name in the field. When her oldest friend's picture popped up, Petra's stomach flipped. It felt wrong to continue. But Petra's hesitance was short-lived.

A tightness built up in her chest as she began scrolling through Kate's profile. Shuffling over to the couch, Petra sat down and got lost in the timeline.

Kate was more beautiful than she remembered. Her jet-black hair was longer now and fell below her shoulders in waves. Her skin was still flawless. Her beautiful eyes shone in the photos where she smiled.

There were pictures of Kate with family, and pictures of her with friends. There were pictures of Kate on sandy beaches, and pictures of her hiking. There were pictures of Kate dining out, and pictures of her bumming it at home.

What did not escape Petra's notice was that there were no pictures of Kate with a partner, despite her status stating that she was in a relationship. There was also no mention of who Kate was with.

Petra gritted her teeth. Was Kate with a man? A woman? She felt a burning need to know.

Why do I even care? It's been so long. Petra sighed and pinched the bridge of her nose.

Shaking her head, Petra closed her eyes. *What would things be like if my mother was still alive? Would Kate and I be together? Would we do all the things we swore to do?*

They'd frequently talked about travelling the world, and Japan had been their number one destination as it was the origin of their favourite things: manga, anime, and instant ramen.

The irony that Petra would be going to Japan with the creature she hated most, instead of with Kate, was not lost on her.

"Who's that? She's pretty."

Petra nearly jumped. She hadn't heard the fang's approach. She hadn't heard the bathroom door open. She scolded herself for being distracted. How had she let herself get so distracted?

Tossing a look over her shoulder, she scowled at Vy, who stood inches behind the couch and was leaning over her shoulder.

"A girlfriend?" Vy probed further.

Petra didn't owe the fang a response. Irritated, she closed the application and tossed the phone on the empty cushion seat beside her. When Vy made no motion to move, Petra spat, "You're wasting time. Shouldn't you be getting ready?"

The fang had a white towel wrapped around her slim body. Beads of water glistened on her bronze skin and dripped from the tangles of her wet hair. A pleasant floral scent came off of her, perfuming the air.

Petra's eyes followed a drop of water that slipped from the fang's bared shoulder, rolling down her collarbone, and disappearing between the crease of her breasts.

Petra's breath caught. The towel was too fucking short. Too much of the fang was on display, and she was mesmerized by the smoothness of the vampire's skin and the curve of her thighs.

She remembered the way Vy's fingers had felt inside her. Petra's face heated. "Why are you just standing there?" she snapped, waving a hand to tell the fang to go somewhere else—anywhere else.

Amusement was written on the fang's face, and Petra's ears and neck burned with embarrassment.

"The way you were looking at me, I figured you wanted me to stick around," she chirped, her tone light and teasing.

Petra scowled and said nothing.

"You should shower too," Vy said next. "I am sure I have some clothes that will fit you."

"No."

"You can't wear that—it's stained with blood."

"Just give me the clothes. I'll change."

"Suit yourself." The fang shrugged and walked away towards the bedroom. The door clicked shut behind her. She emerged about twenty minutes later with a bundle of folded clothes in hand.

The fang had dressed in the kind of outfit that would look ridiculous on most people, but looked perfectly suitable on her. The black bra she was wearing peeked beneath a netted top stitched with white rhinestones. Over that, she sported a leather trench coat paired with slim fitting black pants that were shiny as if made from latex—and maybe they were. Her accessories included thin gold hooped earrings, thick rimmed sunglasses, and a braided gold necklace.

Petra stood from her seat on the couch and crossed her arms. "Took you long enough."

"I was packing and looking for something for you to wear." The fang lifted her sunglasses so they sat at the top of her head and tossed the bundle she held.

Petra caught the clothes. There was a pair of large grey sweatpants and an oversized black hoody.

Turning, Petra walked to the bathroom, where she stripped and pulled on the clean clothes that—to her irritation—smelled like the fang.

Petra stepped back into the main room just as Vy was coming out of her bedroom carrying a backpack.

"So what's the plan?" Petra asked. "How are we going to make it halfway across the world?"

"I know a hopper," Vy replied, biting down on her lip. She frowned.

Petra leaned against a wall and hugged her soiled clothes. "Okay, so what happens when we get to Japan?"

"Once we are in Japan, I just need to locate Itachi Yamamoto's resting place and—"

"You still expect me to believe you can raise the dead," Petra scoffed, raising a brow.

"I haven't in a long time, but I don't anticipate having much trouble," the fang said, sounding annoyed.

"I saw you use magic to fix the door. You looked like you wanted to pass out," Petra said. "I am having a hard time believing you can perform any form of sorcery."

"Have a little faith. I can do it," the fang assured. "Trust me."

Petra snorted, "I will never trust you, fang."

Chapter Fifteen

The spring air smelled like rain was coming. Vy walked on the sidewalk, hyper aware of Petra stalking behind her. She hated that Dustin's feelings were still influencing her, making her heart titter every time she caught Petra's eyes on her.

Vy only fancied herself in love once before, and Alice had rejected her advance so wholly and bluntly that Vy had gone out of her way to ignore her friend for almost a year.

Vy and Alice were good now, but she still remembered how wrecked she'd been. She never wanted to feel that way again.

There has to be a way to rid myself of these unwanted feelings, Vy thought before coming to an abrupt stop.

A tight knot formed in her stomach. Up ahead, she saw the weathered red bricks of Nick's apartment building. Vy's fingers bit into the foamy straps of the backpack she wore.

Petra stopped walking when she reached her side. Shoving her hands into the front pocket of the black hoodie, she turned towards Vy. "Are we here?"

Blinking, Vy shook her head. "It's that red building ... just after the crosswalk."

Petra shot her a dark look. "Why are we stopping here?"

"Because I need a moment."

"For what?"

"To compose myself." Vy released a deep breath and then another.

Petra arched a brow. "Why?"

"I haven't seen Nick in over two months," she explained. "Let's just say we didn't part on the best terms."

Petra frowned. "What did you do?"

"I didn't do anything. He ..." Vy's teeth mashed together. She didn't owe the SOL an answer. "Let's just go and get this over with."

In the short time it took them to reach the building, Vy had worked herself into a bit of rage. She welcomed the anger, preferring it over the sorrow she was used to.

Vy muttered a quick spell to disengage the lock and threw open the clunky metal entrance door. Stepping inside, she headed for the stairs and briskly climbed up three flights. Vy's ascent was silent while Petra's boots clapped on the treads.

The two women stepped into a shadowy hallway that smelled distinctly of cigarettes and kitty litter. Vy's nose wrinkled as she continued down the corridor.

Arriving at Nick's unit, she sensed his presence inside. Her ears pricked, picking up the beat of two hearts beyond the door—he was not alone.

Vy didn't bother knocking—Nick would not willingly let her inside. He was a grown man, but he acted like a little boy. Though he had no right to be upset, he liked to play the victim. He blamed Vy for their falling out and didn't acknowledge his role.

Vy held back a snort.

In a barely audible voice, she unlocked his door with a spell. Turning the handle, she and Petra stepped into Nick's chaotic apartment.

Vy had never liked going to Nick's place. Even in the thick of their friendship, she had avoided going over. She didn't like that the floors were sticky and that the walls were stained and had peeling paint. She didn't like the stacks of old pizza boxes and takeout cartons dumped everywhere. But most of all, she hated the roaches.

Vy hated bugs. Just the sight of a creepy crawly set her in a panic, and if one happened to touch her, she just about lost her mind.

Her phobia stemmed from one of Camellia's many lessons. When Vy had been five years old, her mother had locked her in a tiny room wriggling with what had to be a million long-legged centipedes. "I have taught you the words and the technique," her mother had said. "Now use that knowledge to cast an invisible forcefield about yourself. Do not let them touch you."

A cold shudder ran up Vy's spine as she recalled the sensation of an infinity of tiny legs crawling over every inch of her skin. They had touched her. For more than twenty-four hours the segmented arthropods had scuttled over her lips, down her shirt and into her curly hair. It had been torture.

Another tremor ran through her as she pushed the memory aside and walked towards Nick's bedroom.

Vy's former friend lay in bed. A naked brunette covered more of his body than the thin beige sheet. Given that he didn't stir upon her approach, she assumed he must be encumbered by chem or some other concoction.

Where Vy only used the dust to stifle her cravings, Nick overindulged in everything spellcasters cooked up. He had once told her that life was too unpleasant to navigate sober.

Vy cleared her throat to rouse the entangled lovers.

"Fuck," Nick cursed, rubbing at his face. He sat up and blinked away any lingering fatigue. When he looked up and took notice of Vy, his hands crumpled the bedsheets tight in his fists.

Their eyes met, and suddenly Vy felt very small. The fury she'd been stoking died down as if smothered by ash.

In that moment, she felt like a tree standing bare in winter. Without her leaves, she could not hide her broken branches—she could not hide her pain.

Nick broke eye contact first. He looked down at the woman, still deep in sleep, and pushed on her shoulder. "Wake up," he rasped.

Groaning, the woman lifted herself up, massaging her neck with her fingers. Her lustrous dark hair curtained most of her face but did nothing to obscure her nakedness.

Vy's gaze dropped to the taut rosy nipples before admiring the woman's gorgeous face. Nick's steely grey eyes took in the way Vy looked at his lover, and his face reddened. Vy recognized the reaction for what it was, and her anger sparked anew.

Nick pushed the woman away from him. "I need you to go—now," he snapped. His chin cocked towards Vy. "Seems that I have a visitor."

The brunette went very still, and then she scurried out of bed as if she just realized bedbugs lived within the folds of the mattress. Vy would bet there were.

Nick's lover tugged on her clothes in record time and pushed past Vy and Petra. The apartment door slammed shut a moment later.

Nick rose up from the bed. The muscles of his tattooed arms bulged as he stretched his hands over his head and yawned. Naked, he turned to face Vy. "Why the fuck are you here? You change your mind?"

"Fuck no." Vy gritted her teeth. Her anger reignited.

"Then why the fuck are you here?"

"I need a favour."

Nick chuckled. The sound was cold. "I would rather cut off my dick than help you."

"You owe me."

He arched a quizzical brow. "I don't owe you shit. Get the fuck out," he ordered, waving her off with a hand. "Now."

"You. Owe. Me."

They looked at each other, exchanging silent words with their eyes. Nick told her that he still wanted her. Vy told him to fuck off.

"I don't owe you shit," he repeated.

"When Alice found out what you did, she was going to tear your throat out," Vy said. "I called her off. You. Owe. Me." Vy knew how much Alice terrified Nick. The first and only time he had met

Alice, she'd broken both his arm because he'd made a snide remark. Vy was banking that his fear of the older fang would make him put aside his pride and hop them to Tokyo.

Nick yawned. "And what do you want? A thank-you?"

Vy shook her head and folded her arms over her chest. "I need you to hop us over to Tokyo. Preferably a main hub or station."

Nick seemed to just have noticed Petra standing just behind Vy in the doorframe. His face flamed, red creeping up his neck. "This is who you're fucking?" He spat, his eyes glowed, hinting at the beast within. "She looks like the fucking Hulk."

If the insult got to Petra, she didn't show it. A quiet observer, the SOL's expression was blank.

"Can you quit acting like a little kid for once?" Vy scolded. "I get it—you hate me. You probably never want to see me again."

Nick snorted and crossed his arms. "Got that right."

"If you take us, I'll make sure you never do," Vy said softly. Despite her ire, a hard ball formed in her throat. She could feel her eyes burning.

Nick stayed quiet for several seconds before throwing up his hands in defeat. "Fine, I'll do it. But after I do this, we are done. Never come back here."

"I won't," Vy promised, her voice cracking.

Nick stepped towards her and held out his hand for Vy to take. She hesitated, but soon grasped it. Sparing a glance at Petra, Vy extended her own hand.

Petra's jaw clenched. Her green eyes glittered with her disdain, but she took Vy's hand. And when she did, Vy felt her chest grow warm.

In less time than it took to blink, Nick hopped them out of the filthy Toronto apartment.

Chapter Sixteen

They stood together on a summit with blistering night air whipping around them. At such an elevation, the wind was cutting and the soft black hoodie was doing nothing to retain any of Petra's warmth.

"Fucking asshole," Vy cursed, kicking a stone. "He hopped us on top of Mt. Fuji. I swear, when I get back to Toronto, I'm going to fucking kill him."

Though Petra tried her best to conceal her discomfort, her teeth began to chatter at their own volition. The fang noticed and stepped towards her.

"You're cold."

"You're stating the fucking obvious," Petra spat, rubbing her hands over her arms.

"May I?"

"May you what?"

"Warm you?" Vy said. "It is very cold—you might get sick."

Petra did not want Vy casting any spells on her. "No," she replied sharply.

Vy sighed. "If you change your mind, let me know."

"I won't," Petra said, almost regretting the words as they left her lips. It was freezing at the top of the mountain. "It is so dark—how the fuck are we going to get down?"

"I think I can get us down in one piece," Vy responded. "But I don't think you'll like my method."

"What method is that?"

"There are some perks to being a fang—I should be able to get us down easily enough, but the ride will probably not be fun for you."

It dawned on Petra what the fang was insinuating, and she scowled. "I will not let you carry me down this fucking mountain in your arms."

"I had no intentions of carrying you in my arms," Vy said. Petra saw the playful smirk form on her lips in the moonlight. "I was thinking more along the lines of a piggyback ride."

"Fuck no."

"Look, it's your funeral if you insist on being difficult," Vy said. "Try to think of it this way. We both want the same things: we want off Mt. Fuji, we want to find the hourglass, and we want to change the past. If we set aside our differences, we will be sure to achieve our aims faster."

The fang's arguments were sound. But Petra did not want to be carried; she didn't want any physical contact with Vy. Petra stewed on the situation and felt her hands freezing painfully. Her nose dripped from the cold. Finally, she mumbled, "Okay, fine—whatever."

Vy nodded and removed the backpack she wore. "Mind wearing this?" she asked, holding the bag out.

Petra took the knapsack and slung her arms through both straps after loosening them enough to accommodate her larger size. "How will this even work?" she asked. "I'm like double your size."

"I can probably bench press a Toyota if I set my mind to it. Your weight shouldn't be a problem," Vy replied, patting a shoulder. "Come now, SOL, your chariot awaits."

"Fuck you, fang." Petra balled her hands into fists. "You're enjoying this too much."

"Am not. This is the last place I want to be," she replied. "And believe me when I say that I'm not happy about being stuck with you either."

Petra exhaled a deep breath, and it came out as a cloud. Moving towards the fang, she hesitated before climbing onto Vy's back. She became hyperaware of the fang's hands propping up her thighs in support.

"Are you ready?" Vy asked, craning her neck to look back at Petra.

"Never. This is fucking ridiculous."

"I'll take that as a yes. Try to hold on." With those last words, the fang took off down the mountain with a speed that kicked Petra's head back and made her stomach flip. Vy's feet barely made a sound as she ran over the gravelly terrain, leaping now and then to avoid obstacles in her path.

Petra would have liked nothing more than to hold on to her sour mood, but exhilaration got the better of her. She felt like she was on the world's fastest and jankiest roller coaster. And, after ten years of monotony, the thrill felt good. Too good.

All in all, it didn't take long to reach the bottom.

Petra hopped down from the fang's back, feeling the rush of excitement pulsing in her ears.

At the lower elevation, the temperature was moderate, and Petra felt her body warming back up.

Unburdened of Petra's weight, the fang squatted into a resting position and pinched her eyes closed as if in pain.

"You good?" Petra asked a little breathlessly.

"I exerted a lot of energy ... very quickly. I'm just trying to catch my breath," Vy wheezed.

The world around them was quiet, with the exception of the buzzing of insects. In the not so far distance, Petra could make out some streetlights.

"What happened between you and the hopper?" Petra asked suddenly. She was curious. Back at the filthy apartment, the tension between the fang and the hopper had been palpable.

"I think I preferred it when you didn't talk," Vy mumbled.

"That fucktart dropped me on the peak of a fucking mountain," Petra said. "I'd like to know why."

The fang stood up and met Petra's gaze. "I met Nick about a year ago, and we hit it off right away ..." Vy stared off to the side, as if recalling a fond memory. Sighing, she continued, "Like me, he's different—an illblood. And just like me, she knows what it is like to be an outcast, an untouchable. Our friendship was immediate. We latched on to each other as if our lives depended on it. But ultimately, he wanted more than friendship, and when I said no ..." Tears sprang to Vy's eyes. Sniffling, she wiped them away with her fingers and then shrugged. "Let's just say this isn't the first time he left me stranded somewhere."

Petra didn't know what to make of the fang's raw display of emotion. It had to be an act. Lightless didn't feel things the way humans did.

Vy sniffled again and flashed Petra a faltering smile. "I'm blown. We should try to find a place to rest."

Petra nodded, and they began walking down the empty road towards the distant lights.

They walked a long time before arriving at a hotel. Upon entering, they were informed that there were no available beds. The second establishment they reached was also full. By the time they found a third inn, Petra's feet were crying, and she was hungry to the point of feeling sick. She chastised herself for not taking up the fang's earlier offer to order food.

Stepping into the quaint foyer of the inn, Vy approached the front desk and smiled at the uniformed Japanese woman standing behind it. In fluent Japanese, the fang began to converse with the hotel agent. Magic allowed her to understand and speak any language. With each skill the fang revealed, Petra became more and more awed by what magic could accomplish.

When Vy turned towards Petra, the look on her face was somber, which led Petra to believe that this hotel was also fully booked.

"So, they have a room," Vy said. That was good news. Petra wondered why the fang looked so dismal. She found out soon enough when Vy bit her lip and said, "There's only one bed. It's a double—but I fear even a king wouldn't be large enough for you."

Petra froze.

"Should we try another place? There's another hotel about a ten minutes walk from here that we can look at," Vy offered.

"No more walking." Petra shook her head. "You can always sleep on the floor."

A look of disgust crossed Vy's face. "I will not."

"Then I can," Petra said with a shrug.

"Okay—so to confirm you want me to take the room?" Vy asked.

"Yes."

Minutes later, Vy slid a key card into a slot, and pushed open the door leading into the hotel room.

Both women stilled upon noting the obvious. "There's no floor space?" Petra said with utter shock. She had heard about how tiny the spaces were in Japan, but this went beyond what she could have ever imagined. The double bed took up the entire room, nearly touching both sides of the walls. There was barely enough room to walk in front of it.

Vy began to snicker.

Petra's brows creased together as the door clicked shut behind them. "Why are you laughing? This is not funny."

The fang continued to giggle as she pushed her way to the bathroom, carrying her knapsack with her.

Still standing near the door, Petra watched as Vy turned on the faucet, washing her hands before sloshing water on her face. The fang then removed a toothbrush from her bag and began brushing her teeth vigorously.

Petra stared at the space and tried to figure out a solution to their predicament. She couldn't think of anything, and her frustration made her want to punch something.

When the fang exited the bathroom, Petra took her turn using it.

Shutting the door, she used the toilet, washed her hands, and then her face. In a cylindrical holder, the hotel had disposable toothbrushes in clear packaging. Grabbing one, Petra removed the plastic and squeezed on some complimentary toothpaste. She brushed her teeth, shut off the lights, and exited the bathroom.

The room was dark, and Vy lay under the covers, seemingly asleep.

Petra's eyes adjusted, and she noted that the fang's clothing was folded neatly on the narrow surface of a ledge jutting over the mini fridge. Absentmindedly, Petra touched the netted fabric of the stoned top. When she noticed what her hand was doing, she snapped her hand back.

Clenching her jaw, Petra marched towards the empty side of the bed that was near the window. For many moments, she stood near the glass and peered out over the landscape, obscured by the night. She leaned her forehead against the cool window and closed her eyes. Petra didn't see how she'd ever fall asleep.

Chapter Seventeen

Kayla stared at her son. She could tell from the look on his face that he was lying, or at least keeping something from her.

She cleared her throat. "So, to clarify, you and Malkovitch were en route with the fang, and then … nothing." Crossing her arms, Kayla leaned against the large desk in her office and gave him a dressing-down with her eyes.

He looked up at her from the armchair. "Yes, we nabbed the illblood, and we were bringing her back. One minute, I'm driving. The next thing I know, I'm waking up in a ditch."

"And you have no idea where Malkovitch is?"

He shook his head. "No. Maybe the illbood made off with her."

Yes, that was likely the case. But how? The not knowing irritated her. "You know that what you are telling me is rather unbelievable?" Kayla arched a brow.

Her son kept to his story. "It's what happened."

"So Malkovitch did not take off on her own to take care of the illblood."

There was a twitch of hesitation on his face. "I don't think so."

"Don't think so sounds like it might be a possibility," Kayla said. "Now, Dustin, I will give you one more opportunity—tell me what happened. And don't leave anything out. I will know if you are lying to me."

His jaw set.

"You will only be telling me what I already know to be true," Kayla added. "I know that Malkovitch went rogue and made a move to kill the fang."

Dustin's blue eyes widened. "How did you know?"

"Because you just told me."

His mouth gaped, and she could tell that he was cursing himself internally.

Kayla's back was starting to ache, so she pushed off the desk and walked towards the large windows. For a moment, her gaze swept over the view beyond, taking in the church. She hated that blasted building. She hated the memories it evoked.

Kayla took pride in her ability to maintain control and reign in the ever-present fury that simmered beneath her skin, but whenever she looked at the church, she was reminded of the last time she'd snapped. Before that incident, she'd often let her emotions drive her decisions. After it, she'd worked hard to remain cool and level-headed.

Shaking her head, she moved away from the window, her long strides taking her back to her son. "I have a meeting soon," she said, stopping herself from frowning. She was not looking forward to the video chat. "Tell me what happened now."

Dustin looked down at his lap. Kayla almost thought he'd refuse to say anything more on the topic, but then he sighed and said, "Malkovitch did try to kill the fang, but I stopped her. I shot her with the tranquilizer gun."

Did he now? Kayla almost smirked. *Perhaps there is hope for my boy.*

Her son ran a hand through his wavy blond hair and then rubbed the back of his neck. "Why'd you send her to tag and bag that fang? Like, of all the tests to put her through, why that one?" His tone was accusatory.

Kayla had her reasons, but she didn't owe it to Dustin to tell him anything. "So you knocked out Malkovitch," she said, dismissing his question, "and then what?"

Dustin's blue eyes glinted with annoyance, but he answered, saying, "I shot the fang with the tranquilizer gun, and I got them both into the SUV." Dustin licked his lips. "I was worried that if Petra woke up before we got to the base, she'd try again to …"

"To kill the fang?"

He nodded. "So, I handcuffed and put leg irons on her. I was driving back to the base, and she woke up about a couple of hours into the drive. We chatted a little—she was pissed at me. Anyhow, I was driving, and then I woke up in a ditch. That's what happened— that's all of it."

Kayla believed him. But what he was telling her still didn't add up. Nothing was adding up. It made no sense that Malkovitch's GPS coordinates registered her as being in Japan. And how did one just wake up in a ditch?

Beyond pissed, Kayla wanted to punch something. Or better yet, she wanted to go on the hunt for lightless. It had been so long since she'd last killed. Her bloodlust was an itch begging to be scratched.

She should have never sent Malkovitch. Dr. Raz had been very clear that he needed the illblood for his research. Now, the illbood might be lost to them.

Clenching and unclenching her hands, Kayla marched behind her desk where she paced.

When she got a handle on her emotions, she looked at her son and said, "You've passed your final."

"I ... what?" He frowned.

"You're an SOL now," she confirmed.

"But ... but I didn't ... bring the illblood back," he stammered.

"You stood up to Malkovitch. That counts for something," Kayla replied. She waved for him to leave. "You can go now."

Dustin opened his mouth to say something more, but apparently thought better of it. He stood up and left.

Before the door closed behind him, Olivia slipped inside and stalked towards the desk. As always, her uniform was out of sorts, but Kayla was not in the mood to bicker with her—she didn't have the time to. In five minutes, she had a meeting with her father.

Just thinking about his sour old face made her want to grimace. To say that their relationship was strained was to put it lightly.

Cornelius Clay had always wanted a son, but he'd gotten a daughter instead. But being a girl wasn't Kayla's worst sin. Her greatest offence was being born.

Shortly after giving birth, Kayla's mother had died of pregnancy complications. Her life had cost Cornelius the love of his life

In her developing years, Kayla's father did everything in his power to avoid her. Back then, she had thought that if she only tried hard enough, he'd change his tune towards her. But nothing she did ever warranted his acknowledgement or praise.

Kayla had one of the best records in the Order. She'd been promoted from SOL to sergeant to commander, and he'd not once congratulated her on her achievements. Around her mid-thirties, Kayla made peace with the fact that they would never have a cordial relationship.

And so, she was really looking forward to the day when she turned the tables. Soon, she'd have all the power. The day when she fucked over the board of directors—her father being one of them—and the chief commander, couldn't come soon enough.

Once the serum was stabilized, all that would be left to do was convince Dr. Raz to join her effort, which she didn't see as being a hurdle. Kayla knew that Raz, ultimately, wanted to see to it that the earth was rid of every last lightless. Their goals were aligned.

Emerging from her thoughts, Kayla shot Olivia a dark look. "What could you possibly want?"

"I want to chat with you about something."

"I have a meeting starting soon," Kayla said.

"It won't take long. I just want to chat about me being on light duties," she stated, throwing herself down into one of the two armchairs in front of the desk and propping her feet up on the desk.

"Put your feet down."

Olivia obliged her. "So, a little birdie told me that the SOTU crew is gearing up to fly out to Tokyo."

Of course, someone in SOTU had told her. Kayla wanted to roll her eyes, but she refrained from doing so. "Yes, they are."

"I am feeling better—much better. I'd like to go out with them." Olivia straightened in her seat. "Also, I had an idea. I know that in order for them to head out that way, you'll need approval from the commander in Japan—might be kind of embarrassing for you to specify why you need to send an SOTU crew out that way."

Olivia was pointing out the obvious. Kayla was not looking forward to ringing up Commander Ishida. However, she would not state that outright. "What is your idea?" she asked.

Cracking a smile, Olivia replied, "Why not hop SOTU out to Tokyo? Sure, the hopper might take a day or two for the sedative to get out of his system. But once he is clearheaded, SOTU can use him to get in and out of Japan quickly. You won't have to bother with protocol because the Japanese commander will never know that your agents were on his turf. It'll save you an awkward conversation and time."

Annoying as she was, Kayla had to give it to the girl—she was resourceful, and the solution she offered was a good one. Kayla just wished that she had thought of it. Crossing her arms, Kayla looked down at Olivia. "Thank you for proposing this strategy—I think I will be using it, but you are still on light duties."

Olivia shot up out of her seat, her hands balling at her sides. "The fuck I am. I told you I feel better." Her face was bright red.

"Language," Kayla said curtly, before adding, "you need to give your body time to rest. Cardiac arrest is no joke, even if you are …" She decided not to finish the statement.

But Olivia caught wind of where she had been going with her words, and her face flamed further. Her body shook with her anger, and Kayla fully expected her to lash out, which was common for her. Surprisingly, she didn't. Instead, she turned on her heel and stormed out of the office, slamming the door behind her.

Kayla knew that she would have to hunt the girl down later to address the tantrum, but her meeting was about to start. She would have to deal with Olivia's behaviour later.

Moving behind her desk, Kayla sat down in the executive chair and signed into her laptop. A minute later, she was in a video chat with her father.

It surprised her to see that his background showed him to be in his study at his Muskoka home. She hadn't known he had returned to Canada. For the last decade or so, he'd been living in the UK, where he'd purchased and renovated a lavish estate Kayla had only seen in pictures.

Kayla didn't comment about him being back. She didn't speak. He'd been the one to request this meeting, so she'd let him do the talking. Her tight muscles just hoped he kept it quick. Already, she could feel discomfort building in her neck and shoulders.

Cornelius was a thin and wrinkly faced man. He was balding, with a neatly trimmed grey beard. On the cusp of hitting eighty years old, the man shouldn't have come off as intimidating, but he did. Even on a computer screen, his presence was overbearing, and the intensity of his blue eyes had the effect of making Kayla feel small.

"I've heard some very disturbing news," he said, jumping right to business. "It's come to the board's attention that you have been turning down contracts."

"Yes," Kayla said flatly, not offering up an explanation.

"We are not in the business of turning down money—good money," her father berated. "Given how behind you are on your quota, I would say that you are in no position to decline a client request."

"I've only turned down requests that were too dangerous to execute," she responded, trying her best to keep any signs of defensiveness from her tone. "Clients have been asking us to nab live demons and beasts for their fighting rings. We aren't in the business of selling livestock."

"That doesn't change the fact that you are not meeting your quota."

"There are several commanders who don't hit their numbers," Kayla shot back. "Not to forget that I am still cleaning up the mess Folkes left for me. The Canadian region is finally in the black, thanks to me."

"Profitable, but not profitable enough." Her father stroked his beard. "When you were voted into your role, it was for a reason. The board felt that given your track record, you were the best person to get results, but now they are thinking they were wrong."

Cornelius was not telling her anything new. Kayla already understood that the board was not happy with her. She knew that come next fiscal they had every intention of removing her from her role, and that was why she was so desperate to see the serum completed before then.

Her father spoke again, breaking her train of thoughts, "There is to be a vote in a month's time."

"A vote?" Kayla repeated. "For what?"

"To replace you," her father said.

Kayla's entire body went rigid. Blood ran hot in her body. The ringing in her ear grew louder.

"This call was just a courtesy," Cornelius said. He ended the call, and the screen went black.

Kayla rocketed from her seat and hurled her laptop. It crashed against a wall, and the screen splintered away from the keyboard, clattering to the floor. Her breathing was ragged.

The door to her office opened, and Richardson popped inside. The expression on the older woman's face was one of shock.

"Get out," Kayla barked.

Richardson jumped, and scampered out the office, shutting the door quietly behind her.

Kayla pressed her palms to her forehead as a means to quell her building headache. The ringing in her left ear was so intense it stung. She felt off balance and leaned against the desk.

Everything was going to shit. *Fucking Malkovitch! Fucking board! Fucking Cornelius!* Her bastard of a father was probably the one who'd pushed to board into having this ridiculous vote.

It took a long time for Kayla's temper to drop down from a boil to its usual simmer. When it did, when she was able to think straight, she grabbed her phone and texted Tim.

Kayla Just now

> 250 million. That's my price for the hopper

Tim's response came almost immediately.

Tim Just now

> I thought you didn't sell livestock?

Kayla

> I changed my mind. 250 million is my price

Tim

> I told you what my highest offer was

Kayla

> It was a low ball and you know it

Tim

> Fine ... 250 million. You have a deal.

Kayla

> Get in touch with Richardson to schedule an appointment with me. We will iron out the details of the purchase when we meet.

Kayla slid her phone back in her pocket. She was not happy about the impending transaction. Livestock should not be sold. Lightless were too dangerous to keep as pets. But all the fucking board cared about was money. In a month's time, if she showed up an extra two-hundred and fifty million in the black, there was no way they'd vote her out of her position.

So, Kayla would do this one sale, and hopefully it would buy her the time she needed to get Raz the illblood.

Once the serum was completed, she'd be the one calling all the shots. No one would be able to stand in her way then, and it'd be game over for all lightless filth.

Chapter Eighteen

"I can't believe Kris dumped you—and right before we ring in the New Year," Kate Chen said, pausing the anime they were streaming on Petra's laptop. Her dark eyes flared with anger. "What an asshole. I'm going to hire a hitman to kick his scrawny ass."

"Kris didn't dump me."

Kate frowned. "You just told me you guys broke up."

"I broke up with him," Petra clarified.

"I thought you were mad about him?" The crease between Kate's dark brows deepened.

Petra looked down at her hands folded in her lap. Her right foot began to rock anxiously. She had a secret that she was bursting to spill, and the need to tell her best friend was intense. She just hoped Kate didn't think anything less of her afterwards. "I think I'm gay," Petra blurted, shooting her pal a quick look before staring back down at her lap. Her heart raced in her chest, and she felt out of breath even as she sat still.

Kate knelt in front of her, placing her long delicate fingers on her own. It was the sign of understanding Petra had been seeking.

Petra met her friend's eyes.

"Gay," her friend repeated. A mischievous smile tugged at the edges of Kate's full lips, which glittered from the application of cherry-scented lip gloss. She arched an inquisitive dark brow. "Prove it to me—kiss me."

Petra tensed. She blinked and then began to laugh. "You're joking, right?"

Everyone knew that Kate was an obnoxious flirt, and Petra had always found it amusing to watch her friend turn confident boys into stammering balls of putty that she so easily moulded at her whim.

But Petra was not amused now. She didn't like being on the opposite end of Kate's teasing. It made her think that it was all a joke—that her friend wasn't taking her disclosure seriously. She didn't want to be clay that Kate toyed with artistically and then never fired in the kiln.

"Quit teasing me," Petra said tightly.

Kate's face sobered. "So, you don't want to kiss me—you don't think I'm pretty?"

"That's not what I—"

Before Petra could finish her sentence, Kate smothered her words with a kiss that undid her. It was the kind of kiss that poets wrote about—the kind that turned her body into a gong and rang pleasure to every nerve ending. It was the kind of kiss that made her toes curl. It was like nothing Petra had felt before.

In the early stages of the morning, sunlight crept its way into the hotel room and shone on Petra's face. With dreams of Kate still steeping in her mind like a strongly brewed tea, Petra unconsciously moved closer to the soft body beside her and encircled her arms around bare shoulders, pulling the woman in close.

Petra awoke to the caress of curly dark hair brushing against her cheeks and the warmth of another body pressed against her. Blinking her eyes open, it took her a moment to place herself. Her heart arrested when it dawned on her where she was and who she was with.

Disgusted, Petra recoiled and shot out of bed. Heart racing, she rushed to the bathroom and slammed the door behind her.

Closing her eyes, Petra leaned against the wall and crumpled to the floor. She hugged her knees and bit back a cry.

Petra could feel the veneer of strength she had fostered for so long fracturing. She wanted so much to hold on to it, but some floods were inevitable.

It was all too much. So much was happening. And so fast. Petra couldn't keep up.

For ten years, her days had been methodically plotted with very little variation. For ten years, she'd stacked her bricks, erecting a wall between herself and others, suppressing her sexual thoughts and urges. And for ten years, she'd been comforted by her anger and plans for vengeance.

Now, everything was upside down. In less than a day, she'd been torn from her routine, she'd given into her sexual desire, and she'd turned her back on her brothers and sisters back at the Order.

Fuck, she'd agreed to work with the fang she'd vowed to kill!

It was too fucking much, and Petra couldn't fight the tears. They rolled down her cheeks and dripped from her chin. She hated being unable to stop the outpour of emotion. Her only solace was that she wept in silence.

Petra wanted to put all the blame on the fang, but she couldn't. She was the one at fault. She'd allowed the fang to fuck her, and just now she'd snuggled up to the fang.

A new fear gripped her suddenly. Despite everything, was it possible that she wanted the fang?

Impossible. Shaking her head, Petra wiped her eyes with the back of her hands. *No, I don't want her. I'm missing Kate. Especially now with the promise of a new reality.*

But even as Petra told herself this, she remembered the taste of the Vy's lips, and the feel of Vy's hands on her thighs as they had descended the mountain. Why did the fang have to be so goddamn beautiful?

Petra knocked her head against the wall and stared up at the ceiling. She wasn't crying anymore, but she was nowhere near feeling normal.

After a time, Petra rose and tore out of her clothes. She stepped into the shower, notching the heat to the highest level. Over and over, she scrubbed at her skin with soap as if to rid herself of the memory of Vy's touch.

By the time she finally exited the tub, every inch of her skin was red and raised.

Pulling back on her clothes, she walked back into the bedroom. It was empty—the bed neatly made up. It was a relief to see that the fang was not there.

She moved towards the window and stared out.

The sky was very blue without a single cloud. Mt. Fuji loomed in the backdrop—a picture of beauty, but also an omen of destruction.

Petra stood looking out of the glass until the door to the hotel room clicked open. She didn't want to look over her shoulder, but she knew that her dread would only build the longer she chose not to face the situation.

Petra turned and folded her arms over her chest. She didn't meet the fang's gaze, choosing instead to focus on the tray of food she held in her hands.

It was a beautiful arrangement of tiny bowls of rice, miso soup, pickled vegetables, grilled fish, and tea.

While Petra was starving, she knew that anything she tried to eat would come back up. Her stomach was wrecked with knots.

Vy set down the tray on the narrow ledge over the mini fridge, and Petra's eyes swept over her. The fang had donned the same fashionable outfit from the other day, and her black bra peeked through the sparkling netted chemise as if laughing at Petra.

Vy's face looked rested and full, hinting that she had fed.

Petra grimaced and decided that she needed more time with the view outside the window. She faced the scenery again with her heart pounding in her ears.

"She's really beautiful. The girl you were looking at yesterday—Kate," Vy said, clearing her throat. Her tone was cheery, without any awkwardness. "You said her name in your sleep. It must have been quite some dream."

Petra didn't respond, but she got the feeling that Vy was trying to put her at ease—rationalizing what had happened that morning. Surprisingly, her words did have the effect of loosening the jumble in her stomach.

"I was looking into the route to get to Tokyo from here. We are about a fifteen-minute walk from Gotemba Eki station. There's a bus we can catch there. It'll be about a two-hour ride, but it will drop us near Shibuya. There's a bar in Tokyo where I think I might be able to get information about Itachi's final resting place. Considering that earth demons are very ritualistic, I am sure that Itachi's ashes would have been interned at a gravesite or ancestral shrine." The fang was rambling, as if nervous. "But if we can't find a gravesite, so long as we find something that belonged to him, the spell should still work. Anyhow, once you finish eating, we can go—"

"I'm not hungry. Let's just go," Petra said. She turned from the window, shouldering the fang out of her way as she exited the room.

Chapter Nineteen

It was a beautiful day for humans. The sun was out and shining; it was warm with a gentle breeze.

Vy would have preferred it to be overcast. She made sure to keep her skin out of direct sunlight. While she wouldn't spontaneously combust into flames in the daylight, like a normal fang would, she was still sensitive to the rays.

Her skinned blistered if not covered, and bright days rendered her near blind unless she wore heavy tinted sunglasses.

Despite having been in the country less than a day, Vy was taking a liking to Japan. The roads and sidewalks were orderly and clean. The people were very polite and kept to themselves.

Vy had fully expected the nationals to stare and gawk at her and Petra. Together they made an odd pair, and they both stood out. Petra towered over everyone, and Vy's skin tone was shades darker than the homogenized population.

But nobody stared. Nobody spared them a second glance. Frankly, it seemed to Vy that the Japanese went out of their way to not acknowledge them.

Vy and Petra proceeded in silence towards the station. Once there, they boarded a bus headed for Tokyo.

Vy sat at the window seat. Petra took the aisle seat.

The human was still in a dark mood. She hadn't said a word since they'd left the hotel room, and Vy knew Petra's sour disposition had everything to do with what had happened that morning.

Closing her eyes, Vy recalled being awoken to strong arms wrapping around her, pulling her in close. At the time, Vy had been shocked, and the urge to pull away had been immediate. She'd thought about wriggling out of the embrace, but only for a second.

Where cuddles were concerned, Vy's will was always weak. Starved for connection as she was, Vy looked forward to postcoital snuggles with her lovers as much as the act of sex itself.

Though Dustin's influence on her was likely the only reason she hadn't bolted the moment Petra's hard body had pressed against her back. It was maddening how much Vy had wanted Petra. Vy wasn't used to being in bed with someone she couldn't have. It had taken every ounce of her resolve to not act on what her body desired.

But then, Petra had whispered the name "Kate" in her sleep, and Vy's senses had returned along with a searing jealously.

Kate was beautiful. Kate mattered to Petra. Kate was human. Vy could not compete—not that she should even want to.

Petra had stabbed her. Petra wanted her dead. Petra was the last woman Vy should want.

Not long after uttering the name, Petra jerked awake and dashed into the bathroom.

Her retreat had been a relief for Vy, who had needed time to herself to sort out her own feelings from Dustin's. The task had proved impossible.

Staring out of the large bus window, Vy watched the passing rural landscape. It was agrarian and lush, but the beauty of the scenery was not enough to hold Vy's attention. Her mind kept turning to Kate—the stunning Asian woman she'd caught Petra social media stalking.

Vy's fingers itched to swipe her phone open and sign into the popular app. She wanted to do a little stalking herself. She wanted to know who Kate was. And more importantly, she wanted to know who Kate was to Petra.

Vy had never been jealous before—at least, not to this degree. She decided that the emotion was only surfacing because of Dustin. *How irritating.*

Turning in her seat, Vy looked at Petra and bit her lip. "Who's Kate?"

Petra met her eyes. Her expression was unreadable, and Vy fully expected her to not answer. So, it was a surprise when Petra said, "She was my best friend in high school."

"Lover?" Vy probed, unable to help herself.

Petra nodded, but offered nothing more.

Vy wrung her hands. Her curiosity wasn't satisfied, but something told her that Kate was a slippery topic for Petra.

So, Vy asked the other question that tugged on her mind. "Is there someone back at the Order—a lover?" From Dustin, she had insights about another woman whom Petra seemed overly chummy with—Yasmin Khan. The trainee was smart and beautiful. While Dustin hadn't put the pieces together where Khan and Petra were concerned, Vy had observed from his memories that there had been more than a few lingering gazes and touches exchanged between the two women over the years.

Petra arched an eyebrow. "Why so interested in my love life?" Her tone was direct but lacked the harshness it normally carried. She sounded tired.

"I'm not," she lied. "Just trying to make small talk."

Vy decided that she didn't need a response to make a determination about Petra and Khan's relationship. She could read the room, and it was telling her that they'd definitely been hooking up over the years. Vy didn't like this revelation. Her chest felt tight and heavy.

Ugh, she could do without these feelings of envy and possessiveness. And what right did Vy have to be this annoyed by the knowledge that Petra had a lover back on the base?

Frankly, Vy had no business being bothered. It was hypocritical. After all, she couldn't put a number to how many women she'd taken to bed.

Sighing, Vy tried to steer her thoughts away from Petra. Her restraint lasted less than five minutes.

How could she focus on anything else when the woman sat right next to her? Petra was so close that Vy could feel her radiant body heat—she burned hot like a furnace.

Vy looked at Petra whose arms were folded over her broad chest. Her green eyes were impassive, but there was the slightest crease between her brows.

What was she thinking about? Did she ever think about their kiss—how electric it had been?

Likely not. Vy frowned. She wished she had the self-control to not revisit the memory, but it played in her mind constantly.

With a slight shudder, Vy recalled the graze of Petra's lips and teeth on her neck. She recalled Petra's hands exploring her body with confident expertise. She recalled how wet Petra had been, and how Petra's body had reacted to Vy's fingers inside her. Petra had liked the way Vy had fucked her.

Their chemistry had been off the charts. Petra had been so receptive to her touch. And it wasn't Vy's imagination—in that moment Petra had wanted her.

Feeling her face flush, Vy leaned her head against the cool glass of the window. She chastised herself for her building desire.

Petra was off limits; she needed to drill that in her head. The woman had stabbed her, and she'd likely do it again. These were dangerous waters that Vy was in. She needed to tread carefully.

"I have some questions of my own," Petra said suddenly, pulling Vy from her thoughts.

"Like what?" Vy turned towards her.

"You've aged. Ten years ago, when …" Petra's brows creased, and her face reddened. "You're older—how is that possible? I thought fangs didn't age."

"I don't know," Vy replied honestly. "Maybe it has something to do with me being an illblood."

Petra's eyes narrowed on her, and a second question fired from her mouth. "Why don't you feed on humans anymore?"

Vy blinked her surprise at the question. "I ... I get sick—really sick."

Petra snorted. "I've never heard of such a thing—a fang who gets sick from blood."

"I'm an enigma," she replied with a shrug. Of course, it wasn't all blood that made her ill. She could feed from small animals. But she didn't bother elaborating.

Petra's eyes darkened. Her expression became menacing. "I don't recall you looking sick that night—the night you ..." Petra's words trailed off.

Vy sighed. Truth was, she had gotten ill that night. So ill, in fact, she'd thought she was dying. If Alice hadn't found her, maybe she would have died.

Staring up at Petra's face, so filled with hate and pain, Vy wished there was something she could say that could make things right, but no such words existed.

There was no changing the fact that she had killed Petra's mother. Yes, it had been a mistake, but that didn't make it right.

Chewing on her lower lip, Vy said the only thing she thought would help, "Everything will be reversed as soon as we find the hourglass."

"It better," Petra muttered, clenching her fists.

They spent the rest of the bus ride in silence. At Ikejiri Ohashi station, they got off.

Standing on the curb near a sewer grate, Vy looked around and was once again impressed with the cleanliness and order of the sprawling city that bustled with foot and road traffic.

Petra stood about six feet away from Vy with her arms crossed. "What now? Where's this bar?" she asked.

"It's in Shinjuku—about a twenty-minute commute by train from here," Vy replied. "Thing is … it opens at 8pm."

Petra made a face.

"I've heard Japan is really cool—we can maybe walk around, see the sights … Or we can do nothing. It's up to you," Vy rambled.

Petra looked like she wanted to punch something. Vy was at a loss. It was going to be a very long day. She just hoped that Petra's mood didn't continue to deteriorate.

Vy's ears perked at the sound of buzzing coming from the grate. She stilled and felt her body grow cold when a large Yamato roach flew out of the sewer and landed on her boot.

Squealing, Vy shook her foot. The movement made the bug take flight again, and Vy went into a full-blown panic when it fluttered in front of her face.

"Fuck! Get it off me! Get it off me! Get it off me!" She shut her eyes and tears sprang to them. Her hands covered her ears, and she balled herself up to protect herself.

Suddenly, all she could see were centipedes. And while there were none, she felt the weight of millions of legs crawling on her skin. "Get them off me! Get them off—please! Let me out!"

Vy felt hands on her shoulders. "I killed it—it's gone."

Vy continued to shake. Her breaths were quick.

"Seriously, you are being fucking ridiculous. It's just a bug," Petra said disapprovingly, though her tone was soft. "Come on, people are staring."

"I ... I just ... need a moment," Vy stammered. Slowly, she rose to her full height and tried to shake off her terror. She wiped her wet eyes.

Vy began walking. She had no clue where she was going, but moving was helping.

Petra followed beside her. "What the fuck was that about? Don't tell me that you're scared of that little thing?" She chuckled.

"Little?" Vy stopped in her tracks. "Please don't remind me of it—I just can't." A tremor ran through her body.

Petra began to laugh. Her face glowed with amusement.

Vy's mouth became a thin line. "I'm glad my torment brings you joy."

"It really does," Petra said, almost teasingly. "If someone ever told me that I'd meet a lightless who feared insects, I'd never believe it."

"Unhumans and humans are not all that different. We aren't the monsters you think we are," Vy spat. "We feel the full range of emotions—maybe even on a deeper level, since we live so long."

Petra's face sobered, the mirth dying from her eyes. "I am not inclined to believe that," she said in a flat tone. "You're putting on an act—I just don't know why."

"Act?" Vy scoffed. She shook her head in disbelief. She decided to enlighten Petra. "When I was five years old, my mother locked me in a room crawling with centipedes. She left me in there for over a day."

Petra's brows drew together. "Fuck. Why?"

"My mother had very unconventional training practices," Vy replied stiffly. "She thought that the best way to teach me how to do something was by making the situation so uncomfortable that I had no choice but to learn how to do it."

"Sounds like she was a piece of work." A noticeable change crossed over Petra's features—a look of empathy.

Wanting to change the topic from her mother, Vy asked, "Are you hungry yet?"

Petra nodded. "Yes."

"Okay, let's find you something to eat."

Chapter Twenty

Petra slurped back the last of the noodles before raising the ramen bowl to her lips, finishing off the cloudy white tonkotsu broth. Rich in collagen, pulled from pork bones simmering for hours, the soup had the texture of velvet, and when coupled with the stringy noodles and slice of tender chashu, made for possibly the most delicious meal Petra ever had.

For years, anything she had put in her mouth tasted like ash.

Sure, the food fare at the base was shit, but even on the few occasions where she had used her vouchers to order something from the outside, her taste buds seemed to not notice.

But with the hope of a new life, Petra found that she was already perceiving the world in a new light. For the first time in over a decade, Petra found herself enjoying eating.

Setting the empty bowl down on the wooden counter, Petra wiped her mouth before adjusting slightly on her stool to peer at the fang. "I'd like another," she said.

Vy stared up from the glass of water she cupped in her hands and looked at her. "Sure," the fang said, removing a stack of neatly folded Japanese yen from her pocket and handing Petra a five-thousand-yen note.

Taking the money, Petra rose to her feet and walked down the narrow walkway towards the front entrance where the vending machine was located. She fed the bill into the machine and made her selection. The machine printed her a ticket, and she pocketed the change.

Petra went back to her booth and pushed a tiny button that blinked upon being pressed.

Seconds later, a panel in front of her slid open briefly and hands grabbed the order ticket. Minutes later, the panel opened again and hands pushed a bowl of steaming ramen towards her.

The restaurant was odd in that the servers remained hidden behind a partition, but the food was delicious, so Petra had no complaints.

Petra's mouth watered. Grabbing her chopsticks, she dug into the bowl with fervour.

Beside her, the fang sat quietly, staring unblinking at a cup of water.

Over an hour had passed since the incident with the bug, and Vy was apparently still shaken by it. If Petra hadn't witnessed the event, she would have never believed it. That a lightless could fear something so small was quite shocking.

The Order had taught her that lightless were soulless and

incapable of feeling anything too deeply. It had been one of the few teachings she hadn't questioned.

Petra wanted to believe Vy's breakdown had been an act, but it had seemed all too real. There'd been real terror in the fang's eyes.

"Wow, you finished that already," the fang said when Petra set down another cleaned bowl on the counter.

Petra licked the soup coating her lips, and she noted the way Vy watched her intently through heavy lids. Her stare discomforted Petra.

"So, have you decided what you want to do?" the fang asked.

Petra raised a brow.

"We have a few hours to burn. Did you want us to split up, and meet up at the bar—"

"No." Petra didn't trust the fang not to run off.

"Okay …" Vy rotated her stool so they face each other. "Any idea what you'd like to do? I can look up a travel site—scope out some tourist attractions."

There were a million things Petra wanted to do and see in Tokyo—things she and Kate had planned to experience together. But Petra was not going to tell the fang that. Instead, she rose from her seat and said, "Let's just walk around."

The fang shrugged and hopped off her stool. She began walking towards the exit, and Petra followed behind her.

They exited the ramen shop that was a few steps away from the great Shibuya crossing.

From where Petra stood on the pavement, she could see the growing mass of people gathering on the curb, waiting for the light to change. She'd read somewhere once that more than two and a half million people crossed the intersection in a single day—more than two thousand pedestrians on every crossing.

The light turned, and Petra watched as the herds made their trek to the other side of the road.

Vy started walking the direction opposite the busiest intersection in the world, and Petra followed her.

With her stomach full, and with the sun beating down on them, Petra found that her steps felt oddly light.

After what had happened that morning, Petra hadn't been sure how she'd ever manage to face the fang with a straight face, but Vy seemingly thought nothing of it. At least, she hadn't thrown the incident in Petra's face, which was a relief. Even so, whenever Petra's mind ticked back to that moment, her gut wrenched with embarrassment.

She was pissed that it had happened at all. How had she even allowed herself to fall asleep next to her greatest enemy?

Petra stared at Vy's back. The fang had thrown on a wide-brimmed hat to complete her outfit. Underneath the hat, her long hair cascaded over her shoulders and down the length of her back.

Petra's face grew hot as she recalled the soft caress of that curly black hair against her cheek.

Gritting her teeth, she forced the thought from her mind—as she had forced out countless others out over the past few hours. Part of Petra wondered if Vy had cast some sort of enchantment on her—the kind that suppressed her anger while augmenting her other feelings—like lust. She knew spellcasters were capable of such magic. It was why they could be so dangerous.

Following the narrow and winding Tokyo streets, the first point of interest they reached was a grand wooden construction—a Torii gate.

As Petra notched her head back to get a good look at it, she felt a sense of awe laced with melancholy. She recognized the sight from photos she and Kate had perused on the internet. It saddened her to know that she was seeing it for the first time without her best friend.

Attention glued to her phone, Vy said, "Google says it leads to Meiji Jingu—a shrine." She cocked her head towards the path beyond the gate. "Would you like us to see it?"

"Sure." Petra shrugged, feigning disinterest.

They began walking down the trail. Giant trees canopied the path, obscuring the sun and making the air feel cooler.

Beneath the shade, the fang removed her shades with a sigh and clipped them on her shirt. She was grinning.

"What the hell are you so happy about?" Petra asked.

Vy looked at her with a blank expression.

"Don't play dumb, I saw you smiling."

"Oh, I was just thinking that …" The fang toyed with a lock of hair, and Petra's gaze dropped to the fingers playing with the dark curls. "I was just thinking that I quite like Japan. It's amazing how busy it is, while also being so orderly—and quiet. It's nothing at all like Toronto."

"You don't like Toronto?" Petra arched a brow.

"I do. It's all I've really known, but it's kind of dirty, and …"

"And what?"

The fang bit her lip. "I don't know. It's home, but sometimes it also feels like the loneliest place on the planet."

Petra frowned. The fang's answer was unexpected. The response seemed too human—too emotional.

"Did you grow up in Toronto?" Vy asked.

Petra nodded.

"What part?"

"Rosedale."

"Nice neighbourhood," Vy acknowledged.

It had been nice. Petra had loved her family home. With its weathered grey bricks and drafty windows, it hadn't been the best maintained, but her mother made sure to keep the yard neat.

What Petra always remembered about it was the intricate designs plastered on the ceilings. And she'd loved the spacious backyard where her mother had set up a hammock between two maple trees. Petra had spent way too much time on that hammock, digesting stacks of manga she'd checked out from the library. The memory of her childhood home was sweet, but also bitter.

Petra sighed.

They passed over a small bridge, and after walking a little farther, they came to an installation of neatly stacked sake barrels. At that point, Vy signalled to Petra that she needed a minute and disappeared into the thick of the trees in less time than it took to blink. It was crazy how fast she was.

Left alone, Petra took time observing the beautifully decorated barrels before continuing on down the trail. She came to a fork in the road, and decidedly chose to walk towards yet another Torii gate.

When Petra reached the shrine, the fang returned with an influx of colour in her cheeks and a bright sheen to her brown eyes.

Petra scowled her disgust and looked away from the fang.

They came across a family with three young boys—all toddlers. One of the kids pointed at Vy and said something that made her laugh. Whatever had been said, the parents hadn't found it funny, and they quickly dragged their son away.

"What'd he say?" Petra asked.

"He called me cute and dark. His parents weren't happy with that." The fang smiled brightly, and Petra felt perplexed.

"Almost appears like you like kids," Petra said curtly.

Vy stopped walking and frowned at her. "I do like kids."

"Even little boys." Petra arched a brow, halting her steps.

"Yes."

"I thought you spellcasters threw all newborn sons into a pit of fire."

"That's a myth." Vy rolled her eyes. "Spellcasters drink a magical potion before conception to ensure a daughter is birthed."

"Sure." Petra snorted.

"It's the truth, but you can go ahead and believe what you want to believe," Vy retorted.

"What is the reason for that anyways—pure hatred for men?" None of the textbooks or teachings at the Order provided rationale for why there were no wizards. Everything was left to speculation. Where spellcasters were concerned, so much was unknown. After the fae, their kind were the most mysterious.

"Spellcasters don't hate men," Vy said, throwing Petra an

annoyed look. "We are just wary of them because of the witch hunts. Anyways, there is a sort of prophecy—"

"Of course, there's a prophecy," Petra said, rolling her eyes.

"I don't have to tell you."

"I want to know—go on."

"As I was saying, there's a prophecy. It was foretold over a millennium ago by one of the greatest soothsayers of all time," Vy said. "She foretold that a wizard would bring about the extinction of the spellcaster race. Hence, there are no wizards."

"That was positively the most riveting story ever," Petra said, and for a moment, she almost found herself chuckling, which gave her pause.

Again, she wondered if Vy had bewitched her in some way. Because it made no sense—Petra was too at ease, and when she looked at the fang, she no longer felt anger's immediate grip. She was way too relaxed. It unnerved her.

Vy began walking towards the Shinto shrine, and Petra fell into step behind her. The sacred monument was a beautiful wooden construction. Despite the many visitors wandering about the courtyard, the atmosphere was serene.

They didn't stay long at the shrine. Before long, Petra and Vy found themselves journeying towards a main road.

Feeling hot from the walk and the sun, Petra opted to get a drink from one of the many vending machines set up just outside the path. Reaching into her pocket, she removed some of the change she'd gotten back at the ramen shop. Petra scrutinized the rows of drinks she'd never seen before. They all looked interesting, and she wasn't sure which one she should try.

Vy came up beside her and leaned against the vending machine. She looked as if she wanted to say something, but she didn't. Instead, her brown eyes swept over Petra. The fang's gaze felt weighted like a caress, which made Petra uneasy.

Shoving some coins into the machine, Petra selected a green tea. The plastic bottle clunked into the pick up slot. Petra grabbed it, twisted off the lid, and gulped down half of the refreshing beverage.

Wiping her mouth, she noticed that the fang was still looking at her. Petra's body tensed. "What do you want?"

"Nothing." Vy pushed off the vending machine and smiled.

"Then quit staring at me. I don't like it."

The fang's expression dimmed as she looked away.

Vy withdrew her phone from her pocket to briefly consult with a navigation app. Stowing her phone away, she said without looking at Petra, "If we head back in the direction we came from, we will arrive at Takeshita Street. It's apparently a famous tourist destination. You interested?"

Petra was very familiar with Takeshita Street and the Harajuku area—known for its colourful street art and distinct fashion. It was yet another place she and Kate had dreamed of visiting together. But Petra was not going to tell the fang that. So, she simply shrugged and said, "Sure, why not," before taking another sip of her drink.

Takeshita Street was a tight walkway brimming with tourists and locals. As Petra waded through the swarm of people, her eyes had trouble digesting a percentage of what they saw.

A lover of fashion, the fang paraded them through countless

boutiques where she bought anything that sparked her fancy. With every ticking minute, Petra found it a little harder to keep on her apathetic mask.

Japan lived up to the hype her teenage mind had conjured. It was so vibrant and eclectic, and a part of Petra wanted to drop her guard and immerse herself in it all.

What a pity that she found herself there with her greatest enemy.

At one point, they ventured down a narrow flight of stairs flanked by graffiti, leading to what Petra could only describe as a fashion dungeon. The store's vibe was very intense with its black walls, harsh fluorescent lighting, chain-link fences, and blaring electronic music.

Looking around and taking in the taxidermy birds and the stacks of static tube televisions, Petra decided that the shop was definitely tailored to the fang's tastes with its racks of unconventional clothing.

"This place specializes in vintage remake–style clothing," Vy said excitingly. "Basically, they curate pieces and combine them together."

Petra crossed her arms. "I don't care."

"We can leave if you want," Vy said without looking at Petra, her concentration was focused on the racks.

The fang had heeded the demand to quit staring and appeared to be making a deliberate effort to avoid making eye contact with Petra.

They'd barely exchanged a word since leaving the shrine. But there'd been too many times where Petra's mouth had opened to say something only for her to snap it shut. The compulsion to stir up conversation was mystifying. Even more disturbing, Petra kept catching her own gaze drifting towards Vy.

It was the outfit, Petra told herself. The ensemble demanded attention.

Vy looked like she'd stepped out of a kinkier version of the Matrix. Barely any of her skin was exposed, but the leather trench coat and tight-fitting latex pants were form fitting.

Wasn't she hot? Did fangs get hot?

The heat of the day was getting to Petra. Sweat drenched the back of the hoody she had on. She was grateful for the store's air conditioning.

Vy found a top she liked and held it up towards Petra. "This would look so good on you. Want to try it on? I think it might actually fit you," she said, her dark eyes flickering over Petra's tall frame.

"No."

"You're no fun," Vy said. Rolling her eyes, she hung the shirt back up on the rack. Seconds later, her excited hands pulled a jacket off the rack. "I don't care what you say. I'm going to get this for you. You'll look so hot in it, and I can't have you looking scruffy when we go out tonight."

Hot? Petra stiffened. Her face flushed. "I said no."

The fang pouted. "I'm buying it—and the shirt. You don't have to wear them, but I'm buying them."

Minutes later, they walked back up the narrow staircase with the fang carrying two additional bags. In total, the fang had accumulated four bags during their walk-through Harajuku. Petra was starting to get annoyed with her shopping spree.

After all, they were in Japan for one specific reason—and it was not to expand Vy's closet.

Chapter Twenty-One

"I thought you were on light duties?" Bowmaster said.

Olivia threw him a dirty look. "There's nothing wrong with me," she replied, sliding into her tactical vest. She clipped it around her waist and tightened the shoulder straps.

"It'll be your funeral if you come," Bowmaster said with a chuckle. He was a hulking man—very wide and very tall—but he had a prepubescent face. The man couldn't grow facial hair to save his life, and his light-brown eyes were too large for his head.

After Raz, if Olivia had to call anyone else on the base a friend, it'd be Bowmaster. It wasn't that they hung out or anything. There were two specific reasons Olivia liked him. First, he'd been the only SOTU member who hadn't given Olivia shit when she'd been promoted to the Special Ops unit. Second, he was the best shot on the base, and he'd always been willing to give Olivia pointers on how to improve her aim. She'd learned a lot from him. Because of him, using the right scope, Olivia could bring down a target from a thousand yards.

Standing to her left, Mambwe grabbed an M16 rifle off the gun rack and did a function check on the weapon. Mambwe was the most senior SOTU agent on their squad. He was a silent man—a stern man. Olivia had no beef with Mambwe as he kept to himself for the most part, and he was great at what he did.

A year back, Mambwe had even saved Olivia's life. Their SOTU squad had been tasked with hunting two class B fangs—each with over a century under their belt. One almost killed her; its teeth had been inches away from tearing out her neck. Mambwe had shot it in the head a flash before its fangs sunk in.

Olivia looked back at Bowmaster. "So, when are we heading out?"

"The hopper is still a little loopy," he replied. "Maybe in a few more hours the lightless will be operational."

Olivia nodded. "Do we have Malkovitch's coordinates?"

Bowmaster nodded. "The commander sent us a link to access her GPS coordinates."

Few on the base knew about the trackers. Trainees definitely weren't advised. Some SOLs knew, while others speculated.

When Olivia had found out about the trackers, she had asked Raz how she could go about removing hers. She didn't like knowing her movements could be followed. Raz had informed her that there was no way to remove it.

Apparently, the devices were implanted in the brain. They were used to location trace and to also measure vitals. "It's important for the Order to know where their people are, and whether they are alive or dead," Raz had told her.

Olivia was not sure when or how hers had been implanted. She couldn't remember ever undergoing such a surgery. According to Raz, the way the tracker was installed made it incredibly risky—possibly lethal—to take out. So Olivia was stuck with it.

"I'm tryna wrap my head around how Malkovitch wound up in Tokyo," Bowmaster said, drawing Olivia out of her thoughts.

"Who the fuck knows," Olivia said. "We will find out soon enough." At least, she hoped their retrieval mission proved successful. Petra had really fucked things up.

What had Clay been thinking, sending Malkovitch to tag and bag the fang who'd killed her mother? The commander had compromised Raz's work by sending her. Olivia should have been tasked with capturing the illblood. What if Petra had blown their chance at nabbing the lightless? Oliva's hands clenched.

Clay might have a stellar reputation, but a strategist she was not. And it was going around that the commander was going off her rocker again. Rumour had it that she'd thrown her laptop at Richardson in a fit. Olivia would have loved to see that. Clay loved to play the role of having it all together, but her control was a stretched rubber band on the brink of snapping.

Pretty much everyone knew that Clay used to have several tantrums in her heyday, but she'd gained a cool head after the incident with the late chief minister.

It wasn't talked about a lot, but Olivia had read the sorry excuse of a report Clay had written up for the occurrence, and she could read between the lines. The commander had killed Wu, likely in a rage.

Just then, Ferguson barged into the armoury. Yawning, he stretched his arms over his head. His grey eyes narrowed when he saw Olivia. "I thought the runt was on light duties," he said, looking at Bowmaster and then at Mambwe.

Bowmaster simply shrugged. Mambwe didn't acknowledge the statement, instead he hung the M16 he'd been holding back up and reached for another one to check.

Olivia didn't like being called runt or brat or girl or any of the others names that many on the base used to reference her short stature. Throwing Ferguson a dark look, her mouth set in a thin line, and she arched a challenging brow. "This runt bagged a hopper. This runt has taken down ten fangs, seven demons, and one beast in the past year alone," she said, crossing her arms over her chest. "Besides jerking yourself off to Richardson's thick ankles, what have you done lately?"

Bowmaster grunted with amusement. Mambwe was the picture of indifference. Ferguson's face burned red. "Why you ... I swear, I—"

"Don't start something you can't finish," Olivia said. "We both know I'm better at this game."

Ferguson opened his mouth and then shut it. He stormed over to his locker, threw it open, and removed his tactical vest.

Olivia watched him for a moment. She still couldn't believe that she'd once hooked up with him. Remembering made her want to gag, and it wasn't because he was unpleasant to look at. After

Dustin, with his shaggy brown hair and chiselled features, Ferguson was one of the best-looking men on the base. But where Dustin was a gentleman and sweet, Ferguson was a pig.

Then again, the fact that Ferguson was a pig also didn't bug Olivia all that much. What bothered her was that his cockiness and bravado were not backed by competence.

Ferguson was dead weight. Actually, he was worse than dead weight because he actively got in the way.

Since Olivia had joined SOTU, there had been several times where Ferguson's fuck-ups had nearly cost them everything. Ferguson needed to be booted from SOTU. He didn't have the skills their unit demanded.

Olivia grabbed an M16 rifle from the rack and inspected it. Noting that it was in optimal condition, she slid its strap over her shoulder and headed for the door to exit the armoury. Before leaving, she called to Bowmaster, "I'm heading for the cellblocks. Let's agree to meet at the hopper's cell in four hours. Hopefully, by then the sedative will be out of his system."

"Ten-four," Bowmaster said in acknowledgement.

Olivia threw open the door and left, heading for Raz's lab. She wanted to let him know that she was going to track down Malkovitch and figure out what happened with the illblood.

Chapter Twenty-Two

After their day of sightseeing, Vy and Petra stood crammed together on a train headed for Shinjuku. The Yamanote car got more suffocating as more exhausted workers and students, loathe to wait for the next crowded train, forced themselves inside.

As more bodies squeezed on, Vy's chest pressed further into Petra, and the feeling of being that close was torture. Her fingers itched to reach out and touch Petra. Her skin burned to feel Petra's hands on her body. Her mouth craved Petra's lips on her own.

Except for Alice, Vy was unused to desiring someone who didn't want her back. Being in love was a foreign and inconvenient experience for her.

Throughout the day, Vy had tried to think up ways to rid herself of Dustin's stupid feelings, but no solutions came to mind.

Worst of all, Vy was now having difficulty differentiating her own emotions from Dustin's. She no longer felt them clinging.

Instead, they seemed to have dissolved into her system, becoming one with her.

Vy didn't like it. She didn't like how her heart sped up whenever she felt Petra's eye on her—and they'd been on her a lot, she'd noted. The feelings were consuming, and it hurt to know they'd never be reciprocated.

Vy gritted her teeth, remembering how wrecked she'd been when Alice had coldly rejected her. She never wanted to go through that kind of pain again.

Hopefully they found the hourglass before things ever got to that point, because Vy wasn't sure how long she'd be able to restrain herself around Petra.

Tilting her head back, Vy looked up at Petra who was staring at the train car's ceiling with her hand tight on the handrail and her jaw set tightly. She could hear Petra's heart beating hard and fast. Vy wondered what was going on in the human's mind.

Vy was tempted to find out. She had the means to do so. But, she was wary of using the spell after what had happened with Dustin. Not to mention that she needed to conserve whatever energy she had. Necromancy was draining. On the off chance they found Itachi's gravesite that night, Vy needed to be prepared.

The train stopped. More people pushed on. Their bodies were forced even closer together, and Petra sucked in a breath, her gaze dropping from the ceiling. Their eyes met.

Vy's heart stuttered.

"How many more stops?" Petra asked sharply.

"It's the next stop."

Petra's eyes closed briefly, and she released a frustrated exhale. "This ride is taking forever."

"It's been less than ten minutes," Vy said.

They were travelling from the hotel Vy had booked for them in Ginza. There, Vy had dropped off her spoils, showered and changed into something more appropriate for the bar. Her plan for the night was simple. She'd go to the bar incognito, masking her vampiric aura behind a shield of glamour.

The establishment they were going to was the most popular girl bar in Tokyo, and Vy was banking that a spellcaster would turn up at some point. If one did, Vy would dazzle them and get the information she needed to find out the location of Itachi's gravesite.

Sure, it probably wasn't the most thought-out plan, but it should work. Spellcasters loved night life, and they loved women. In Toronto, those of her mother's faction flocked to the Sappho lounge in droves. Vy was pretty sure that the same would happen in Tokyo.

Vy's attention returned to Petra. She was pleased that the human had changed out of the hoodie and put on the shirt and jacket she'd bought for her. She'd been right about the garments being the right size.

The cut of clothing was flattering, accentuating Petra's broad shoulders and her tapered waist. The jacket was cropped and olive green with gold trim and two large offside pockets. The top was black and somewhat asymmetrical with edgy stitching.

Vy hadn't been able to find any pants to complement the ensemble—Petra was too tall. Everything she'd found had been too short.

Beneath the jacket, Vy could see the outline of Petra's holster. The SOL had insisted on bringing her gun. Luckily, the jacket hid it pretty well. Someone would have to look very closely to spot a flash of metal.

Absentmindedly, Vy brought a hand to the black fabric of Petra's shirt and trailed her fingers upward.

"What are you doing?" Petra snapped.

Vy's hand stilled, and she met Petra's glaring green eyes. "The shirt looks good on you—I knew it would."

Petra sucked in a breath. Her gaze dropped to Vy's mouth and lingered. "Get ... your hand ... off me."

As they stared at each other, Vy swore she saw a trace of something other than anger on Petra's face. Maybe Petra did think about their time together before she'd stabbed her.

Dropping her hand, Vy smiled smugly. Was it possible that Petra might want her too?

There had been several times throughout the day where Vy had questioned some of the looks Petra sent her way, but none had been so revealing. The look Petra was giving her now seemed more hungry than pissed.

The trained stopped.

Before Vy could fully unpack her theory, her focus was directed to forcing her way out of the train car.

Vy and Petra shuffled with the herd of passengers onto the station platform and briskly followed the crowd of commuters down the stairs.

A few minutes later, they stepped out of the hectic Shinjuku station and into fresh night air.

Vy took out her phone and consulted her navigation app.

One of the first things she had realized upon arriving in Japan was that there was little to no signage. Frequent check-ins with her phone were needed to ensure that they were on the right path.

There had been a few occasions during the day where Vy had gotten them a bit lost. But, after a quick look at Google Maps, she'd been able to guide them back on course.

They'd managed to see a lot over the last few hours. After shopping in Harajuku, Vy had referred to TripAdvisor for recommendations on what to do next. The list of options had been endless, and Vy had told Petra to pick.

Petra had opted to go to Akihabara—an area famous for its arcades, electronics, and shops devoted to manga and anime paraphernalia.

To get there, they had found their way back to Shibuya station, crossing the busiest intersection Vy had ever seen.

When Petra had noticed a dog statue, near the station entrance, she had intentionally steered them towards it.

"What's the deal with the dog?" Vy had asked, not understanding Petra's keen interest in the statue.

Petra had tossed her an annoyed look before recounting the tale of Hachiko, the loyal Akita dog.

According to Petra, Hachiko would accompany his owner to the train station every day and wait for him to return from work. Sadly, one day, Hachiko's owner passed away while on the job and never came back for a final goodbye. For ten years, Hachiko continued to visit the station every day until he too passed away. The statue was a commemoration.

Vy had found the story touching, and she had started to wonder if she should get a dog—an animal that would love her, no matter what. A dog wouldn't judge her for being an illblood.

Once they'd reached Akihabara, they had walked around for a bit before Vy got the sense—from the way Petra eyed a giant red Sega building—that Petra was interested in checking out an arcade. Vy had casually asked Petra if she wanted to go to the arcade.

In response, Petra had given one of her signature shrugs. So, they'd gone to the red Sega building.

At the arcade, Vy discovered that Petra was quite the sore loser. They'd played a few rounds of a gruesome fighting game called Mortal Combat. Vy had not been familiar with the game, but Petra had seemed to know all the combos and moves. She had crushed Vy in every round. And with each win, Petra's smug expression grew worse.

But then they had tried out a rhythm game called Maimai that Vy picked up very quickly and destroyed Petra in.

To Vy's disappointment, Petra hadn't taken the defeat well and refused to play another game.

From Akihabara, they had travelled to Asakusa, where they saw the Sensoji temple and perused the souvenir stalls.

Departing Asakusa, they wound up in Ginza—a district devoted to upmarket boutiques and ritzy dining spaces.

There, they had sat down at a sushi restaurant. Petra had racked up quite the bill, ordering pretty much everything on the menu and wolfing it down. The woman's stomach was seemingly endless, but Vy determined that it made sense given her size.

Also, Vy understood that the food fare back on the base was horrible, so Petra was probably starved for good food. In any case, Vy had been more than happy to sit back and watch Petra devour platter after platter.

Vy felt pathetic for loving every second they'd spent together, but she got the notion that Petra had enjoyed exploring Tokyo too.

While Vy hated to admit it, her day with Petra was possibly one of the best days of her life—regardless of Petra's sulking mood, and her ominous glares.

"So, we need to go this way," Vy said, slipping her phone back into her pocket. When Petra made no move to acknowledge her, she started walking in the direction of the bar. She heard Petra's heavy boots fall into step behind her.

They were headed to Shinjuku Nichome—referred to by the locals as simply Nichome.

A search on Google had informed Vy that Nichome was the buzzing queer quarter in East Shinjuku, boasting hundreds of small bars and nightclubs in the stacks of multistory buildings.

That night, the gay district was alive with the hum of chatter and music. Neon signs highlighted the streets littered with bar hoppers and partygoers.

When Vy spotted a set of bright-red doors and a giant rainbow flag draped across a front facade, she announced, "We're here," and stepped into a vacant alley. She leaned against a wall and crossed her arms.

"So, that's it?" Petra asked, gesturing with a nod at the red doors just across the thin road.

"Yeah, it opens in a few minutes."

"This better work," Petra said.

Though Vy had gone over her plan with Petra earlier, she wanted to re-establish how it'd go down. "We can't look like we are together. So, come in a few minutes after me, okay? Try to sit as far away from me as possible. Try to blend in—order a drink and mingle."

"I know how to operate covertly. Don't lecture me." Petra shot her an intense look that made Vy's skin tingle.

Vy bit her lip. "I wasn't."

"You were," Petra said, taking a step forward in her direction. Her green eyes were still on her. They emoted irritation, but also the same undertone Vy had seen on the train car.

Vy couldn't help herself. Throwing reason to the wind, she closed the distance between them and placed her hands on Petra's hips, brushing her thumbs over the waistband of her pants. "You've been staring at me all day, don't deny it," Vy stated. "Don't worry, I don't mind."

Green eyes widened, and Petra's heart accelerated. A mix of panic, anger, and hunger flashed on her face. *I'm not wrong. She wants me too.*

Petra made a move to shove her off, but Vy was much stronger than her and didn't budge. Vy tugged on Petra's waist, bringing her in close. The press of their bodies together made Vy want to groan.

"Let me go," Petra said through gritted teeth.

Wearing heels, Vy was easily able to reach Petra's neck. She brushed a kiss against Petra's throat. "Do you really want me to?" she murmured.

The response she got was Petra's hand clamping around her throat. Vy's back was driven into the opposing wall. Vy allowed it. She didn't fight.

Petra's breaths came quick. There was a wildness in her eyes. Vy feared she'd read everything wrong. Had she pushed her luck?

But then, Petra's mouth took her own with such unexpected savagery that Vy was left gasping, fighting for breaths.

The kiss was like nothing Vy had ever experienced. It was mad and selfish and rough. Vy was living for it, and she gave back as hard as she got.

Petra's hand dropped from Vy's neck and dug into her hair, pulling to the point of almost being painful. Vy liked it, and she moaned.

Petra's leg wedged between Vy's thighs and moved against her. Vy responded by pushing her hands up the back of Petra's shirt and digging her nails into her back.

Petra tore away from her mouth and hissed in her ear, "I fucking hate you so much," before biting Vy's earlobe.

Pleasure shot hot through Vy's body, and she rode Petra's thigh, grinding down hard and fast. Her dress notched up her body. "Fuck me like you hate me," she rasped.

Vy felt Petra's lips on her neck, nipping and biting. Petra's hand in her hair dropped to her breast and squeezed. Vy gasped and knocked her head back against the wall, clenching her eyes shut.

"Petra—I need you to fuck me." She grabbed Petra's free hand and brought it to where she needed it. She was so wet. Her need was so extreme that it hurt.

But Petra pulled away from her. Stumbling more than stepping back. She stabbed a hand through her short red hair. With heaving breaths, Petra's gaze rake over Vy's body with desire, and Vy knew that Petra wanted her just as badly. So, why had she stopped?

Petra's back sagged against the opposite wall, and she crossed her arms.

Vy groaned her frustration and stared Petra down with disbelief. She wanted to scream or hit something. Why had Petra stopped? She almost asked but decided against it.

Exhaling deeply, Vy forced herself to stand straight. She righted her dress.

Maybe it was a good thing they'd stopped. Now that the bar was open, they needed to move forward with the plan.

Removing a compact mirror and tube of lip gloss from her purse, Vy assessed the damage and applied a new coat of gloss. She threw the items back in her purse and strutted towards the red doors without another look spared at Petra.

Vy was horny and a little pissed. But mainly with herself.

Petra was off limits. What had she been thinking?

Chapter Twenty-Three

It wasn't until Vy disappeared behind a red door that Petra let out a loud groan. Throwing her head back, she slumped against the alley wall and shut her eyes.

Gritting her teeth, Petra thought back to the look Vy had given her when she'd forced her against the wall. It had been a mix of fear, excitement, and desire. The expression had the effect of undoing Petra's ability to think rationally.

It was so fucked up—Petra shouldn't want Vy the way she did. She hated herself for the way she'd reacted so senselessly. Kissing Vy was possibly the stupidest thing she could have done. But in that moment, Petra had been possessed, overwhelmed by an urge to take what she wanted and satisfy her own desire that had built up over the last few hours.

All throughout the day, Vy's beauty had teased her cruelly. The fang was too goddamn pretty. It was unnerving.

And it didn't help that Petra was starting to question everything she had come to believe.

For years, she'd been convinced that the lightless were soulless creatures without any redeeming qualities—that they were a stain on the earth that needed removal.

But now, she was wondering if she'd been wrong. All day, Petra had waited for Vy to exhibit behaviours that could support the narrative she wanted so badly to hold on to. Instead, Vy had shown vulnerability, kindness, and thoughtfulness.

In the span of a few hours, Petra's worldview had begun to fray. And after that kiss, she could feel the tapestry of her convictions unravelling. The anger she'd clung to for so long was unspooling, and she didn't want to let go of it.

She didn't know who she was without it. And wouldn't losing that part of herself be a betrayal to her mother?

Petra inhaled a deep breath. Tuning out the sounds of nearby chatter, laughter, and muffled music, she exhaled and willed her body to relax.

After a few more deep breaths. Petra regained some composure, and she stepped away from the wall. With long strides, she crossed the thin road and swung open a red door.

Stepping inside the dimly lit establishment, Petra was immediately greeted by the two Japanese women with edgy haircuts who operated the bar. In unison, they both robotically shouted, "Irasshaimase!"

Petra's gaze immediately went to Vy. She sat alone at a high-top table near the back of the room. Vy didn't look up at her. Her gaze was fixed on a glass of white wine in front of her. Slender fingers fiddled with the glass stem, and there was a look of irritation on her face. Her dark brows were slightly creased, and her glossy lips were set in a flat line.

Vy had removed her thin leather jacket, and it was slung across the back of her chair. The fang was a vision in the strapless black dress she'd put on for the night. Petra couldn't stop herself from drinking in the sight of the smooth bronze skin of her arms and shoulders.

Shaking her head, Petra turned towards the bar. She pulled out a stool and sat. Briefly, she scanned the area.

Inside was dark and narrow. The bar top was red, and it ran the length of the room, taking up about a third of the space. The ceiling was painted black and so were the walls. Hip-hop played from speakers mounted in the upper corners of the room. The music was loud, but not to the point where conversation was impossible.

Relatively early, the bar was dead. Besides her and Vy, there were only three other patrons.

One of the bartenders approached Petra and bowed her head as she set down an English menu in front of her. Petra eyed the selection, pointed at a random beer and handed over some cash. Moments later, a bottle of Asahi was cracked open and set down in front of her. Petra grabbed the bottle and took a long swig. The carbonated drink did nothing to erase the lingering taste of Vy's lips.

The lure to look at Vy tugged on Petra, and she despised it. In her annoyance, she began tearing at the beer label to occupy herself.

Scenes from the day rolled over in her mind like a movie. She saw Vy's excitement during her shopping splurge and the cocky look Vy had thrown her way when she'd annihilated Petra in that stupid hand tapping rhythm game at the arcade. Petra remembered how both she and Vy seemed to revel in the beauty of the Sensoji Temple.

A sigh escaped Petra's mouth. She looked up at a clock mounted over shelves holding an array of liquor. It was only twenty minutes past eight.

Something told Petra that she'd be forced to sit there, with the pull of Vy's presence at her back, for at least another hour or two.

Finishing her beer, Petra ordered another. The bartender set down another bottle and removed the empty one.

The bar didn't start to fill up until almost ten, and by that time Petra had knocked back three beers. She could feel the effects of the alcohol numbing her, but also making her feel more frustrated and antsy. A part of her wanted to stomp over to Vy and tell her that this whole plan of hers was stupid, which it was. But she didn't. Instead, she settled for shooting the fang a quick look.

Petra frowned when she saw that Vy was beaming at someone. Whipping her head in the other direction, Petra focused her attention on the woman Vy was smiling at. The lines between her eyebrows deepened.

The woman was a gorgeous Japanese woman with jet-black hair that fell very straight past her shoulders. Her face was very fair. Her lips were painted red. Her dark eye makeup was applied thickly but expertly. She was dressed in a formfitting cream pantsuit.

There was a fierce energy about her that captivated the eye and made Petra want to stare. She was so very alluring. Petra found it hard to look away. When she managed to, Petra noticed that everyone in the bar seemed to watch the woman as if in thrall.

It dawned on Petra what was happening—the Order had taught her about it. *She's a spellcaster casting a type of glamour magic.*

The glamour cloaked spellcaster made a beeline for Vy's high-top table, and the two women seemed to hit it off immediately. Vy said something that made the spellcaster laugh. The spellcaster put a hand on Vy's arm and traced a path down its length with a finger.

Petra felt a twinge of something in her chest, and she moved to face the bar again.

"Seems Yumiko has found a new mark," a woman beside her said in a bitter tone with the slightest bit of an accent.

Blinking, Petra looked at the stranger who sat on her left. "Yumiko?"

"The chick in white who's working on the hottie you've been discreetly eyeing all night," she said, taking a sip of dark liquid from a glass.

"I wasn't eyeing anybody," Petra muttered.

The stranger snorted. "Sure."

"I wasn't."

"If you say so." The woman took another sip from her drink. Dressed in a stylish black track suit, wearing the barest of makeup and sporting long dark hair with a crisp undercut, she was … cute.

"You don't seem to like her," Petra stated, cocking her head towards the spellcaster, Yumiko, who was flirting shamelessly with Vy. The fang seemed to be enjoying the banter. Her face was animated, and her hands were playing with the ends of her hair.

Petra's jaw clenched.

"I don't," she confirmed.

Petra didn't bother asking her why. Petra didn't care. Petra didn't want to be conversing with her. She wanted to leave the fucking bar.

"You ever been cheated on?" the stranger asked suddenly, finishing the rest of her drink and slamming the glass down on the red bar top. Not waiting for a response, she continued, "I have. My girlfriend and I were together for five years—five fucking happy years. I moved here from Seoul to be with her—and then she meets Yumiko ..." The woman signalled for the bartender to bring her another glass of whatever she'd been drinking. Her slender fingers slipped into her pocket and withdrew a package of cigarettes. She popped a cigarette into her mouth and lit up, blowing out a cloud of smoke.

A few other patrons were smoking. The air inside the bar was filled with haze.

The woman held out the carton. "Want one?" When Petra shook her head, the woman shrugged and tossed the carton onto the bar top, took a deep drag, and leaned back on her stool. "I'm Ji-woo."

So, we are exchanging names now. "I'm Petra." It stunned Petra that she had answered. She blamed her loose lips on the alcohol.

"Petra," Ji-woo repeated, as if to lock the name into her memory. "Where are you from?" she asked.

"Canada."

"Vancouver? I have an aunt in Vancouver."

"Toronto," Petra corrected. Her gaze drifted over to Vy again, and her eyes narrowed.

Vy and Yumiko were making out. Their hands were all over each other.

Petra darted her eyes back to the bar top. Her stomach felt unsettled. The room suddenly felt a little too hot. She rubbed the back of her neck.

"Seems you're out of luck where that hottie is concerned." Ji-woo chuckled, putting out her cigarette in an astray. "But I'm available if you wanted to get out of here," she said boldly, placing a hand on Petra's thigh.

Petra looked down at the hand on her thigh and then gave Ji-woo a questioning look.

Ji-woo seemed to misread Petra's confusion for something else because she rose off her stool seat and kissed her.

Surprisingly, Petra allowed it. It wasn't an unpleasant kiss, but it left Petra unstirred and empty. It was so unlike the heated kiss she'd exchanged with Vy in the alley, and she didn't want to dwell on that fact.

Ji-woo pulled away and sat back down in her seat with a grin. "So, you wanna get out of here?"

"Yes," Petra said, "but not with you—sorry."

Lines of dissatisfaction etched into Ji-woo's features, but only for a moment before she said, "Sure, whatever," and returned to her drink.

The stool scraped against the floor as Petra stood up. She scowled when she saw that Vy was still at it with the spellcaster. The two women were pawing at each other like dogs in heat. Petra turned her back to the scene.

The air in the bar was suddenly asphyxiating. Petra needed some fresh air—immediately.

Petra left the bar, and her legs took her all the way to the main road before she felt herself start to calm.

Exhaling a deep breath, she pivoted and strode back in the direction of the bar, but she didn't go back inside. She walked past the red doors and over to a vending machine. She fed some money into it and purchased a water.

Twisting the top off the bottle, she chugged half of it down and then leaned her back against a brick wall.

Petra could smell rain coming. The air was thick with moisture, but looking up, she couldn't see any evidence of clouds. The sky was just black.

"There you are."

Petra's head turned in the direction of Vy's voice. The fang approached her. She had put her jacket back on.

Stopping a few feet away, Vy propped a shoulder against the vending machine and crossed her arms. "I see you had fun," she said in a flat tone.

Petra rolled her eyes and put the water bottle back to her lips. She finished the rest of it. Crushing the bottle, she tossed it into the recycling bin near the vending machine.

Vy's eyes were still on her. "So, you're back to not talking to me?"

"Don't you have work to do, or have you forgotten why we fucking came here?"

"You'd think with all the action you're getting, you'd be less pissy," Vy said, her tone edged with bitterness. "Of course, I haven't forgotten."

"Then why are you out here?" Petra sneered, clenching her teeth. "Shouldn't you be in there dry-fucking the information we need out of that spellcaster?"

"Dry-fucking?" Vy arched a brow and chuckled.

Petra didn't understand what the fang found so funny, and her face reddened as her anger flared. "Why the fuck are you laughing, fang?"

Vy pushed off of the vending machine and stepped towards her. "You sound jealous."

Petra snorted. "You're fucking delusional." She shook her head at the absurdity of the fang's words. She was not jealous—definitely not. Petra couldn't give a fuck.

"Am I?" Vy asked, closing the distance between them. She looked up at Petra, and her eyes brimmed with intensity. Her hands reached out to take Petra by the waist.

Glowering, Petra brushed off Vy's advance and stook a step back. "I swear, fang, I am not in the mood for your games."

Vy sighed and ran a hand through her long dark hair. "Seriously. SOL, I wish you'd learn to lighten up." They stared at each other for several moments. Then Vy released a breath and said, "I got the information we need."

Petra blinked at her in surprise. "What? When?"

"Apparently, when I was dry-fucking the spellcaster." Vy said. "Anyways, the Yamamoto estate is not that far from here—just a little outside of Tokyo. We can get there by taxi. But I smell rain."

"Rain," Petra repeated.

"Rain can disrupt the spell," Vy clarified. "Hopefully it holds off for a couple more hours."

"We should get going then," Petra said.

Chapter Twenty-Four

The taxi's wheels slowed and came to a stop. Vy paid the driver and exited the cab. The night air smelled thick. She hoped there was enough time to complete the spell before it began to spit.

Magic was so finicky. The last thing she needed was for the weather to impact her ability to channel its flow.

Petra climbed out of the vehicle next, closing the door with more force than needed. Vy looked at her as the taxi drove away, its lights disappearing as it rounded a corner.

It was late and quiet. The streets were empty.

They stood in front of an imposing stone wall that rose well over nine feet in height. The rocks that built it up had been piled on each other in their natural unprocessed form, fitting together like pieces of a puzzle. A thick green moss coated most of the stones. Beyond it lay the ancestral estate of the Yamamoto clan and hopefully Itachi's final resting place.

Vy and Petra hadn't spoken during the drive. Nor had they exchanged words after Vy had announced that she knew where the Yamamoto estate was. Vy was growing to dislike it when silence yawned between them. Still confused about what had happened in the alley, she wanted to talk about it.

It was obvious to Vy that they were mutually attracted to each other, and she felt that they could save each other a lot of grief if they just talked about it. But she also wasn't sure how to broach the topic, especially with Petra being in possibly the darkest mood Vy had ever seen her in.

Petra stood ramrod straight with her arms crossed over her broad chest. Her green eyes had an "I'm pissed off" gleam to them.

Vy was pretty sure she knew why Petra was pissed—it was the same reason she was a little on edge. She'd been more than a little jealous when she had seen Petra kissing some random at the girl bar. The feeling had been searing—possibly more intense than the wave of jealously that had washed over her that morning when Petra had whispered "Kate" in her sleep.

From Petra's earlier tone and from the way she'd rushed out of the bar, Vy was willing to bet that Petra also hadn't liked seeing Vy with Yumiko. Or maybe she just wanted to believe that.

Wringing her hands, Vy bit her lip. She opened her mouth to say something, but Petra turned and began scaling the wall with an ease that was impressive for a human.

Vy easily leapt over the wall, landing softly on the bed of grass on the other side.

Reaching the top, Petra launched herself towards the ground

and landed in a soft crouch beside Vy. She rose to her full height. "I can barely see anything," she confessed, looking around her.

Like all unhumans, Vy had excellent night vision, and so it didn't matter to her that there were no lamps on the other side of the wall.

Muttering a few choice words, Vy summoned an orb of light to hover just above Petra's head. When the light appeared, Petra shrank away from it, and tried to bat it away with her hands. "What the fuck?"

"It's just light," Vy said, chuckling. "Nothing to get worked up over."

Petra snorted. "Sure, it is," she said, her tone hinting that she was unconvinced.

"What's that supposed to mean?" Vy frowned. "Would it hurt you to say thank you once in your life?"

Still waving the light away, Petra stared at Vy intently. "What other magic have you used on me?"

"I've used magic around you, but never on you," Vy corrected.

"Like glamour?"

"Yes, I have used glamour, but—"

"To allure me, make me fond of you?" Petra snapped. She seemed to forget about the light and stepped towards Vy. They were suddenly standing very close, and Vy's heart began to race.

"No, I haven't." Vy tilted her head back to meet Petra's eyes. Her body itched to close the distance between them. "If I had, you wouldn't be asking me these questions."

"I don't know about that," Petra said. "I knew what the spellcaster was about back at the bar."

Vy wrinkled her nose at the memory of Yumiko. The reek of glamour had been strong on her. She hadn't been a very competent spellcaster, and Vy had been able to easily see her for what she was under her magical guise.

Like Vy and all spellcasters, Yumiko's skin was naturally bronze—she was not Japanese as she appeared.

Passing for other races was a commonplace practice amongst spellcasters. In the pre-modern era, lightening one's complexion or masking one's gender offered protection from societal horrors and inequities. Now, the practice was purely for aesthetics. Though, while changing appearance was acceptable, spellcasters now shunned those in their faction who preferred to masquerade as the opposite sex. Vy wasn't sure why this was, and she didn't think it should matter how one opted to present themselves.

Even so, it had always bothered Vy that she and Camellia looked so different. Camellia chose to pass for white.

Once, Vy had been bold enough to ask her mother why it was that she continued to hide herself when there was no need to. Oddly, her mother had answered, telling her that she had grown so accustomed to her white pigmentation over the centuries and could not recognize herself without it. When Vy had asked if she could change her skin tone too, Camellia's response had been a curt no.

Other than that, Vy had never sought to alter her physical appearance with magic. She liked her face and her hair and her body. If only loving one's physical appearance had the effect of making one also love themselves.

"That spellcaster has a lot to learn where glamour magic is

concerned. I am not surprised you picked up on it," Vy replied finally. "But I haven't used any magic on you. If I had, let's just say you wouldn't have stopped in the alley. Whatever attraction you have for me is all you. I've never had to trick someone into sleeping with me, and I never will. I don't want someone who doesn't want me back." Vy's gaze dropped to Petra's lips.

She heard Petra's heart rate increase. A flush crept up the human's neck. Vy's eyes landed on the pulse fluttering under the thin layer of skin at her jugular.

Vy's fangs began to throb. She had fed moments before they had left for Shinjuku, but she was already hungry. She peeled her eyes away from Petra's throat. Backpedaling, she put some distance between them.

Clearing her throat, Petra looked upward. "It's going to rain," she said, changing the subject. Her voice was tight. "We should get this over with."

Though Vy wanted to finish their conversation, she decided they could pick it back up at the hotel. Nodding her agreement, Vy looked away from Petra and scanned the area.

There was a footpath just behind the main house that led to the gravesite. It was flanked by expertly sculpted Japanese pines known as *matsu*, whose horizontal branches hovered parallel to the ground below.

The light Vy had summoned guided them down the path. Soon, they arrived at a small gravesite.

Vy began examining the names upon the gorintō—Japanese grave markers. Gorintō were composed of stacked geometric stone forms. Each shape represented one of five elements.

It didn't take Vy long to find Itachi's—his was one of the smaller markers.

Kneeling on the ground before the stone structure, Vy felt more than heard Petra at her back.

"So this is it?" Petra asked. "I'm still not buying that you can pull off necromancy."

Vy shot her a look over her shoulder and arched a brow. "Are you willing to bet on it?"

Petra shook her head. "No."

"So you do have some faith in me?" Vy smiled.

"I want to. I want this to all be real," Petra admitted. Her voice was soft. "I want the promise of a new life."

"It is real," Vy said. "When we find the hourglass, we will both get what we want."

"And you're so sure this person can help you cure your vampirism?"

Vy nodded. "Yes."

"How can you be so sure?"

"It's my mother—she knows everything there is to know," Vy replied.

"Your mother," Petra repeated, gritting her teeth. "Why do you need the hourglass to find her?"

"Because the only way to find her is in the past," Vy said, curtly. It still hurt to think of her mother's abandonment. Camellia had left all those years ago without a word and without a clue to her whereabouts. Vy had tried searching for her, but she'd given up when all her leads had dried up. Of course, Vy had always known that Camellia would never be found if she didn't want to be. Going back into the past was the only way.

"Sure," Petra said, shoving her hands into the front pockets of her sweatpants. "If you can pull this off, hopefully Itachi can point us in the right direction."

"Hopefully," Vy whispered. She turned her attention back to the marker.

She looked at the nail of her right index finger, and channelled magic to it so that it grew long and sharp as a razor. For a moment, Vy recalled all the times she'd cut herself with the delicate porcelain handle knife.

Vy shuddered. She despised blood magic.

Camellia had often said that practice made permanent, and Vy hated to acknowledge that her mother had been right. While it had been years since she'd last raised the dead, the ancient words tumbled from her mouth with a confidence and a precision that could only come with years of practice.

Magic buzzed in the air from the utterance of the spell, and it wasn't long before Vy could feel it building in her core and flowing in her veins. She felt the magic weighing down her body, making each word of the spell harder to say. But she ignored the discomfort and barrelled on until she neared the part she dreaded. Closing her eyes, Vy slashed her sharp nail across her flesh without hesitance. She gasped a sound of release as the power poured out of her.

Blood trickled down her arm, falling onto the ground in the particular dribble that the magic demanded.

Leaning over, Vy dipped a finger into the dark ink that hummed with power. She then painted a red marking upon the cold stone of Itachi's grave marker.

A rush of wind encircled her, sweeping up her hair. The blood ink upon the grave began to glow a brilliant white, and the ground shook ever so slightly as the gate to the spiritual world collided with that of the natural world.

"Fuck," Petra swore. Her awe was evident. "What's happening?"

Vy smirked. "I'm raising the dead." After healing the cut on her arm, she made an attempt to stand up, but stumbled. Petra reached out and grabbed her arm to stabilize her.

"You okay?" she asked, helping Vy to her feet.

The feel of Petra's hand on her arm made Vy's heart jump. Nodding, she said, "I'm just a little lightheaded. Blood magic is a huge energy suck, and I'm …"

"You're what?"

"I never have enough energy."

Petra arched a brow and dropped her hold on Vy's arm. "Because you don't feed from humans?"

Remembering how their conversation had turned for the worse the last time they'd broached the topic of her diet, Vy kept her response to a minimum, saying a quick yes.

Bending, Vy dusted the dirt from her legs and from the hem of her dress.

"What now?" Petra cocked her head towards the grave that still glowed ethereally. "I don't see Itachi."

"That's because I haven't called for him." Vy's eyes snapped closed when the world began to spin, but her weakness wasn't the worst thing. The thirst was raging all of a sudden—her teeth throbbed and her throat burned.

Petra's hands were on her shoulders, keeping her upright. Vy opened her eyes and tried to smile. "I just need a moment. The feeling should pass soon." She hoped.

The look on Petra's face wasn't angry for once—it was concerned. "Will you have trouble raising him?"

Vy shook her head. "No, the hard part is done. I just ... I just need the world to stop spinning."

"You can lean on me if that will help," Petra said. Not waiting for an answer, she pulled Vy against her.

Vy's head collapsed on Petra's chest. She closed her eyes, and her body relaxed somehow.

Vy knew better than to wrap her arms around Petra, but she did it anyway. It was what she wanted to do, and surprisingly, Petra allowed it. But what was even more astonishing was how the thirst seemed to retreat.

They stood like that for many moments.

Besides the wind rustling through the trees, all was still. Vy usually abhorred quiet. For years, silence acted as a constant reminder of all she had lost and all she would never have. A life of silence was a life alone.

But, she didn't feel alone with Petra. Her presence was a comfort, and her radiant body heat warmed Vy from the inside out.

Even as her dizziness dissipated, Vy held on. She didn't want to let go. She wanted to hold on forever.

"Are you feeling better?" Petra asked. Her voice was so soft it was almost a whisper.

Vy wanted to lie, but she didn't—it wouldn't do to press her luck. She withdrew her arms from around Petra and took a step back. "Yes," she said, tucking a lock of hair behind her ear. "I feel better."

"Good." Petra's expression was unreadable, but it wasn't angry.

With a sigh, Vy turned back to the grave that was still illuminated. She walked over to the Gorintō and placed her hands upon the cold stone. "Itachi Yamamoto, I summon you."

The earth around the gravesite shuddered, and an apparition came with a gust of wind.

Itachi's holographic ghost appeared as a muscular and handsome man with black hair pulled back into a tight bun. He wore a white-collared dress shirt tucked into a pair of jeans and a pair of black and white Adidas. He stood frozen as a statue.

Vy knew he awaited orders.

If it weren't for her utter exhaustion, Vy definitely would have inspected her creation from all angles. It had been so long since she'd raised a ghost, and a part of her wanted to rate her conjuring, but she was too tired.

Vy felt herself leaning against the hardness of Petra's body once more. To her satisfaction, Petra didn't move away.

"Holy fucking shit! You did it," Petra said, sounding amazed. "What now?"

Vy cleared her throat. "I ask him some questions. He responds. Hopefully, we get our next clue. I send him back to wherever the hell he came from."

"Sounds simple enough."

"Should be." Vy craned her head back to meet Petra's stare. In the subtle glow of the light orb, Petra's green eyes seemed to sparkle. Vy's gaze dropped to her full lips.

Petra seemed to notice where Vy was looking. She coloured a bit, her muscular body tensing. Vy didn't know if that was a good thing or not. She took it as a sign to get back to work.

With a deep exhale, Vy pulled away and stepped towards the spirit. "Hey there, Itachi," she said.

Upon hearing his name, Itachi's ghost blinked, but remained still—too still.

Vy bit her lip. "Itachi, I need you to tell me everything you know about Present's Gate," she commanded.

The apparition looked down and seemed to be thinking. Then he began to shake his head profusely. His hands flew to his ears and his spectre body quivered. "NO—NO—NO," he shouted, over and over.

"Is this supposed to happen?" Petra asked.

"No," Vy said, remembering the report she had read on the Order's database. "It's likely that whatever mental ailment he'd been suffering from followed him into death. I don't think I will be able to get him to tell me anything."

Petra's fists clenched. "Fuck—if we can't get information from him, where the fuck does that leave us?" She began to pace. Anger rolled off her in waves. Whipping towards Vy, she pointed a finger and shouted. "I knew you were playing fucking games—this whole thing is a trick."

"It's not." Vy shook her head.

"Then do something!"

Vy pressed her hands to her face as she tried to think of something. She had an idea, but it was risky. After what happened with Dustin, she was wary of using the dark magic again—especially when her energy levels were so low.

Petra was still pacing. Her strides were long and urgent. Vy could sense that Petra's mind was whirling, and she remembered that Petra carried her gun. The possibility that Petra might still try to kill her was not lost on her, and the reality of that was crushing.

Vy didn't want Petra's hate, and Vy despised that she was the reason for Petra's pain and grief.

What if this is the only way? Vy bit her lip. "Look Petra, I have an idea."

Petra stopped and glared at her. "Good."

"But I need time to think about it," Vy said. "We can come back tomorrow."

"No." Petra snorted. Her face was very red, and she looked feral and ready to pounce. "If you can do it tomorrow, you can do it now."

Vy shook her head. "I'm very weak—it's risky."

"Sometimes you need to take risks," Petra snapped. "Stop making excuses."

"If this doesn't work … I don't know what would happen."

"Then why don't you find out? If you don't do something, it will not turn out well for you," Petra stated. Her green eyes glinted dangerously.

Vy's stomach churned. She didn't like that Petra was putting her in this position, and remembering how Dustin's thoughts had clung to her, she feared what might happen if Itachi's madness touched her. She remembered her mother's warning about living too many lives.

"I can't. Not tonight—I just don't have it in me."

"You can and you will," Petra said. "If you don't, we are done—I'm done with this."

Vy felt her eyes sting. "Done," she repeated. "And what does done mean? You going to try to kill me again?"

"I'll have no choice." Petra's nostrils flared. "You killed my mother!"

"I didn't mean to. It was an accident … a horrible accident." The tears started, and Vy couldn't stop them. She wiped them away, but more kept coming. There wasn't a word that Vy could use to describe what she felt. Her heart was battered, and her body felt just as beaten.

Maybe she should just let Petra kill her. What was her life anyway? How many years had she thought of putting herself out of her own misery—maybe now was the time to just give up.

Sniffling, Vy met Petra's eyes, and she stilled.

Petra didn't look as angry anymore. Instead, the human's expression appeared almost thoughtful. Her brows were furrowed together. "I need you to take the risk," she said, bringing a hand to her chest. "If this whole thing isn't a twisted game, this is where you prove it to me."

Vy stared at her. She thought again about her mother's warning, and about Dustin's clinging feelings, and about her worries about

Itachi's madness. But Petra's words seemed to matter more.

Exhaling a deep breath, her shoulders sank in defeat as she decided to take the risk. Rubbing the tears from her eyes, she said, "Fine, I will try."

Petra didn't say anything. She just watched her.

Vy turned away from Petra and fixed the ghost with a stare. Then, she said the words and launched herself into its soul.

On impact, Vy was met with a turbulent ocean of chaos. She couldn't wade through it. The tide of Itachi's thoughts was high, and it crashed down on her.

Vy drowned beneath the current.

Chapter Twenty-Five

With wide eyes, Petra watched Vy collapse to the ground.

The holographic spectre stopped its shaking and mutterings of "no" and it looked up, seeming to smirk with satisfaction. Its expression made a chill run up Petra's spine.

With a sinister curling of its lips, Itachi's ghost floated over Vy's unconscious body and slithered within her, disappearing.

Instantly, Vy began to convulse, her head slamming against the ground and her limbs quivering.

Goosebumps broke out over Petra's skin. Her heart raced. She rushed to Vy's side, hoisting her writhing body in her arms.

What do I do? Petra wasn't sure what she could do. She wasn't sure what she had seen exactly.

"Wake up," Petra said, at first softly. Then, her grip on Vy tightened, and she spoke louder, "Hey, come on, enough of this. Wake up."

Petra bit her lip and looked down at Vy's face—so very pale in the soft glow of the orb she had cast. Her cheeks were still wet from her tears.

"Come on now, Vy, snap out of this." But the fang didn't. If anything, her condition worsened. Her eyes rolled to the back of her head, and her trembling intensified.

Fuck ... I don't know what to do. Petra had some medical training, but she had no idea what to do in a situation involving magic.

As Vy continued to shake, a fear took root in Petra's gut. *Can she die from this?* Strangely, that was the last thing she wanted. In fact, the thought of that end made something twinge in her chest.

Petra hadn't liked the look on the spectre's face. She wondered if the ghost was doing something to Vy. Was possession possible? She hoped it wasn't. Because, whether she liked it or not, she needed Vy—without her, without the hourglass ... *Fuck.*

In such a short time, Petra started to want her new promised life more than anything, and she didn't want to see her hopes perish. Her outlook had changed. Her goals were no longer aligned with the Order. She didn't want to be an SOL and couldn't see herself going back to the way things were. It would be impossible.

She'd come to believe that there was a chance of having everything she ever wanted—her mother back and a future with Kate. Petra wasn't ready to give up that dream of a new reality—not now when the world had just begun to feel brighter and worth living again.

"You have to wake up." Petra whispered, gently cupping Vy's face. "Wake up."

As if heeding the command, Vy finally grew still, and the curtains of her thick dark lashes lifted to reveal eyes shot black without a hint of white. The expression on Vy's face was strange, but it was a look not foreign to Petra.

Vy was gone. In her place was the monster with obsidian eyes who had haunted Petra for more than a decade.

Razor-like fangs protruded from its mouth. Its demeanour was feral.

Petra motioned to defend herself, but the fang was too quick, snapping at her like a viper. Sharp teeth tore into Petra's shoulder.

Crying out, Petra tried to extricate herself from its grasp, but the fang's strength was formidable. Whereas Petra could feel her own strength diminishing with every second it fed.

Petra tried again to dislodge herself. She pummelled the creature with blows to its side. The vampire was unfazed.

Refusing to succumb to panic, Petra leaned on her training and kept calm. She was not the same scared girl. She would not freeze. She was a soldier. Death did not scare her. Failure was far worse. Petra would not suffer the same fate as her mother.

She reached for her gun, and once her fingers curled around its handle, she shoved the barrel into the fang and squeezed the trigger.

A thunderous bang disrupted the silence of the night.

The shot had the desired effect of stunning the fang. Feeling its hold slacken, Petra shoved it off of her and put some distance between them while aiming her weapon.

The fang hissed. Spittle flew from a mouth smeared with Petra's blood.

Shoot it—kill it! Petra directed her gun at its head. But her fingers were stiff on the trigger.

Healing rapidly, the fang's thigh smoked and fizzled at the site of the wound. The silver bullet was pushed out of its flesh and thunked to the ground.

Petra waited for it to come at her again. She told herself that if it did, then she'd shoot.

But it didn't make a move towards her. Instead, it shook its head as if struggling with something internal.

Petra's shoulder burned where she'd been bitten. Her gun seemed to weigh fifty pounds, and her aim wavered slightly.

The fang looked towards the ground and blinked. When it looked up, its irises were back to brown. There was confusion reflected in their depths.

Vy was back. Her eyes narrowed on Petra's gun aimed at her head, and then they widened upon seeing the blood on Petra's neck.

Her knees hit the floor, and she retched—over and over.

Petra watched in disbelief. She'd thought Vy had lied about getting sick from drinking human blood, but she was witnessing it for herself.

As Vy continued to heave, the seal of the sky finally broke. Rain came down hard and heavy. They were both soaked in an instant, and Vy's pinkish spew was washed away.

When Vy was finished vomiting, she looked up at Petra with sorrowful eyes and wiped her mouth.

Even with the rain, Petra could tell that she was crying. Her bottom lip quivered, and her whole body shook.

With a quick motion, Petra brought up a second hand to support her hold on the gun. The pain in her shoulder was excruciating. A multitude of emotions swirled in her mind. Her past anger flared, mixing with panic and other feelings she couldn't name.

Petra didn't know how this situation would play out, and the unknown was somewhat terrifying. She wasn't in the right mind to think.

Vy struggled to her feet, and when she tried to take a step forward, Petra was quick to stop her. "Take another step, fang, and I'll blow your fucking head off!"

Vy clutched her chest with two hands. "Petra, I am so sorry. I'm so sorry—you have to believe me. I don't know what happened. I lost control. It was an—"

"An accident," Petra spat, finishing for her. "Where have I heard that before?"

"You're in pain." Despite the warning, Vy moved towards her. "I can heal you."

"I said don't fucking move!" Petra's double-handed grip on her weapon tightened. She hated the part of herself that felt relief to see that the fang was okay.

Vy was dangerous. Vy was volatile. Vy was a stain on the earth that needed to be eradicated. And Petra owed it to her mother to see that the fang was finally put down. But could she do it? Could she kill Vy?

Vy disobeyed Petra's order and shuffled forward. "You're bleeding. I can help."

In an automatic reaction, Petra fired a shot into Vy's knee. The fang buckled and dropped to the wet ground.

Petra winced, and her heart seemed to as well.

Horrified, Vy looked up at Petra, bringing a hand to touch her bloody knee. She stared at the red painting the tips of her fingers before the rain cleaned it away. "You shot me?" Her voice was a cocktail of hurt and puzzlement. The bullet ejected quickly, and the wound healed over.

"And you bit me," Petra said in a tone so raw and icy that she barely recognized it as her own.

Vy stood up and balled her hands into fists. "I warned you that I was weak—I told you that it'd be a risk."

"You—bit—me!"

"All I can say is that I am sorry," Vy whispered. She bit her lip. "Where does this leave us?"

The question made Petra blink. She snorted. "I don't know. What did you find out from Itachi?"

"His mind was chaos—there was nothing to find."

"So, I guess that's our answer."

"Petra, you can't mean to ..." Vy's words came out in sobs, and she shook her head. "I need to find that hourglass. I can't go on without it."

Ironically, Petra felt the same, but she could see no way of moving forward from this—even as she determined that she might not be able to pull the trigger again.

It didn't matter that she was angry at Vy for biting her. It didn't matter that Vy was dangerous. It didn't matter that Vy had killed her mother. Petra didn't have it in herself kill Vy—at least, not now.

In the distance, something caught her eye, and Petra saw five figures drop from out of nowhere. They landed on the path with a thud—the Order.

How? Petra's heart arrested in her chest.

Vy looked over her shoulder and cursed before turning her eyes back to Petra.

Petra recognized the individuals toting semi-automatic assault rifles, but she didn't recognize the man who was restrained.

She deduced quickly who he might be. Obviously, they'd been hopped, so it was likely the unknown man in the orange jumper was the hopper Olivia had bragged about bagging.

Thick shackles hugged the hopper's wrists and ankles, and one of the SOTU agents, Mambwe, clamped his arm tightly.

"Of course, it is fucking raining," Petra heard Olivia shout. The two other SOTU agents Petra recognized as being Bowmaster and Ferguson.

The squad clicked on their tactical flashlights that were clipped to their belts, flooding the area in concentrated rays of light. Petra squinted from the brightness.

"Well, look there. If it isn't Malkovitch?" Olivia called out, taking in the scene before her with amusement. "It seems Malkovitch is once again thwarted from her ultimate goal."

Petra was unsure how the Order had found them. Their presence made things more complicated than they already were.

All she knew was that she didn't want them to take Vy. At the same time, she was not in a position to fight them. But even if she was, Petra didn't want to hurt them. For years, she had eaten with them and trained alongside them. They were her brethren by association.

Even Olivia, whom she hated, she didn't want to see dead. Petra had only ever wanted to get back at Olivia—put the bitch in her place for once.

Petra's gaze drifted back to Vy, whose eyes were wide and still full of tears. "Petra, let me go," Vy said softly. She eyed Petra's gun, which was still aimed at her head. She was fast, but not fast enough to evade the shot. It was likely Vy knew that, which was why she didn't flee.

"I can't," Petra said flatly. The statement was true. She couldn't drop her aim. Not while Olivia and the others watched. If she did, and Vy attempted to escape, there was a very good probability that SOTU agents might be able to take her down. Bowmaster was a ridiculously good shot. His reflexes were otherworldly. If Vy bolted, she'd likely die.

The only thing Petra could do was let them take her back to the base. The commander wanted Vy alive. It was the only option.

"Petra," she whispered, "don't do this."

"I have no choice," Petra muttered under her breath.

"Please."

"She's part spellcaster," Petra shouted, ignoring Vy's plea. "Bind and gag her quickly, before I do something we may all regret."

In response, someone—Bowmaster—fired a weapon. A tranquilizer dart pierced Vy's back. Before she collapsed to the ground, shocked and hurt eyes looked up at Petra.

Petra lowered her weapon. Her gaze drifted to Vy, who lay very still and seemed so small and fragile. Her black dress was ruined with mud. Her long black hair was a wet tangle around her. Her limbs looked crumpled like an action figure whose extremities had been manipulated by a sadistic toddler.

All the while, the rain pelted down on her. The tableau was depressing, and Petra's chest ached in a way she'd not felt in years. She told herself that she was mourning the loss of her new reality. No, her heart wasn't splitting because she cared for Vy.

The light orb Vy had cast burned out, fizzling away with all of Petra's hopes.

A hard lump lodged in Petra's throat. She looked away from Vy and watched Olivia stalk towards her. The bitch was humming some sort of cheery melody as her fingers drummed on the rifle slung over her shoulder. Petra wanted so badly to knock out her teeth.

When Olivia reached Petra, she stopped humming and adjusted her gun so it hung across her back.

Olivia crouched over Vy's body and slapped handcuffs over her small wrists before securing a shock collar around Vy's neck. Looking over her shoulder, Olivia snapped her fingers at Bowmaster, "Gag!"

Bowmaster reached into his vest and removed a gag. He threw it at Olivia, who caught it and proceeded to shove the material into Vy's mouth, tying it tight. "My, my, she's pretty—the boys in the cellblocks are gonna love her," Olivia mused. Eyeing Petra, she asked, "Why so sad, Malkovitch?"

Petra threw her a sharp look, but said nothing.

"If you are worried that the fang won't get what she deserves, I can promise you she'll get that and more," Olivia said. She looked up at Petra and her eyes roamed over the blood oozing from her shoulder. "I see you got bit. How pathetic."

Petra gritted her teeth.

Olivia smiled. It was a cruel smile and full of teeth. "What the fuck are you wearing? And how the fuck did you end up in Japan?"

Petra didn't answer. She holstered her gun, and her body began to shiver, but she didn't think it had anything to do with the rain.

Olivia's words were replaying in her mind, making Petra's stomach twist. What had Olivia meant by the boys in the cellblocks loving Vy? What would happen to Vy?

"What are the commander's plans for her?" Petra asked.

"I would love to tell you." Olivia chuckled. "But you're still a trainee. You don't have the clearance for that information."

Chapter Twenty-Six

Olivia sat on the top of the commander's giant desk with her feet dangling. She chewed gum, blowing large pink bubbles that she'd pop with a snap.

With each snap, Petra felt her patience erode. How much longer would Clay be? How much longer would she have to endure the company of Olivia and her squad?

Bowmaster, Ferguson, and Mambwe lounged quietly in the seating area near the large gas fireplace. They all wore a stern look that expressed that they'd rather be somewhere else.

The commander's office might have been large, but it wasn't large enough. In that moment, Petra needed space. She needed time alone. She needed to go to sleep and never wake back up.

Once, Petra had wanted to become a member of SOTU and bare the tattoos of the rank. Now, she could think of nothing worse. Working alongside Olivia would have been as bearable as swallowing broken glass.

Olivia continued to clap her mouth and snap her gum. Her boots knocked against the side of the desk. All the while her hazel eyes scrutinized Petra, who sat in one of the two armchairs.

Petra's shoulder throbbed where Vy had bitten her. Earlier, she had visited the medical unit where a nurse had disinfected the area and covered the bite with a bandage. She had also changed out of her wet clothes before coming to the commander's office.

Her standard uniform didn't feel right on her skin. The fitted collared shirt and cargo pants were constricting and uncomfortable—likely because it felt wrong to wear them. Petra no longer belonged. She was a traitor.

Not only had she agreed to work with a lightless, but she'd been enlightened too. She no longer bought into the narrative that the only good lightless was a dead one. Lightless didn't mean souless. Or, at least, Vy didn't fit that brief.

At the thought of Vy, Petra sighed and rubbed her eyes. Her chest was achy and heavy, and she didn't want to unpack why it felt that way.

Olivia continued staring at her, and the weight of her gaze was an irritant. The clapping of her mouth seemed louder. She popped a very big bubble.

Petra exploded. "Why the fuck are you looking at me?"

"I am trying to make sense of it all," Olivia said with a smirk. "The math isn't mathing."

"What the fuck does that even mean?"

"It means that I'm not buying your bullshit," Olivia replied, withdrawing the ball of gum from her mouth and sticking it underneath the desk.

Petra's jaw clenched. She knew her story wasn't as tight as it could be, but there was no changing it now.

About an hour earlier, before she'd been afforded the opportunity to change into dry clothes, Bowmaster had asked how Petra had ended up halfway around the world.

Petra had responded that the fang had been holding her hostage and had gotten a hopper to teleport them to Japan. When Bowmaster had asked what for, she'd told him that she didn't know why. At that point, Olivia had interjected, wanting to know how they'd happened upon Petra in the cemetery with her gun aiming down the illblood. Petra's reply had been short. "I saw an opening to escape, and I went for it."

When Olivia had tried to push for more information, Petra had ignored her.

Bowmaster, Ferguson, and Mambwe seemed to believe her. They didn't seem to care that her story was vague. Petra could only hope that the commander bought her retelling of events and didn't go hunting for specifics.

Olivia's fingers rapped on the white desktop. She opened her mouth to say something but closed it when the door to the commander's office opened.

Clay walked in, and everyone but Olivia rose to their feet to salute her.

The commander's gaze swept over Petra and narrowed on Olivia. "What have I told you about sitting on my desk?"

"My bad." Olivia hopped off. "I forgot."

"You seem to be forgetting a lot of things," Clay said.

Olivia smirked. "Only the things that don't matter."

The tension between Olivia and the commander was palpable.

"Leave—all of you, except Malkovitch." The commander's lips thinned into a flat line of annoyance as she walked behind her desk. "Olivia, don't go far. After I speak with Malkovitch, we need to have a discussion."

Olivia rolled her eyes and started for the door. Her unlaced boots thunked as she walked away.

Soon, Petra was alone with Clay, and she felt like a kid being brought to the principal after committing the worst schoolyard offence. Could Clay sense that Petra was a traitor?

The commander gestured for Petra to sit back down, and so she did, resting her arms on the armrest and leaning back into the seat.

Clay's blue eyes fixed on her face. They seemed icier than usual. In fact, the commander's whole demeanor seemed off—colder.

Where Olivia's stare had been annoying, Clay's was penetrating. Petra began to fidget, her nails scratching the white fabric of the armrests.

The commander cleared her throat and at last spoke. "I remember the day I found you in that park. I hadn't seen the point in recruiting you. You were such a scrawny and pretty thing. I didn't think you had what it took to become an SOL." Clay shook her head. "But you proved me wrong. You shattered my expectations, and I saw you going very far in this organization."

She did? Petra went very still.

The commander moved away from the desk, her long legs taking her to the panel of windows that overlooked the base. It was early in the evening, and the sky was a blend of blues and pinks and purples.

Petra stared at Clay's back as she waited for more words to fill the silence. She wanted the commander to get to the point so she could climb into her bunk and curl into the fetal position.

The last twenty-four hours had done a number on her, and Petra wasn't sure she'd ever really recover from having her newfound hopes dashed away. For a while, she'd really come to believe in the power of the hourglass and Vy's promise of a new reality. She was a fool.

"But the moment you went against my directive and tried to kill the illblood, you demonstrated that you have no loyalty to the Order or to me," Clay said, turning away from the scenery to face Petra. She crossed her arms over her chest. "I think I always knew this, but I needed to see it for myself."

"You set me up. Why?" Petra asked.

"Isn't that the question," Clay said. "The short answer is that I have plans, and I need strong and trustworthy people at my side. It'd been my hope to mentor you."

"Mentor me," Petra repeated, feeling the weight of the words on her tongue. She'd always admired the commander, and it was a shock to know that Clay had regarded her so highly. The realization made her treachery feel even worse.

"But I will not mentor someone who lies to my face," the commander continued, shaking her head. "I cannot reward insubordination."

"I understand."

"Of course you do." Clay snorted. "Tell me, how is it that you arrived in Japan?"

Petra rehearsed the same story she had fed to Bowmaster and the others, praying that the commander wasn't as critical as Olivia.

To her luck, Clay nodded her acceptance of the story and didn't probe. Instead, she moved to a different line of questioning. "Dustin tells me that the illblood had been secured and that you had been driving back to the base. He says that he blinked and found himself lying in a ditch. He doesn't know how this happened. Can you shed any light on this?"

"No. Sorry," Petra replied, shaking her head. She was happy she didn't have to lie. It was still a mystery to her how Vy had managed to escape. Although she now suspected that magic was involved.

"I guess that is to be expected," Clay said. She made her way back towards the desk and leaned against the edge nearest to Petra. Sighing, the commander rubbed her chin and then set her large hands down on her knees. "It's such a shame. You have such promise, but I cannot swear you in as an SOL at this time."

Even though Petra didn't have the right to feel upset, she felt a twinge of it. If she wasn't to be an SOL, what was to be her fate? Dustin had inferred that insubordination wasn't taken lightly.

With her next words, Clay explained what was to be done with her. "For the next year, your post will be in the cellblocks where you will operate the control room. Your first shift will begin tomorrow night."

Petra frowned. "The cellblocks control room," she repeated with dismay. It was the most insulting of posts. There was no real purpose to a job that consisted of monitoring cameras and opening doors.

Petra, who had ranked highest in her class year after year, was too ambitious and too proud for such an assignment. Clay must know that, and so it was the perfect punishment.

Still, working in the cellblocks didn't sit well with Petra. But she didn't have a say. She'd made her bed, and now she'd have to lie in it—for an entire year.

Petra could already anticipate how the news would be taken by her peers. They'd revel at the situation. She knew how much they resented her for how well she'd done in training, and she wasn't looking forward to being the butt of their jokes.

"You should be grateful that I am only giving you a year there," Clay said, pulling Petra from her thoughts. "If you were anyone else, I would have you ousted from the Order. But you are skilled, and so I will give you another chance to prove yourself."

"You set me up, and now I am being punished for acting just as you knew I would," Petra said, gritting her teeth. "Doesn't seem fair."

"Life's not fair," Clay said, rising off the desk. There was a sorrowful look in her blue eyes. "The worst part is that if you had only followed my orders, I would have given you exactly what you wanted. If you only brought the illblood back as directed, I would have let you kill her in any way your vengeful heart desired. Because I know how it feels to lose someone to lightless filth, and I know there's no better medicine than revenge."

Petra looked down at her lap. She didn't know how to respond.

"You can leave now," Clay said with a wave of her hand. "Tell Olivia to come back in."

Nodding, Petra rose to her feet and proceeded towards the door. She stepped outside the office and found Olivia leaning her back against the wall near the door.

"The great Malkovitch isn't so great no more," Olivia said with a cruel smirk as she pushed off the wall. "I've heard working in control is a riveting as watching paint dry. You're sure to love it."

Petra's hands clenched at her sides. She wanted to take a verbal shot at Olivia, but her mind was working too slow for a comeback.

Olivia bumped her as she moved to enter the office, but Petra's hand clamped down on her wrist, preventing her. "Get your fucking hand off me," Olivia said.

Petra didn't. Instead, she squeezed.

"I can see you're dying for round three. But now's not the time." Olivia twisted her wrist in the direction of Petra's thumb and yanked her arm away to break the hold.

She blew Petra a kiss as she disappeared behind the office door.

Chapter Twenty-Seven

Were she a sack of potatoes, Vy felt the Order would have handled her with more care. It didn't matter that she was a sentient and feeling being; she was not human, and that alone justified being shoved, tossed, and kicked. It justified having her dress torn from her body and having a hose turned on her, its frigid spray pelting against her skin like a rain of thin needles. It justified being shocked by the collar and subsequently struck in the face when she struggled against the two female SOLs who worked to dress her in an oversize and itchy orange jumper.

Once the jumper was on, and Vy was fitted with a pair of laceless black shoes, they escorted her through a hallway so white that Vy's sensitive eyes, which preferred darkness, had to squint against the brightness.

Even with her legs and arms shackled, the female SOLs found it necessary to firmly grip Vy's upper arms as they paraded her through the building.

Vy's gaze darted in an effort to track their movements and gain further understanding of her predicament. Unfortunately, she couldn't lean on Dustin for any helpful information. Vy assumed she was in the cellblocks, and as a trainee, Dustin wasn't privy to what went on there.

There was an unsettling and sterile feeling to the institution.

It was very silent. The only sounds being the whizzing and slamming of mechanized doors, the distant rattling of keys, and the clacking of boots on floors.

They stopped at an elevator. One of Vy's chaperones scanned their security card and called for the lift. With a ding, the elevator doors opened, and Vy was nudged inside. The doors closed, and the lift rose with a creak before opening onto the fifth floor, which look identical to the floor they had left behind.

Vy was steered down a hallway, and then she was made to stand before a sallyport.

While they waited for the first door to open, Vy peered inside. She saw that they were about to enter some sort of lab.

On the other side of the thick glass and metal doors, bright overhead lights shone on a display of beakers, flasks, and tubes. An arrangement of desks and tables boasted thin computer monitors. A long shelf was completely stocked with nitrile glove cartons.

Were it not for the gag, Vy would have anxiously gnawed on her bottom lip. Were it not for the gag, she would have been able to escape.

Legend had it that there once existed spellcasters so powerful that they did not need to utter a word to manipulate magic, but Vy did not possess this ability, and she wouldn't even know where to start. To cast a spell, she needed to be able to speak.

One of Vy's escorts began tapping her foot. The woman had a mean look to her and had a temper to match—she'd been the one who had smacked Vy in the face earlier. "Those fucking goofs in control have one job," she said to her partner.

The other SOL, an older woman with thick glasses and cropped blond hair, shrugged. "In time, you'll learn to live and even accept their incompetence."

The younger SOL snorted and proceeded to stab an intercom button. "Open the doors, you lazy shits!"

An exasperated sigh escaped her partner's lips. "You shouldn't have done that, Maple. Now they won't let us in."

Maple rolled her eyes. "Whatever."

If Vy had to guess, maybe three minutes passed before the first door finally whirred open, allowing them to enter the enclosure. The first door glided and slammed close, but it took another two or three minutes for the second door to open.

As they waited, Maple's face grew redder. Vy found subtle pleasure in her irritation. But her dread for what was coming next didn't let her bask in the feeling.

When they were finally admitted into the lab, Maple turned towards the security camera and threw up a middle finger, which made the older SOL shake her head.

Vy was ushered over to an exam table in the middle of the room. Her body tensed.

"Fucking lightless—move!" Maple urged her forward. When Vy didn't budge, the neck collar activated and sent a burst of electric fire through her nerves. Vy yelped and her knees buckled. While Vy was still processing the pain, she was dragged over to the table and strapped down.

Vy heard the mechanized door whir open, and she turned her head towards it. The collar went off again, but the shock was not as bad as the first, so she bared it better.

A tall muscular woman stepped through the sallyport, and Vy recognized her immediately. It was Dustin's mother—the commander. Vy understood that Kayla was a formidable soldier. She had one of the best records in the organization. She was as cold as she was competent.

Dustin couldn't recall a single time she had hugged him or spared him a kind word. But that wasn't why he hated her. He hated her for killing Chief Minister Wu—the man who'd raised him.

Kayla strode into the lab with a stern expression. Maple and the older SOL saluted her, but Vy could tell their gesture had more to do with procedure rather than respect. The commander nodded her acknowledgement, and said, "You two can go now."

Vy's escorts followed the directive, heading for the sallyport. It took a long time for them to make their exit, likely because of Maple's earlier antics.

The commander came to stand over Vy. Her weathered and wrinkled face was set hard like cement. Her eyes were very blue and did not hint at what she was thinking. In some ways, she reminded Vy of Petra.

The thought of Petra made Vy frown. Her chest ached from the betrayal even as she knew that she had no right to feel that way. Of course, Petra had let the Order take her. She shouldn't be surprised.

Petra hated her. Petra wanted her dead. Petra had always made her intention known to Vy. But that didn't make Vy feel any less hurt over what had happened.

"So, you're what all the fuss is about," the commander said, meeting Vy's eyes. "You'd better be worth it."

Vy's eyes widened as she contemplated Kayla's words.

A door clicked open and a middle-aged man with greying hair, thick black glasses, and a neat goatee step into the lab. He wore a long white lab coat, a crisp white shirt, and black slacks.

She knew his name was Raz and that he had a special relationship with Olivia—a belligerent woman with whom Dustin slept with every now and then. Dustin didn't like Raz. Dustin felt that Raz hurt Olivia. There'd been several occasions where Dustin had disrobed Olivia to find her skin covered in bruises, but she was tight-lipped—she'd tell him it was none of his business.

Raz's eyes narrowed on the commander, and Vy noticed his jaw clench ever so slightly. "Clay," he said, checking his watch. "You already made your visit to the lab today."

"I came to see the illblood."

"And now that you have seen her, you may leave," he said curtly. "I have a lot of work to do."

The commander didn't budge.

Raz looked up at her. A glint of annoyance registered on his face.

"Just so you know, Olivia is banned from the lab. Control staff have been advised not to let her in."

"I've heard," Raz said through tight lips. "You shouldn't have done that."

"She went against my orders."

"She was cleaning up your mess." Snorting, the doctor walked towards a counter and grabbed a steel tray. A large syringe with a fine pointed needle was arranged on it along with a set of powder blue nitrile gloves and a vial containing a clear fluid. "You put my whole project at risk when you sent Malkovitch."

Kayla's nostrils flared. She didn't acknowledge the doctor's statement and changed the subject. "I want Olivia off this project. Do not test any new formulations of the serum on her."

A cart was positioned near the head of the examination table that Vy was strapped to. Raz slammed the steel tray down on the cart, making the vial topple over and bounce onto the floor with a clink. Raz cursed as he bent over to pick it up.

As Vy's luck would have it, the vial survived without a single scratch. She didn't want to be injected with whatever was in it.

"Confirm that you have heard me," Kayla said.

"You will not dictate how I run my experiments," Raz responded, jabbing his glasses up the bridge of his nose with an index finger. "Olivia has been crucial to my work. I will not cut her out."

"I've been pushed to my limit, and I am done playing nice," Kayla stated. "I am the commander. You will do as I say."

Raz's hands balled at his sides, and he stood very straight as he fixed Kayla with his darkest look. "I will not be bullied."

"I am not bullying you. I am telling you how it is," Kayla said. "Olivia is off the project. Her blood is tainted, and she is out of control."

"Is that so?"

"Yes," Kayla said. "SOTU members have been advised that they are to make themselves available to you. Test subjects will not be an issue."

"I need Olivia." The doctor angled his chin defiantly. "Without her, I will stop working on this project."

"Do that Raz," Kayla dared. "See if I don't destroy everything that you have created. See if I don't pull all your resources."

"You wouldn't."

"Are you willing to bet on it?"

"I know how much you hate them. You wouldn't pull the plug on this project," he said.

"I think the same could be said for yourself," Kayla countered. "At the end of the day, I have done everything you've asked. I have filled your impossible requests. I have stretched my budget to accommodate your research. And now that you have all that you need, you will stabilize the serum, and you will do it without Olivia."

Raz gritted his teeth.

"Confirm that you have heard me."

"I have heard you," he said stiffly.

"Good." Kayla crossed her arms. If she was happy about the outcome of their exchange, Vy couldn't tell.

It didn't escape Vy that this was a conversation not meant to be overheard. The fact that Kayla indulged in such a discussion in

Vy's presence was worrying. It meant they didn't care if she was a witness. Did that mean that she wouldn't be around long enough for it to matter? Or did they intend to keep her gagged for the rest of her unhuman life?

Vy wondered about the serum. What did it do, and why was it so important to Kayla and Raz?

Raz snapped on a pair of blue nitrile gloves, and Vy flinched. Hovering over the examination table, Kayla stared at Vy like she was dog crap embedded in the treads of her combat boots. Being an illblood, it was a look Vy had grown accustomed to. It was the same look Poppy and several other spellcasters had given her. It was a look Petra had often displayed.

Vy's thoughts were interrupted when gloved hands suddenly pressed against her cheeks, jaw, and chin before moving to feel the pulse at her neck.

Raz's fingers trailed lower, examining every square inch of her body. His touch was surgical and rushed. Vy contemplated whether every unhuman that was brought to him had to endure such treatment.

The doctor moved away from her to write something down on a chart, and then he picked up the vial and shook it. Grabbing the syringe, he flicked off the needle cap and proceeded to fill up the barrel.

Raz stepped forward and bent over the examination table. The tip of the needle was a breath away from Vy's left ear, and she shrank back, making the collar buzz painfully. Vy squeezed her eyes shut.

"Don't worry. It'll only be a prick." Raz said to her in a tone that was soft and lacked the bite she'd noticed during his exchange with

Kayla. "This is a strong sedative that I have developed for the use on lightless. I have plans for you, but I promise you won't feel a thing."

The needle was pushed into Vy's neck, and the contents of the syringe burned as they were plunged into her system. Vy couldn't dwell on the discomfort. Before she knew it, she was unconscious.

Chapter Twenty-Eight

Petra bolted awake, breathing heavily. Sweat drenched her shirt and the bedsheets.

She'd had a nightmare.

Her eyes darted to the large wall mounted clock—it was 1833hrs. In less than four and a half hours, she would start her first shift in control. She was not looking forward to it.

Her mind was still reeling from the vividness of her dream.

In her dream, she had been back at the cemetery, but a different scenario had played out—instead of letting SOTU take Vy, Petra fought against her brethren in a Mortal Combat style fight.

Petra managed to defeat Ferguson, and then Mambwe, and then Bowmaster. Olivia was supposed to be the final boss, but then the Commander showed up.

"You're a fucking traitor," Clay had said before squeezing the trigger and unloading an entire M16 clip into Petra's body.

Sitting upright in her tiny bunk, Petra tried to shake off the nightmare.

Hopelessness sat heavy in her chest, and Petra felt like she was sinking. Ten years ago, on that cold winter night, she had felt the same.

In a way, it made sense. Though the situation was different, she was losing her mother all over again, and she wished she knew what to do.

Petra had mulled over her options for hours. All were difficult. There was no winning.

Her first option was to live out her days with the Order until retirement. It was the least appealing choice because she knew that she'd forever be haunted by the question she hated most, "what if?"

In the second option, Petra found a way to break Vy out. But there were several unknowns and problems. Would Vy even agree to team up again? Or would Vy turn on her?

Petra also wasn't sure she had it in herself to betray the commander again. She didn't like feeling like a traitor, and she felt an obligation to repent for her previous treachery.

Sure, her worldview was no longer aligned with the Order's, but that didn't change the fact that the organization had taken her in. It had trained her. It had fed her. It had become her home.

Sighing, Petra laid back down on the mattress and stared up at the ceiling. She wondered how long she had to make a decision. Without knowing what went on in the cellblocks, it was impossible to know. Maybe Vy was already dead and the choice had already been made for her.

The thought that Vy might be dead made Petra's heart sink deeper into the abyss of her hopelessness.

Sighing, Petra shook her head.

Deciding that there was no way she would be able to go back to sleep, she swung her legs over the bunk and hopped down—her bare feet hitting the cold white floor.

As it was dinner hour, she was alone in the barracks. Twenty-three bunks were neatly made up, and Petra proceeded to make her bed up too.

Once the corners were all neatly folded and tucked, Petra removed her damp shirt and opened her laundry bag. Her eyes caught sight of the rain-drenched black shirt and jacket Vy had bought her. She brought her fingers to the jacket and gently rubbed the material.

Petra remembered putting the items on back at the Ginza hotel. Looking at her reflection, she had thought Vy right—she had looked kinda hot. The shirt and the jacket had fit her like a glove, and the cut of the clothes gave her the appearance of a Marvel superhero or villain. Her shoulders had looked broader, while her waist had looked tapered.

When Vy had seen her in the new clothes, Vy's expression had been pleased, but also ravenous. Petra recalled how she had felt branded by the fang's heated gaze. In that moment, she had told herself that she hadn't liked being eye-fucked by Vy, but there was no point in being dishonest with herself anymore. Petra had liked the way Vy had looked at her.

Back at the hotel in Ginza, she had also wanted Vy in the worst way. How could she not have? Vy had exited her hotel room, entering the hallway in that strapless black dress with her jacket slung over a shoulder, and she'd been so beautiful. Petra had been so angry at herself for desiring the fang.

Petra was still annoyed with herself for not being able to tamp down the part of herself that wanted to be with Vy in that way.

Tossing her sweat-drenched shirt into the laundry bag, Petra went to her locker. She pulled out and donned her standard uniform—a crisp white collared shirt that snuggly fit over her chest and biceps, and a pair of grey tactical pants that she bloused over black boots that were polished to shine.

Petra exited the female living quarters building and walked out into the cool evening breeze.

As she passed the chapel, heading for the main building, she noticed a few stares directed her way, subsequently followed by intense whispering and some giggling. Petra clenched her jaw.

The rumour mill was greased and running at full speed. The word was out, and everybody knew. Her peers were taking great delight in Petra's assignment to the cellblocks control module for a year.

Petra's embarrassment stung, and her face coloured as she continued to advance towards the main building.

Petra wasn't sure what was more discomforting—that she had been knocked off her pedestal or that her mind was still treacherous.

She thought over her options again, and she thought about Vy. She wondered if Vy was all right. She wondered if Vy's capture had solely been to test Petra, or if there was an alternate reason for her being brought back to the base.

Pulling open a door, Petra stepped into the main building.

She wasn't hungry, but she decided that she could at least try to eat something before her shift.

When Petra got to the cafeteria, she grabbed a tray and a plate before taking a spot in the line.

The room was alive with chatter, and it appeared to Petra that she was the main topic. Trainees, SOLs, and sergeants openly gawked at her. Hell, even the kitchen staff had the audacity to eye her strangely as they spooned slop on her plate.

Petra tried to ignore everyone as she took a seat at an empty table near the back. Grabbing her fork, she began moving the lumpy brown meat mixture around.

In the past, she'd not given a second thought to the unappetizing food fare. But now, she wasn't sure she had the stomach for the shit on her plate—her tastebuds yearned for another bowl of ramen from the joint in Shibuya.

Petra recalled how quiet and shaken the fang had been at the noodle shop, and it still surprised her that a lightless could be terrified by something as menial as a cockroach. Then again, what kind of mother locked a five-year-old in a room crawling with bugs?

Petra had a few choice words for Vy's mother.

As Petra continued to absently play with her food, her thoughts again became consumed with Vy.

She had questions about Vy's upbringing—about her mother's unconventional training practices. Petra also wanted to know how Vy became a fang without dying. From what she knew, there was no such thing as a naturally born vampire. If Petra was to believe her,

Vy just woke up one day with fangs.

"Malkovitch!"

Petra looked up from her plate and saw Dustin. She'd heard that the commander had passed him through his final. He was now an SOL. Her teeth gritted.

"I am glad to see you are okay," he said, smiling brightly. "I was … I was really worried about you."

Petra didn't say anything.

"Look, I get it, you probably hate me." Dustin nervously rubbed the back of his neck.

"I'm not in the mood for this discussion right now."

Dustin's smile faltered. "I get that," he said with a slow nod. "All the same, I am glad to see you back." He left her then, walking away with slumped shoulders.

Deciding that she wasn't going to eat, Petra stood up and ridded herself of her tray. As she exited the dining hall, she felt the weight of eyes on her back.

Seeking some form of solace, Petra headed over to the gym.

As it was the peak of dinner time, the fitness centre was near empty. There was a group of SOLs sparring on the mats.

Upon Petra's entrance, they paused, exchanged words with each other, and then began laughing. Petra turned her gaze away from them.

Petra's gym routine always began with a ten-kilometre run on the treadmill, which she usually completed in under forty minutes. That afternoon, however, she clocked in what had to be her worst time in years, forty-two minutes.

Dialling the machine down to a slow pace, she wiped the sweat from her brow and took a swig of water from her bottle. Her gaze hovered over the fitness equipment. In that moment, she couldn't fathom completing a strength training circuit. She was demotivated.

The run hadn't helped calm her mind, and she doubted strength training would help.

Just then Khan entered the gymnasium. They locked eyes almost immediately, and Khan headed towards the row of treadmills.

"Malkovitch," Khan greeted in a flat tone that was unusual for her.

"Hey," Petra replied, stopping the machine and taking another sip from her bottle. Screwing the lid back on, she stepped off the treadmill and looked blankly at her peer. There was a dark bruise around her eye, where Petra had hit her during their last sparring session.

"I heard what happened." Khan tucked a locked of dark hair behind her ear. "For what it is worth, I would have done the same thing," she said.

"Done what?"

"Tried to kill the fang," she replied. "It's fucked up that Clay set you up that way."

"It is what it is." Petra shrugged. "I assume you passed your final."

Khan's gaze fell to the floor. "I wasn't given a final," she mumbled.

Petra frowned with confusion. "What?"

"Apparently, I am too smart for my own good and my assistance in the lab is critical to Raz's research." Khan's hands balled into fists at her side.

"I'm sorry, Khan," Petra said, meaning it. Sure, Khan wasn't the best at combat, but Petra knew how much she'd wanted to be an SOL. "That's really shitty."

"Yeah," A sad chuckled escaped her lips. "And it doesn't help that the cellblocks are worse than I ever imagined."

"How's that?" Petra sat on a bench and wiped the sweat from her face with a towel.

"I'm not supposed to say anything. You don't have lab clearance, and I'm bound by confidentiality," Khan stated, crossing her arms. She shot a look over her shoulder and stared at the retreating group who were done sparring on the mats. When they exited the gym, Khan turned her attention back on Petra and said, "But I don't care. I need to vent."

"I'm all ears, and you know I won't say anything," Petra said.

Khan took a seat beside her on the bench, and their legs brushed. In the past, whenever they'd touched, Petra had always felt a jolt, but she didn't at that moment. Whatever romantic interest she'd harboured for Khan was gone.

A loud sigh escaped Khan's mouth, and then she said, "I always wondered what kept the lights running. Like, an operation like this must cost a fortune."

Petra nodded. She had often wondered the same.

"I know now," Khan said. Her body stiffened, and her dramatic eyebrows drew together. "Today I had the pleasure of assisting with draining a fang and removing its teeth."

"Draining?" Petra repeated. Her heart stopped. "Was it the illblood?"

Khan shook her head. "Nope—it was a male fang that was recently brought in by some trainees for their final. Word on the street is that Raz is running tests on the illblood."

Intense relief flooded Petra system. "What kind of test?"

"Dunno," Khan said. "But Raz is working on a secret project, and only SOTU and the commander know what it's about."

"This organization loves to keep us in the dark," Petra said, taking another swig of water. "Is draining what I think it is?"

"Yes," Khan confirmed with a nod. "Fang blood fetches a pretty penny on the black market apparently. But I've been told that fang teeth are worth more."

Petra grimaced. "The Order sells fang blood and teeth?"

"Not just that—pelts from beasts and horns cut off from demons. But it's even worse than that, sometimes live lightless are sold at auction," Khan said bitterly. "Clarks, who has worked down in the cellblocks longer than anybody, told me that there are gambling circles for captive lightless fighting matches."

"So, we are like lightless traffickers?"

"Not us. Clay doesn't sell livestock. But the other regions do."

Petra snorted. "It's sick."

"It is." Khan nodded her agreement. She sighed again and looked down at her hands. "I wish that was it." She began to tremble, and Petra wasn't sure if it was from anger or sadness. There were tears in her eyes, but her mouth was set tightly.

Instinctively, Petra wrapped a supporting arm around her

comrade's shoulder. "What is it?"

Khan sniffled. "The guards in the cellblocks are fucking pigs."

"What'd they do to you?" Petra's brows pinched together.

"Nothing," Khan said, wiping her eyes. "I just overheard something, and I ..."

"You what?"

"Forget I said anything." She shook her head.

Petra's grip on Khan's shoulder tightened. "No, tell me. I want to know."

"You probably do," Khan agreed. "But I don't want to hear you say that the illblood deserves it. Nobody deserves it. Not even lightless filth."

Vy? Petra stilled. "Deserves what?" she said, her tone stronger than she meant it to be.

Khan met her eyes. "I always thought we were the good guys. How many times were we told that we are the champions of the Light destined to eviscerate the Darkness?" Cold laughter escaped Khan's lips as she bent over and massaged her temples.

"Tell me what you overheard," Petra said, trying her best to sound compassionate even as she wanted to shake the words out of Khan.

"The guards talk. They talk about things they want to do—things they've done," Khan said. "Let's just say that there have been a lot of pretty lightless women locked up and sedated out of their minds."

Petra felt a tightness in her chest. She hadn't thought her heart could sink further. "Have they touched her?" she asked through gritted teeth, her tone guttural.

Khan looked up at her with surprise. "I don't think so ... I just heard them saying what they'd like to—"

"You need to report what you heard." Petra snapped.

"Already did. I wrote up Officer Green." Khan snorted. "But Raz thinks I am making shit up to get reassigned. Everyone knows that I am pissed about being assigned to the lab."

"That's fucked up."

Khan nodded. "I am thinking about quitting."

Petra's eyes widened. It was common for trainees to drop out of the SOL program. In such cases, the Order would see their memories wiped, and they'd be plopped back into the real world dazed and confused. But someone leaving the organization after serving over ten years was almost unheard of.

"You have to do what you think is right for you." Petra found herself saying.

"Yeah." Khan smiled sadly, and then she moved closer to Petra. Arching her head up, she brushed her lips over Petra's gently. She pulled away from Petra and stood up. "I've wanted to do that for years," she said, looking nervous.

Petra almost said, "Me too," but she didn't. Instead she said, "Why now?"

"Nothing seems to matter anymore," she said, turning away and walking out of the gym.

At 2255hrs, Petra showed up to control for her first shift and was buzzed into the small room by Gladwell.

That she was being scheduled for a graveyard shift was not surprising. Seniority counted for something in the Order. Newbies got the hours no one else wanted.

Petra entered and nodded at the two officers inside.

Gladwell wheeled his chair around to face her and to return her salutation, but Rogers didn't budge. The older man had made a makeshift lounger for himself between two chairs. His eyes were closed, and his hands rested comfortably on his stomach.

"Did you want me to review the controls with you?" Gladwell asked her with a smile.

"No need, I recall from training."

Gladwell rose from his seat and stretched. He leaned over and jostled his partner's shoulder. "Relief is here. Time to go."

Rogers yawned and blinked his eyes opened. "About time," he said. The older man stood up and yawned again. Then, his eyes narrowed on Petra with confusion. "What the hell is she doing here? Ain't this Malkovitch—the apple of Clay's fucking eye?"

Petra crossed her arms over her chest. "I failed my final."

"How the fuck did you do that?"

"Insubordination apparently."

"Well, that would do it." Rogers sniffled and wiped his nose with the back of his hand. "An ambitious one like you … I am not sure you'll enjoy it up here in control. There's not much to do, especially at night. But then, you can always sleep. If someone needs you to open the door, they'll press the intercom button, which will alert you."

When Petra didn't respond, Rogers grunted and headed for the door.

"You sure that you don't want me to run through the screens and icons with you?" Gladwell asked.

Petra shook her head. "There's no need."

Nodding, Gladwell signed himself out of the system and handed Petra the emergency key. "I think Connors will be providing you with your break later. From what I know, he usually swings by the module around 0400hours."

Petra signaled that she understood.

"Well, have a good shift," Gladwell stated, heading over to the door where Rogers waited.

Petra buzzed them out, and she observed their departure from the cellblocks building on one of the many visual displays, which broadcasted camera footage.

The control room was not that big of a space—a large curved desk and giant computer screens overwhelmed it. Each screen had a layout of thirty-six frames, displayed in a six-by-six format. However, it was not a fixed setting, and the displays could be customized to the control officer's preference.

The room was warm to the point of discomfort. The radiant heat emanating from computers was partly to blame, but the air circulation was also horrendous.

With a sigh, Petra grabbed a chair with a mesh back and wheeled it towards the desk. She took a seat and scanned the camera frames. She spotted a guard walking towards a door, and she opened it.

When he had passed through, she closed it.

Another sigh escaped her lips. She wasn't sure how she would last a year in there.

Her eyes roamed the displays, and her breath caught when she happened upon the footage of Vy's cell.

The fang was curled up on the thin pad that was meant to be a mattress. She appeared to be sleeping.

Petra clicked on the frame and made the footage bigger. Her eyes lingered on Vy's face, and she knew with certainty what path she would take.

Chapter Twenty-Nine

Olivia laid on the patch of grass behind the main building. With her hands behind her head, she gazed up at the stars and desperately hoped she'd be able to quiet the thoughts in her mind and sleep.

Usually, she spent her nights in Raz's office, where she would watch sitcoms, and she'd be able to drift off for a few hours. But the bitch commander had banned her from the lab.

Olivia had tried her luck, but fucking Malkovitch was up in control and had denied her entrance. *Fucking Malkovitch.*

It had been years since Olivia had slept outdoors. When she had first arrived on the base, she had always slept outside if the weather permitted. Back then, she had found the barracks stifling, and it had been impossible to rest in a room with twenty-three girls, many of whom snored and farted under their sheets.

Leaving the barracks after curfew was against the base guidelines, but Olivia had never been one to follow rules. She had first met Raz while making her exit one night.

When he saw her, he had smiled, and before Olivia knew it, they were deep in discussion. He had asked her about her story, and surprisingly, Olivia had spilled everything.

She'd told him that her mother killed herself months after being exiled from the pack—an outcome that was quite common for lone wolves. Olivia had fully expected Raz to recoil at hearing that she was the product of a human and beast copulation, but he hadn't.

If anything, he'd seemed empathetic, and when he had said, "I'm sorry," Olivia had believed him.

In response, Olivia had shrugged sadly. "It is what it is—though I can't say I understand why she did it. Being alone is not so bad."

"It's different for beasts, especially wolves," Raz had said. "They are not meant to be alone."

"I am happy I am not one," Olivia had said. "Then again, if I was, my mother would be alive."

"How's that?" Raz had asked.

"When I hit fifteen years old and still hadn't changed, my father realized that I wasn't his, and that I must be part human. He had my mother kicked out of the pack shortly after," Olivia had responded. "I hate him. I hate them all. I want to kill them all."

"Maybe one day you can," Raz had said, looking down at her. Behind his thick black glasses, his eyes had been warm and kind.

To this day, Olivia wasn't sure why she had told him, but it had been the right decision. Their friendship began that night, and soon they spent many nights talking.

Raz would bring her to the lab, and he'd often give her an Oh

Henry! chocolate bar or some other snack. When he couldn't talk, because he needed to finish work on something, he had granted Olivia access to his office, telling her that she could play on the computer. And so it went for years.

No one understood Olivia the way Raz did, and Olivia felt that she knew Raz better than anyone. He was a sad and determined man. She knew that he felt a sort of kinship for Olivia because she reminded him of his little sister, who had passed away long ago. Olivia knew that his sister had been killed by some spellcasters for a reason Raz kept to himself.

Raz hated all lightless, but he especially despised spellcasters. Like many who joined the Order, Raz sought to avenge a loved one. It was why he was so devoted to his research. It was why he was so committed to the development of the serum that had the potential to finally put humans on the same level as lightless.

Olivia reached into her pocket and removed the capped syringe that Raz had handed her that morning behind the main building, away from prying eyes. "It's done," he had said, smiling brightly. "I believe it is stable now—the pressures on the body should not be as harsh."

"Congratulations," Olivia had said, beaming at him and then hugging him. "You've been working on this for years. I can't wait to test it out."

"I was thinking you could use it when they deploy you for your next assignment," He had said, pulling away from her embrace. "When are you off of light duties?"

"Who the fuck knows? Clay has a giant stick up her ass where I am concerned. I still can't believe she banned me from the lab—all because I went to retrieve the illblood." Olivia had let out a snort. "She should have never sent Malkovitch in the first place."

"Yes, Clay has been notably brusque lately. Though, I agreed with her that you needed to recover. Now, she is just being irrational. You are my best tester. You need to be a part of this," Raz had said, pushing his glasses up the bridge of his nose. "Well, when you do have the opportunity to test it, let me know. In the meantime, make sure you hide it."

Olivia had agreed, and they had parted ways.

Sitting up from the grass, Olivia observed the syringe. The fluid within it was an iridescent green, and it glowed subtly in the night.

Olivia had almost died the last time she had taken the serum. She'd had a heart attack, and Raz had had to resuscitate her. Ever since, she still suffered some pains in her chest, and her body was covered in bruises. Her legs looked and hurt the worst. She was good at ignoring her pain though. Besides moving a little slower, Olivia gave nothing else away.

In the grand scheme of things, a heart attack was nothing. Olivia didn't care if she had another. Frankly, she didn't care if she died, if it meant that Raz succeeded in his endeavour as his dreams had become her own.

Olivia slipped the syringe back into her pocket and nestled back down on the grass. She closed her eyes and willed herself to sleep, but sleep wouldn't come.

Thoughts of Malkovitch buzzed in her head. Something was off. Olivia had picked up on it the moment the hopper had teleported them all back to the base. And when she replayed the events at the Japanese cemetery, it became even more apparent that the math was indeed not mathing.

At the same time, what she had deduced could not possibly be true. There was no possible way that Malkovitch could have feelings for the fang who slew her mother. But then, there was no other explanation for the look that had been on Petra's face.

And Olivia wasn't buying the bullshit tale Petra was spinning. It was too sparse. There were holes that needed filling. Even so, she wasn't sure what the truth could even be. Though her leading theory was that the illblood had bewitched Malkovitch somehow.

Olivia had flagged her concerns to Clay, but the commander ignored them. When it came to Malkovitch, the commander seemingly lost all ability to reason.

Olivia rubbed her eyes. *Fucking Malkovitch.*

Standing to her feet, Olivia stretched her hands over her head and yawned. Restless, she began walking.

Making her way around the main building, her boots felt weighted. Every step took effort. Her knees hurt—the joints were stiff.

Heading south towards the cellblocks, the gravel crunched under her boots. The night was quiet, but dark it was not. The base was kept well-lit at night.

Lampposts decorated the ringed road. Spotlights highlighted the front, side, and rear elevations of all buildings. Though, it was the chapel that shone brightest.

As Olivia approached the place of worship, its front door opened and out stepped Clay Junior.

Their eyes met.

Olivia smirked. Dustin looked away.

Such an encounter was not rare. There had been many nights when they happened upon each other. Olivia often walked the grounds at night, and Dustin was quite the night owl. He often spent long hours at the church. Olivia didn't know what he did in there—she didn't care enough to ask.

"Fancy seeing you out here," she said, casually shoving her hands in her pockets.

"Olivia—I can't tonight."

"If I recall, you owe me for picking you up from the side of the road."

Dustin sighed. "I haven't forgotten."

"Why do you always have to act like you don't want to be with me?" Olivia chimed before saying, "You know, Sergeant Parker recently retired so her room is empty."

Dustin's face coloured.

"Or, we can always fuck on the dais again," Olivia said, cocking her head towards the chapel.

Dustin's face reddened further, but there was also something glinting in his eyes—something that looked like anger.

While Olivia pretty much hated everyone, she had come to tolerate Dustin. He was different from everyone else—he was too good. Maybe that was why she was drawn to him. He was kind, almost like Dr. Raz, but he was her age.

Olivia turned and headed for the barracks. "So, are you coming or what?" she called when she didn't hear Dustin move.

"I'm not in the right head space," he said.

"I'm not either, but it isn't every day that there's an empty room to defile."

When he chuckled, Olivia knew that she had won him over. He began following her.

They walked towards the two long rectangular structures that were built closely to each other. One housed the women, and the other housed the men.

Together, they entered the building allocated to female personnel.

Three floors made up the barracks. Trainees lived on the first floor, SOLs lived on the second floor, and sergeants and the deputy commanders were on the third floor.

As it was well past midnight, the halls were empty. In silence, Olivia and Dustin climbed the staircase.

Upon reaching the highest landing, Olivia interlaced her fingers with Dustin's and guided him to Parker's old room. She picked the lock and swung open the door.

Once inside, Olivia shut the door and threw herself down on the firm mattress. When Dustin joined her, she tussled his soft blond hair with her hand. "Anyone ever tell you that you're so pretty you look gay."

"Yes, you have," Dustin mumbled. "Anyone ever tell you that you need a filter?"

"Yes, everyone."

Dustin laughed.

Olivia leaned over and kissed him. He kissed her back. It was nothing amazing, but it was nice.

Olivia was hoping that any release from orgasm would help her sleep. But they didn't get that far. Dustin pulled away from her the moment her pants were slid down.

"What is that sick fuck doing to you?" Dustin said through clenched teeth. He rolled off her and sat up in the bed.

Olivia knew Dustin was referring to Dr. Raz. "Nothing that I haven't signed up for," she said with a shrug. "Why does this always have to be an issue?"

He threw up his hands. "And what exactly is it that you have signed up for?"

"You don't have the clearance for me to tell you."

"When did you start caring about rules?" he asked. "Does my mother know?"

"You know I love it when you talk about your mother when my pants are down," Olivia chirped. "Of course, Clay knows. She knows everything."

Dustin stared at her. Olivia stared right back.

Just then, there was a buzzing. It was his phone. Dustin reached into his pocket and looked at the screen. He went very still and then smiled dumbly. Olivia guessed who the caller was. It was the smile that gave it away. *Of course, she would be calling him at this very moment.*

"I know you are dying to take the call. Don't hold off because of me," Olivia said, looking down at her fingers to inspect her nails.

Dustin didn't hesitate a second more. He took the call, bringing the phone to his ear. "Hey … yeah, sure … no problem. I will be there soon."

Olivia folded her arms over her chest. "What the fuck does Malkovitch want?"

"She needs to be relieved for a bit. Makes sense. She is new to the graveyard shift."

Olivia arched a brow. "I am sure there is someone assigned to give her a break at some point during her shift. You shouldn't have to."

"Seriously, Olivia, I'm not interested in hearing it."

"Whatever, just go." Olivia waved for him to go, and he did.

She felt an urge to follow him.

Chapter Thirty

The sedative was crushing. Vy couldn't lift a finger—she couldn't feel her fingers. But if she focused hard enough, she could crack her eyes open.

Whenever she did, the brightness of the room had her cursing internally. Her eyes were too sensitive. Her head spun. She couldn't think clearly. Somewhere a voice called for her to sleep.

Vy didn't want to heed the call, but she was quickly losing the battle against the heaviness. Unwillingly, she let go and fell.

For a second everything went dark. Then, there was light. Everywhere around her was white, and the flat plane seemed to go on forever.

Vy stood up and began to walk in vast emptiness. As she progressed towards no end, she felt adrift and aimless like a raft lost at sea.

There was so much space, but the environment was oddly

claustrophobic. Vy hugged herself as she stopped to examine the void. "Where the fuck am I?"

"You are exactly where you need to be," someone said, making her jump from the unexpectedness of the reply.

Vy whirled around to find a man sitting cross-legged on the floor. He was handsome with a strong jawline dotted with stubble. His black eyes were intense, and his long black hair was pulled back into a tight bun. He wore a white-collared dress shirt tucked into a pair of jeans and a pair of black and white Adidas. She recognized him instantly.

"Itachi?"

The man nodded with a grin.

Vy's feet shuffled towards him. "How am I exactly where I need to be?"

"Your choices led you here. This is exactly where you should be right now."

Vy frowned and gestured around her. "And where exactly is this?"

He smirked. "I am surprised you do not know, considering your propensity to barge into such a sacred place when it belongs to another."

Vy blinked. "I'm inside my soul?"

"Not inside—merely seeing into it."

"I am not sure I understand. Why are you here? Or maybe the better question is: how are you here?"

"I see your mother has taught you nothing," he said with a laugh.

Vy's brows drew together. "My mother? You knew her?" She

sat down on the floor just opposite him and drew her knees into her chest.

Itachi's expression grew somber. "Yes, I *knew* your mother very well. You could even say we were friends."

"My mother has no friends," Vy scoffed. She eyed Itachi suspiciously. "She never mentioned you to me."

"She wouldn't," he said.

With an answer like that, maybe he did know Camellia well. Her mother had always made a point of keeping the past in the past. "You didn't answer my question. How are you here?"

"That spell is a two-way door. When you open the door to someone's soul, you also open a path into your own. I decided to enter. We are connected until I decide to leave," he replied. "I am surprised Camellia never mentioned this to you."

Vy was surprised as well. She wondered what else her mother had kept from her. Looking at Itachi, she had a million questions for him.

As if reading her mind, he said, "Your time with me is limited. After all these years in limbo, I am tired. I want to finally find peace. I will only answer three of your questions. So, think wisely," he warned before adding, "and I have a favour to ask of you as well."

Vy nodded. "Sure, of course."

"When you see Camellia, let her know that I understand," he said. "You can tell her that I forgive her."

"What did she do?" Vy blurted.

"She betrayed me," he replied curtly. "You have two more questions."

Vy cursed herself. She needed to think before she spoke. She considered her options and then decided to ask, "What do you know about the Architect's hourglass?"

"I know that it is not an hourglass and that it has taken on many forms. I know that it was lost for some time. I know that your mother sought it and found it. I know that it was broken. I know that your mother tried for more than a century to fix it. I know that she enlisted my help to fashion a device to repurpose it, which I did. I now know that she was successful in her endeavor." He paused and then said, "That is what I know."

It was a lot of information, but Vy made sure to digest his every word. A part of her wanted to confirm with him that she had heard right—that her mother had been in possession of the talisman. But to do so would be to forfeit her last question.

Frowning, Vy contemplated what to ask him next. She determined that it made sense to probe him more about the hourglass. If she had something more concrete, perhaps there was a way to get through to Petra.

Vy knew it was a longshot, but she felt that Petra was the only hope she had of escaping her predicament. She needed out of the Order's base.

Releasing a sigh, Vy asked her final question, "What device did you fashion?"

Itachi's lips curled. "A pendulum," he said.

A pendulum? No fucking way! Vy wanted to smack herself. How had she not known? It was so obvious now.

"That seems to be the answer you were looking for." Itachi rose to his feet and bowed his head slightly. "It was a pleasure meeting you, Violet. I can tell that your mother's efforts were not in vain."

Vy wondered what he meant by that, but she didn't bother to ask. He'd made it clear that he'd only be answering three questions. "It was great meeting you too. I hope you can find peace."

"Me too," he said. "Remember what I have asked of you."

Vy nodded. "Of course. I will tell her."

Itachi bowed again before vanishing into what looked like a cloud of vapour. As the mist dispersed and disappeared, Vy willed herself to rise—to wake.

Blinking her eyes open, Vy felt like an elephant sat on her chest. She squinted against the brightness of the room.

The sedative still weighed her down, but she could feel the hard mattress beneath her back, and she could perceive her fingers and toes, which meant the effects were starting to subside.

Nothing about her current situation was in her favour, but there was a light at the end of the tunnel. Vy knew where the hourglass was. She needed to find a way to tell Petra. But how?

Vy hadn't seen Petra since she'd been brought to the base. Gagged and sedated as she was, her situation seemed impossible.

Alone, she was laid up in what looked to be a tiny cell with white walls and ceilings. Vy tried to lift her head to get a better look of her surroundings, but she couldn't.

In the near distance, boots clomped, and the sound of footsteps grew closer until they stopped outside the door to her cell.

Keys jingled as they were forced into the lock. There was a distinct click of the lock being turned over.

When the door scraped open, Vy tried again to lift her head to see who it was. Her attempt was in vain. Moving was impossible.

A musky scent hinted that the visitor was a man, and Vy wondered if he had come to parade her back to the lab.

The man was suddenly standing over her. His pot belly jutted over the waistband of his grey tactical pants, and the buttons of his collared shirt threatened to burst. He looked to be middle-aged, and he had more hair on his jaw than on his head. There was a mean sparkle in his beady brown eyes, but it was his smug expression that told Vy what he was about.

Spit welled in Vy's mouth as her stomach rolled over.

"Never had myself a witch," he muttered, firmly grabbing her chin.

Vy wished she had the strength to turn her head. Or even better, the strength to cast a spell that would set his body on fire. He was so lucky she was drugged and gagged.

Releasing his hold on her face, he sat down on the edge of the cot and tore open the front her jumpsuit, exposing her breasts to the cold air of the cell.

Vy's flesh prickled in horror and disgust as he fondled her breasts with abrasive hands. Every fibre of her being wanted to scream and fight against him, but she was a hostage in her body and couldn't move.

The fat man repositioned himself on top of her. Vy's mind screamed her protest. She shut her eyes and felt tears roll down her cheeks.

The weight of his body was yanked off her. There was a thud of human mass hitting the ground.

Vy's eyes flew open. She could not angle her head enough to get a look at what was happening, but her ears perceived a struggle. Skin smacked against skin. A breath hitched and then gurgled. Finally, there was a snap.

A moment past and then Petra stood over her, red faced and breathing heavily.

Relief washed over Vy.

Leaning over, Petra made quick work of righting Vy's clothes, and then lifted Vy into her arms. From her new viewpoint, Vy saw the fat guard sprawled on the floor. He didn't have a pulse.

"We don't have much time." Petra stated, sounding a bit panicked. "I will have to remove the gag and collar later."

Bending, Petra snatched the dead guard's keys. She then shouldered them through the door and began to run down the well-lit hallway. To where, Vy wasn't sure. But she was impressed by Petra's speed and the ease with which she carried her.

Petra abruptly stopped at another cell door. Vy caught a glimpse inside. A man in an orange jumper sat on the edge of a cot. When he looked up, Vy recognized him as the hopper from the cemetery.

Petra adjusted her hold on Vy so that she could handle the keys. When she found the right key, she popped it into the lock. But before she could turn it, a voice halted her.

"Fancy seeing you here, Malkovitch." Vy felt Petra's body stiffen. Turning, Petra faced the speaker.

Olivia stood down the hallway with her hands shoved into her pockets.

Petra gently set Vy on the floor, propping her up against the door of the hopper's cell.

The air fizzled with tension.

Vy was aware of the feud between Petra and Olivia. She understood that, for years, almost everyone on the base looked forward to the day when the two women would go at it again.

Petra and Olivia were finally going to finish what they started years ago.

Chapter Thirty-One

Of course, it was Olivia.

Of all people, it had to be her who happened upon Petra in her moment of treason. Fate was definitely cruel.

While Olivia stood in a relaxed pose—hands in pockets and shoulders slanted back—the animalistic glint in her eyes, paired with the self-righteous set of her mouth, made for an ominous portrait. "Why am I not surprised to see you here, Malkovitch?"

Petra squared her shoulders towards Olivia and met the feral stare that was directed at her. She noticed that the bags under Olivia's eyes seemed darker than usual.

"What, nothing to say?" Olivia cocked her head to the side. "Come on, throw me a fucking bone. I'd love to hear you try to talk yourself out of this one."

"There's nothing to say. I am doing what's right for me."

"And what's that, exactly?" Olivia asked, rocking on her heels.

"You in love with her? The illblood put a spell on you? She convince you that she'll make your wildest dreams come true? She promise to satisfy all of your sick sexual fantasies?" Olivia arched a sinister brow.

Petra clenched her teeth. Olivia was wrong, but her words still hit home. It unnerved her that Olivia could perceive things so clearly.

"Ding, ding, ding. Point for me, right?" Removing a hand from a pocket, Olivia pretended to unholster an imaginary gun and aimed it at Petra's head. "I hit it on the mark. Bullseye!" she said, firing the invisible weapon. She blew on its muzzle and chuckled menacingly.

Petra could tell that Olivia was more off her rocker than usual. And time was ticking. She needed to deal with her rival—and quickly.

At any moment, Dustin might start questioning what was taking her so long to return from her "quick break." Or worse, what if he began fiddling with the cameras and discovered that a few feeds weren't showing up on the display? If Dustin corrected Petra's manipulation of the footage, the jig would be up and he'd most definitely sound the alarm.

"Enough chatter." Petra dropped into her fighting stance and matched the intensity in Olivia's eyes with her own. "Let's settle things—once and for all."

"Oh, Malkovitch, I thought you'd never ask," Olivia squealed. Squatting down into her own combat position, she smirked. "I feared you were too scared to dance with me again."

Petra grunted. She was suddenly looking forward to wiping the overconfident look from Olivia's twisted face.

Immediately, Petra went on the offensive. Rushing forward, she launched a fist at her opponent's head. Olivia managed to dodge the punch, but her movements were off. Like their last bout in the gym, she was moving slower than normal.

Speed had always been one of Olivia's greatest assets, and at that moment, Olivia seemed to be having difficulty keeping up with Petra's onslaught of hand strikes and kicks.

It shouldn't be this easy. Petra wondered what ace Olivia had up her sleeve. There had to be a trick coming; her challenger was sneaky.

Petra broke through Olivia's defences, smashing an elbow into her jaw. The blow made Olivia stagger, but not long enough for Petra to land another hit.

Olivia continued to bob and evade the bombardment of Petra's attacks. Even so, it didn't take long for the second strike to land. Petra's kick connected hard with Olivia's right thigh.

Crying out, Olivia crashed down on the floor.

Without hesitation, Petra jumped on her and began to pummel Olivia's face in. Her small body squirmed to escape, but there was no getting away.

Soon, Olivia stopped moving entirely. Her breathing was gargled. Blood and pulpy skin made Olivia's face unrecognizable.

Petra eased off her adversary.

Spitting up blood, Olivia began to cough incessantly. She was incapacitated and going nowhere.

Petra untangled herself and stood up. Olivia continued to cough, but started again with her taunts. "Why'd … you stop?" She hacked up a glob of blood. "Weren't we having fun?"

"You're fucked up," Petra said.

"No, Peter, you're ... you're the one who's fucked."

Peter? Olivia is really out of it. Petra looked down at her and decided that the taste of victory was not so sweet. There were no feelings of triumph; there was just pity.

Petra was about to turn and head back to Vy when Olivia began to laugh maniacally. For the life of her, Petra couldn't understand what was so funny. But then, she saw it.

There, in Olivia's hand was a tiny syringe containing a fluorescent-green liquid. With a quick movement, Olivia flicked off the cap and stabbed her leg with the needle.

A strange thing happened next.

Olivia's eyes began to glow with a green incandescence that traveled down her body, highlighting the symbols of the tattoos that marked her as a member of SOTU. Her body began to morph, snapping and crackling as bones popped out of place to extend and realign. The transition was monstrous and like nothing Petra had seen before.

What the fuck? Petra took a step back.

Olivia sat up. Her lips curved with amusement.

Petra gasped. Olivia's face had completely healed.

"Amazing, eh?" Olivia snickered, wiping the blood from her mouth with the back of her hand. She stood up. In her new form, she stood almost as tall as Petra, and her lean body had filled out with muscle. "Dr. Raz is a fucking genius."

"What the fuck did he do to you?" There was a bit of a tremble in Petra's voice.

"He made me indestructible," Olivia said. She raised a brow. "Ready for the next round?"

Before Petra could even think to reply, Olivia's fist connected with her abdomen. Petra sucked in a breath as her body curled in on itself and she dropped to her knees. "How ... how are you so ... fast? What's ... in the syringe?" she said, hugging her stomach. Her insides were on fire. She wanted to hurl.

"It's the thing that will finally level the playing field," Olivia replied, launching a knee into Petra's face.

On impact, Petra's head flew back with a crack, and her body slumped to the floor. The world swam around her and was littered with black dots.

When she looked up, her eyes connected with Vy's. Petra grimaced. She couldn't see a scenario where they left together in one piece. *Fucking Olivia.*

Olivia seemed to have noticed Petra exchanging looks with Vy, for she commented, "The lightless has got you whipped. Disgusting. Time to end this enchantment." Hopping over Petra, Olivia moved towards Vy, who was still too sedated to do much of anything.

"Leave her the ... fuck alone!" Petra began to cough. It was hard to breathe. Her lungs felt heavy with fluid.

Olivia ignored her, and with unnatural strength, she lifted Vy up by the collar of the orange jumper. "Raz doesn't need you anymore. You're expendable."

Petra tried to crawl towards them. "Olivia ... please ... let us go."

"Shut it, you're so fucking pathetic—you're ruining my vibe," Olivia said, hoisting Vy even higher off the floor, making her feet dangle.

"Let us ... go," Petra pleaded again. "The fang ... promised me my life back—my mother back."

"Your mother is dead!" Olivia snapped. "Just as my mother is dead. There is no bringing them back."

"Please, Olivia, don't do this." Petra could barely get the words out. It was taking a lot of effort to speak.

"But I want to. I really want to snap your girlfriend's pretty neck," Olivia said, wrapping her hands about Vy's throat and squeezing. She began to hum cheerfully. The hum soon became a horrendous melody to which Olivia sang, "Momma had a baby and her head popped off."

Petra tried to say something else, but she couldn't. The black dots in her vision multiplied until there was only darkness.

Chapter Thirty-Two

The night's events were a roller coaster, and Vy's ride was about to end.

Olivia was still humming that dreadful tune as her monstrous hands tightened around Vy's neck.

Frustration far outweighed any pain Vy felt—or maybe it was the drug in her system, dulling sensation.

Vy had always been able to rely on her magic and her strength to get herself out of trouble. Sedated and gagged, she couldn't use either.

Her gaze drifted to Petra's limp body. She still had a heartbeat, but Vy could perceive it growing fainter by the second.

If only there was something Vy could do other than scream at her body to move. *If only I could speak.*

"Look at me, fang!" Olivia slammed Vy's head against the hopper's cell door. "I want to see the light go out from your eyes."

Vy looked up.

Olivia's glowing green eyes were wild, and the bloodlust registering on her face was unfamiliar. Through Dustin, Vy had a connection to Olivia, and it was hard to recognize this version of the woman.

Olivia's crude tattoos were glimmering, and Vy couldn't quite believe what she was seeing. The markings were a conduit for magic, and Olivia was channelling it in a way that shouldn't be possible for a human. How Dr. Raz had devised such a technique, Vy couldn't even imagine. It must have taken years of experimentation and research. If this was what the Order was up to, the organization was a bigger threat to unhumans than Vy had ever imagined.

The bones in Vy's neck began to fissure under the pressure of Olivia's intensifying grip. Now, she felt pain. Her eyes squeezed shut. *Why is she prolonging this? Why doesn't she just kill me already?*

Then, without warning, Olivia's hands about her throat disappeared. Vy collapsed to the ground.

Olivia's severed head thumped to the floor and rolled towards her, spurting blood all over her orange jumpsuit.

Shocked, Vy's eyes widened.

Vy's saviour stood over her, decked in leather, and sporting the blankest of expressions. Blood dripped from her delicate fingertips. Lifting her hand, Alice licked the blood clean with her tongue.

She came for me? How did she know where to find me? Vy couldn't believe it. Both gratitude and love for her friend surged through her system.

Stepping over Olivia's headless body, Alice knelt down beside Vy. Bending her blond head, she bit into the flesh of her wrist. Blood welled to the surface of her pale skin.

With a quick movement, Alice snapped off the shock collar and ripped the gag from Vy's mouth. "No arguments—drink," she said, pressing her wrist to Vy's mouth.

As the blood slid between her unmoving lips and trailed down her throat, Vy could feel the sedation wearing off. Her hands became mobile, and she clutched Alice's arm tightly as she fed.

All injuries to her neck repaired, and any lingering pain vanished. All Vy could feel was hunger, and she drank her fill with gusto.

"Enough," Alice said.

Vy didn't stop. She couldn't stop. She was so thirsty.

An alarm sounded, and Vy became somewhat conscious of the fact that the hallway lights blinked to flag an emergency.

"I said enough!" Alice forcefully shoved Vy away.

Blinking, Vy came to her senses. Wiping her mouth, she looked up at her friend. "You came for me?"

Alice frowned at her. "Did you ever doubt it?"

Vy had. Not once had she considered that her friend would come for her. But she didn't reveal the thought. Instead, she said, "I thought you were in New York?"

"I was—briefly," Alice replied. "Turns out Silas might have made a deal with the devil, or maybe he is just lucky. Anyhow, the movement is dead—for now. But now is not the time for a discussion."

Vy didn't have time to fully digest her friend's words as her ears picked up the thunder of boots on the ground—lots of them.

Alice turned toward the sound of the approaching enemy. "We must go."

Vy scrambled to her feet and cocked her head in the direction of the cell. In the tiny rectangular window was the hopper's face. He'd apparently been a witness to all that had transpired. "He's a hopper," Vy stated.

Alice nodded in acknowledgement and proceeded to tear the cell's door off its hinges. She flung the door and it clattered to the floor.

Vy rushed over to Petra's side.

"What are you doing?"

Vy hoisted Petra into her arms. "I am not leaving her."

The boots on the ground were louder.

"She's an SOL. Her place is here," Alice said.

"I am not leaving without her."

Alice's eyes narrowed on her, but knowing there was no time to argue, she turned away from Vy, entering the cell.

Hoisting Petra into her arms, Vy ran into the hopper's cell.

With little effort, Alice broke the shock collar from the hopper's neck. She then set to destroying the shackles from the unhuman's ankles and wrists. "Thanks so much," he said with a grin, rubbing his freed wrists.

"Take us away from here," Alice commanded.

The hopper nodded. "Where to?"

"Toronto."

The hopper took hold of Vy's and Alice's arms. In less time than it took to blink, he teleported them away from the carnage, alarms, and flashing lights. They landed in front of the CN Tower.

Though it was not the most inconspicuous of places, given the late hour, there was no one to witness their miraculous arrival.

As always, Vy felt a little disoriented from the hop, but she recovered quickly.

The hopper smiled at them, flashing white teeth. "I can't thank you enough—"

"I see no reason for gratitude," Alice said stiffly. "We did you a favour, and you returned it."

The hopper chuckled. "If you say so."

"I do."

"Well, then—goodbye." The hopper saluted them and hopped away.

Vy set Petra down on the concrete. She uttered a quick spell, which made her palms glow. Setting her hands on Petra's abdomen, she proceeded to heal her.

"Now is not the time for that," Alice snapped. "Someone might see."

"She might die if I don't tend to some of her injuries."

"She is an SOL." Alice snorted. "The world would be all the better if she passed."

Vy's jaw clenched. She removed her hands from her patient. "Look, I have stabilized her. I think it might be risky to take her to my place. We need a place to stay—"

"Absolutely not!"

"Please, Alice."

"You are asking for too much." Alice paced a bit, and then stopped to point an accusatory finger in Vy's direction. "I do not think you grasp the gravity of what I did for you."

Vy frowned. "You're right, I don't understand."

"Exactly." Alice shook her head. "It is one thing to kill an SOL when they are the ones on the hunt. It is another thing entirely to kill their own on their territory."

"They started it."

"No, they did not. You have no affiliations, Vy. The same cannot be said for myself."

"What are you saying?"

"I am saying that the Order will rain down on this city. They will want blood. Belisarius will have my head for this." For the first time ever, Vy sensed a vulnerability in her friend's disposition.

"What if I told you that all of this doesn't matter?" Vy said.

"You make no sense. Of course, it matters."

"I know where the hourglass is."

Alice went still—very still. "You do not."

"I do."

For a moment, all was silent. Then, Alice said, "And you mean to use it?"

Vy nodded.

More silence ensued, and then Alice said, "Fine, you can stay with me. But you are to leave before I am reanimated with the sun's descent."

"Wouldn't want to overstay," Vy murmured just as Alice took off. With gentle hands, she picked up Petra and took off after her friend at a blurring speed.

While Alice swore allegiance to Belisarius, she was one of the few fangs who did not quarter with the coven. Even so, Alice's luxurious penthouse was only a hop and a skip away from the coven leader.

When the elevator dinged open, Alice stepped inside the grand and open space. "Bring her to your old room," she said. "And take care—I do not want her blood soiling my floors."

Alice's curt tone rubbed Vy the wrong way, but she also knew that her friend had every right to be annoyed. So, she said nothing and carried Petra to her old bedroom.

Vy carefully set Petra down on the mattress. She was glad to see that the colour was returning to Petra's face. Her ears noted that Petra's heartbeat was stronger as well.

Without much of a thought, Vy brushed a hand along Petra's cheek. With her eyes closed, she looked much younger.

Vy shook her head and rubbed her temples. There was a dull ache in her chest that she wanted to disregard.

Rolling up Petra's shirt to expose the skin of her stomach, Vy grimaced. The bruising was severe. Luckily, Petra was in good hands. Vy could heal her, and for once, she had enough juice to do the job without a hitch.

Vy spoke the words of a spell. When her palms glowed, she placed one on Petra's head and the other on her abdomen.

"I do not understand why you are caring for her," Vy heard Alice say. Turning her head, she saw her friend leaning on the door frame with arms crossed. "Why such concern for an SOL?"

"I killed her mother—I owe her."

"I did not know the woman had a daughter." Alice said. Stepping into the room, she observed the human closely. "I have some shackles—"

"We don't need them."

"If you killed her mother as you say, will she not want to see your head mounted on a pike the moment she rouses?"

"No. We have a deal."

Alice arched a brow. "The hourglass?"

Vy nodded. "Yes."

"How did you find it?"

"A conversation with an old friend of my mother's."

Alice frowned. "Who?"

"Itachi Yamamoto," Vy replied. "Know him?"

"I never met the man," Alice said. She sighed. "I do not think you will get what you seek from this endeavor."

"Why do you say that?"

"There is no cure for vampirism," Alice said flatly. "And as I told you before, your aversion and sickness is all in your head. Note that you fed from me, and you did not suffer your usual malady. Your mind was far too pre-occupied with what was going on that you could not focus on your revulsion to feeding."

That was true. The realization made Vy still. For the first time, she really considered Alice's words. All this time, had it all been in her head?

Vy didn't want to think that she had been living a lie for over a decade. Instead of acknowledging her friend's statement, she said,

"You can't possibly know that there isn't a cure."

"I do," Alice said. "And even if there existed such a thing, your mother would not cure you."

Vy pulled away from Petra, and her hands stopped glowing. "How could you possibly know that?"

Alice turned away from her and paced the room. "I knew your mother," she finally confessed.

Vy frowned. Alice had never mentioned knowing Camellia before. The fact that she had kept this from Vy felt like a betrayal. "You knew my mother?" Vy repeated softly.

Alice nodded, but said no more.

Another question formed in Vy's mind. One she had always wanted to ask but thought it implausible. Now, it seemed like the only answer. It would explain how Alice always knew how to find her. "Are you my donor?"

"Yes," Alice answered. "Do not give me that look. Do not look at me as if this is a revelation. You have always known it, Vy. You simply refused to recognize it."

Was that true? She didn't think so. Vy's fists clenched. "You could have told me."

"It was best not to say it aloud. You can never be too sure who is listening," she explained. "As you are well aware, mixing bloodlines is greatly frowned upon."

"Why'd you turn me then? When did you turn me?" Vy asked. She felt the sting of tears in her eyes. She found she couldn't stand, and slunk down to the floor, leaning her back against the bedframe.

Alice had been the one to turn her and had known her mother.

What else had her friend kept from her? Could she even be called a friend? "I trusted you more than anyone. How could you have kept all this from me?" Vy asked, her voice cracking.

Alice did not meet her eyes when she responded, "It is not my place to say."

"What? Why?" The tears sprang free and trickled down Vy's face.

"Your mother never wanted you to learn the truth." Alice shook her head. "For once, I would hope that you listen to me. Do not do it—do not use the hourglass. I can sort out this mess with the Order."

"I don't have a choice." Vy wiped her eyes and looked at Petra. "But, even if I did …"

Alice sighed and moved towards the door. Before leaving, she threw Vy a look over her shoulder and said, "In some ways, you are just like Camellia—stubborn."

Vy watched Alice go, and then wiped her eyes. Rising to her feet, she took a place on the bed beside Petra. Though she knew that she shouldn't, she propped her head on Petra's shoulder and found comfort.

Chapter Thirty-Three

Kayla's ear rang fiercely as she took in the carnage. Her mask of composure hadn't slipped, it was off. Her staff made sure to stay out of her way.

Her face burned from the heat of her rage. The last time she'd been this angry had been when she'd heard a rumour that her best friend was having a sexual relationship with a lightless and had been preaching to her son that the lightless could be reformed to accept the Light Almighty as their saviour.

Kayla had killed Wu for his alleged indiscretion, and it was only after she'd shot him that she'd realized that she ought to have investigated the matter first. As it turned out, it hadn't been Wu who had been sleeping with the lightless captive.

Ever since that blunder, Kayla tried to keep a cool head. But she couldn't reign in her temper now—not after all that had happened.

The illblood was gone, and so was the hopper. Olivia was

dead—decapitated. A fang had infiltrated the base and had made quick work of two other SOLs who had been unfortunate to cross its path.

Kayla hands balled at her sides.

The white floors and walls were spattered with blood. Around her, many SOLs were panicking or talking in hushed whispers. They were shocked, and they were scared.

An attack like this had never happened before, and it had happened under Kayla's watch.

Her career would not survive this. Even if the hopper were still here and she finalized the deal with Tim, she would still be deemed unfit.

Kayla whirled on Dukes. In a cold tone she repeated what she had heard him say, "Dustin was operating control when this happened?"

"Yes," he confirmed.

"Find my son and tell him to wait for me in my office," Kayla barked.

Dukes nodded and left her side.

Kayla purposefully strode out of the blood splattered hallway and made her way to the control room. There, she ordered the control officer to replay the footage. She wanted to see Malkovitch's treachery for herself.

On video, she saw Malkovitch strangle Officer Green and then heft the illblood in her arms. Malkovitch made a run down the halls, heading, she knew, for the hopper's cell. That was when Olivia stepped into the picture, and there was a fight between the two women.

Olivia fought valiantly, but she fell when Malkovitch's kick connected with her leg.

So headstrong—she was not fit to fight yet. Kayla gritted her teeth. It was hard to watch Malkovitch pummel Olivia's face in. Had Olivia been in better shape, she might not have fallen so easily. Perhaps she would have even won.

On the video, Malkovitch was seen extracting herself from her downed opponent. The two women began to exchange words that could not be heard, as there was no recorded audio. Olivia began to laugh, and Kayla's eyes narrowed as she saw Olivia extract a syringe and inject the contents of what had to be Raz's serum. What happened next was miraculous, but Kayla could not bask in the success of it because Olivia's victory was short-lived.

A female fang with short blond hair flashed into the frame and severed her head.

Headless, Olivia's body crumbled to the floor. The head rolled for a bit, gushing blood everywhere. Even as seasoned as Kayla was, the sight made her stomach turn. Bile rose in her mouth.

Kayla swallowed it down and looked away from the monitor. "I have seen enough," she said.

The control officer closed out of the video feed, and Kayla motioned towards the door. She was buzzed out of the room, and she left in somewhat of a hurry.

Searing anger coursed through her veins as she strode out of the cellblocks and headed towards the main building. Her fury acted somewhat like a time warp, and she reached her office without realizing it.

Her dreams were shattered. It didn't matter that the serum had been stabilized. She would be demoted for what had happened on her base. Without her title as commander, she wouldn't be able to execute her plans. *I was so close ...*

In the space of a few hours, everything had gone to shit, and her son was partly to blame.

Throwing open her office door, Kayla stormed inside. When she spotted her son's grief-stricken form, she felt herself get even angrier.

Dustin stood up from the armchair by the giant desk. He wrung his hands as he stared at his feet.

"Look at me!" Kayla commanded.

Her son shook his head.

"I said, look at me!"

He did, and she saw that his blue eyes were red from crying. Dustin had always been weak and being confronted with his ineptitude in that moment stoked Kayla's fury hotter. Why couldn't she have birthed a stronger man—a man who wasn't led by his heart? Or was it that Dustin was compromised?

Olivia had mentioned that she thought Malkovitch might have been enchanted by the illblood. Could it be that her son was as well? It was impossible to know, and not knowing made Kayla's head spin. The ringing in her ear grew louder.

"I'm so sorry," Dustin said. "I didn't mean to—I didn't know that—"

"That Malkovitch was a traitor," she finished for him. "Would you have told me if you had known?"

"Of course, I would have." His voice was wavering.

"I don't think you would have. You've lied to me before," Kayla said with a sneer. She stepped towards her son and looked down at him, showing him every bit of disgust she felt towards him. "You're a liar, and you're an idiot, and worst of all, you are weak."

He turned his head away from her.

"Look at me when I am talking to you." When he didn't heed her directions, something within Kayla snapped and she backhanded him hard. The blow made Dustin stumble, and his head struck the sharp edge of the desk. His body collapsed to the floor.

Meanwhile, Kayla heaved. Her breaths were quick. Her heart hammered in her chest. Her blasted ear wouldn't stop ringing.

She eyed her son's limp body with annoyance. "Get up," she ordered, nudging his leg with her foot.

When he made no move to do so, Kayla reached down and hefted him up by his collar. In doing so, she saw the blood coating his wavy blond hair.

All of a sudden, the spinning in her head stopped. Her heart stopped. Everything stopped except the ringing.

Kayla brought two fingers to her son's neck. Pressing against his skin, she checked for a pulse that was not there.

Stunned, she set his limp body down gently on the floor and staggered back. *What have I done?*

Her dizziness returned, and this time when the bile rose, she vomited.

Once the retching subsided, Kayla sat down on the floor. She couldn't bring herself to look at Dustin, and so she didn't.

Her mind couldn't register anything, so she just sat. And even as her injuries cried out at her, she stayed seated.

Kayla wasn't sure how long she stayed like that—immobile and unthinking. The sun rose, which gave her some indication of the time. But what did time matter? Did anything matter?

Kayla was starting to think that nothing mattered.

In her life, Kayla had seen a lot of death. She'd lost colleagues. She'd lost friends. She'd even lost a lover. Every time, she'd managed to pick herself up and move forward.

For the most part, her hate for the lightless motivated her to live. But it wasn't until she discovered what Raz had been working on that she found her true purpose. Kayla had been so sure that if she took all the right steps, she'd be the one to finally see the Order's goal realized—the extermination of all lightless. She'd envisioned a world where humans finally possessed the power to fight them on equal footing.

But that dream was dead, and she'd lost her son—the last remnant of the only man she'd ever loved.

Her muscles screamed at her, begging her to move. She told herself that she deserved the pain. Frankly, she deserved worse.

She had killed her son. Was there any greater sin? Yes, it had been an accident, but that didn't change a thing. Dead was dead—it was permanent.

From the moment Dustin had been born, Kayla had loved him with all her heart. To anyone looking, it might have seemed like she didn't care about him, but they were wrong.

It had been because Kayla cared about him that she kept him out of her reach. She hadn't wanted to coddle him—she'd wanted him to be strong. But her approach hadn't worked. Instead of becoming strong, Dustin had latched on to the church, and his head became filled with nonsense. Instead of wanting to fight the good fight, Dustin sought to bring more light into the world.

How stupid and naive her son had been. But his greatest shortcoming had been falling for Malkovitch.

Malkovitch. The name rolled over in Kayla's mind. She clenched her fist.

Suddenly, Kayla found that she couldn't sit another minute. She struggled to her feet and her stiff muscles cried. Without sparing her son's lifeless body a second glance, Kayla left her office.

Dead was dead, but she wasn't the only one to blame for Dustin's death. If it wasn't for Malkovitch's treachery, he'd still be alive.

Malkovitch had killed him, and Kayla knew from experience that revenge was the best medicine.

Chapter Thirty-Four

Petra's eyes cracked open; warm light cast from a nearby lamp made her squint. Blinking a few times, she sat upright and rubbed the sleep from her eyes. The bed was plush and richly outfitted. She looked around in bewilderment. *Where am I? How did I get here?*

The room was large and immaculately designed, but tailored to a very specific taste. Textured black wallpaper was framed by ornate white trim. The high ceilings were white and coffered. Dark solid wood floors with considerable grain and a matte finish gave the opulent space an air of warmth.

Petra sat on what had to be the comfiest mattress, and she noted that the bed was by far the most prominent feature in the bedroom. It was large and canopied with black linen that felt like silk and probably was. Lush cushions were piled high against a panelled headboard.

On the opposite end of the room, there was a tiny seating area and a gas fireplace. Thick blackout curtains were drawn closed along one wall, blocking the windows and making it impossible to know what time of day it was.

For a brief moment, Petra wondered who could afford to live in such lavishness. But then an array of images of the night flickered in her mind, pulling her attention elsewhere. As Petra pieced the memories together, she remembered everything: working the doors in control and spotting Officer Green on camera, making his rounds. Recalling her conversation with Khan, a panic had gripped Petra. The thought of Green laying a finger on Vy had incensed Petra to a degree that set her down the path of frantically drafting a plan to break them out of the base.

The scheme had come to her quickly. Knowing how Dustin felt about her, and knowing he felt he owed her for having thwarted her revenge efforts, Petra had decided that she could use him. She'd been right. Not only had he picked up his phone almost immediately, but he had rushed over to relieve her for a quick break.

And so, everything seemed to have gone her way. She had caught up with Green, and she'd had the satisfaction of strangling the life out of him.

Yes, everything had been going her way—until Olivia had showed up.

Wait, how am I alive? Petra frowned.

Lifting her shirt, Petra noted that her skin was unblemished. She touched her shoulder and realized that there was also no indication of Vy's bite. The bandage was gone, and her skin wasn't raw and oozing. Her brows furrowed further in her confusion.

"You're finally up."

Petra jolted, and she turned her head in the direction of the voice. Her heart began to race.

Vy stood in the door frame. A hint of a smile played on her lips.

A flush of warmth spread throughout Petra's body, and she sat up straighter in the bed. "Yeah," Petra said, rubbing the back of her neck. "I thought … I died."

"You almost did," Vy admitted. "But nothing I couldn't handle."

She saved my life. Petra's mouth opened to utter her thanks, but the words got stuck in her throat. Perhaps it was embarrassment that kept her quiet. She'd been trying to save Vy, but in the end, she'd been the one who'd needed saving.

Petra shouldn't have extended mercy to Olivia. She should have killed the girl while she'd had the chance. Then again, how could she have ever guessed at the ace Olivia had been holding?

A shudder tore through Petra as she recalled the change Olivia had undergone—the way she'd packed on muscle and height in an instant. The transformation had been unnatural. How had it been possible? What exactly was Raz up to in his lab?

"What happened to Olivia?" Petra asked.

"She's dead. Alice, my friend, came to our rescue—right in the nick of time, I'd say."

Olivia's dead. Petra didn't know how she felt about that. She should be happy, right? Oddly, she wasn't. She felt numb.

Nodding, Petra didn't ask for details. She didn't want to know. After clearing her throat, she asked, "How long have I been out for?"

"Hard to say. Give or take three hours," Vy replied.

"Where are we?"

"Alice's place," Vy said. Approaching the bed, she shoved her hands in the pockets of tight-fitting leather pants. She also wore a body-hugging leather corset that pushed up her breasts in a way that made it impossible not to look at them.

Swallowing hard, Petra looked down at the bedsheets balled in her fists. "What the hell are you wearing?"

"Alice is fond of leather," she explained. "I thought the top look cute on me."

Cute was not how Petra would describe it. Sexy was probably also too tame a word. Why couldn't Vy dress normally? She made it impossible to not take notice of her.

Stopping at the edge of the bed, Vy said, "Anyways, I needed out of that hideous orange jumper. Not only is orange not my colour, but I wanted no reminders of ..." As her words trailed off, her gaze lowered, and Petra understood where her thoughts had gone.

Without really thinking, Petra shifted out of bed and took Vy into her arms. "It's okay." Her words were a whisper of assurance that brushed against Vy's curly black hair. "He's gone. He can't hurt you." Petra inhaled the flowery scent of Vy's hair. Vy always smelled good.

Vy sniffled and looked up at Petra. "I am being silly." She wiped her wet eyes. "It was just really fucking scary. I couldn't move, I couldn't scream, I couldn't do anything. I was trapped in my own body, and I could only watch ..."

"You are not being silly," Petra said, finding it ironic that she was comforting the very creature who had once made her feel the same way—trapped and frozen. But then, Vy was not the monster Petra had thought her to be.

In that moment, a part of Petra wanted to say all the things that went unsaid. But how could she even begin? And maybe now wasn't the time to tell Vy that she'd been wrong all this time. Wrong to think of Vy as a senseless fiend for all these years. Wrong for thinking that killing Vy would be the antidote to cure her pain. Wrong for allowing SOTU agents to take her in the first place.

Then again, maybe she didn't have to say it for Vy to recognize the change in her. Maybe Petra's earlier actions spoke for her. Perhaps they could move forward and go back to how things were before.

It suddenly dawned on Petra that she was still holding on to Vy. She could feel Vy's heart beating against her chest and she could feel her own quickening.

When Petra peered down into Vy's dark eyes, she saw a flicker in them that took her back to their moment in the alley just outside the girl bar, and then she remembered their indiscretion back at Vy's condo. Petra's face flushed.

Swallowing, Petra's gaze drifted downwards to Vy's slightly parted lips. She licked her own.

Vy smiled impishly up at her and ran fingers up her torso. The touch was light but overwhelmed Petra with sensation.

Somehow, against all the odds, it no longer felt wrong to want Vy as she did. Petra didn't fight against the pull. She leaned forward, and when their lips touched, Petra felt her heart jumpstart.

Their kiss started off slow and deep, but quickly became urgent and crazed, and it wasn't long before Petra was gasping and fighting for air.

Breaking away from Vy, Petra swept kisses down the span of Vy's neck, and her hands went to cup breasts that jutted out of the corset. Vy moaned, and she recaptured her lips.

Petra's hands went to undo the back laces of the leather corset, and she struggled. Annoyed and needing it off, she ripped the garment apart and tossed it to the floor.

Vy pulled away from her, and her eyes narrowed on the discarded top. "Alice is going to kill you for that," she said, smiling.

"I don't care." Petra grabbed Vy by the waist and drew her towards her until their bodies were pressed firmly together. Bending her head, she laid a kiss on one of Vy's shoulders and then ran her tongue downwards. When she brought her mouth to Vy's breasts, she felt Vy tremble. Petra looked up and met Vy's eyes. They were dilated with lust.

"I want this off," Vy murmured, tugging at Petra's shirt. Her hands flew to undo the buttons of Petra's bloodstained shirt.

Soon, Petra's shirt and sports bra were on the floor with the corset, and Vy's hands were exploring her bared skin. "Your body is incredible."

The compliment made Petra feel good, but she also felt slightly self-conscious. While she liked the way she looked, she was also aware that she didn't have the average female body. She was all hard muscle. She lacked softness and curves.

Whatever insecurities Petra had disappeared the moment she

felt the heat of Vy's mouth on her abdomen.

Closing her eyes, she revelled in the bath of kisses on her skin, and she groaned her pleasure.

Vy's hands went to her belt and then her zipper. Petra assisted with the removal of her grey tactical pants, and then she lifted Vy into her arms, setting her back down on the bed.

Settling on top of Vy, Petra relished the feeling of skin touching skin. Vy was so soft, and her scent was intoxicating. The press of her breasts against her own aroused Petra to no end. She was so wet, and she ached between her legs.

Petra retook Vy's lips. She needed Vy so badly. Even more than that, she wanted to please Vy. She wanted to make Vy writhe with pleasure. She wanted to see Vy's eyes roll back in her head as she came.

The only problem was that she wasn't entirely sure how to do that.

She'd only had sex once with Kate, and while it had been a wonderful experience, awkward was probably the best word that could be used to describe her first time. Petra had never made anyone orgasm before, and Vy wasn't a fifteen-year-old Kate. Vy was very experienced.

Petra's mind flew back to Dustin, scrolling through the list of Vy's conquests on the tablet. Not only had it been long, but the women on it had been gorgeous. How could Petra match them? How could she compete with a smoke show like Isabella?

"Petra," Vy said, her voice hoarse and breathy. "You're frowning. We can stop. You know, we don't have to do anything."

Blinking, Petra met concerned brown eyes. "I don't want to stop. I want you. I just don't—I've never …" Petra ran a frustrated hand through her short red hair and then collapsed beside Vy on the mattress. She stared up at the coffered ceiling, feeling quite dejected and a little mortified.

Vy rose on an elbow and looked at Petra. Her brows furrowed together. "You're a virgin?"

Petra shook her head. "No, I've had sex once—a long time ago," she replied, before adding, "when I was fifteen. And maybe you have forgotten already, but you fucked me a few nights back." Heat creeped up Petra's neck at the memory of Vy's fingers inside her.

"Oh yeah, and I haven't forgotten." Vy's face softened, and she traced a finger gently over Petra's collarbone. "But from the way you kiss and touch me, I would have never guessed that."

"Haha, very funny," Petra said, rolling her eyes.

"I'm being serious," Vy said, resting her head on Petra's shoulder. She brought a hand to Petra's jaw and met her eyes. "I've never felt chemistry like this with anyone before."

Petra wrapped an arm over Vy and pulled her in closer. She found Vy's confession highly unlikely. "I don't want to suck," Petra said aloud before realizing that she'd wanted to keep that last thought to herself.

Vy chuckled. "I think that would be impossible."

"Easy for you to say."

"It is," Vy said. "There's no wrong way to do it. Whatever feels right, you do it. It's more intuition than anything, and I'd say you've got great intuition, but I can always guide you if that's your preference. At the same time, I don't want to push you to do anything you're not ready to do."

"I don't think there's anything I don't want to do with you," Petra admitted.

"Same," Vy said. Her expression grew intense once more, and she brought her lips to Petra's neck, grazing the sensitive area and making Petra's thoughts muddle. Then, she crawled on top of Petra, straddling her hips.

Vy's mouth moved away from Petra's neck, and she kissed down the length of Petra's chest while her expert hands slid over her sides and stomach. The brush of Vy's hair on Petra's skin felt delectable.

Petra sucked in a breath and arched her back when Vy's tongue circled her nipple. "Fuck, your tits are perfect," Vy muttered. Her hands were suddenly where her mouth had been, and she cupped and brushed her thumbs over Petra's breasts.

Petra motioned to sit up, and her hands went to Vy's ass. She stared into Vy's brown eyes, and then grabbed her dark hair and pulled her in for a kiss. Vy moaned into her mouth and then broke away from her lips to whisper against her ear. "Hmmm ... I like it when you take charge." Vy's teeth tugged on her earlobe, and Petra shuddered.

Her words evoked the memory of how badly Vy had seemed to want her in the alley. She'd seemed to really be into it when Petra had forced her against the wall.

Was it that Vy liked rough sex? Deciding to test her theory, Petra gripped Vy by the neck and rolled her over onto her back.

Looking down at Vy, she could tell that her guess had been right. Vy's pupils were blown. Her breathing was rapid. "Fuck. Petra," she said, licking her lips. "I want you to take me."

Petra couldn't stop the smug smile from curving on her lips. "Oh yeah," she said, dropping her hand from Vy's throat.

Petra secured Vy's wrists with her hands and held them firmly down at Vy's sides. She brought her mouth to Vy's chest and kissed her breasts passionately. Beneath her, Vy writhed and moaned and pleaded.

"Please," Vy said desperately, with a groan. "I … need you to touch me."

Petra let go of Vy's wrists and peeled off the leather pants Vy still had on. Then, kissing her way down Vy's smooth thighs, she ran her hands over the soft expanse of her skin. "Your skin feels like silk," she said breathlessly, stroking the back of her fingers over the inner area of Vy's thighs.

Vy trembled under her touch. Petra's confidence boosted a bit from seeing Vy's want for her, but she still felt rather anxious as she slid Vy's panties off. A gasp escaped Petra when she saw the slick evidence of Vy's longing.

Suddenly, all her apprehension dissolved as she became consumed with the need to know how Vy tasted.

Bending her head, Petra brought her mouth to kiss Vy's thighs, and she slowly inched her lips closer to her destination. As she did so, Vy whimpered and gasped and spasmed. Petra thrilled in Vy's reactiveness, and her excitement only intensified when she brought her tongue to Vy's clit, making Vy hiss and buck her hips unabashedly against Petra's face.

Petra rode the wave of Vy's building desire, kissing, suckling, and licking her. All the while, Vy's fingers dug into her hair as she arched and thrashed her head. "Fuck, Petra, you're going to make me come," Vy said, her voice rough with need.

Petra felt Vy's body going tense. Her back arched higher and higher. Crying out, Vy crashed down onto the mattress with ragged breaths.

Withdrawing from between her legs, Petra pulled Vy into her arms, and they lay on their sides facing each other. Petra beamed.

"What are you so happy about?" Vy asked in a teasing tone.

"Who says I'm happy?" Petra tried to retract her smile, but she couldn't—she was far too pleased with herself.

Bringing a hand to her cheek, Vy brushed her lips over Petra's and said, "You're so beautiful when you smile. You should do it more."

A feeling of warmth blossomed in Petra's chest. "I'm sure I'll be less of a curmudgeon when we find the hourglass."

Vy's eyes shifted, and her expression grew somber. Her hand dropped from Petra's face.

"What is it?"

Vy shrugged and sighed.

Petra wondered if Vy's mind had turned back to what had happened at the base, and she blamed herself. She pulled Vy even closer to her and kissed her forehead. "I shouldn't have let them take you back in Japan. I was conflicted, and I made the wrong choice. If I could go back …"

"It's okay, Petra."

Petra gave her a doubtful look.

"Really, it's water under the bridge." Vy sighed again. "I understand why you did what you did."

"I'm sorry."

Vy brought a finger to her lips. "No more talking. Just kiss me."

Chapter Thirty-Five

Vy's head rested on Petra's chest, rising and falling with each breath her lover took.

After hours of fucking and curled up as she was in Petra's strong arms, Vy ought to have felt calm. But she didn't. Dread nestled in her chest and twisted her stomach.

The hourglass was within her reach, and she would have to tell Petra, but she didn't want to.

Vy wasn't good at letting go, but she had promised Petra a new life. She would not go back on her word.

Also, after her discussion with Alice, Vy's resolve to find her mother had tripled. Confused couldn't begin to explain her feelings. She had so many new questions for Camellia.

Vy's fingers traced the solid outline of Petra's abs. She wanted to stay in bed forever. She wanted to remain in the bubble that she and Petra had created for themselves over the last few hours. More than anything, she wanted to be with Petra.

When they used the hourglass, and changed everything, the version of Petra she'd grown to care about would cease to exist. Knowing that was unbearable.

Tears stung Vy's eyes, and she sighed.

Petra shifted and looked down at her. "Hey, what's wrong?"

Vy wiped her eyes with the back of her fingers and turned her gaze downward and away from Petra's face. "It's nothing. I'm just being emotional."

"Want to talk about it?"

How could Vy even begin to do so? She couldn't tell Petra what was going on in her mind, and she wasn't ready to bring up the hourglass. And so, she just said no.

Petra's arms tightened around her. "Why not?"

"Because it is stupid—I am being stupid."

Petra drew Vy up in her arms and kissed her lightly. "I'm sure it isn't stupid. Talk to me."

Vy exhaled a deep breath. She decided to share one of the many things on her mind. "I found out who my donor is. It's Alice."

"Alice—your friend?"

Nodding, Vy said, "She kept it from me for all these years. And, apparently, she knows my mother."

"Why do you think that is?"

"I can't even begin to guess. It feels like the greatest betrayal. I thought Alice was my friend. I thought she cared about me. Turns out, she probably only had my back for all of these years out of a sense of duty to my mother."

"I don't think that's the case," Petra said. "She came for you—rescued you from the Order. I don't think she would have done that out of obligation."

"Perhaps, but I don't know what to think anymore." Vy stared up at Petra, who was frowning. "What are you thinking?"

"I'm thinking that if you have a donor that means that you would have died at some point," Petra replied.

"Perhaps—who knows? I'm an illblood. Maybe I'm the exception to the rule?"

"Maybe." Petra's hands ran down the length of her body, stoking a fire within Vy that had been dwindling. Vy kissed Petra, and soon the two were at it again. Their appetite for each other was seemingly insatiable. Vy feared that she would never get enough of Petra while also understanding that she would soon lose her.

They came together—almost in sync. Then, Vy again found her head burrowed against Petra's chest.

Humans had a saying that insanity was doing the same thing over and over and expecting a different result. Vy wanted to believe that she could fuck Petra out of her system and move on with her plans. But each time she found herself spent and entangled in Petra's embrace, her dilemma worsened.

Maybe it was time to burst the bubble. Perhaps, if they had a change of scenery, Vy could finally tell Petra that she knew where the hourglass was—that it had been hiding in plain sight for her entire life.

Lifting her head, Vy looked at Petra and asked, "Are you hungry?"

"Famished," she replied, smiling sheepishly.

Petra's smile had the effect of knotting Vy's insides. Biting down her lip, Vy sat up and scooted towards the edge of the bed. "Let's get you something to eat. I doubt Alice has anything in her kitchen. We'll have to eat out."

Vy slid off the bed. She found her underwear and put them on. Then, she bent over and grabbed the leather pants.

Petra watched her closely. Her green eyes were smouldering with a hunger that Vy didn't think had anything to do with food. "How about we order in? I'm not ready to get up yet," she said.

"Alice wants us gone before the sun sets," Vy stated. "It's probably best that we go now. I also need to … feed too."

Vy fully expected Petra's face to turn up with disgust, as it had every other time she'd been reminded of Vy's squirrel diet, but it didn't. Petra's expression remained unchanged—she still looked like she wanted to devour her. "What time is it?" she asked.

"I have no idea." Vy shrugged and pulled on the leather pants. "If I had to guess, late afternoon."

Petra sat up in the bed and raked a hand through her tussled red hair. "Come here," she said, grinning devilishly.

Vy shook her head. "I know what you're about, so I'm not going to."

Arching a brow, Petra said, "You're no fun."

"And when exactly did you become fun?" Picking up Petra's discarded clothes, Vy threw them at her. "Put on your pants. I'll try to find you a fresh shirt that isn't covered in blood. Alice must have something that'll fit you in that giant closet of hers."

"I don't do leather," Petra said.

"You might not have a choice," Vy replied. An image of Petra in a tight leather shirt popped in her mind. She suppressed a giggle. "I'll be back."

Vy exited her old bedroom. Crossing the hallway, she entered the master bedroom.

Like most fangs, the bedroom was more for show than anything. Alice rarely used the space, and when she did, it wasn't for sleeping but for play.

The massive bed, in the center of the room, was perhaps the equivalent of two kings. Alice loved a good orgy. The giant bed was only ever used when she had company.

Fangs were very much defenceless when the sun rose, especially, the younger ones. Older vamps were able to rise and regain some of their strength before nightfall. But they thrived in the dark. For that reason, fangs usually tucked themselves away in a hidden and secure area at dawn. Alice's fortified space, Vy knew, was behind the bookcase in the office.

Vy headed for the walk-in closet, and her mind turned again to the conversation she'd had with Alice. How did Camellia and Alice know each other?

Her hands skimmed over a few hung items and removed a black tank top, which she put on. Then, she grabbed a thin black jacket made of smooth leather and stuffed her arms through it.

Finding a shirt for Petra proved difficult, but Vy did find one. As Petra's luck would have it, it wasn't leather.

Tucking the oversized cotton top under her arm, Vy went back to her old bedroom. She entered just as Petra was exiting the bathroom.

Petra smiled at her.

Butterflies batted in Vy's stomach.

Vy tossed the shirt, and Petra caught it, slipping it over her head. "Have you thought about what you want to eat?" she asked.

"Anything is fine," Petra replied, closing the distance between them and bringing her hands to Vy's waist. She bent her head and kissed her.

More than anything, Vy just wanted to let go and let things get out of hand again, but she knew that the longer she prolonged not telling Petra about the hourglass, the harder it'd be.

Vy felt that she'd be in a better position to tell Petra about it when they were out in public. Or perhaps her tongue would loosen when they got outside and the fresh air hit her, clearing her brain.

Vy pulled back. Stepping away from Petra, she leaned her back against a wall and crossed her arms.

Petra frowned. "Did I do something?"

"No, I just think we need to go."

"Okay, let's go."

Leaving the bedroom, Petra laced her hands through Vy's as they proceeded down a long corridor that led to the main living area.

They were about half a dozen steps away from the private elevator when it dinged open, and Kayla shot out of it with her assault rifle aimed and a bloodcurdling expression on her face.

Chapter Thirty-Six

Clay's cold blue gaze dropped to Petra's hand that was interlaced with Vy's. In a quick motion, she aimed her gun at Vy's head and squeezed the trigger.

Petra shoved Vy out of the line of fire and launched herself at the commander's legs, taking the beastly woman down.

The assault rifle clattered to the floor. Clay reached for it, but Petra knocked it away. The two women wrestled each other.

On top, Petra had the advantage. However, she was finding it hard to maintain her position. Clay was stronger than she'd ever imagined. She felt outmatched.

Petra cocked a fist back to throw a punch. Before the blow could land, the commander headbutted her in the face.

There's was a distinctive crunch, followed by blinding pain. Petra's nose was broken.

Before she could recover, Clay bucked her hips and flipped

Petra over onto her back. Now, she was the one at a disadvantage.

Clay's large hands wrapped around Petra's neck and squeezed. The look on Clay's face was wild and frenzied. And Petra couldn't quite believe it. The commander had always been so calm and put together. But now, with the buttons of her uniformed shirt popped open and the sleeves of her shirt rolled up, the crazed woman bent on strangling her seemed like a stranger.

"You bitch—fucking bitch. I should have listened. Olivia warned me about you. Fucking lightless filth," Clay screamed, spittle flying from her mouth and landing on Petra's face. "He's dead. You're dead. You cost me everything. You killed my son!"

Dustin's dead? A picture of Dustin flashed in Petra's mind—his boyish face and wavy blond hair. He'd annoyed her endlessly with his smiles and his puppy dog eyes, but the knowledge of his death pricked Petra's heart. Tears pricked her eyes.

"Why'd you do it?" Clay demanded. "Tell me why you betrayed us!"

"To get my mother back," Petra choked out.

"Dead is dead," Clay sneered. Her handhold tightened, cutting off Petra's breath entirely.

Petra tried to manoeuvre out of the death-grip, but the more she struggled the tighter it got.

Her ears picked up Vy's voice. She couldn't hear what was being said, but the next instant, Clay went completely still and collapsed on top of her.

Gasping for air, Petra pushed the commander off of her and sat up. Blood dripped from her nose. She wiped it away with the back of her hand.

Hurrying over to her, Vy knelt by her side, and when Vy reached for her face, Petra batted her hands away. "What did you do to her?"

Vy shrank back. "I put her to sleep."

"You shouldn't have interfered," Petra said. "I was handling it."

"She was going to kill you."

Petra tried to snort but winced instead. Her nose fucking hurt.

Vy reached for her face again. Once again, Petra wouldn't let her. It pissed her off that she'd had to be rescued—again. And the rush of adrenalin wasn't helping. Her mind was reeling over what had just happened, and she need space to think and decompress.

"Why are you being so difficult?" Vy asked. "You're hurt. I'm trying to help you."

Behind them, someone tittered.

Turning her head, Petra's eyes narrowed on a delicate blond woman with icy blue eyes. She assumed it was Alice. The fang was gorgeous and was dressed in a black satin negligee that left nothing to the imagination. Even in her state of discomfort, Petra couldn't help but stare.

Beside her, Vy's mouth thinned with annoyance.

Alice crossed her arms over her chest. Her expression was blank. "I believe I was abundantly clear that I wanted no blood soiling my floors and that you were to depart before I roused," she said in a tone that made the room feel like it dropped several degrees in temperature. "I want an explanation for this ruckus."

Vy cocked her head in the direction of Clay's sleeping form. "The commander of the Order's Canadian base came here looking for a fight," she replied in voice that was just as frosty.

The fang sauntered towards them and lifted the commander with a single hand. "I loathe uninvited guests," Alice hissed, flashing sharp teeth. She angled her blonde head down and opened her mouth wide to bite Clay's neck.

Petra shot to her feet. "No, don't!"

Alice drew away from her prey, her eyes glinting with irritation. "I will not be dictated to in my home. Control your human, Violet, or I will put her in her place."

Vy placed a hand on Petra's arm as if to assure her. "Alice doesn't kill her meals," she said.

"And that's supposed to make me feel better." Petra shrugged her off. "Don't let her bite her."

"I can't tell Alice what to do."

"Don't let her bite her," Petra repeated. "Please."

Sighing, Vy looked at Alice. "Could you not feed on her?"

For a second, Alice seemed to contemplate the request, but then she smirked and struck down, piercing Clay's neck.

Petra lurched forward. Vy was quick to grab her wrist, holding her back. Petra tried to free herself, but Vy's grip was incredibly strong. "Let me go, fang!"

Vy shot her a hurt look, but Petra was too angry to care.

Petra continued to struggle to free herself as she watched Alice feed from the woman she'd once admired to no end. It pissed her off that she couldn't break Vy's hold.

It pissed her off that she was in this situation. It pissed her off that her peers were dropping off like flies.

Olivia was dead. Dustin was dead, and the commander blamed her for it. Petra was an enemy of the organization she'd once wanted to swear her life to, and they'd likely continue to hunt her down. They wouldn't let her get away with her betrayal. And depending on how long it took to find the hourglass, she'd likely have to fight more of her brothers and sisters—people she ate with, trained with, lived with.

Everything was a fucking mess.

The burden of it all weighed on Petra, and tears of frustration cascaded from her eyes. She rubbed them away with her freehand. She didn't want Vy or Alice to see her cry.

But to her dismay, Vy's expression made Petra want to bawl all the more. "Petra," she whispered.

Ashamed, Petra turned her face away.

Alice finished feeding and discarded the commander's limp body on the floor. She wiped blood away from her mouth with her fingers and then licked it off.

Old memories and pain resurfaced, making Petra tremble with rage. She welcomed the anger. It was familiar and a comfort. She found it preferable to the feelings of loss and sadness that also took residence in her heart.

"I forgot how delectable the blood of an Order agent is," the fang purred, before her face took on a chilling countenance. "It does not please me that the Order has been led to my front door."

"They've known where you live for years. They've been watching and documenting our movements for over a decade," Vy said.

The barest frown etched on Alice's face. "Is that so?"

"Yes," Vy confirmed. "But I told you already that it doesn't matter. I will fix everything."

"Ah, yes, because you have found the hourglass, and you intend to go against my better judgement and use it."

Petra stilled.

Surely, she had heard wrong. Vy would have told her if she knew where the hourglass was. She looked down at Vy. "You know where the hourglass is?"

Finally, Vy dropped her hold on Petra's arm. She bit her lip. "Yes."

"How? When?" Petra huffed, taking a step back.

"I managed to connect with Itachi," she explained, wringing her hands. "We spoke, and he gave me some information. I know where it is."

"And you didn't tell me …" Petra made a face, and she was reminded that her nose was broken. Wincing, she cradled the bridge of her nose.

"Let me heal your face." Vy took a step towards her.

Petra waved her away. "I don't want you touching me. How could you have kept this from me?"

"I was going to—"

"When?"

"As soon as we left here," Vy said.

"I don't believe you," Petra replied sharply.

"Of course, you don't believe me. I'm a fang after all—a lightless—a creature without a soul," Vy fumed, her nostrils flaring.

"I was going to tell you. But I just wanted to forget about the damn hourglass for a bit. I just wanted to ..." Sighing, Vy shook her head.

"If you know where it is, I'd like to get going. I need this to be over," Petra snapped, shoving past Vy and hunkering down beside Clay.

Petra was not going to leave the commander here. The woman might want her dead, but she didn't deserve to be left in a fang's den. She hoisted the larger woman onto her back.

"Let's go," Petra said.

Vy rubbed her temple and turned to her friend. "Can I borrow a car?"

Alice seemed to mull over the question for far too long. The fang's silence grated on Petra's nerves. "You may borrow the Cayenne. I do not care for that vehicle much," she eventually said.

Alice left the main room and came back with a key fob. When she dropped the device in Vy's outstretched palm, she said, "You ought to listen to me. Nothing good will come of seeing Camellia again. Your mother is wicked. She cannot be trusted."

Vy scowled, her hand closing tightly over the fob. "That's rich coming from you."

Alice opened her mouth to say something, but apparently decided not to waste her words. She said nothing and crossed her arms.

Vy went to the elevator. She pushed the button, and when the doors opened, she stepped inside.

Petra followed her into the lift. The doors closed.

They didn't speak as it descended.

Chapter Thirty-Seven

From the passenger window, Petra eyed Vy's childhood home.

The cape cod house was picturesque in the sense that it was familiar. With its wood siding painted white, symmetrical facade boasting large windows fringed by dark shutters, and pitched wooden shingled roof, it was the type of dwelling that hearkened to the American dream. The only element that stood out was its very red door.

Trees of varying varieties towered over the home, casting it in shade. The front yard was very green and neatly manicured. Shrubbery flanked a paved driveway that led to a three-car garage. A silver Subaru was parked out front, but aside from that, there was no other indicator of someone being home.

The commander dozed in the backseat. According to Vy, she would stay asleep until released from the spell, and Petra found that rather unsettling. She had greatly misjudged Vy's abilities. From what she had observed, Vy was likely a class B or even a class A lightless. In other words, she was incredibly powerful.

Sparing a glance at Clay, Petra couldn't help but feel a mixture of heavy emotions. Dustin was dead, and the commander blamed her. She'd never liked Dustin. In a lot of ways, he'd been like an annoying little brother, following her around and hanging on her every word. But knowing that he was gone ate at her.

Vy's fingers drummed on the steering wheel, and she was biting her lip. She seemed anxious.

While Petra wanted to ask Vy what was wrong, she kept her mouth shut. It was always hard to break a long-stretched silence. Their drive to the affluent suburb had been spent in an uncomfortable quiet. They hadn't said much since they'd left Alice's place.

Petra touched her nose and winced. She had avoided looking at her face in any of the car's mirrors. She was sure she looked a mess.

It irritated Petra that Vy was mad at her. What right did she have being angry?

Vy had been the one who had withheld information. There had been several opportunities where she could've told Petra.

Just thinking about it, Petra felt her own anger stoke again. "Why didn't you tell me about the hourglass?" she asked suddenly, breaking the silence.

Vy's fingers stilled on the steering wheel. Instead of answering, she opened her car door and hopped out of the Porsche, slamming the door behind her.

Petra spared the commander another quick glance. An ache bloomed in her chest from knowing her betrayal, but from also knowing that it couldn't be helped. Vy was offering her the chance at a new life. It was what she wanted—more than anything.

Exiting the vehicle, Petra chased after Vy down the sidewalk. Grabbing her wrist, Petra tried to pull Vy towards her. But Vy wasn't having it. She resisted being tugged.

"Let me go before I make you," Vy said through clenched teeth.

"I am the one who should be mad—not you," Petra stated, dropping Vy's wrist. "You lied to me."

Vy shook her head. "I didn't lie to you. I was going to tell you. I just …"

"You just what?"

"Has it even occurred to you what will happen when we do this?"

Petra frowned. "Of course I have."

"Have you thought about what it means for the current version of yourself?" Vy asked. Her voice was very soft.

"No, I haven't," Petra admitted.

"Well, I have," Vy whispered, turning to face her. Petra saw that her brown eyes shimmered. "Anyways, I had every intention of telling you today. I just wanted to be with you in that moment, okay."

"Vy, I—"

"I don't want to talk about this." She held up a hand. "I think that I just need this over with too." With those words, she wiped her eyes and hurried for the red door. She opened it and disappeared behind it.

Petra stared at the red door for a moment and replayed the

conversation they'd just had. It hadn't occurred to her that by changing everything, she'd essentially be erasing the person she was. The thought was disturbing.

Releasing a deep exhale, Petra tried to shake off the dismal feeling in her stomach. She approached the front door, turned the handle, and stepped inside.

The home's interior was almost as cookie cutter as the exterior, with its earth tones, warm wooden floors, open concept layout, and contemporary furnishings.

Walking into the living room, Petra noted that a middle-aged man and a younger woman were deeply asleep on the grey sectional. It occurred to Petra that Vy must have enchanted them in the same way she had done to Clay.

Petra scanned the area, looking for Vy. She called out for her but did not receive a response.

Her gaze landed on a wall where many photographs were hung. It did not pass Petra's notice that Vy was not in a single one.

There were some more pictures on the mantle above the fireplace. Similarly, none of them showed Vy. A brunette, in varying stages of life, was the subject of the majority. Petra guessed her to be Vy's half-sister.

Petra's stare ventured over to the winding staircase with its white banister and carpeted treads. She moved towards it and ascended to the second floor.

Arriving at the top landing, she briefly poked her head into rooms, discovering the main bathroom, laundry area, and master bedroom. But Vy was nowhere. She called out for her again. As before, she did not receive a response.

When she opened a fourth door, she felt herself drawn inside.

The room's air was stale and musty. A thin layer of dust coated every visible surface. Thick drawn curtains blocked out the sun.

By the looks of it, it had been a very long time since anyone had stepped foot into Vy's childhood bedroom.

The room felt like a time capsule devoted to the early 2000s and late '90s. In the dim lighting, Petra made out posters of Destiny's Child, P!nk, and Britney Spears. Issues of *Seventeen* magazine and *Vogue* were scattered on the tiny desk.

Intricate floral wallpaper made the room feel smaller than it was. The bed was tiny with a gold barred frame and headboard. Its pink blanket looked just as dusty as the rest of the room.

Walking towards a dresser, Petra's fingers toyed with bottles of Victoria Secret body spray, and she recalled how obsessed Kate had been with the same ones.

Her eyes landed on a photo, and she picked up the frame. In the picture, Vy was perhaps thirteen. Her father stood in the middle of the photo with his arms around his two girls. Vy's half-sister was smiling brightly, but Vy's grin looked forced.

Petra's gaze landed on a second frame. Vy was alone in the picture. She looked a little older, and in it she wasn't even trying to smile. Her lips were a thin line. Her expression seemed haunted, and her posture was rigid.

Petra wondered if it was that the photographer had caught her in a bad moment or if something had happened to make Vy look so miserable.

"What are you doing in here?"

Petra jolted. She hadn't heard Vy's approach. Setting the picture frame back on the dresser, she turned to face Vy, who stood in the doorway. In her arms, she carried a long rectangular box.

"I was looking for you," Petra replied. "What's that?" She cocked her head at the black box.

"It's what we need to get the talisman working," she said flatly. "If you're done snooping, we can go and do this."

Petra didn't budge. Raking her fingers through her hair, she sighed and slumped a bit. "I thought about what you said, and ..." She shook her head. "It never occurred to me what a new life would cost."

Vy shrugged with indifference. "Anything worth having takes sacrifice." She stared off into the hallway.

"Vy?"

"What?"

"Can you look at me? I'm trying to have a conversation with you."

Vy looked at her. "What could you possibly want to talk about?" Her tone was wary.

"I want to thank you for saving my ass back there."

"Sure, whatever. You're welcome. Is that all?"

"No. I ..." Petra licked her lips. "I want you to know that I don't think you're soulless. I want you to know that I'm sorry for being such an asshole. I want you to know that I wanted to be with you in that moment too."

Vy stood very still. Her beautiful face was unreadable.

Petra held her breath as she waited for Vy to say something—anything.

Setting down the box, Vy leaned against the doorjamb and rubbed her forehead. "I kind of wish you hadn't told me that," she finally said.

Petra frowned. "Why's that?"

"It would have been easier to say goodbye if you didn't." She sighed and dropped her head in her hands.

Petra stepped towards Vy, pulling her into her arms. She planted a kiss in her curly black hair. "Does it have to be goodbye?"

"It will have to be," Vy confirmed. She dropped her hands from her face, revealing that she was crying.

The raw emotion in her eyes baffled Petra. Was it possible that Vy cared for her—even after everything she'd put her through? Petra found it hard to believe, but maybe it wasn't as impossible as she imagined.

After all, she would have never thought in a million years that she would have forgiven Vy. And never in a million years would she have imagined that she could care for her as much as she did.

But thinking back on their time together, it was easy to see how Petra had begun to fall for her. Vy was possibly the most gorgeous woman Petra had ever laid eyes on. She was kind and strong. Her touch made Petra feel more alive than she had the right to feel.

Petra found her own eyes stinging, and she tightened her embrace. "I wish it didn't have to be over," she said, touching her forehead to Vy's.

"Me too." Vy looked up at her with wide tear-filled eyes. She brought a hand up to Petra's face. Her palm glowed, and Petra could feel the heat of her touch healing her face.

Soon, Petra's nose didn't hurt, but a new pain gripped her heart.

Bending her head, she kissed Vy wholly and deeply—like it was the last time. Because it would be.

Chapter Thirty-Eight

November 2007

When Vy had made the decision to give up her family out of fear for their safety, she had thought that would be the most difficult decision she'd ever make.

But as she had stepped through the time portal with the taste of Petra still fresh on her lips, she'd known that leaving her in that moment had been harder.

Maybe it was because Dustin's feelings were still there somewhere. But perhaps it had more to do with the fact that while she had given her family up, she'd always been able to check in on them from her favourite perch in the backyard tree.

Unlike her father and half-sister, Petra—the version of her that Vy had come to care about—would be gone. Petra as she knew her would cease to exist, and the pain of that knowledge was overwhelming.

While Vy knew that she was exactly where she needed to be, she felt more lost and alone than ever before.

Soon, she'd be seeing her mother for the first time in over twelve years, but Vy felt no sense of victory or excitement. There was just emptiness.

Shaking her head, she tried to dispel the thoughts that told her that she'd made the wrong decision. Leaving Petra had been the right choice.

They could never have made it together. They couldn't build a life together—not with the Order constantly hunting Petra down, not with Vy's assurance to Alice that everything would be sorted out, not with Vy's thirst worsening with each year, and definitely not with Petra's mother's death hanging over them.

Vy had told Petra as much when they'd been lying naked and entangled in her childhood bed. Petra had looked at her with wide green eyes, and had asked, "Should we really go through with this?"

Vy remembered how she had cupped Petra's face with her hands, staring into her eyes deeply and with incredulity. Vy remembered how she had brushed her lips against Petra's before snuggling her head into the curve of Petra's neck and nodding. Vy remembered the long length of Petra's sigh before she had said, "I know we have to do it. I'm a little scared."

"Me too," Vy had murmured.

They had withdrawn from the cocoon of their arms and the musty pink blanket shortly after exchanging those words.

Both had gotten dressed. Vy had lifted the long rectangular box in her arms. And together, in rueful silence, they had walked down the stairs and to the dining room where Vy set the box down beside the broken grandfather clock.

Within the box contained the pendulum Itachi had referenced. Vy had found the missing part in the basement amongst the many worthless possessions her mother had left behind.

Given that her mother had taken everything that seemed to matter with her, Vy couldn't help but speculate on why she'd left the pendulum behind. Had Camellia wanted her to find and use it?

Her mother had the sight, so it was a possibility. And there was a reason for everything her mother did.

In Vy's youth, she had always wondered why it was that the grandfather clock remained in the dining room—even as it couldn't tell time—and when all of Camellia's other things had been banished to the darkest corner of the house.

Now, Vy was certain that her mother had seen to it that the clock would not have been moved.

It hadn't taken Vy long to affix the pendulum and set the clock moving once more. With the ticking of its hands, Vy had felt power humming from it.

In that moment, she had scolded herself for not knowing sooner that the talisman had been within her reach the entire time. She should have known or at least guessed.

Camellia had often spoken about the hourglass. On the few occasions that she had opted to indulge her daughter with a story, she had told the tale of the hourglass more than any of the others—perhaps five times as many.

Yes, Vy should have known that Camellia had found it, given her mother's obsession with uncovering relics and ancient wisdom.

When Vy had finally unlocked the time portal—Present's Gate—she'd felt a sinking feeling in her chest.

Her time with Petra had been too short. They'd been together less than a week, but something had told Vy that she'd miss Petra for a lifetime.

Presently, Vy stared at the portal.

It was a vortex of black, grey, and shades of purple. Its force could tear a human apart upon entry. It hissed liked a radio without reception.

Vy wondered what was happening on the other side. Was Petra standing in the future watching the spiralling mess with the same vexation and loss?

Vy blinked back tears as she thought of their final goodbye. It hadn't been sweet, but it had been a reflection of their entire time together—bitter, tense, and slightly violent.

Their last kiss had been charged and bruising. Fingers had dug into skin, not wanting to let go. Lips had smashed together. Breathing had become as impossible as moving apart.

But they had come apart, and Vy had stepped into the portal. Now, she stood in the dining room, but in the past. It was the night Vy's world had first started to fall apart—the night her mother had left.

Outside was dark, and Vy could tell from the silence that everyone was asleep—everyone except her mother, who she heard conspiratorially descending the staircase.

All at once, with Camellia's presence so near, Vy's heart began to race. Moving her feet away from the portal and out of the dining area became her hardest challenge, but she managed to do it.

When Vy saw her mother, she froze.

Her mother looked at her, and there was no indication of surprise on her beautiful face. If anything, her mother's expression was colder than Vy ever remembered it being.

Vy opened her mouth to say something, but she became mute. She forgot the rant she'd rehearsed in her mind for this encounter.

An unexpected thing happened—Camellia's red painted lips curved into a mocking smile, and she chuckled. "It would seem that my days are numbered," she said, flashing white teeth.

Huh? Vy's brows came together. It was such an odd thing for her mother to say. Her words made no sense.

Unfazed by the older rendition of her daughter, Camellia brushed past Vy, walking towards the living-room area.

She waved for Vy to follow her. "Come now, I expect you have questions for me, and our time is limited."

It would seem that her mother had been expecting her, but Vy wondered how. Then again, maybe the answer was easy. While Vy didn't have the sight, Camellia did.

"You should know that the time portal only operates for a half-hour window before disappearing, and then it cannot be summoned again for a year's time," her mother said next.

Only thirty minutes? Vy frowned. She hadn't known that. The new information unsettled her. How could she even begin to say everything she needed to say? She had so many questions. Thirty minutes was not long enough.

Per Camellia's instructions, Vy trailed after her mother.

With a dramatic sweep of her hand, Camellia ignited the fireplace before gracefully taking a seat down onto the sofa and crossing her legs. "Why do you stand there like a sad kicked puppy?" Camellia scolded. "I did not raise you to be like this."

Vy exhaled a deep breath and strode towards the seating area. She didn't sit. Instead, she hovered awkwardly near her mother.

Knowing her time was ticking away, Vy forced her nervousness away and asked the question she'd been wanting to ask for over a decade. "Why are you leaving?"

"I left for the same reason you will need to one day," her mother replied in a tone as bitter as a juniper. "While the stewards are slow to stir, the only thing one can do is flee when they wake."

Stewards? Vy sucked in a breath. "As in the Architect's stewards."

"Who else would it be?" Her mother snapped, face flashing with annoyance.

Vy shrank back, like she had when she'd been a child. Some reactions were so ingrained they returned automatically. Even after all these years, her mother's vehemence made Vy want to curl into herself and disappear.

Vy wished it wasn't so. She'd hoped to have some agency in this encounter. But even after everything, she was still that unsure and anxious little girl inside.

Camellia looked just as she recalled. Flawless white skin and eyes so dark they looked black. Long black curling hair, so much like

Vy's, cascaded down Camellia's back. She sat upright like royalty. Anyone looking would think the beautiful enchantress owned the world, and they'd be right. Camellia was all-encompassing. Her very presence stole all the oxygen in the room.

Vy had always felt choked in her mother's presence. Some things never changed. But Vy couldn't dwindle her time. She needed to push past her reservations. She needed to find her voice. She'd come all this way for a reason.

"Why didn't you tell me? Why just leave without a word?" Vy looked at her mother, and she tried her best to meet her mother's very dark eyes. She succeeded, but found she wanted to look away from Camellia's penetrating stare.

"I saw no need to, and it was easier."

Of course it was. Her mother's response was not surprising. "Easier for who? Because it definitely wasn't for me."

"For me," Camellia confessed. The sorceress looked away from her daughter. Her eyes went to the flames dancing in the fireplace. "I know you will not believe this, but leaving you was possibly the hardest decision I have ever had to make."

Vy grimaced. "Bullshit!" she said, the harshness of her voice catching her off guard.

Surprise registered on Camellia's face—only for a moment—but it was enough to root some confidence in Vy. Maybe she could do this. Maybe she could muscle the courage to speak frankly with her mother.

Camellia sighed. "It is not."

"You're a liar," Vy snapped, finding more sureness with the

newfound anger stoking in her belly. She didn't believe Camellia. Not for a moment. Her mother had never cared for her. Her mother had only ever cared about power. Her mother had left her behind, likely because she saw Vy as a hinderance. "Don't you sit there and say that. You left me because I held no value in your eyes. I was never good enough for you. I could never learn fast enough. I was holding you back, and that is why you left me."

Camellia shook her head. "That is simply not true, Violet. How can you say that? Of course, you have value. You're my only daughter." Her mother rose to her feet and came to stand in front of her. "I sacrificed everything for you."

Sacrificed? Vy scoffed. She remembered her conversation with Alice, and her rage burned hotter. Her entire body shook from it. "You turned me into a monster—an abomination!"

"So that's what this is about? You are upset that you are part-vampire?" It was her mother's turn to scoff. "Your mixed blood is a gift. Your anger is misguided."

"Gift—more like a curse. You doomed me to a life of rejection. I am a leper among unhuman factions. Do you know how that feels? To fit in nowhere? To be hated and shunned?" Vy spat.

Tears stung her eyes, but she wouldn't let them fall. Not here. Not now. She'd cried enough because of the woman in front of her. She wouldn't spill anymore for her. Wiping her eyes, she went on the rant she'd contrived years ago, "When the change first started, I thought I was going crazy. I remember drinking glass after glass of water, but I was always thirsty. Then, for weeks, I threw up anything I ate and a chill took over me—I thought I was dying. It didn't matter how many blankets dad wrapped me in. It didn't matter how much he cranked the space heater. I was so cold, and achy, and thirsty. I had no fucking clue what was going on. I was so scared. And then, I blacked out, and it was only after I snapped out of my delirium with blood dripping from my mouth and a dead woman laying at my feet that the truth settled in. Can you even imagine what that did to me? I had no idea—never in my wildest dreams would I have ever guessed that I was a fang."

A loud sigh escaped her mother's lips, but there was no remorse on her face. "I probably should have told you the truth about what you are. Upon reflection, yes, it might have been good to warn you that the seal holding back your fang tendencies would weaken with puberty," Camellia said finally. "But, I hadn't wanted to get into it then. I didn't want to answer the questions that I knew you would ask."

Her mother turned away, giving Vy her back. She sauntered towards the fireplace and stared down into the pit. Her profile glowed in the orange tint cast from the crackling flames.

"What hadn't you wanted to tell me then?"

Her mother didn't motion to look at her when she replied, "Everything."

"Well, I am here, and I want to hear it," Vy said. "Tell me everything."

Her mother seemed to change the topic, stating, "I wish you could see the beauty in what you are instead of rejecting it." She paused momentarily before adding, "I have always taught you that, where unhumans are concerned, all that matters is power. And yours can be endless, but it won't if you continue this crusade to fit in. Fitting in is for the weak. Fitting in means those beneath you can walk all over you. Fitting in is the worst possible fate." Vy saw her mother's hands ball into fists, and she wondered what thoughts incited such a reaction.

"Where are you going with this?" Vy asked, because she really wasn't sure.

"In the end, all that matters is power and the respect that comes with it," she answered, her fists uncoiling. "How easily you have forgotten my teachings. I taught you better than this. Taught you to—"

"The only thing you taught me was that I was not good enough."

"If that is what you heard, then you were not listening," Camellia stated. "I was always so proud of you—of your progress in the art of magic."

So it seemed Camellia was back to lying to her. "You're such a liar."

"I am not lying. I sacrificed everything for you. I can't even begin to name the trials I went through to bring you into this world." Camellia shifted towards her with a face flush with emotions. Her mother's dark eyebrows drew close together. It was a raw expression. It looked out of place. "You were—you *are* everything to me."

It was too much, and Vy closed her eyes, knowing in her heart that the attestation was untrue. Those words ... how long had she dreamt of hearing such words come from her mother's lips? *Too many times,* she told herself, feeling again the prickle in her eyes.

"I can tell you do not believe me, but maybe if I show you, I can make you understand," her mother said, beckoning with a hand for Vy to join her by the fireplace.

Vy shuffled towards her, though she didn't want to.

Once at her mother's side, Camellia motioned with a single hand towards the blaze, transforming the chaotic dance of red, orange, and yellow into a tangible image.

Vy was met with the burning portrait of Camellia, who stood in the clearing of a forest.

"I was one and twenty when my sister, in her jealousy, cursed me," her mother said, and with the snap of her fingers, the picture began to play out like a movie.

Camellia was seen kneeling and picking herbs when she was shoved from the back. The fire changed, showing the figure who pushed her.

Vy gasped. "Mistress May?"

"Is that what Iris is going by now?" her mother said, voice clipped.

"She's the Grand Sorceress of Toronto," Vy stated.

"Of course, she is." Camellia snorted. "Even after all these centuries, she still seeks to ruin me. I know she has corrupted you, weakening your resolve with chem."

Embarrassment and shame scorched Vy. She couldn't help the embarrassment she felt. She didn't like her mother knowing about her chem habit. "How do you know?"

Her mother arched a brow. "Who do you think taught Iris the sight?" Gesturing towards the fire, the image changed again, showing Mistress May/Iris shouting with a pointed finger directed at Camellia, who was rising to her feet and brushing the dirt from her skirts.

"She was so mad over nothing," Camellia said, "and I was shocked that my sister finally found her spine. I was even more shocked when she spoke dark words against me—dark words that I would not use against my greatest enemy—and then she prophesized that I would only bear sons until I bore a single daughter, who would draw one breath before passing."

The fire shifted, showing a sped up time-lapse of Camellia going about her life. The whir of it all was almost too much for Vy to decipher.

"My sister and I parted ways. I embarked on a journey to uncover magic long forgotten, and in my quest I never thought once about the curse—until the day came when I did. It occurred to me that should something befall me, all the knowledge that I had accrued would be lost again," her mother said. "At first, I contemplated that I could foster a young spellcaster and take her on as a protégé, but that seemed rather precarious to me. It didn't take long for me to realize that I could only bequeath my wisdom to a daughter—my daughter. At that time, it never occurred to me that Iris had actually managed to curse me. I drank the magical tonic to ensure I birthed a daughter, but to my surprise I birthed a son. And I birthed several more—all male. I think something broke in me when I culled my second son minutes after giving birth."

Vy's eyes were transfixed to the story playing out before her in the fire. She saw the breaking that her mother spoke about reflected in the flames. Her mother's fire-drawn expression truly looked crazed, and Vy's heart ached for her. She couldn't imagine the agony her mother must've felt—killing a child she'd carried in her womb for nine months.

Her mother continued, saying, "I must have visited every sorceress from every corner on the planet—all told me it would be impossible to break the curse, and even if Iris were to try to retract her words, that would not change my fate. In my stubbornness, I refused to be told that there was nothing I could do. I refused to acknowledge that none could *see* a path where I bore a daughter who lived past the first breath. It became an obsession of mine, trying to find a way to subvert the curse. But as years became decades, and decades became centuries, I did begin to lose hope, and I thought that perhaps it was impossible. Then came the day when you came into the world—and you were so perfect and so beautiful ..."

The fire showed a baby Vy still and quiet in Camellia's arms. In the flames, Vy watched, aghast, as her mother was shown crying, cradling the lost child in her arms.

"In that moment, holding you in my arms, I knew that I had to save you," Camellia said, "and the plan came to me to find the Architect's hourglass to go back to the moment you were birthed. It dawned on me that one breath was more than enough to preserve you. One breath was all that was needed to bring you back to life."

"Alice ..." Her friend's name fell from Vy's lips.

Her mother nodded. "Yes, Alice agreed to change you."

The image in the fire retreated, and Vy stared towards her mother. "Why didn't you tell me?"

"I did not want to speak about it. That was such a dark time in my life," Camellia admitted. Her dark eyes took on a far away look. "I wanted to forget. But I have told you now, and now you see."

My mother loves me? Without really thinking, Vy motioned towards her mother and hugged her. The tears were back, and they flowed freely. Her mother was stiff in her arms, but Vy didn't care. It was enough to just hold her.

Camellia patted her daughter's head. The gesture felt unnatural. "Come now, Violet, your time is running out, and I know you have more work to do still."

Vy shook her head. How could she let go of her mother now?

"You need to let me go," her mother said, pulling away and taking a measured step back.

Vy sniffled and wiped her eyes. "Where are you headed?"

"It is better for you not to know."

"Why?"

"You mustn't go looking for me again. To do so would be your undoing," Camellia warned.

Vy frowned. "How?"

"You must know that the sight has its limits—even for me. I do not know everything. What I do know is that your path is brighter without me in it," Camellia said. "You must learn to accept yourself—all of yourself—and you mustn't stop pursuing knowledge. There are trials on the horizon, but if you are strong enough, there is nothing you cannot overcome."

"What trials?"

"Humans," her mother said curtly. "And their weapons."

Vy's mind took her back to the Order's base. She recalled the syringe in Olivia's hands and the monstrous change that the girl had undergone. Was that what her mother referenced?

Vy watched as her mother walked towards the front door, and she followed her.

Camellia's hand turned the knob, opening it.

"You said the stewards were after you?" Vy asked.

Her mother halted in the doorframe. "They are," she confirmed.

"You said that your days were numbered?" Vy bit her lip. "Is there a path where we ever meet again?"

"Perhaps, but it is unlikely," her mother replied. "Even so, I would hope that day comes. It would mean you listened to me and became all you were meant to be."

When her mother turned to leave again, Vy remembered her promise to Itachi. "Wait. I forgot to tell you, Itachi told me to tell you that he understands and he forgives you."

For a moment, her mother seemed to go really still, and then her lips curled into a thin smile. "Goodbye, Violet." With those final words, her mother disappeared in a flash that mimicked a hopper's hop, which shouldn't be possible.

For a few moments, Vy stared at the empty doorway. She felt heavy all over.

Seeing her mother had answered so many questions, yet presented many more. Vy wanted to reflect further on it all, but now was not the time. She did have other work to do, and she needed to do it before the time portal vanished.

Climbing the stairs, Vy pushed open the door to her bedroom, closing it softly behind her.

She walked the short distance to the bed, took a seat on the edge of it, and looked down at her younger self.

Sound asleep, little Vy appeared to be the bastion of innocence. Vy felt a sense of protectiveness for the child.

Part of her did not want to impart all the hurt and pain from the future, but it was the only way to change Vy's trajectory and give Petra her life back.

Brushing a hand through the girl's hair, Vy sought to gently wake her. "Violet," she said.

Her younger self stirred, blinking her eyes open. "Mom?" The girl blinked again, and then her eyes narrowed with suspicion, which quickly morphed into fear. The girl sat up and drew the blanket to her chin. "Who ... are you?"

"I am you—from the future."

"Impossible. Get out of here before I scream. I will do it—I will scream."

"Don't do that. There's no need for dramatics."

Her younger self pouted and crossed her arms, making the sheet drop. "I am not dramatic." She looked at Vy strangely as if seeing her for the first time. "You look like me, but like way, way older."

"That's because I am you." She tried not to let the "way, way older" part get to her.

"So cool!" Her younger self jumped out of bed. "You've gotta tell me what the future is like. How hot is my future girlfriend—like really hot, right? Am I a model? Do I travel the world in private jets and—"

"How about I show you?" Vy said, her tone flat and laced with sadness. It hurt her to know that the moment she shared everything, her younger self would be changed—and not for the better. But what mattered was that she would be better for it. Everyone would be.

Her younger self squeezed her hands together. By the expression on her face, you'd think she'd won the lottery. "Really?!"

"Yeah, sure."

"I'm so down."

Of course I am. Sighing, Vy began to speak the words of the spell she knew so well, but the last words she inverted, making it so that instead of marching into her younger self's soul, her younger self marched into hers and saw and felt it all—her mother's departure, her monstrous change, the slaying of Petra's mother, Alice taking her in, her wasted years, the fallout with Nick ... her love for Petra. All the pain and rejection. The scorn and the bitterness. The loneliness.

She shared it all in a quick and fleeting moment—her entire existence.

When the transfer finished, Vy couldn't stand to see the look of shock on her younger self. She used magic to force the girl back to sleep and hurried downstairs—back to the dining room.

Time was ticking, and the portal had shrunk considerably in the short time Vy had spent in the past. Its hiss was weak. Its swirls of purple were muted. It was starting to close.

Without hesitation, Vy stepped through the vortex to meet her new reality.

Epilogue

Fall 2019

Fall leaves of different shades of yellow, red, and orange carpeted the dog park. A cool breeze blew. The sun was hidden behind a curtain of clouds.

Vy sat on a bench. Her loyal companion sat near her and keenly observed the other dogs frolicking, sniffing, and digging.

There was one particular dog that caught Vy's attention. An energetic toy poodle with a shiny brown coat whose name was Dumpling.

Vy's gaze drifted away from the poodle and focused on his humans. Her breath caught—as it always did.

As she watched the lovers talking and laughing several metres away, Vy recalled a statement from Alice. In a past life, Alice had told her that she was addicted to her own misery. Maybe that was true. There was no other rationale to explain why Vy went so out of her way to take Archie to the dog park in Rosedale.

Leaning over, Vy scratched Archie's red head, which made the Akita turn to look at her.

"You need to go and run, Archie, you're getting fat," Vy said. She knew her dog understood her well, but Archie was as stubborn as she was loyal. The Akita would only go off and play if she was in the mood to do so.

The crinkling sound of paws on leaves drew Vy's gaze away from Archie. She looked up and saw Dumpling dashing towards the bench—towards her, which had never happened before.

The poodle came to a stop about a foot away from Archie, who was uninterested and kept seated.

Vy bent over and presented her hand to Dumpling to sniff. The animal was perceptive and could tell instantly that Vy was not what she appeared—that she was a threat.

The poodle growled, baring its teeth, and began kicking up dirt and leaves.

"Whoa, whoa, Dumpling, what has gotten into you?"

Vy froze at the voice.

Petra ran over to the bench and knelt down to comfort the dog. "I am so sorry," she said, meeting Vy's eyes. "He is usually so friendly. I am not sure why he is acting like this." When her efforts to calm the poodle didn't work, she picked him up.

Vy shrugged and pushed back a string of her loose hair behind an ear. "It's fine," she said, trying to sound normal. She'd been coming to the park for months now, and while she'd sighted Petra on several occasions, they'd never interacted before.

Coddled in Petra's arms, the poodle quieted. Meanwhile, Vy felt the world go still as she stared into the woman's green eyes.

Petra frowned. "Do I know you?"

Vy blinked. Looking away, she shook her head. "No." It wasn't a lie. She didn't know *this* Petra. "But I come here often. I think I have seen you around."

The woman standing in front of her was slim, with long hair that looked more auburn than red. She was very pretty in a girl-next-door kind of way. Her green eyes were so soft and lively. There wasn't a hard edge to her. The woman was a stranger.

Kate joined them then, and Dumpling was set back down on the ground. Petra laced her fingers with her girlfriend's. Vy tensed.

Archie yawned, as if sensing the change in Vy's mood.

"Your dog's coat is beautiful," Kate said.

Vy nodded and forced a smile. "Thanks."

"Akita's are my favourite breed of dog," Petra stated. "They are so loyal and loving. Do you know the story of Hachiko?"

"Yes, someone told me about it once," Vy said, feeling a lump begin to form in her throat. She rose to her feet and pushed her arms in the pockets of her wool coat. "It was nice meeting you," she said, gesturing to Archie that it was time to leave, and it was.

Ginger wanted Vy home at six for dinner, and Vy had promised that this time she would make it.

In a way, it was kind of ironic. In her previous life, all she had wanted was her family back and a place at the dining table. Now, Vy had a seat and she had a family, but she never had the time to see them.

So much was different. So much had changed. And still, so much remained the same.

Vy still found herself quite lonely—possibly even lonelier in this rendition of her life, where Alice wasn't a friend but an acquaintance of sorts. Possibly not even that.

On the positive side, her mother had been right about power and respect. In her new life, Vy had learned to accept herself, and she no longer battled thirst. She kept a clear head as she no longer had use for chem. And she was more powerful now than she ever imagined being, and the factions had taken notice.

Respect meant that people didn't dare leer or ignore you. In fact, quite the opposite happened. Belisarius had frequently enquired whether Vy was interested in joining the coven. Spellcasters now fawned over Vy as they sought to become her lover and protégé.

Before, Vy thought that she would have liked such attention. But now, she found it exhausting.

Unearthing ancient knowledge and wisdom was a full-time job Vy had adopted, and she finally understood and appreciated Camellia's devotion and discipline. Finding and learning dark magic was gruelling work. It was the kind that melted your mind with how hard it could be.

But Vy was dedicated to her mission—the one that saw her saving her mother.

Vy just hoped she figured out how to kill stewards before it was too late.

The Order was also keeping her busy, and she was trying to

figure out the best way to get to Raz. The doctor's work needed to be stopped.

Knowing what she knew, Vy couldn't let him stabilize that serum. At the same time, she also sought to understand his methods.

Before exiting the dog park, Vy glanced back over to the happy couple and tried to brush off the familiar pang of regret. She pulled open the wooden gate and stepped through it with Archie, deciding that it was time for her to let go of the past.

Thank you from the Author

Thank you so much for reading Born of Blood and Magic. Your support means the world!

For free bonus content and updates on Book Two of the Lightless Series, sign up for M.C. Hutson's mailing list here: **mchutson.com**

Every review helps, so please review if you can.

About the Author

M.C. Hutson reads, reviews and writes sapphic books. She was born and raised in Toronto, Canada.

For more than a year, M.C. lived in Tokyo, Japan where she worked as a foreign English teacher. Her experiences in Japan highly influenced this story.

When M.C. isn't reading, reviewing, and writing sapphic books, you can find her in the kitchen replicating recipes she finds on YouTube or snuggling on the couch with her morkshire terrier.

Follow M.C. on Social Media

- @mchutsonauthor
- @mchutsonwrites
- M.C. Hutson

Milton Keynes UK
Ingram Content Group UK Ltd.
UKHW020940270224
438492UK00005BA/307

9 781738 253807